The rich and the ruthless!

*Praise for three bestselling authors –
Penny Jordan, Anne McAllister
and Sara Craven*

About THE DEMETRIOS VIRGIN:
'Penny Jordan's latest is a must read with
passionate overtones, powerful characters
and an intense story line.'
—*Romantic Times*

About THE PLAYBOY AND THE NANNY:
'Anne McAllister puts a humorous spin on a
favourite plot featuring irresistible characters, a
meaningful conflict and charming scenes.'
—*Romantic Times*

About THE TYCOON'S MISTRESS:
'Sara Craven pens an intense and
passionate story with fabulous characters
and compelling scenes.'
—*Romantic Times*

Greek Millionaires

THE DEMETRIOS VIRGIN
by
Penny Jordan

THE PLAYBOY AND THE NANNY
by
Anne McAllister

THE TYCOON'S MISTRESS
by
Sara Craven

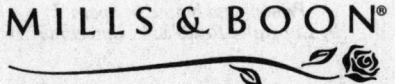

DID YOU PURCHASE THIS BOOK WITHOUT A COVER?
If you did, you should be aware it is **stolen property** as it was reported *unsold and destroyed* by a retailer. Neither the author nor the publisher has received any payment for this book.

All the characters in this book have no existence outside the imagination of the author, and have no relation whatsoever to anyone bearing the same name or names. They are not even distantly inspired by any individual known or unknown to the author, and all the incidents are pure invention.

All Rights Reserved including the right of reproduction in whole or in part in any form. This edition is published by arrangement with Harlequin Enterprises II B.V. The text of this publication or any part thereof may not be reproduced or transmitted in any form or by any means, electronic or mechanical, including photocopying, recording, storage in an information retrieval system, or otherwise, without the written permission of the publisher.

This book is sold subject to the condition that it shall not, by way of trade or otherwise, be lent, resold, hired out or otherwise circulated without the prior consent of the publisher in any form of binding or cover other than that in which it is published and without a similar condition including this condition being imposed on the subsequent purchaser.

MILLS & BOON and MILLS & BOON with the Rose Device are registered trademarks of the publisher.
Harlequin Mills & Boon Limited,
Eton House, 18-24 Paradise Road, Richmond, Surrey, TW9 1SR

GREEK MILLIONAIRES © by Harlequin Enterprises II B.V., 2004

The Demetrios Virgin, The Playboy and the Nanny and
The Tycoon's Mistress were first published in Great Britain by
Harlequin Mills & Boon Limited in separate, single volumes.

The Demetrios Virgin © Penny Jordan 2001
The Playboy and the Nanny © Barbara Schenck 1998
The Tycoon's Mistress © Sara Craven 2000

ISBN 0 263 84072 7

05-0704

Printed and bound in Spain
by Litografia Rosés S.A., Barcelona

Penny Jordan has been writing for more than twenty years and has an outstanding record: over 150 novels published, including the phenomenally successful *A Perfect Family, To Love, Honour & Betray, The Perfect Sinner* and *Power Play*, which hit the *Sunday Times* and *New York Times* bestseller lists. Penny Jordan was born in Preston, Lancashire, and now lives in rural Cheshire.

**Don't miss Penny Jordan's latest red-hot read:
MISTRESS OF CONVENIENCE
On sale August 2004, in Modern Romance™!**

THE DEMETRIOS VIRGIN
by
Penny Jordan

CHAPTER ONE

'FOUR forty-five.' Saskia grimaced as she hurried across the foyer of the office block where she worked, heading for the exit. She was already running late and didn't have time to pause when the receptionist called out. 'Sneaking off early... Lucky you!'

Andreas frowned as he heard the receptionist's comment. He was standing waiting for the executive lift and the woman who was leaving hadn't seen him, but he had seen her: a stunningly leggy brunette with just that gleam of red-gold in her dark locks that hinted at fieriness. He immediately checked the direction of his thoughts. The complication of a man to woman entanglement was the last thing he needed right now, and besides...

His frown deepened. Since he had managed to persuade his grandfather to semi-retire from the hotel chain which Andreas now ran, the older man had begun a relentless campaign to persuade and even coerce Andreas into marrying a second cousin. Such a marriage, in his grandfather's eyes, would unite not just the two branches of the family but the wealth of the family shipping line—inherited by his cousin—with that of the hotel chain.

Fortunately Andreas knew that at heart his grandfather was far more swayed by emotion than he liked to admit. After all, he had allowed his daughter, Andreas's mother, to marry an Englishman.

The somewhat clumsy attempts to promote a match between Andreas and his cousin Athena would merely afford Andreas some moments of wry amusement if it were not for one all-important fact—which was that Athena herself was even keener on the match than his grandfather. She had made her intentions, her *desires*, quite plain. Athena was a widow seven years his senior, with two children from her first marriage to another wealthy Greek, and Andreas suspected that it might have been Athena herself who had put the ridiculous idea of a marriage between them in his grandfather's head in the first place.

The lift had reached the penthouse floor and Andreas got out. This wasn't the time for him to be thinking about his personal affairs. *They* could wait. He was due to fly out to the Aegean island his grandfather owned, and where the family holidayed together, in less than a fortnight's time, but first his grandfather wanted a detailed report from him on his proposals to turn the flagging British hotel chain they had recently bought into as successful an enterprise as the rest of the hotels they owned.

Even though Andreas had become the company's chief executive, his grandfather still felt the need to challenge his business decisions. Still, the acquisition would ultimately be a good one—the chain-owned hotels were very run down and old fashioned, but had excellent locations.

Although officially he was not due to arrive at the chain's head office until tomorrow, Andreas had opted to do so this afternoon instead, and it looked as though he had just discovered one way at least in which profitability could be improved, he decided grimly, if all the staff were in the habit of 'sneaking off early', like the young woman he had just seen...

Sneaking off early! Saskia grimaced as she managed to hail a cruising taxi. If only! She had been at her desk for seven-thirty this morning, as she had been every morning for the last month, and neither had she had a lunch hour, but they had all been warned that Demetrios Hotels, who had taken over their own small chain, were relentless when it came to pruning costs. Tomorrow morning they were all due to meet their new boss for the first time, and Saskia wasn't exactly looking forward to the occasion. There had been a lot of talk about cutbacks and there had also been grapevine rumours about how very formidable Andreas Latimer was.

'The old man, his grandfather, had a reputation for running a tight ship, and if anything the grandson is even worse.'

'They both favour a "the guest is always right even when wrong" policy, and woe betide any employee who forgets it. Which is, of course, why their hotels are so popular... and so profitable,'

That had been the general gist of the gossip Saskia had heard.

Her taxi was drawing up outside the restaurant she had asked to be taken to. Hastily she delved into her handbag for her purse, paying the driver and then hurrying quickly inside.

'Oh, Saskia—*there* you are. We thought you weren't going to make it.'

'I'm sorry,' Saskia apologised to her best friend as she slipped into the spare seat at the table for three in the Italian restaurant where they had arranged to meet.

'There's been a panic on at work,' she explained. 'The new boss arrives tomorrow.' She pulled a face, wrinkling the elegant length of her dainty nose and screwing up her thick-lashed aquamarine eyes. She paused as she saw that her friend wasn't really listening, and that her normally happy, gentle face looked strained and unhappy.

'What's wrong?' she asked immediately.

'I was just telling Lorraine how upset I am,' Megan answered, indicating the third member of their trio, Megan's cousin Lorraine, an older woman with a brisk, businesslike expression and a slightly jaded air.

'Upset?' Saskia queried, a small frown marring the elegant oval of her face as she pushed her long hair back and reached hungrily for a bread roll. She was starving!

'It's Mark,' Megan said, her voice shaking a little and her brown eyes full of quiet despair.

'Mark?' Saskia repeated, putting down her roll so that she could concentrate on her friend. 'But I thought the two of you were about to announce your engagement.'

'Yes, we were...we are... At least, Mark wants to...' Megan began, and then stopped when Lorraine took over.

'Megan thinks he's involved with someone else...' she told Saskia grimly. 'Two-timing her.'

Older than Megan and Saskia by almost a decade,

and with a broken marriage behind her, Lorraine was inclined to be angrily contemptuous of the male sex.

'Oh, surely not, Megan,' Saskia protested. 'You told me yourself how much Mark loves you.'

'Well, yes, that's what I thought,' Megan agreed, 'Especially when he said that he wanted us to become engaged. But...he keeps getting these phone calls. And if I answer the phone whoever's ringing just hangs up. There've been three this week and when I ask him who it is he says it's just a wrong number.'

'Well, perhaps it is,' Saskia tried to reassure her, but Megan shook her head.

'No, it isn't. Mark keeps on hanging around by the phone, and last night he was talking on his mobile when I walked in and the moment he saw me he ended the call.'

'Have you *asked* him what's going on?' Saskia questioned her in concern.

'Yes. He says I'm just imagining it,' Megan told her unhappily.

'A classic male ploy,' Lorraine announced vigorously with grim satisfaction. 'My ex did everything to convince me that I was becoming paranoid and then what does he do? He moves in with his secretary, if you please!'

'I just wish that Mark would be honest with me,' Megan told Saskia, her eyes starting to fill with tears. 'If there *is* someone else...I... I just can't believe he's doing this... I thought he loved me...'

'I'm sure he does,' Saskia tried to comfort her. She had not as yet met her friend's new partner, but from what Megan had told her about him Saskia felt he sounded perfect for her.

'Well, there's one sure way to find out,' Lorraine announced. 'I read an article about it. There's this agency, and if you've got suspicions about your partner's fidelity you go to them and they send a girl to try to seduce him. That's what you should do,' she told Megan crisply.

'Oh, no, I couldn't,' Megan protested.

'You must,' Lorraine insisted forcefully. 'It's the only way you'll ever know whether or not you can trust him. I wish I'd been able to do something like that before I got married. You *must* do it,' she repeated. 'It's the only way you'll ever be sure. Mark is struggling to make ends meet since he started up his own business, Megan, and you've got that money you inherited from your great-aunt.'

Saskia's heart sank a little as she listened. Much as she loved her friend, she knew that Megan was inclined to allow herself to be dominated by her older and more worldly cousin. Saskia had nothing against Lorraine, indeed she liked her, but she knew from past experience that once Lorraine got the bit between her teeth there was no stopping her. She was fiercely determined to do things her own way, which Saskia suspected was at least part of the reason for the breakdown of her marriage. But right now, sympathetic though Saskia was to Megan's unhappiness, she was hungry…very hungry… She eyed the menu longingly.

'Well, it does *sound* a sensible idea,' Megan was agreeing. 'But I doubt there's an agency like that in Hilford.'

'Who needs an agency?' Lorraine responded. 'What *you* need is a stunningly gorgeous friend who Mark hasn't met and who can attempt to seduce him. If he responds...'

'A stunningly gorgeous friend?' Megan was musing. 'You mean like Saskia?'

Two pairs of female eyes studied Saskia whilst she gave in to her hunger and bit into her roll.

'Exactly,' Lorraine breathed fervently. 'Saskia would be perfect.'

'What?' Saskia almost choked on her bread. 'You *can't* be serious,' she protested. 'Oh, no, no way...' She objected when she saw the determination in Lorraine's eyes and the pleading in Megan's. 'No way at all.'

'Meg, this is crazy, you must see that,' she coaxed, trying to appeal to her friend's common sense and her conscience as she added winningly, 'How *could* you do something like that to Mark? You love him.'

'How can she risk committing herself to him unless she knows she can trust him?' Lorraine interjected sharply, adding emphatically, 'Good, that's settled. What we need to do now is to decide just where Saskia can accidentally run into Mark and put our plan into action.'

'Well, tonight is his boys' night out,' Megan ventured. 'And last night he said that they were planning to go to that new wine bar that's just opened. A friend of his knows the owner.'

'I can't do it,' Saskia protested. 'It...it's...it's immoral,' she added. She looked apologetically at Megan as she shook her head and told her, 'Meg, I'm sorry, but...'

'I should have thought you would *want* to help Megan, Saskia, to protect her happiness. Especially after all *she's* done for *you*...' Lorraine pointed out sharply.

Saskia worried guiltily at her bottom lip with her pretty white teeth. Lorraine was right. She *did* owe Megan a massive favour.

Six months ago, when they had been trying to fight off the Demetrios takeover bid, she had been working late every evening and at weekends as well. Her grandmother, who had brought her up following the breakdown of her young parents' marriage, had become seriously ill with a viral infection and Megan, who was a nurse, had given up her spare time and some of her holiday entitlement to care for the old lady.

Saskia shuddered to think even now of the potentially dangerous outcome of her grandmother's illness if Megan hadn't been there to nurse her. It had been on Saskia's conscience ever since that she owed her friend a debt she could never repay. Saskia adored her grandmother, who had provided her with a loving and stable home background when she had needed it the most. Her mother, who had given birth to Saskia at seventeen was a distant figure in her life, and her father, her grandmother's son, had become a remote stranger to both of them, living as he now did in China, with his second wife and young family.

'I know you don't approve, Saskia,' Megan was saying quietly to her, 'but I *have* to know that I can trust Mark.' Her soft eyes filled with tears. 'He means *so* much to me. He's everything I've *ever* wanted in a man. But...he dated so many girls before he met me, before he moved here, when he lived in London.' She paused. 'He swears that none of them ever meant anything serious to him and that he loves me.'

Privately Saskia wasn't sure that she could even begin to think about committing herself to a relationship with a man without being able to trust him—and trust him to such an extent that there would be no need for her to use any underhand methods to test his fidelity. But then she acknowledged that she was perhaps a trifle more wary of love than her friend. After all, her parents had believed themselves to be in love when they had run away to get married and conceived her, but within two years of doing so they had parted, leaving her grandmother with the responsibility of bringing her up.

Her grandmother! Now, as she looked at Meg's tearstained face, she knew she had no option but to go along with Lorraine's scheme.

'All right,' she agreed fatalistically. 'I'll do it.'

After Megan had finished thanking her she told her wryly, 'You'll have to describe your Mark to me, Megan, otherwise I shan't be able to recognise him.'

'Oh, yes, you will,' Megan said fervently with a small ecstatic sigh. 'He'll be the best-looking man there. He's gorgeous, Saskia...fantastically good-looking, with thick dark hair and the most sexy mouth you've ever seen. Oh, and he'll be wearing a blue shirt—to match his eyes. He always does. I bought them for him.'

'What time is he likely to get there?' Saskia asked Megan practically, instead of voicing her feelings.

'My car's in the garage at the moment, and since Gran's house is quite a way out of town...'

'Don't worry about that. I'll drive you there,' Lorraine volunteered, much to Saskia's surprise. Lorraine wasn't known to be over-generous—with anything!

'Yes, and Lorraine will pick you up later and take you home. Won't you, Lorraine?' Megan insisted with unexpected firmness. 'There's no taxi rank close to the wine bar and you don't want to be waiting for a mini-cab.'

A waiter was hovering, waiting to take their order, but bossily Lorraine shook her head, telling Megan and Saskia firmly, 'There won't be time for us to eat now. Saskia will have to get home and get ready. What time *is* Mark likely to go to the wine bar Megan?' she asked her cousin.

'About eight-thirty, I should think,' Megan answered.

'Right, then you need to get there for nine, Saskia,' Lorraine informed her, 'So I'll pick you up at half-eight.'

Two hours later Saskia was just coming downstairs when she heard the front doorbell. Her grandmother was away, spending several weeks with her sister in Bath. A little nervously Saskia smoothed down the skirt of her black suit and went to open the door.

Only Lorraine was standing outside. They had agreed that it would be silly to take the risk of Megan being seen and recognised. Now, as Lorraine studied her, Saskia could see the older woman beginning to frown.

'You'll have to wear something else,' she told Saskia sharply. 'You look far too businesslike and unapproachable in that suit. Mark's got to think you're approachable—remember. And I really think you ought to wear a different lipstick...red, perhaps, and more eye make-up. Look, if you don't believe me then read this.' Lorraine thrust an open magazine beneath Saskia's nose.

Reluctantly Saskia skimmed through the article, a small frown pleating her forehead as she read of the lengths the agency was prepared to have its girls go to in order to test the faithfulness of its clients' men.

'I can't do any of this,' she told Lorraine firmly. 'And as for my suit...'

Stepping into the hall and closing the front door behind her, Lorraine stood squarely in front of Saskia and told her vehemently, 'You have to—for Megan's sake. Can't you see what's happening to her, the danger she's in? She's totally besotted with this man; she's barely known him four months and already she's talking about handing over the whole of her inheritance to him...marrying him...having children with him. Do you know how much her great-aunt left her?' she added grimly.

Silently Saskia shook her head. She knew how surprised and shocked Megan had been when she had learned that she was the sole beneficiary under her great-aunt's will, but tactfully she had not asked her friend just how much money was involved.

Lorraine, it seemed, had not had similar qualms.

'Megan inherited nearly three million pounds,' she told Saskia, nodding her head in grim pleasure as she saw Saskia's expression.

'*Now* do you see how important it is that we do everything we can to protect her? I've tried to warn her umpteen times that her precious Mark might not be all he tries to make out he is, but she just won't listen. Now, thank goodness, she's caught him out and he's showing his true colours. For her sake, Saskia, you just do everything you can to prove how unworthy he is. Just imagine what it would do to her if he not only broke her heart but stole all her money as well. She'd be left with nothing.'

Saskia could imagine it all too well. Her grandmother had only a small pension to live on and Saskia, mindful of the sacrifices her grandmother had made when she was growing up, to make sure she did not go without the treats enjoyed by her peers, contributed as much as she could financially to their small household.

The thought of losing her financial independence and the sense of security that earning money of her own gave her was one that was both abhorrent and frightening to her, and Lorraine's revelations suddenly gave her not just the impetus but a real desire to do everything she could to protect her friend.

Megan, dear sweet trusting Megan, who still worked as a nurse despite her inheritance, deserved to find a man, a partner, who was truly worthy of her. And if this Mark wasn't... Well, perhaps then it would be for the best if her friend found out sooner rather than later.

'Perhaps if you took off the jacket of your suit,' Lorraine was saying now. 'You must have some kind of sexy summer top you could wear...or even just...'

She stopped as she saw Saskia's expression.

'Summer top, yes,' Saskia agreed. 'Sexy...no!'

As she saw the look on Lorraine's face Saskia suppressed a small sigh. It was pointless trying to explain to a woman like Lorraine that when nature had given one the kind of assets it had given Saskia, one learned very young that they could be something of a double-edged sword. To put it more bluntly, men—in Saskia's experience—did not need the double overload of seeing her body clad in 'sexy' clothes to encourage them to look twice at her. And in most cases to want to do much more than merely look!

'You must have *something*,' Lorraine urged, refusing to be defeated. 'A cardigan. You must have a cardigan—you could wear it sort of unbuttoned...'

'A cardigan? Yes, I have a cardigan,' Saskia agreed. She had bought it halfway through their cold spring when they had been on an economy drive at work and the heating had been turned off. But as for wearing it unbuttoned...!

'And red lipstick,' Lorraine was insisting, 'and more eye make-up. You'll have to let him know that you find him attractive...' She paused as Saskia lifted her eyebrows. 'It's for Megan's sake.'

In the end it was almost nine o'clock before they left the house, due to Lorraine's insistence that Saskia had to reapply her make-up with a far heavier hand than she would normally have used.

Uncomfortably Saskia refused to look at her reflection in the hall mirror. All that lipstick! It felt sticky, gooey, and as Lorraine drove her towards Hilford she had to force herself to resist the temptation to wipe it off. As for the unbuttoned cardigan she was wearing beneath her suit jacket—well, the moment she was inside the wine bar and out of Lorraine's sight she was going to refasten every single one of the top three buttons Lorraine had demanded that she left undone. True, they did nothing more than merely hint at a cleavage, but even that was far more of a provocation than Saskia would normally have allowed.

'We're here,' Lorraine announced as she pulled up outside the wine bar. 'I'll pick you up at eleven—that should give you plenty of time. Remember,' Lorraine hissed determinedly as Saskia got out of the car, 'We're doing this for Megan.'

We? But before Saskia could say anything Lorraine was driving off.

A man walking in the opposite direction paused on the pavement to give her an admiring glance. Automatically Saskia distanced herself from him and turned away, mentally squaring her shoulders as she headed for the entrance to the wine bar.

Lorraine had given her a long list of instructions, most of which had made Saskia cringe inwardly, and already her courage was beginning to desert her. There was no way she could go in there and pout and flirt in the enticing way that Lorraine had informed her she had to do. But if she didn't poor Megan could end up having her heart broken and her inheritance cheated away from her.

Taking a deep breath, Saskia pulled open the wine bar door.

CHAPTER TWO

ANDREAS saw Saskia the moment she walked in. He was seated at the bar, which was now being besieged by a crowd of young men who had come in just ahead of her. He could have stayed in and eaten in the office block's penthouse apartment—or even driven to the closest of their new acquisitions—but he had already endured two lengthy phone calls he would rather not have had this evening: one from his grandfather and another from Athena. So he had decided to go somewhere where neither of them could get in touch with him, having deliberately 'forgotten' to bring his mobile with him.

He hadn't been in a particularly good mood when he had arrived at the wine bar. Such places were not to his taste.

He liked good food served in comfortable surroundings where one could talk and think with ease, and there was also enough Greek in him for him to prefer somewhere more family centred and less of an obvious trawling ground for members of the opposite sex.

Thinking of the opposite sex made his mouth harden. Athena was becoming more and more brazen in her attempts to convince him that they should be together. He had been fifteen the first time he had been exposed to Athena's sexual aggression, and she had been twenty-two and about to be married.

He frowned as he watched Saskia. She was standing just inside the doorway, studying the room as though she was looking for someone. She turned her head and the light fell on her smoothly glossed lips.

Andreas sucked in his breath as he fought to control his unwanted reaction to her. What the hell was he doing? She was so damned obvious with that almost but not quite scarlet lipstick that he ought to be laughing, not... Not what? he asked himself caustically. Not wanting...lusting...

A strong surge of self-disgust lashed him. He had recognised her, of course. It was the girl from this afternoon, the one the receptionist had congratulated on her early departure from work. Then she had been wearing a minimum of make-up. Now... He eyed her lipsticked mouth and kohl-enhanced eyes grimly. She was wearing a suit with a short skirt...a very short skirt, he observed as she moved and he caught sight of the length of her sheer black tights-clad legs. A very, very short skirt!

As the turned-over waistband of her once respectably knee-length skirt made its presence felt, Saskia grimaced. Once she had found Mark she fully intended to make her way to the cloakroom and return her skirt to its normal length. It had been Lorraine, of course, who had insisted on shortening it.

'I can't go out like *that*,' Saskia had yelped.

'Don't be ridiculous,' Lorraine had derided her. 'That's nothing. Haven't you seen pictures from the sixties?'

'That was then,' Saskia had informed her firmly without letting her finish, but Lorraine had refused to give in and in the end Saskia had shrugged her shoulders and comforted herself with the knowledge that once Lorraine was out of sight she could do what she liked with her skirt. The cardigan too was making her feel uncomfortable, and unwittingly she started to toy with the first of its unfastened buttons.

As he watched her Andreas's eyes narrowed. God, but she was obvious, drawing attention to her breasts like that... And what breasts! Andreas discovered that he was starting to grind his teeth and, more importantly, that he was totally unable to take his eyes off Saskia...

Sensing that she was being watched, Saskia turned round and then froze as her searching gaze clashed head-on with Andreas's hard-eyed stare.

For a breath of time Saskia was totally dazed, such was the effect of Andreas's raw masculinity on her. Her heart was pounding, her mouth dry, her body... Helplessly transfixed, she fought desperately against what she was feeling—against what she was not allowed to feel. For this was Megan's Mark—it had to be. She could not really be experiencing what her emotions were telling her she was experiencing, she denied in panic. Not a woman like her, and not for this man, Megan's man!

No other man in the place came anywhere near matching the description Megan had given her as closely as this one did. Mentally she ticked off Megan's euphoric description of him—one Saskia had previously put down to the near ravings of a woman besottedly in love. Gorgeous, fantastically good-looking, sexy... Oh, and he would be wearing a blue shirt, Megan had told her, to match his eyes. Well, Saskia couldn't make out the colour of his eyes across the dimly lit distance that separated them, but she could certainly see that Megan had been right on every other count and her heart sank. So this was Megan's Mark. No wonder she was worrying so anxiously that he might be being unfaithful to her... A man who looked like this one did would have women pursuing him in droves.

Funny, but Megan hadn't mentioned the most important thing of all about him, which wasn't just that he was so spectacularly and sexually male but that he emanated a profound and intense air of authority that bordered almost on arrogance; it had struck Saskia the moment she had looked at him. That and the look of discreet male inspection quickly followed by a reactive resultant look of contemptuous disapproval.

That look... How *dare* he look at her like that? Suddenly all the doubts she had been harbouring about what she had agreed to do were vanquished.

Lorraine was right to be suspicious of such a man's motives, especially where a naïve, gentle, unworldly girl like Megan was concerned. Saskia didn't trust him one little bit. Megan needed a man who would appreciate her gentleness and treat her correspondingly. This man was powerful, daunting, awesome—and looking at him was, as Saskia was beginning to discover, something of a physical compulsion. She couldn't take her eyes off him. But that was just because she disliked him so much, she assured herself quickly, because she was so intensely aware of how very right Lorraine had been to want to test his loyalty to Megan.

Determinedly quelling the butterflies fluttering in

her stomach, Saskia took a deep breath, mentally reminding herself of what she had read in the article Lorraine had thrust under her nose. Then she had been horrified, repulsed by the lengths the girls hired by the agency were prepared to go to in order to entice and entrap their quarry into self-betrayal. It had even crossed her mind that no mere man could possibly find the strength to resist the kind of deliberate temptation those girls offered—everything from the most intense type of verbal flattery right up to outright offers of sex itself, although thankfully offers had been all they were.

A man like this one, though, must be used to women—attractive women—throwing themselves at him. 'He dated so many girls before he met me,' Megan had said innocently.

Saskia would just bet that he had. Megan was a honey, and Saskia loved her with a fierce loyalty, but even she had to admit that her friend did not possess the kind of glamorous instant eye appeal she suspected a man like this one would look for. But perhaps that was what he loved about her—the fact that she was so shy and homely. If he loved her... Well, that was up to Saskia to prove...or disprove...wasn't it?

With the light of battle shining in her eyes, Saskia made her way towards him.

Andreas watched her progress with a mixture of curiosity and disappointment. She was heading for him. He knew that, but the cool hauteur with which she not only ignored the interested looks she was collecting from other men as she did so but almost seemed not to notice them, was every bit as contrived as the unfastened buttons of the top she was wearing. It had to be! Andreas knew the type. He should do. After all, Athena...

'Oh, I'm sorry,' Saskia apologised as she reached Andreas's side and 'accidentally' stumbled against him. Straightening up, she stood next to him at the bar, giving him a winsomely apologetic smile as she moved so close to him that he could smell her scent... Not her perfume, which was light and floral, unexpectedly, but her *scent*, ...the soft, honey-sweet headily sensual and erotic scent that was her. And like a fool he was actually breathing it in, getting almost drunk on it...letting his senses react to it...to her...

Lorraine had coached her on her best approach and Saskia had memorised it, grimacing with loathing and distaste as she did so.

Andreas forced himself to step back from her and put some distance between them, but the bar was crowded and it was impossible for him to move away altogether, so instead he asked her coldly, 'I'm sorry...do I know you?'

His voice and demeanour were, he knew, cutting enough to make it plain that he knew what she was up to. Although why on earth a woman who looked like this one needed to trawl bars looking for men to pick up he had no idea. Or rather he did, but he preferred not to examine it too closely. There were women, as he already knew to his cost, who would do anything for money...anything...with anyone...

But Saskia was facing him now, her lipstick-glossed mouth parting in a smile he could see was forced as she purred, 'Er, no, actually, you don't...but I'm hoping that soon you will.'

Saskia was relieved that the bar was so dimly lit. She could feel the heat of her burning face. She had *never* in her most private thoughts even contemplated coming on to a man like this, never mind envisaged that she might actually do so. Quickly she hurried on to the next part of her prepared speech, parting her lips in what she hoped was a temptingly provocative smile whilst carefully running her tongue-tip over them.

Yuck! But all that lipstick felt repulsive.

'Aren't you going to ask me if I'd like a drink?' she invited coyly, batting her eyelashes in what she hoped was an appropriately enticing manner. 'I love the colour of your shirt,' she added huskily as she leaned closer. 'It matches your eyes...'

'If you think that you must be colour blind; my eyes are grey,' Andreas told her tersely. She was beginning to make him feel very angry. Her obviousness was nothing short of contemptible. But nothing like as contemptible as his own ridiculous reaction to her. What was he? A boy of eighteen? He was supposed to be a man...a mature, sophisticated, experienced, worldly man of thirty-odd—and yet here he was, reacting, *responding*, to the pathetically tired and jaded sexual tricks she was playing on him as eagerly as though... As though what? As though there was nothing he wanted to do right now more than take her to bed, to feel the hot urgency of her body beneath his, to hear her cry out his name through lips swollen with the mutual passion of their shared kisses whilst he...

'Look,' he told her sharply, cutting off the supply of lifeblood to his unwanted fantasies by the simple act of refusing to allow himself to think about them, 'you're making a big mistake.'

'Oh, no,' Saskia protested anxiously as he started to turn away from her. By rights she should simply accept what he was saying and go back to Megan and tell her that her beloved Mark was everything he was supposed to be. But an instinct she couldn't analyse was telling her that despite all the evidence to the contrary he was tempted. *Any* man could be tempted, she tried to tell herself fairly, but something inside her refused to allow her to listen.

'*You* could never be a mistake,' she purred suggestively. 'To any woman…'

Fatuously Andreas wondered if he had gone completely mad. To even think of desiring a woman who was openly propositioning him was anathema to everything he believed in. How could he possibly be even remotely attracted to her? He wasn't, of course. It was impossible. And as for that sudden inexplicable urge he had had to take her home with him, where she would be safe from the kind of attention her make-up and behaviour were bound to attract. Well, now he knew he *must* be seriously losing it.

If there was one thing he despised it was women like this one. Not that he preferred them to be demure or virginal. No. What he found most attractive was a woman who was proud to be herself and who expected his sex to respect her right to be what she was. The kind of woman who would automatically eschew any act that involved her presenting herself as some kind of sexual plaything and who would just as determinedly turn her back on any man who wanted her to behave that way. This woman...

'I'm sorry,' he told her, making it verbally plain that he was no such thing by the cold tone of his voice, 'but you're wasting your time. And time, as I can see,' he continued in a deceptively gentle voice, 'has to be money for a woman like you. So why don't you go away and find someone else who will be... er...more receptive to what you've got on offer than I am?'

White-faced, Saskia watched as he turned away from her and thrust his way towards the door. He had rejected her...refused her. He had... He had... Painfully she swallowed. He had proved that he was faithful to Megan and he had... He had looked at her as though...as though... Like a little girl, Saskia wiped the back of her hand across her lipsticked mouth, grimacing as she saw the stain the high-coloured gloss had left there.

'Hi there, gorgeous. Can I buy you a drink?'

Numbly she shook her head, ignoring the sour look the man who had approached was giving her as she stared at the door. There was no sign of Megan's man. He had gone—and she was glad. Of course she was. How could she not be? And she would be delighted to be able to report to Megan and Lorraine that Mark had not succumbed to her.

She glanced at her watch, her heart sinking. She still had over an hour to go before she met Lorraine. There was no way she could stay here in the bar on her own, attracting attention. Quickly she headed for the ladies. There was something she had to do.

In the cloakroom she fastened her cardigan and

wiped her face clean of the last of the red lipstick and the kohl eye-liner, replacing them both with her normal choice of make-up—a discreet application of taupe eye-shadow and a soft berry-coloured lipstick—and coiling up her long hair into a neat chignon. Then she waited in the ladies' room until an inspection of her watch told her she could finally leave.

This time as she made her way through the crowded bar it was a very different type of look that Saskia collected from the men who watched her admiringly.

To her relief Lorraine was parked outside, waiting for her.

'Well?' she demanded eagerly as Saskia opened the car door and got in.

'Nothing,' Saskia told her, shaking her head. 'He turned me down flat.'

'What?'

'Lorraine, careful…' Saskia cried out warningly as the other woman almost backed into the car behind her in shock.

'You mustn't have tried hard enough,' Lorraine told her bossily.

'I can assure you that I tried as hard as anyone could,' Saskia corrected her wryly.

'Did he *mention* Megan…tell you that he was spoken for?' Lorraine questioned her.

'No!' Saskia shook her head. 'But I promise you he made it plain that he wasn't interested. He looked at me…' She stopped and swallowed, unwilling to think about, never mind tell anyone else, just how Megan's beloved had looked at her. For some odd reason she refused to define just to remember the icy contempt she had seen in his eyes made her tremble between anger and pain.

'Where *is* Megan?' she asked Lorraine.

'She was called in unexpectedly to work an extra shift. She rang to let me know and I said we'd drive straight over to her place and meet up with her there.'

Saskia smiled wanly. By rights she knew she ought to be feeling far happier than she actually was. Though out of the three of them she suspected that Megan would be the only one who would actually be pleased to learn that her Mark had determinedly refused to be tempted.

Her Mark. *Megan's* Mark. There was a bitter taste in Saskia's mouth and her heart felt like a heavy lump of lead inside her chest.

What on earth was the matter with her? She couldn't possibly be jealous of Megan, could she? No! She couldn't be…she *must* not be!

'Are you sure you tried hard enough?' Lorraine was asking her sternly.

'I said everything you told me to say,' Saskia told her truthfully.

'And he didn't make any kind of response?'

Saskia could tell that Lorraine didn't believe her.

'Oh, he made a response,' she admitted grimly. 'It just wasn't the kind…' She stopped and then told her flatly, 'He wasn't interested, Lorraine. He must really love Megan.'

'Yes, if he prefers her to you he must,' Lorraine agreed bluntly. 'She's a dear, and I love her, but there's no way… You don't think he could have *guessed* what you were doing do you? No way he could have known...?'

'No, I don't,' Saskia denied. She was beginning to feel tired, almost aching with a sharp, painful need to be on her own. The last thing she wanted right now was to deal with someone like Lorraine, but she owed it to Megan to reassure her that she could trust Mark.

As they pulled up outside Megan's house Saskia saw that her car was parked outside. Her stomach muscles started to clench as she got out of Lorraine's car and walked up the garden path. Megan and Mark. Even their names sounded cosy together, redolent of domesticity...of marital comfort. And yet...if ever she'd met a man who was neither domesticated nor cosy it had been Megan's Mark. There had been an air of primitive raw maleness about him, an aura of power and sexuality, a sense that in his arms a woman could...*would*...touch such sensual heights of delight and pleasure that she would never be quite the same person again.

Saskia tensed. What on earth was she thinking? Mark belonged to Megan—her best friend, the friend to whom she owed her grandmother's life and good health.

Megan had obviously seen them arrive and was opening the door before they reached it, her face wreathed in smiles.

'It's all right,' Saskia told her hollowly. 'Mark didn't...'

'I know...I know...' Megan beamed as she ushered them inside. 'He came to see me at work and explained everything. Oh, I've been such an idiot...

Why on earth I didn't guess what he was planning I just don't know. We leave next week. He'd even told them at work what he was planning...that was the reason for all those calls. Plus the girl at the travel agency kept phoning. Oh, Saskia, I can't believe it. I've always longed to go to the Caribbean, and for Mark to have booked us such a wonderful holiday... The place we're going to specialises in holidays for couples. I'm so sorry you had a wasted evening. I tried to ring you but you'd already left. I thought you might have got here sooner. After all, once you'd realised that Mark wasn't at the wine bar...' She stopped as she saw the look on both her cousin's and Saskia's faces.

'What is it?' she asked them uncertainly.

'*You* said that you'd spoken to Mark,' Lorraine was saying tersely to Saskia.

'I did...' Saskia insisted. 'He was just as you described him to us, Megan...'

She stopped as Megan shook her head firmly.

'Mark wasn't there, Sas,' she repeated. 'He was with me at work. He arrived at half past eight and Sister gave me some time off so that we could talk. He'd guessed how upset I was and he'd decided that he would have to tell me what he was planning. He said he knew he couldn't have kept the secret for very much longer anyway,' she added fondly.

'And before you say a word,' she said firmly to her cousin, 'Mark is paying for everything himself.'

Saskia leaned weakly against the wall. If the man she had come on to hadn't been Megan's Mark, then just who on earth had he been? Her face became even paler. She had come on to a man she didn't know...a total and complete stranger...a man who... She swallowed nauseously, remembering the way she had looked, the way she had behaved...the things she had said. Thank God he was a stranger. Thank God she would never have to see him again.

'Sas, you don't look well,' she could hear Megan saying solicitously. 'What is it?'

'Nothing,' she fibbed, but Lorraine had already guessed what she was thinking.

'Well, if the man in the wine bar wasn't Mark then who on earth was he?' She demanded sharply.

'Who indeed?' Saskia echoed hollowly.

CHAPTER THREE

TO SASKIA'S dismay she heard the town hall clock striking eight a.m. as she hurried to work. She had intended to be in extra early this morning but unfortunately she had overslept—a direct result of the previous evening's events and the fact that initially she had been mentally agonising so much over what she had done that she had been unable to get to sleep.

Officially she might not be due to be at her desk until nine a.m., but in this modern age that was not the way things worked, especially when one's hold on one's job was already dangerously precarious.

'There are bound to be cutbacks...redundancies,' the head of Saskia's department had warned them all, and Saskia, as she'd listened to him, had been sharply conscious that as the newest member of the team she was the one whose job was most in line to be cut back. It would be virtually impossible for her to get another job with the same kind of prospects in Hilford, and if she moved away to London that would mean her grandmother would be left on her own. At sixty-five her grandmother was not precisely old—far from it—and she had a large circle of friends, but the illness had left Saskia feeling afraid for her. Saskia felt she owed her such a huge debt, not only for bringing her up but for giving her so much love.

As she hurried into the foyer she asked Emma, the receptionist, anxiously, 'Has he arrived yet?'

There was no need to qualify who she meant by 'he', and Emma gave her a slightly superior smile as she replied, 'Actually he arrived yesterday. He's upstairs now,' she added smugly, 'interviewing everyone.' Her smugness and superiority gave way to a smile of pure feminine appreciation as she sighed. 'Just wait until you see him. He's gorgeous...with a great big capital G.'

She rolled her eyes expressively whilst Saskia gave her a wan smile.

She now had her own special and private—very private—blueprint of what a gorgeous man looked like, and she doubted that their new Greek boss came anywhere near to matching it.

'Typically, though, mind you,' the receptionist continued, oblivious to Saskia's desire to hurry to her office, 'he's already spoken for. Or at least he soon will be. I was talking to the receptionist at their group's head office and she told me that his grandfather wants him to marry his cousin. She's mega-wealthy and—'

'I'm sorry, Emma, but I must go,' Saskia interrupted her firmly. Office gossip, like office politics, was something Saskia had no wish to involve herself in, and besides... If their new boss was already interviewing people she didn't want to earn herself any black marks by not being at her desk when he sent for her.

Her office was on the third floor, an open plan space where she worked with five other people. Their boss had his own glass-walled section, but right now both it and the general office itself were empty.

Just as she was wondering what to do the outer door swung open and her boss, followed by the rest of her colleagues, came into the room.

'Ah, Saskia, there you are,' her boss greeted her.

'Yes. I had intended to be here earlier...' Saskia began, but Gordon Jarman was shaking his head.

'Don't explain now,' he told her sharply. 'You'd better get upstairs to the executive suite. Mr Latimer's secretary will be expecting you. Apparently he wants to interview everyone, both individually and with their co-department members, and he wasn't too pleased that you weren't here...'

Without allowing Saskia to say anything, Gordon turned on his heel and went into his office, leaving her with no option but to head for the lift. It was unlike Gordon to be so sharp. He was normally a very laid back sort of person. Saskia could feel the nervous feeling in her tummy increasing as she contemplated the kind of attitude Andreas Latimer must have adopted towards his new employees to cause such a reaction in her normally unflappable boss.

The executive suite was unfamiliar territory to Saskia. The only previous occasions on which she had entered it had been when she had gone for her initial interview and then, more recently, when the whole staff had been informed of the success of the Demetrios takeover bid.

A little uncertainly she got out of the lift and walked towards the door marked 'Personal Assistant to the Chief Executive'.

Madge Fielding, the previous owner's secretary,

had retired when the takeover bid's success had been announced, and when Saskia saw the elegantly groomed dark-haired woman seated behind Madge's desk she assumed that the new owner must have brought his PA with him from Demetrios head office.

Nervously Saskia gave her name, and started to explain that she worked for Gordon Jarman, but the PA waved her explanation aside, consulting a list in front of her instead and then saying coldly, without lifting her head from it, 'Saskia? Yes. You're late. Mr Latimer does not like... In fact I'm not sure...' She stopped and eyed Saskia with a disapproving frown. 'He may not have time to interview you now,' she warned, before picking up the phone and announcing in a very different tone of voice from the one she had used to address Saskia, 'Ms. Rodgers is here now, Andreas. Do you still want to see her?

'You *can* go in,' she informed Saskia. 'It's the door over there...'

Feeling like a naughty child, Saskia forced herself not to react, heading instead for the door the PA had indicated and knocking briefly on it before turning the handle and walking in.

As she stepped into the office the bright sunlight streaming in through the large windows momentarily dazzled her. All she could make out was the hazy outline of a man standing in front of the glass with his back to her, the brilliance of the sunlight making it impossible for her to see any more.

But Andreas could see Saskia. It hadn't surprised him that she should choose to arrive at work later than her colleagues; after all, he knew how she spent her evenings. What had surprised him had been the genuinely high esteem in which he had discovered she was held both by her immediate boss and her co-workers. It seemed that when it came to giving that extra metre, going that extra distance, Saskia was always the first to do so and the first to do whatever she could to help out her colleagues.

'Yes, it is perhaps unusual in a young graduate,' her boss had agreed when Andreas had questioned his praise of Saskia. 'But then she has been brought up by her grandmother and perhaps because of that her values and sense of obligation towards others are those of an older generation. As you can see from my report on her, her work is excellent and so are her qualifications.'

And she's a stunningly attractive young woman who seems to know how to use her undeniable 'assets' to her own advantage, Andreas had reflected inwardly, but Gordon Jarman had continued to enthuse about Saskia's dedication to her work, her kindness to her fellow employees, her ability to integrate herself into a team and work diligently at whatever task she was given, and her popularity with other members of the workforce.

After studying the progress reports her team leader and Gordon himself had made on her, and the photograph in her file, Andreas had been forced to concede that if he hadn't seen for himself last night the way Saskia could look and behave he would probably have accepted Gordon's glowing report at face value.

She was quite plainly a woman who knew how to handle his sex, even if with him she had made an error of judgement.

This morning, for instance, she had completely metamorphosed back into the dedicated young woman forging a career for herself—neatly suited, her hair elegantly sleeked back, her face free of all but the lightest touch of make-up. Andreas started to frown as his body suddenly and very urgently and unwontedly reminded him of the female allure of the body that was today concealed discreetly beneath a prim navy business suit.

Didn't he already have enough problems to contend with? Last night after returning from the wine bar he had received a telephone call from his mother, anxiously warning him that his grandfather was on the warpath.

'He had dinner with some of his old cronies last night and apparently they were all boasting about the deals they had recently pulled off. You know what they're like.' She had sighed. 'And your grandfather was told by one of them that he had high hopes of his son winning Athena's hand...'

'Good luck to him,' Andreas had told his mother uncompromisingly. 'I hope he does. That at least will get her and Grandfather off my back.'

'Well, yes,' his mother had agreed doubtfully. 'But at the moment it seems to have made him even more determined to promote a marriage between the two of you. And, of course, now that he's half retired he's got more time on his hands to plan and fret... It's such a pity that there isn't already someone in your life.' She had sighed again, adding with a chuckle, 'I honestly believe that the hope of a great-grandchild would thrill him so much that he'd quickly forget he'd ever wanted you to marry Athena!'

Someone else in his life? Had it really been exasperation and the headache he knew lay ahead of him with their new acquisition that had prompted him into making the rashest statement of his life in telling his mother, 'What makes you think there *isn't* someone?'

There had been a startled pause, just long enough for him to curse himself mentally but not for him to recall his impetuous words, before his mother had demanded in excitement, 'You mean there *is*? Oh, Andreas! Who? *When* are we going to meet her? Who is she? How did you...? Oh, darling, how wonderful. Your grandfather *will* be thrilled. Olympia, guess what...'

He had then heard her telling his sister.

He had tried to put a brake on their excitement, to warn them that he was only talking in 'ifs' and 'buts', but neither of them had been prepared to listen. Neither had his grandfather this morning, when he had rung at the ungodly hour of five o'clock to demand to know when he was to meet his grandson's fiancée.

Fiancée... How the hell his mother and sister had managed to translate an off the cuff remark made in irritation into a real live fiancée Andreas had no idea, but he did know that unless he produced this mythical creature he was going to be in very big trouble.

'You'll be bringing her to the island with you, of course,' his grandfather had announced, and his words had been a command and not a question.

What the hell was he going to do? He had eight

days in which to find a prospective fiancée and make it clear to her that their 'engagement' was nothing more than a convenient fiction. Eight days and she would have to be a good enough actress to fool not just his grandfather but his mother and sisters as well.

Irritably he moved out of the sunlight's direct beam, turning round so that Saskia saw him properly for the first time.

There was no opportunity for her to conceal her shock, or the soft winded gasp of dismay that escaped her discreetly glossed lips as her face paled and then flooded with burning hot colour.

'You!' she choked as she backed instinctively towards the door, her memories of the previous night flooding her brain and with them the sure knowledge that she was about to lose her job.

She certainly was an excellent actress, Andreas acknowledged as he observed her reaction—and in more ways than one. Her demeanour this morning was totally different from the way she had presented herself last night. But then no doubt she *was* horrified to discover that he was the man she had so blatantly propositioned. Even so, that look of sick dismay darkening her eyes and the way her soft bottom lip was trembling despite her attempts to stop it... Oh, yes, she was a first-rate actress—*a first-rate actress*!

Suddenly Andreas could see a welcome gleam of light at the end of the dark tunnel of his current problem. Oh, yes, indeed, a very definite beam of light.

'So Ms Rodgers.' Andreas began flaying into Saskia's already shredded self-confidence with all the delicacy of a surgeon expertly slicing through layer after layer of skin, muscle and bone. 'I have read the report Gordon Jarman has written on you and I must congratulate you. It seems that you've persuaded him to think very highly of you. That's quite an accomplishment for an employee so new and young. Especially one who adopts such an unconventional and, shall we say, elastic attitude towards time-keeping...leaving earlier than her colleagues in the evening and arriving later than them in the morning.'

'Leaving *early*?' Saskia stared at him, fighting to recover her composure. How had he known about *that*?

As though he had read her mind, he told her softly, 'I was in the foyer when you left...quite some time before your official finishing time.'

'But that was...' Saskia began indignantly.

However, Andreas did not allow her to finish, shaking his head and telling her coolly, 'No excuses, please. They might work on Gordon Jarman, but unfortunately for you they will not work with me. After all, I have seen how you comport yourself when you are not at work. Unless...' He frowned, his mouth hardening as he studied her with icy derision. 'Unless, of course, *that* is the reason he has given you such an unusually excellent report...'

'No!' Saskia denied straight away. 'No! I don't... Last night was a mistake,' she protested. 'I...'

'Yes, I'm afraid it was,' Andreas agreed, adding smoothly, 'For you at least. I appreciate that the salary you are paid is relatively small, but my grandfather would be extremely unhappy to learn that a member of our staff is having to boost her income in a way that can only reflect extremely badly on our company.' Giving her a thin smile he went on with deceptive amiability, 'How very fortunate for you that it wasn't in one of *our* hotels that you were…er… plying your trade and—'

'How dare you?' Saskia interrupted him furiously, her cheeks bright scarlet and her mouth a mutinous soft bow. Pride burned rebelliously in her eyes.

'How dare I? Rather I should say to you, how dare *you*,' Andreas contradicted her sharply, his earlier air of pleasantness instantly replaced by a hard look of contemptuous anger as he told her grimly, 'Apart from the unedifying moral implications of what you were doing, or rather attempting to do, has it ever occurred to you to consider the physical danger you could be putting yourself in? Women like you…'

He paused and changed tack, catching her off guard as he went on in a much gentler tone, 'I understand from your boss that you are very anxious to maintain your employment with us.'

'Yes. Yes, I am,' Saskia admitted huskily. There was no use denying what he was saying. She had already discussed her feelings and fears about the prospect of being made redundant with Gordon Jarman, and he had obviously recorded them and passed them on to Andreas. To deny them now would only convince him she was a liar—as well as everything else!

'Look… Please, I can explain about last night,' she told him desperately, pride giving way to panic. 'I know how it must have looked, but it wasn't… I didn't…' She stopped as she saw from his expression that he wasn't prepared even to listen to her, never mind believe her.

A part of her was forced to acknowledge that she

could hardly blame him...nor convince him either, unless she dragged Lorraine and Megan into his office to support her and she had far too much pride to do that. Besides, Megan wasn't capable of thinking of anything or anyone right now other than Mark and her upcoming Caribbean holiday, and as for Lorraine... Well, Saskia could guess how the older woman would revel in the situation Saskia now found herself in.

'A wise decision,' Andreas told her gently when she stopped speaking. 'You see, I despise a liar even more than I do a woman who...' Now it was his turn to stop, but Saskia knew what he was thinking.

Her face burned even more hotly, which made it disconcerting for her when he suddenly said abruptly, 'I've got a proposition I want to put to you.'

As she made a strangled sound of shock in her throat he steepled his fingers together and looked at her over them, like a sleek, well-fed predator watching a small piece of prey it was enjoying tormenting.

'What kind of proposition?' she asked him warily, but the heavy sledgehammer strokes of her heart against her ribs warned her that she probably already knew the answer—just as she knew why she was filled with such a shocking mixture of excitement and revulsion.

'Oh, not the kind you are probably most familiar with,' Andreas was telling her softly. 'I've read that some professional young women get a kick out of acting the part of harlots...'

'I was doing no such thing,' Saskia began heatedly, but he stopped her.

'I was there—remember?' he said sharply. 'If my

grandfather knew how you had behaved he would demand your instant dismissal.' His grandfather might have ceded most of the control of the business to Andreas, but Andreas could see from Saskia's expression that she still believed him.

'You don't *have* to tell him.' He could see the effort it cost her to swallow her pride and add a reluctant tremulous, 'Please…'

'I don't *have* to,' he agreed 'But whether or not I do depends on your response to my proposition.'

'That's blackmail,' Saskia protested.

'Almost as old a profession as the one you were engaging in last night,' Andreas agreed silkily.

Saskia began to panic. Against all the odds there was only one thing he could possibly want from her, unlikely though that was. After all, last night she had given him every reason to assume…to believe… But that had been when she had thought he was Mark, and if he would just allow her to explain…

Fear kicked through her, fuelling a panic that rushed her headlong into telling him aggressively, 'I'm surprised that a man like you needs to blackmail a woman into having sex with him. And there's no way that I…'

'Sex?' he questioned, completely astounding her by throwing back his head and laughing out loud. When he had stopped, he repeated, 'Sex?' adding disparagingly, 'With you? No way! It isn't *sex* I want from you,' he told her coolly.

'Not sex? Then…then what is it?' Saskia demanded shakily.

'What I want from you,' Andreas informed her

calmly, 'is your time and your agreement to pose as my fiancée.'

'What?' Saskia stared at him. 'You're mad,' she told him in disbelief.

'No, not mad,' Andreas corrected her sternly. 'But I am very determined not to be coerced into the marriage my grandfather wants to arrange for me. And, as my dear mother has so rightly reminded me, the best way to do that is to convince him that I am in love with someone else. That is the only way I can stop this ridiculous campaign of his.'

'You want *me*…to pose…as *your*…fiancée?' Saskia spaced the words out carefully, as though she wasn't sure she had heard them correctly, and then, when she saw the confirmation in his face, she denied fiercely, 'No. No way. No way at all!'

'No?' Andreas questioned with remarkable amiability. 'Then I'm afraid you leave me with no alternative but to inform you that there is a strong—a very strong possibility that we shall have to let you go as part of our regrettable but necessary cutbacks. I hope I make myself clear.'

'No! You can't do that…' Saskia began, and then stopped as she saw the cynical way he was looking at her.

She was wasting her time. There was no way he was even going to listen to her, never mind believe her. He didn't *want* to believe her. It didn't suit his plans to believe her…she could see that. And if she refused to accede to his commands then she knew that he was fully capable of carrying out his threat against her. Saskia swallowed. She was well and truly trapped, with no way whatsoever of escaping.

'Well?' Andreas mocked her. 'You still haven't given me your reply. Do you agree to my proposition, or…?'

Saskia swallowed the bitter taste of bile and defeat lodged in her throat. Her voice sounded raw, rasping…it hurt her to speak but she tried to hold up her head as she told him miserably, 'I agree.'

'Excellent. For form's sake I suggest that we invent a previously secret accidental meeting between us—perhaps when I visited Hilford prior to our takeover. Because of the negotiations for the takeover we have kept our relationship…our love for one another…a secret. But now…now there is no need for secrecy any more, and to prove it, and to celebrate our freedom today I shall take you out for lunch.'

He frowned and paused. 'We shall be flying out to the Aegean at the end of next week and there are things we shall be expected to know about one another's background!'

'Flying out to *where*?' Saskia gasped. 'No, I can't. My grandmother…'

Andreas had heard from Gordon Jarman that she lived with her grandmother, and now one eyebrow rose as he questioned silkily, 'You are engaged to me now, my beloved, surely *I* am of more importance than your grandmother? She will, I know, be surprised about our relationship, but I am sure she will appreciate just why we had to keep our love for one another to ourselves. If you wish I am perfectly prepared to come with you when you explain…everything to her…'

'No!' Saskia denied in panic. 'There's no need anyway. She's in Bath at the moment, staying with her sister. She's going to be there for the next few weeks. You can't do this,' she told him in agitation. 'Your grandfather is bound to guess that we're not…that we don't… And…'

'But he must *not* be *allowed* to guess any such thing,' Andreas told her gently. 'You are an excellent actress, as I have already seen for myself, and I'm sure you will be able to find a way of convincing him that we *are* and we *do*, and should you feel that you do need some assistance to that end…' His eyes darkened and Saskia immediately took a step backwards, her face flaming with embarrassed colour as she saw the way he was looking at her.

'Very nice,' he told her softly, 'But perhaps it might not be wise to overdo the shy, virginal bit. My grandfather is no fool. I doubt that he will expect a man of my age to have fallen passionately in love with a woman who is not equally sexually aware. I am, after all, half-Greek, and passion is very much a factor of the male Greek personality and psyche.'

Saskia wanted to turn and run away. The situation was becoming worse by the minute. What, she wondered fatalistically, would Andreas do if he ever learned that she was not 'sexually aware', as he had termed it, and that in fact her only experience of sex and passion was limited to a few chaste kisses and fumbled embraces? She had her parents to thank for her caution as a teenager where sexual experimentation had been concerned, of course. Their rash behaviour had led to her dreading that she might repeat their foolishness. But there was, of course, no way that Andreas could ever know that!

'It's now almost ten,' Andreas informed her

briskly, looking at his watch. 'I suggest you go back to your office and at one p.m. I'll come down for you and take you out to lunch. The sooner we make our relationship public now, the better.'

As he spoke he was moving towards her. Immediately Saskia started to panic, gasping out loud in shock as the door opened to admit his PA in the same heartbeat as Andreas reached out and manacled Saskia's fragile wrist-bone in the firm grip of his fingers and thumb.

His skin was dark, tanned, but not so much so that one would automatically guess at his Greek blood, Saskia recognised. His eyes *were* grey, she now saw, and not blue as she had so blush-makingly suggested last night, and they added to the confusion as to what nationality he might be, whilst his hair, though very, very dark, was thick and straight. There was, though, some whisper of his ancient lineage in his high cheekbones, classically sculptured jaw and aquiline nose. They definitely belonged to some arrogant, aristocratic ancient Greek nobleman, and he would, she suspected, be very much inclined to dominate those around him, to stamp his authority on everything he did—and everyone he met.

'Oh, Andreas,' the PA was exclaiming, looking in flustered disbelief at the way her boss was drawing Saskia closer to him, 'I'm sorry to interrupt you but your grandfather has been on—twice!'

'I shall ring my grandfather back shortly,' Andreas responded smoothly, adding equally smoothly, 'Oh, and I don't want any appointments or any interruptions from one to two-thirty today. I shall be taking my fiancée to lunch.'

As he spoke he turned to Saskia and gave her such a look of melting tender sensuality, so completely redolent of an impatient lover barely able to control his desire for her, that for a breath of time she was almost taken in herself. She could only stare back at him as though she had been hypnotised. If he had given her a look like that last night... Stop it, she warned herself immediately, shaken by the unexpected thought.

But if his behaviour was shocking her it was shocking his PA even more, she recognised as the other woman gave a small choked gurgle and then shook her head when Andreas asked her urbanely if anything was wrong.

'No. I was just... That is... No...not at all...'

'Good. Oh, and one more thing. I want you to book an extra seat on my flight to Athens next week. Next to mine...for Saskia...' Turning away from his PA he told Saskia huskily, 'I can't wait to introduce you to my family, especially my grandfather. But first...'

Before Saskia could guess what he intended to do he lifted her hand to his mouth, palm facing upwards. As she felt the warmth of his breath skimming her skin Saskia started to tremble, her breath coming in quick, short bursts. She felt dizzy, breathless, filled with a mixture of elation, excitement and shock, a sense of somehow having stepped outside herself and become another person, entered another life—a life that was far more exciting than her own, a life that could lead to the kind of dangerous, magical, awe-inspiring experiences that she had previously thought could never be hers.

Giddily she could hear Andreas telling her huskily, 'First, my darling, we must find something pretty to adorn this bare finger of yours. My grandfather would not approve if I took you home without a ring that states very clearly my intentions.'

Saskia could hear quite plainly the PA's sudden shocked indrawn breath, but once again the other woman could not be any more shocked than she was herself. Andreas had claimed that she was a good actress, but he was no slouch in that department himself. The look that he was giving her right now alone, never mind the things he had said...

After his PA had scuttled out of his office, closing the door behind her, she told him shakily, 'You do realise, don't you, that by lunchtime it will be all over the office?'

'All over the office?' he repeated, giving her a desirous look. 'My dear, I shall be very surprised and even more disappointed if our news has not travelled a good deal further than that.'

When she gave him an uncomprehending look he explained briefly, 'By lunchtime I fully expect it to have travelled at least as far as Athens...'

'To your grandfather,' Saskia guessed.

'Amongst others,' Andreas agreed coolly, without enlightening her as to who such 'others' might be.

Unexpectedly there were suddenly dozens of questions she wanted to ask him: about his family, as well as his grandfather, and the island he intended to take her to, and about the woman his grandfather wanted him to marry. She had a vague idea that Greeks were very interested in protecting family interests and according to Emma his cousin was 'mega wealthy', as was Andreas himself.

Somehow, without knowing quite how it had happened, she discovered that Andreas had released her hand and that she was walking through the door he had opened for her.

'Ready, Saskia?'

Saskia felt the embarrassed colour start to seep up under her skin as Andreas approached her desk. Her colleagues were studiously avoiding looking openly at them but Saskia knew perfectly well that they were the cynosure of their attention. How could they not be?

'Gordon, I'm afraid that Saskia is going to be late back from lunch,' Andreas was announcing to her bemused boss as he came out from his office.

'Have you told him our news yet, darling,' Andreas asked her lovingly.

'Er...no...' Saskia couldn't bring herself to look directly at him.

'Saskia,' she could hear her boss saying weakly as he looked on disbelievingly, 'I don't understand...'

He would understand even less if she tried to explain to him what was *really* happening, Saskia acknowledged bleakly. It seemed to her that it was a very unfair thing to do to deceive the man who had been so kind to her but what alternative did she really have.

'You mustn't blame Saskia,' Andreas was saying protectively. 'I'm afraid I'm the one who's at fault. I insisted that our relationship should be kept a secret until the outcome of our takeover bid became public.

I didn't want Saskia to be accused of having conflicting loyalties—and I must tell you, Gordon, that she insisted that any kind of discussion about the takeover was off-limits between us... Mind you, talking about work was not exactly *my* number one priority when we were together,' Andreas admitted, with a sensual look at Saskia that made her face burn even more hotly and caused more than one audible and envious gasp from her female co-workers.

'Why did you have to do *that*?' Saskia demanded fretfully the moment they were alone and out of earshot.

'Do what?' Andreas responded unhelpfully.

'You know perfectly well what I mean,' Saskia protested. 'Why couldn't we just have met somewhere?'

'In secret?' He looked more bored now than amorous, his eyebrows drawing together as he frowned impatiently down at her. He was a good deal taller than her, well over six foot, and it hurt her neck a little, craning to look up at him. She wished he wouldn't walk so close to her; it made her feel uncomfortable and on edge and somehow aware of herself as a woman in a way that wasn't familiar to her.

'Haven't I already made it plain to you that the whole object of this exercise is to bring our relationship into the public domain? Which is why—' He smiled grimly at Saskia as he broke off from what he was saying to tell her silkily, 'I've booked a table at the wine bar for lunch. I ate there last night and I have to say that the food was excellent—even if what happened later was less...palatable...'

Suddenly Saskia had had enough.

'Look, I keep trying to tell you, last night was a mistake. I...'

'I completely agree with you,' Andreas assured her. 'It *was* a mistake...*your* mistake...and whilst we're on the subject, let me warn you, Saskia, if you *ever* manifest anything similar whilst you are engaged to *me*, if you ever even *look* at another man...' He stopped as he saw the shock widening her eyes.

'I'm half-Greek, my dear,' he reminded her softly. 'And when it comes to *my* woman, I'm more Greek than I am British...very much more...'

'I'm *not* your woman,' was the only response Saskia found she could make.

'No,' he agreed cynically. 'You belong to any man who can afford you, don't you, in reality? But...' He stopped again as he heard the sharp sound of protest she made, her face white and then red as her emotions overwhelmed her self-control.

'You have no right to speak to me like that,' Saskia told him thickly.

'No right? But surely as your fiancée I have *every* right,' Andreas taunted her, and then, before she could stop him, he reached out and ran one long finger beneath her lower eyelashes, collecting on it the angry humiliated tears that had just fallen. 'Tears?' he mocked her. 'My dear, you are an even better actress then I thought.'

They had reached the wine bar and Saskia was forced to struggle to control her emotions as he opened the door and drew her inside.

'I don't want anything to eat. I'm not hungry,' she told him flatly once they had been shown to their table.

'Sulking?' he asked her succinctly. 'I can't force you to eat, but I certainly don't intend to deny *myself* the pleasure of enjoying a good meal.'

'There are things we have to discuss,' he added in a cool, businesslike voice as he picked up the menu she had ignored and read it. 'I know most of your personal details from your file, but if we are to convince my family and especially my grandfather that we are lovers, then there are other things I shall need to know…and things you will need to know about me.'

Lovers… Saskia just managed to stop herself from shuddering openly. If she had to accede to his blackmail then she was going to have to learn to play the game by his rules or risk being totally destroyed by him.

'Lovers.' She gave him a bleak smile. 'I thought Greek families didn't approve of sex before marriage.'

'Not for their *own* daughters,' he agreed blandly. 'But since you are *not* Greek, and since *I* am half-British I am sure that my grandfather will be more…tolerant…'

'But he wouldn't be tolerant if you were engaged to your cousin?' Saskia pressed, not sure why she was doing so and even less sure just why the thought of his cousin should arouse such a sensation of pain and hostility within her.

'Athena, my cousin, is a *widow*, a previously married woman, and naturally my grandfather…' He paused and then told her dryly, 'Besides, Athena herself would never accept my grandfather's interference in any aspect of her life. She is a very formidable woman.'

'She's a *widow*?' For some reason Saskia had assumed that this cousin was a young girl. It had never occurred to her that she might already have been married.

'A widow,' Andreas confirmed. 'With two teenage children.'

'Teenage!'

'She married at twenty-two,' Andreas told her with a shrug. 'That was almost twenty years ago.'

Saskia's eyes widened as she did her sums. Athena was obviously older than Andreas. A lonely and no doubt vulnerable woman who was being pressurised into a second marriage she perhaps did not want, Saskia decided sympathetically.

'However, you need not concern yourself too much with Athena, since it is doubtful that you will meet her. She lives a very peripatetic existence. She has homes in Athens, New York and Paris and spends much of her time travelling between them, as well as running the shipping line she inherited.'

A shipping line and a hotel chain. No wonder Andreas's grandfather was so anxious for them to marry. It amazed Saskia that Andreas was not equally keen on the match, especially knowing the hard bargain he had driven over the takeover.

As though he had guessed what she was thinking, he leaned towards her and told her grittily, 'Unlike you, *I* am not prepared to sell myself.'

'I was *not* selling myself,' Saskia denied hotly, and then frowned as the waiter approached their table carrying two plates of delicious-looking food.

'I didn't order a meal,' she began as he set one of them down in front of her and the other in front of Andreas.

'No. I ordered it for you,' Andreas told her. 'I don't like to see my women looking like skinny semi-starved rabbits. A Greek man may be permitted to beat his wife, but he would never stoop to starving her.'

'Beat...' Saskia began rising to the bait and then stopped as she saw the glint in his eyes and realised that he was teasing her.

'I suspect you are the kind of woman, Saskia, who would drive a saint, never mind a mere mortal man, to be driven to subdue you, to master you and then to wish that he had had the strength to master himself instead.'

Saskia shivered as the raw sensuality of what he was saying hit her like a jolt of powerful electricity. What was it about him that made her so acutely aware of him, so nervously on edge?

More to distract herself than anything else she started to eat, unaware of the ruefully amused look Andreas gave her as she did so. If he didn't know better he would have said that she was as inexperienced as a virgin. The merest allusion to anything sexual was enough to have her trembling with reaction, unable to meet his gaze. It was just as well that he knew it was all an act, otherwise... Otherwise what? Otherwise he might be savagely tempted to put his words into actions, to see if she trembled as deliciously when he touched her as she did when he spoke to her.

To counter what he was feeling he began to speak to her in a crisp, businesslike voice.

'There are certain things you will need to know about my family background if you are going to convince my grandfather that we are in love.'

He proceeded to give her a breakdown of his immediate family, adding a few cautionary comments about his grandfather's health.

'Which does not mean that he is not one hundred and fifty per cent on the ball. If anything, the fact that he is now prevented from working so much means that he is even more ferociously determined to interfere in my life than he was before. He tells my mother that he is afraid he will die before I give him any great-grandchildren. If that is not blackmail I don't know what is,' Andreas growled.

'It's obviously a family vice,' Saskia told him mock sweetly, earning herself a look that she refused to allow to make her quake in her shoes.

'Ultimately, of course, our engagement will have to be broken,' Andreas told her unnecessarily. 'No doubt our sojourn on the island will reveal certain aspects of our characters that we shall find mutually unappealing, and on our return to England we shall bring our engagement to an end. But at least I shall have bought myself some time...and hopefully Athena will have decided to accept one of the many suitors my grandfather says are only too willing to become her second husband.'

'And if she doesn't?' Saskia felt impelled to ask.

'*If* she doesn't, we shall just have to delay ending our engagement until either she does or I find an alternative way of convincing my grandfather that one of my sisters can provide him with his great-grandchildren.'

'You don't *ever* want to marry?' Saskia was startled into asking.

'Well, let's just say that since I have reached the age of thirty-five without meeting a woman who has made me feel my life is unliveable without her by my side, I somehow doubt that I am likely to do so now. Falling in love is a young man's extravagance. In a man past thirty it is more of a vain folly.'

'My father fell in love with my mother when he was seventeen,' Saskia couldn't stop herself from telling him. 'They ran away together...' Her eyes clouded. 'It was a mistake. They fell out of love with one another before I was born. An older man would at least have had some sense of responsibility towards the life he had helped to create. My father was still a child himself.'

'He abandoned you?' Andreas asked her, frowning.

'They both did,' Saskia told him tersely. 'If it hadn't been for my grandmother I would have ended up in a children's home.'

Soberly Andreas watched her. Was *that* why she went trawling bars for men? Was she searching for the male love she felt she had been denied by her father? His desire to exonerate her from her behaviour irritated him. *Why* was he trying to make excuses for her? Surely he hadn't actually been taken in by those tears earlier.

'It's time for us to leave,' he told her brusquely.

CHAPTER FOUR

IF SOMEONE had told her two weeks ago that she would be leaving behind her everything that was familiar to fly to an unknown Greek island in the company of an equally unknown man to whom she was supposed to be engaged Saskia would have shaken her head in denial and amusement—which just went to show!

Which just went to show what a combination of male arrogance, self-belief and determination could do, especially when it was allied to the kind of control that one particular male had over her, Saskia fretted darkly.

In less than fifteen minutes' time Andreas would be picking her up in his Mercedes for the first leg of their journey to Aphrodite, the island Andreas's grandfather had bought for his wife and named after the goddess of love.

'Theirs was a love match but one that had the approval of both families,' Andreas had told Saskia when he had been briefing her about his background.

A love match...unlike *their* bogus engagement. Just being a party to that kind of deceit, even though it was against her will, made Saskia feel uncomfortable, but nowhere near as uncomfortable as she had felt when she had had to telephone her grandmother and lie to her, saying that she was going away on business.

Andreas had tried to insist that she inform her grandmother of their engagement, but Saskia had refused.

'*You* may be happy to lie to your family about our supposed "relationship",' she had told him with a look of smoky-eyed despair. 'But I *can't* lie to my grandmother about something so...' She hadn't been able to go on, unwilling to betray herself by admitting to Andreas that her grandmother would never believe that Saskia had committed herself and her future to a man without loving him.

Once the fall-out from the news of her 'engagement' had subsided at work, her colleagues had treated her with both wary caution and distance. She was now the boss's fiancée and as such no longer really 'one of them'.

All in all Saskia had spent the week feeling increasingly isolated and frightened, but she was too proud to say anything to anyone—a hang-up, she suspected, from the days of her childhood, when the fact that her parents' story was so widely known, coupled with the way she had been dumped on her grandmother, had made her feel different, distanced from her schoolmates, who had all seemed to have proper mummies and daddies.

Not that anyone could have loved her more than her grandmother had done, as Saskia was the first to acknowledge now. Her home background had in reality been just as loving and stable, if not more so, than that of the majority of her peers.

She gave a small surreptitious look at her watch. Less than five minutes to go. Her heart thumped heavily. Her packed suitcase was ready and waiting in the hall. She had agonised over what she ought to take and in the end had compromised with a mixture of the summer holiday clothes she had bought three years previously, when she and Megan had gone to Portugal together, plus some of her lightweight office outfits.

She hadn't seen Andreas since he had taken her out for lunch—not that she had minded *that*! No indeed! He had been attending a gruelling schedule of business meetings—dealing, if the trickles of gossip that had filtered through the grapevine were anything to go by, heroically with the problems posed by the challenging situation the hotels had fallen into prior to the takeover.

'He's visited every single one of our hotels,' Saskia had heard from one admiring source. 'And he's been through every single aspect of the way they're being run—and guess what?'

Saskia, who had been on the edge of the group who'd been listening eagerly to this story, had swallowed uncomfortably, expecting to hear that Andreas had instituted a programme of mass sackings in order to halt the flood of unprofitable expenses, but to her astonishment instead she had heard, 'He's told everyone that their job is safe, provided they can meet the targets he's going to be setting. Everywhere he's been he's given the staff a pep talk, told them how much he values the acquisition his group has made and how he personally is going to be held responsible by the board of directors if he can't turn it into a profit-making asset.'

The gossip was that Andreas had a way with him that had his new employees not only swearing allegiance but apparently praising him to the skies as well.

Well, they obviously hadn't witnessed the side to his character she had done, was all that Saskia had been able to think as she listened a little bitterly to everyone's almost euphoric praise of him.

It was ten-thirty now, and he wasn't... Saskia tensed as she suddenly saw the large Mercedes pulling up outside her grandmother's house. Right on time! But of course Andreas would not waste a precious second of his time unless he had to, especially not on her!

By the time he had reached the front door she had opened it and was standing waiting for him, her suitcase in one hand and her door key in the other.

'What's that?'

She could see the way he was frowning as he looked down at her inexpensive case and immediately pride flared through her sharpening her own voice as she answered him with a curt, 'My suitcase.'

'Give it to me,' he instructed her briefly.

'I can carry it myself,' Saskia informed him grittily.

'I'm sure you can,' Andreas agreed, equally grimly. 'But...'

'But what?' Saskia challenged him angrily. 'But Greek men do not allow women to carry their own luggage nor to be independent from them in any way?'

Saskia could see from the way Andreas's mouth tightened that he did not like what she had said. For some perverse reason she felt driven to challenge him, even though a part of her shrank from the storm signals she could see flashing in his eyes.

'I'm afraid in this instance you should perhaps blame my English father rather than my Greek mother,' he told her icily. 'The English public school he insisted I was sent to believed in what is now considered to be an outdated code of good manners for its pupils.' He gave her a thin, unfriendly look. 'One word of warning to you. My grandfather is inclined to be old-fashioned about such things. He will not understand your modern insistence on politically correct behaviour, and whilst you are on the island...'

'I have to do as *you* tell me,' Saskia finished bitterly for him.

If this was a taste of what the next few weeks were going to be like she didn't know how she was going to survive them. Still, at least there would be one benefit of their obvious hostility to one another. No one who would be observing them together would be surprised when they decided to end their 'engagement'.

'Our flight leaves Heathrow at nine tomorrow morning, so we will need to leave the apartment early,' Andreas informed Saskia once they were in the car.

'The *apartment*?' Saskia questioned him warily immediately.

'Yes,' Andreas confirmed. 'I have an apartment in London. We shall be staying there tonight. This afternoon we shall spend shopping.'

'Shopping...?' Saskia began to interrupt, but Andreas overruled her.

'Yes, shopping,' he told her cautiously. 'You will need an engagement ring, and...' He paused and gave her a brief skimming look of assessment and dismissal that made her itch to demand that he stop the car immediately. Oh, how she would love to be able to tell him that she had changed her mind...that there was no way she was going to give in to his blackmail. But she knew there was no way she could.

'You will need more suitable clothes.'

'If you mean holiday clothes,' Saskia began, 'they are in my case, and...'

'No, I do not mean "holiday" clothes.' Andreas stopped her grimly. 'I am an independently wealthy man, Saskia; you don't need me to tell you that. Your department's investigations prior to our takeover must have informed you to the nearest hundred thousand pounds what my asset value is. My grandfather is a millionaire many times over, and my mother and my sisters are used to buying their clothes from the world's top designers, even though none of them are what could be considered to be fashion victims or shopaholics. Naturally, as my fiancée...'

Without allowing him to finish Saskia took a deep, angry breath and told him dangerously, 'If you think that I am going to let *you* buy my clothes...'

With only the briefest of pauses Andreas took control of the situation from her by asking smoothly, 'Why not? After all, you were prepared to let me buy your *body*. Me or indeed any other man who was prepared to pay for it.'

'No! That's not true,' Saskia denied with a shocked gasp.

'Very good,' Andreas mocked her. 'But you can

save the special effects for my family. I know *exactly* what you are—remember. Think of these clothes as a perk of your job.' He gave her a thin, unkind smile. 'However, having said that, I have to add that I shall want to vet whatever you wish to purchase. The image I want you to convey to my family as my fiancée is one of elegance and good taste.'

'What are you trying to suggest?' Saskia hissed furiously at him. 'That left to my own devices I might choose something more suited to a...?' She stopped, unable to bring herself to voice the words burning a painful brand in her thoughts.

To her bemusement, instead of saying them for her Andreas said coolly, 'You are obviously not used to buying expensive clothes and there is no way I want you indulging in some kind of idiotic unnecessary economy which would negate the whole purpose of the exercise. I don't want you buying clothes more suitable for a young woman on a modest salary than the fiancée of an extremely wealthy man,' he informed her bluntly, in case she had not understood him the first time.

For once Saskia could think of nothing to say, but inside she was a bundle of fury and shame. There was no way she could stop Andreas from carrying out his plans, she knew that, but she fully intended to keep a mental record of everything he spent so that ultimately she could repay him, even if doing so totally depleted the small nest egg she had been carefully saving.

'No more objections?' Andreas enquired smoothly. 'Good, because I promise you, Saskia, I mean to have my way—even if that entails dressing you and undressing you myself to get it. Make no mistake, when we arrive on Aphrodite you will be arriving as my fiancée.'

As he drove down the slipway onto the motorway and the powerful car picked up speed Saskia decided diplomatically that quarrelling with him whilst he was driving at such a speed would be very foolish indeed. It was over half an hour later before she recognised that, in her anxiety to reject Andreas's claimed right to decide what she should wear, she had neglected to deal with the more important issue of her discomfort at the idea of spending the night with him.

But what did she really have to fear? Certainly not any sexual advances from Andreas. He had, after all, made it shamingly plain what he thought of her sexual morals.

She had far too much pride to admit to him that she felt daunted and apprehensive at the thought of sharing the intimacy of an apartment with him. On the island it would be different. There they would be with his family and the staff who ran the large villa complex he said his grandfather had had built on it.

No, she would be wise to grit her teeth and say nothing rather than risk exposing herself to his disbelief and mocking contempt by expressing her anxieties.

As she waited for the chauffeur to load her luggage into the boot of her hired limousine Athena tapped one slender expensively shod foot impatiently.

The moment she had heard the news that Andreas was engaged and about to bring his fiancée to

Aphrodite on an official visit to meet his family she had sprung into action. Fortunately an engagement was not a marriage, and she certainly intended to make sure that *this* engagement never made it as far as a wedding.

She knew why Andreas had done it, of course. He was, after all, Greek to the very marrow of his bones—even if he chose to insist on everyone acknowledging his British blood—and like any Greek man, indeed any *man* he had an inborn need to be the one in control.

His claim to be in love with this other woman was simply his way of showing that control, rejecting the marriage to her which was so very dear to his grandfather's heart and to her own.

As the limousine sped away from the kerb she leaned forward and gave the driver the address of a prestigious apartment block overlooking the river. She herself did not maintain a home in London; she preferred New York's social life and the Paris shops.

Andreas might think he had outmanoeuvred her by announcing his engagement to this undoubtedly cold and sexless English fiancée. Well, she would soon bring an end to that, and make sure that he knew where his real interests lay. After all, how could he possibly resist *her*? She had everything he could want, and he certainly had everything *she* wanted.

It was a pity he had managed to prevent her from outbidding him for this latest acquisition. Ownership of the hotels themselves meant nothing to her *per se*, but it would have been an excellent bait to dangle in front of him since he obviously set a great deal of store by them. Why, she could not understand. But then in many ways there were a considerable number of things about Andreas that she did not understand. It was one of the things that made him so desirable to her. Athena had always coveted that which seemed to be out of reach.

The first time she had realised she wanted Andreas he had been fifteen and she had been on the verge of marrying her husband. She smiled wantonly to herself, licking her lips. At fifteen Andreas, although a boy, had been as tall as a man and as broad, with a superbly fit young body, and so indescribably good-looking that the sight of him had made her melt with lust.

She had done her best to seduce him but he had managed to resist her and then, within a month of deciding that she wanted him, she had been married.

At twenty-two she had not been a young bride by Greek standards, and she had been carefully stalking her husband-to-be for some time. Older than her by a decade, and immensely wealthy, he had played a cat and mouse game with her for well over a year before he had finally capitulated. There had certainly been no way she was going to give up the marriage she had worked so hard for for the passion she felt for Andreas, a mere boy.

But then fate had stepped in. Her husband had died unexpectedly and she had been left a widow. A very rich widow…a very rich and sexually hungry widow. And Andreas was now a man—and what a man!

The only thing that was keeping them apart was Andreas's pride. It had to be. What other reason could he possibly have for resisting her advances?

As the limousine pulled up at the address she had

given the driver Athena examined her reflection in the neat mirrors fitted into the Rolls's interior. That discreet nip and tuck she had had last year had been well worth the prince's ransom she had paid the American plastic surgeon. She could quite easily pass for a woman in her early thirties now.

Her jet-black hair had been cut and styled by one of the world's top hairdressers, her skin glowed from the expensive creams lavished on it, her make-up was immaculate and emphasised the slanting darkness of her eyes, her toe and fingernails gleamed richly with dark red polish.

A smile of satisfaction curved her mouth. No, there was no way Andreas's dreary little fiancée—an office girl, someone he had supposedly fallen in love with during the negotiations to buy out the hotel chain—could compete with her. Athena's eyes hardened. This girl, whoever she was, would soon learn what a mistake she had made in trying to lay claim on the man *Athena* wanted. What a very, very big mistake!

As she left the limousine the perfume she had especially blended for her in Paris moved with her, a heavy, musky cloud of sexuality.

Her teenage daughters loathed it, and were constantly begging her to change it, but she had no intention of doing so. It was her signature, the essence of herself as a woman. Andreas's English fiancée no doubt wore something dull and insipid such as lavender water!

'I'll leave the car here,' Andreas told Saskia as he swung the Mercedes into a multi-storey car park right in the centre of the city. Saskia's eyes widened as she saw the tariff pinned up by the barrier. She would never have dreamed of paying so much to park a car, but the rich, as they said, were different.

Just how different she came to realise during the course of the afternoon, as Andreas guided her into a series of shops the like of which Saskia had never imagined existed. And in each one the very aura of his presence seemed to draw from the sales assistants the kind of reverential reaction that made Saskia tighten her lips. She could see the female admiration and speculation in their eyes as a series of outfits was produced for his inspection. For *his* inspection— not *hers*, Saskia recognised and her sense of helpless frustration and resentment grew with each shop they visited.

'I'm not a doll or a child,' she exploded outside one of them, when she had flatly refused to even try on the cream trouser suit the salesgirl had gushingly declared would be perfect for her.

'No? Well, you're certainly giving a wonderful imitation of behaving like one,' Andreas responded grimly. 'That suit was—'

'That suit was over one thousand pounds,' Saskia interrupted him grittily. 'There's no *way* I would ever pay that kind of money for an outfit... not even my wedding dress!'

When Andreas started to laugh she glared furiously at him, demanding, 'What's so funny?'

'You are,' he told her uncompromisingly. 'My dear Saskia, have you really any idea of the kind of wedding dress you would get for under a thousand pounds?'

'No, I haven't,' Saskia admitted. 'But I do know that I'd never feel comfortable wearing clothes the cost of which would feed a small country, and neither is an expensive wedding dress any guarantee of a good marriage.'

'Oh, spare me the right-on lectures,' Andreas broke in in exasperation. 'Have you ever thought of how many people would be without jobs if everyone went around wearing sackcloth and ashes, as you obviously would have them do?'

'That's not fair,' Saskia defended herself. She was, after all, feminine enough to like good clothes and to want to look her best, and in that trouser suit she *would* undeniably have looked good, she admitted inwardly. But she was acutely conscious of the fact that every penny Andreas spent on her she would have to repay.

'I don't know why you're insisting on doing this,' she told Andreas rebelliously. 'I don't *need* any clothes; I've already told you that. And there's certainly no need for you to throw your money around to impress me.'

'You or anyone else,' Andreas cut in sharply, dark bands of colour burning across his cheekbones in a visual warning to her that she had angered him.

'I am a businessman, Saskia. Throwing money around for *any* reason is not something I do, least of all in an attempt to impress a woman who could easily be bought for less than half the price of that trouser suit. Oh, no, you don't,' he cautioned her softly, reaching out to catch hold of the hand she had automatically lifted.

He was holding her wrist in such a tight grip that

Saskia could actually see her fingers going white, but her pride wouldn't allow her to tell him that he was hurting her. It also wouldn't allow her to acknowledge that she had momentarily let her feelings get out of control, and it was only when she suddenly started to sway, white-faced with pain and shock, that Andreas realised what was happening. He released her wrist with a muffled curse and then start to chafe life back into her hand.

'Why didn't you *tell* me I was hurting you so much?' he grated. 'You have bones as fragile as a bird's.'

Even now, with his dark head bent over her tingling hand whilst he massaged it expertly to bring the blood stinging back into her veins, Saskia couldn't allow herself to weaken and claim his compassion.

'I didn't want to spoil your fun,' she told him sharply. 'You were obviously *enjoying* hurting me.'

She tensed when she heard the oath he gave as he released her completely, and tensed again at the sternness in his voice, one look of grim determination in his eyes as he said, 'This has gone far enough. You are behaving like a child. First a harlot and now a child. There is only *one* role I want to see you play from now on, Saskia, and that is the one we have already agreed upon. I'll warn you now. If you do or say *anything* to make my family suspect that ours is not a true love match I shall make you very sorry for it. Do you understand me?'

'Yes, I understand you,' Saskia agreed woodenly.

'I mean what I say,' Andreas warned her. 'And it won't just be the Demetrios chain you won't be able to work for. If you flout me, Saskia, I'll see to it that you will never be able to work *anywhere* again. An accountant who can't be trusted and who has been dismissed on suspicion of stealing is not one that anyone will want to employ.'

'You can't do that,' Saskia whispered, white-faced, but she knew all too well that he could.

She hated him now...really hated him, and when in the next shop he marched her into she saw the salesgirl's eyes widening in breathless sexual interest, she reflected mentally that the other girl was welcome to him...more than welcome!

It was late in the afternoon before Andreas finally decided that Saskia had a wardrobe suitable for his fiancée.

At their last port of call he had called upon the services of the store's personal shopper who, with relentless efficiency, had provided Saskia with the kind of clothes that she had previously only ever seen in glossy magazines.

She had tried to reject everything the shopper had produced, but on each occasion apart from one Andreas had overruled her. The only time they had been in accord had been when the shopper had brought out a bikini which she had announced was perfect for Saskia's colouring and destination. The minuteness of the triangles which were supposed to cover her modesty had made Saskia's eyes widen in disbelief—and they had widened even more when she had discreetly managed to study the price tag.

'I couldn't possibly swim in that,' she had blurted out.

'*Swim* in it?' The other woman had looked stunned. 'Good heavens, no, of course not. This isn't for *swimming* in. And, look, this is the wrap that goes with it. Isn't it divine?' she had purred, producing a length of silky fragile fabric embellished with sequins.

As she'd seen the four-figure price on the wrap Saskia had thought she might actually faint with disbelief, but to her relief and surprise Andreas had also shaken his head.

'That is *not* the kind of outfit I would wish my fiancée to wear,' he had told the shopper bluntly, adding, just in case she had not fully understood him, 'Saskia's body is eye-catching enough without her needing to embellish it with an outfit more suitable for a call girl.'

The shopper diplomatically had not pressed the issue, but instead had gone away, returning with several swimsuits.

Saskia had picked the cheapest of them, unwillingly allowing Andreas to add a matching wrap.

Whilst he'd been settling the bill and making arrangements for everything to be delivered to his riverside apartment Saskia had drunk the coffee the personal shopper had organised for her.

Perhaps it was because she hadn't really eaten anything all day that she was feeling so lightheaded and anxious, she decided. It couldn't surely be because she and Andreas were now going to go to his apartment, where they would be alone—could it?

'There's an excellent restaurant close to the apartment block,' Andreas informed Saskia, once they were in the car and he was driving her towards the dockland area where his apartment was situated. 'I'll arrange to have a meal sent in and...'

'No,' Saskia protested immediately. 'I'd rather eat out.'

She could see that Andreas was frowning.

'I don't think that's a good idea,' he told her flatly. 'A woman on her own, especially a woman like you, is bound to attract attention, and besides, you look tired. I have to go out, and I have no idea what time I will be back.'

Andreas was going out. Saskia could feel her anxiety easing. Her feet ached from the unaccustomed pavement-pounding and her brain was exhausted with the effort of keeping a running tab on just how much money Andreas, and therefore she, had spent.

Far more than she had wanted to spend. So much that just thinking about it was making her feel distinctly ill. Wretchedly she acknowledged that there would be precious little left of her hard-earned little nest egg once she had repaid Andreas what he had spent.

Tiredly Saskia followed Andreas through the underground car park and into the foyer of the apartment block. A special key was needed to use the lift, which glided upwards so smoothly that Saskia's eyes rounded in shock when it came to a standstill. She had not even realised that they were moving.

'It's this way,' Andreas told her, touching her arm and guiding her towards one of the four doorways opening off the entrance lobby. He was carrying her case, which he put down as he unlocked the door, motioning to Saskia to precede him into the elegant space beyond it.

CHAPTER FIVE

THE first thing that struck Saskia about Andreas's apartment was not the very expensive modern art hanging on the hallway's walls but its smell—a musky, throat-closing, shockingly overpowering scent which stung her nostrils and made her tense.

That Andreas was equally aware of it she was in no doubt. Saskia could see him pause and lift his head, like a hunting panther sniffing the air.

'Hell… Hell and damnation,' she heard him mutter ferociously beneath his breath, and then, to her shock, he thrust open the door into the huge-windowed living space that lay beyond the lobby and took hold of her. His fingers bit into the soft flesh of her arms, his breath a warning whisper against her lips as his eyes blazed down into the unguarded shocked softness of hers, dark as obsidian, hard as flint, commanding…warning…

'Alone at last. How you have enjoyed teasing me today, my loved one, but now I have you to myself and I can exact what punishment on you I wish…'

The soft crooning tone of his voice as much as his words scattered what was left of her senses, leaving Saskia clinging weakly to him as the shock ripped through her in a floodtide. Then his mouth was covering hers, silencing the protest she was trying to make, his lips moulding, shaping, coaxing, *seducing* hers with an expertise that flattened her defences as effectively as an atom bomb.

Incoherently Saskia whispered his name, trying to insist on a cessation of what he was doing and an explanation for it. But her lips, her mouth, her senses, unused to so much sensual stimulation, were defying reason and caution and everything else that Saskia's bemused brain was trying to tell them. Her frozen shock melted beneath the heat of the pleasure Andreas's hungry passionate expertise was showing her, and her lips softened and trembled into an unguarded, uninhibited response.

Without being aware of what she was doing Saskia strained to get closer to Andreas, standing on tiptoe so that she could cling ardently to the delicious pleasure of his kiss. Her hands on his arms registered the sheer size and inflexibility of the muscles beneath them whilst her heart pounded in awed inexperienced shock at the intensity of what she was feeling.

Even more than she could smell that musky, overpowering female perfume, she could smell Andreas himself. His heat...his passion...his maleness... And shockingly something in her, something she hadn't known existed, was responding to it just as her lips were responding to him...just as *she* was responding to him, swaying into his arms compliantly, her body urging him to draw her close, to let her feel the rest of his male strength.

Dizzily Saskia opened the eyes she had closed at the first touch of his mouth on hers, shivering as she saw the sparks of raw sensuality darting like lightning from his eyes as he stared down at her. It was like hanging way above the earth in a dizzying, death-defying place where she could feel her danger and yet at the same time know somehow she would be safe.

'You love like an innocent...a virgin...' Andreas was telling her huskily, and as he did so the sparks glittering in his eyes intensified, as though he found something very satisfying about such a notion.

Helplessly Saskia stared back at him. Her heart was thudding frantically fast and her body was filled with an unfamiliar shocking ache that was a physical need to have him touch her, to have his hand run slowly over her skin and reach right through it to that place where her unfamiliar ache began, so that he could surround and soothe it. Somehow just thinking about him doing such a thing *increased* the ache to a pounding throb, a wild, primitive beat that made her moan and sway even closer to him.

'You like that... You want me...'

As he spoke to her she could hear and feel the urgency in his voice, could feel his arousal. Eagerly she pressed closer to him, only to freeze as she suddenly heard a woman's voice demanding sharply, 'Andreas? Aren't you going to introduce me?'

Immediately she realised what she was doing and shame flooded through her, but as she tried to pull away, desperate to conceal her confusion, Andreas held on to her, forcing her to stay where she was, forcing her even more closely into his body so that somehow she was leaning against him, as though...as though...

She trembled as she felt the powerful thrust of his leg between her own, her face burning hotly with embarrassed colour as she realised the sexual connotation that their pose suggested. But it seemed that the woman who was watching them was not similarly self-conscious.

Saskia caught her breath as Andreas allowed her to turn her head and look at the woman.

She was tall and dark-haired, everything about her immaculately groomed, but despite the warmth of her olive skin and the ripe richness of her painted mouth and nails Saskia shivered as she sensed her innate coldness.

'Athena,' Andreas was demanding shortly, 'how did *you* get in here?'

'I have a key. Have you forgotten?' the other woman purred.

The sloe-eyed look she gave Andreas and the way she was managing to totally exclude Saskia both from their conversation and from her line of vision left Saskia ruefully reflecting on her earlier mental picture of a devastated widow being too grief-stricken at the loss of her husband to prevent herself from being bullied into a second marriage.

No one would ever bully *this* woman into anything...and as for her being grief-stricken—there was only one emotion Saskia could see in those dark eyes and it had nothing to do with grief.

She forced down the sudden surge of nausea that burned in her throat as she witnessed the look of pure condensed lust that Athena was giving Andreas. Saskia had never imagined, never mind seen, a woman looking at a man in such a powerfully and openly predatory sexual way.

Now she could understand why Andreas had felt in need of a mock fiancée to protect himself, but what she could not understand was how on earth Andreas could resist the other woman's desire for him.

She was blindingly sensually attractive, and obviously wanted Andreas. And surely that was what all men fantasised about—a woman whose sexual appetite for them could never be satiated.

Naively Saskia assumed that only her own sex would be put off by Athena's intrinsic coldness and by the lack of any real loving emotion in her make-up.

Andreas had obviously kissed Saskia because he had guessed that Athena was in the apartment, and now that the other woman was standing so close to them both Saskia knew how he had known. That perfume of hers was as unmistakable as it was unappealing.

'Aren't you going to say how pleased you are to see me?' Athena was pouting as she moved closer to Andreas. 'Your grandfather is very upset about your engagement. You know what he was hoping for,' she added meaningfully, before turning to Saskia and saying dismissively, 'Oh, I'm sorry. I didn't mean to hurt your feelings, but I'm sure Andreas must have warned you how difficult it is going to be for all his family, especially for his grandfather, to accept you...'

'Athena,' Andreas was saying warningly, and Saskia could well imagine how she *would* have felt to be confronted by such a statement, if she and Andreas were genuinely engaged.

'But it's the truth,' Athena was continuing unrepentantly, and she shrugged her shoulders, the movement drawing attention to the fullness of her breasts. Breasts which Saskia could quite easily see were naked and unfettered beneath the fine cotton shirt she was wearing.

Quickly she averted her gaze from the sight of Athena's flauntingly erect nipples, not daring to allow herself to look at Andreas. Surely no man could resist the demand that those nipples were making on his attention…his concentration…his admiration for their perfection and sexuality. Her own breasts were well shaped and firm, but her nipples did not have that flamboyant fullness that the other woman's possessed and, even if they had, Saskia knew that she would have felt embarrassed about making such a public display of them.

But then perhaps Athena's display was meant *only* for Andreas…perhaps it was meant to be a reminder to him of intimacies they might already have shared. She did, after all, have the key to his apartment, and she certainly seemed to want to make it plain to Saskia that there was a very special intimacy between the two of them.

As though in confirmation of Saskia's thoughts, Athena suddenly leaned forward, putting one manicured hand against Andreas's face and effectively coming between them. With a sultry suggestiveness she said softly, 'Aren't you going to kiss me? You normally do, and I'm sure your fiancée understands that in Greece family relationships…family *loyalties* are very, very important.'

'What Saskia understands is that I love her and I want her to be my wife,' Andreas informed Athena curtly, stepping back from her and taking Saskia with him. As he held her in front of him and closed his arms around her, tucking her head against his shoulder, Saskia reminded herself just *why* he was doing so and just what her role was supposed to be.

'How sweet!' Athena pronounced, giving Saskia an icy look before turning back to Andreas and telling him insincerely, 'I hate to cast a shadow on your happiness, Andreas, but your grandfather really isn't very pleased with you at all at the moment. He was telling me how concerned he is about the way you're handling this recent takeover. Of course *I* understand how important it must be to you to establish your own mark on the business, to prove yourself, so to speak, but the acquisition of this hotel chain really was quite foolhardy, as is this decision of yours to keep on all the existing staff.

'You'll never make a profit doing that,' she scolded him mock sweetly. 'I must say, though, having had the opportunity to look a little deeper into the finances of the chain, I'm glad I pulled out of putting in my own bid. Although of course I *can* afford to lose the odd million or so. What a pity it is, Andreas, that you didn't accept my offer to run the shipping line for me. That would have given you much more scope than working as your grandfather's errand boy.'

Saskia felt herself tensing as she absorbed the insult Athena had just delivered, but to her astonishment Andreas seemed completely unmoved by it. Yet *she* only had to make the merest observation and he fired up at her with so much anger.

'As you already well know, Athena,' he responded, almost good-humouredly, 'It was my *grandfather's* decision to buy the British hotel chain and it was one I endorsed. As for its future profitability... My research confirms that there is an excellent market for a chain of luxurious hotels in Britain, especially when it can boast first-class leisure facilities and a top-notch chef—which is what I am going to ensure that our chain has.

'And as for the financial implications of keeping on the existing staff—Saskia is an accountant, and I'm sure she'll be able to tell you—as you should know yourself, being a businesswoman—that in the long run it would cost more in redundancy payments to get rid of the staff than it will cost to continue employing them. Natural wastage and pending retirement will reduce their number quite dramatically over the next few years, and, where appropriate, those who wish to stay on will be given the opportunity to relocate and retrain. The leisure clubs we intend to open in each hotel alone will take up virtually all of the slack in our staffing levels.

'However, Saskia and I are leaving for Athens tomorrow. We've had a busy day today and, if you'll excuse us, tonight is going to be a very special night for us.'

As Saskia tensed Andreas tightened his hold on her warningly as he repeated, 'A *very* special night. Which reminds me...'

Still holding onto Saskia with one hand, he reached inside his jacket pocket with the other to remove a small jeweller's box.

'I collected this. It should be small enough for you now.'

Before Saskia could say anything he was slipping

the box back into his jacket, telling her softly, 'We'll find out later…'

In the living area beyond the lobby a telephone had started to ring. Releasing her, Andreas went to answer it, leaving Saskia on her own with Athena.

'It won't last,' Athena told her venomously as she walked past Saskia towards the door. 'He won't marry you. He and I were destined to be together. He *knows* that. It's just his pride that makes him fight his destiny. You might as well give him up now, because I promise you *I* shall never do so.'

She meant it, Saskia could see that, and for the first time she actually felt a small shaft of sympathy for Andreas. Sympathy for a man who was treating her the way Andreas was? For a man who had misjudged her the way he had? She must be crazy, Saskia derided herself grimly.

Apprehensively Saskia watched as the new suitcases, which were now carefully packed with her new clothes, were loaded onto the conveyor belt. The airline representative was checking their passports.

On her finger the ring Andreas had given her the previous evening glittered brilliantly.

'It's amazing how good fake diamonds can look these days, isn't it?' she had chattered nervously when Andreas had taken it from its box. She'd tried to disguise from him how edgy and unhappy she felt about wearing a ring on the finger that she had imagined would only ever bear a ring given to her by the man she loved, a ring she would wear forever.

'Is it?' Andreas had responded almost contemptuously. 'I wouldn't know.'

His comment had set all her inner alarm bells ringing and she had demanded anxiously, 'This... It isn't real, is it?'

His expression had given her her answer.

'It *is*!' She had swallowed, unable to drag her gaze away from the fiery sparkle of the magnificent solitaire.

'Athena would have spotted a fake diamond immediately,' Andreas had told her dismissively when she'd tried to protest that she didn't want the responsibility of wearing something of such obvious value.

'If she can spot a fake *diamond* so easily,' she had felt driven to ask him warily, 'then surely she will be able to spot a fake fiancée.'

'Athena deals in hard facts, not emotions,' had been Andreas's answer.

Hard facts, Saskia reflected now, remembering that brief conversation. Like the kiss Andreas had given her last night, knowing Athena would witness it. Andreas himself had made no mention of what he had done, but Saskia had known that her guess as to why he had done it was correct when, immediately after he had ended his telephone call, he had switched on the apartment's air conditioning with the grim comment, 'We need some fresh air in here.'

Later, Andreas had gone out, as promised, and, after picking at the meal he had ordered her, Saskia had gone to bed—alone.

'How long will it take us to reach Aphrodite?' Saskia asked Andreas as they boarded their flight.

'On this occasion it will take longer than normal,'

Andreas answered as the stewardess showed them to their seats—first-class seats, Saskia noted with a small frisson of nervous awe. She had never flown first class before, never really done anything that might have equipped her to feel at home in the rarefied stratosphere of the mega-wealthy that Andreas and his family obviously inhabited.

'Once we arrive in Athens I'm afraid I shall have to leave you to occupy yourself for a few hours before we continue with our journey. That was my grandfather who rang last night. He wants to see me.'

'He won't be at the island?' Saskia asked.

'Not immediately. His heart condition means that he has to undergo regular check-ups—a precautionary measure only, thank goodness—and they will keep him in Athens for the next day or so.'

'Athena told me she doesn't believe that our relationship will last. She believes that the two of you are destined to be together,' Saskia said.

'She's trying to intimidate you,' Andreas responded, the smile he had given the attentive stewardess replaced by a harsh frown.

Impulsively Saskia allowed the sympathy she had unexpectedly felt for him the previous evening to take precedence over her own feelings. Turning towards him, she said softly, 'But surely if you explained to your grandfather how you feel he would understand and accept that you can't be expected to marry a woman you don't...you don't want to marry...'

'My grandfather is as stubborn as a mule. He's also one hell of a lot more vulnerable than he thinks...than any of us want him to think. His heart condition…' He gave a small sigh. 'At the moment it's stable, but it is important that he—and we—keep his stress levels down. If I told him that I didn't want to marry Athena without producing you as a substitute he would immediately become very stressed indeed. It isn't just that by marrying Athena as he wishes I would attach her fortune and assets to our own, my grandfather is also a man to whom male descendants are of paramount importance.

'My elder sister already has two daughters, and Athena also has two. My grandfather is desperate for me, as his direct male descendent, to produce the next male generation…a great-grandson.'

'But even if you did marry Athena there would be no guarantee that you would even have children, never mind sons,' Saskia protested.

'Why are you laughing at me?' she demanded in chagrin as she saw the mirth crinkling Andreas's eyes and a gust of warmly amused male laughter filled the small space between them.

'Saskia, for a woman of your experience you can be very, very naïve. You should *never* suggest to any man, and most *especially* not a Greek one, that he may not be able to father a son!'

As the plane suddenly started to lift into the sky Saskia automatically clutched at her arm-rests, and then tensed in shock as she felt the hard male warmth of Andreas's hand wrapping around her own.

'Scared of flying?' he asked her in amusement. 'You shouldn't be. It's the safest form of transport there is.'

'I know that,' Saskia responded waspishly. 'It's

just…well, it's just that flying seems so…so unnatural, and if…'

'If God had intended man to fly he'd have given him wings,' Andreas offered her wryly. 'Well, Icarus tried that option.'

'I always think that's such a sad story.' Saskia shivered, her eyes shadowing. 'Especially for his poor father.'

'Mmm…' Andreas agreed, before asking her, 'Am I to take it from that comment that you're a student of Greek mythology?'

'Well, not precisely a student,' Saskia admitted, 'but my grandmother used to read me stories from a book on Greek mythology when I was little and I always found the stories fascinating…even though they nearly always made me cry.'

Abruptly she stopped speaking as she realised two things. The first was that they were now completely airborne, and the second was…her own bemused awareness of how good it felt actually to have Andreas's large hand clasping her own. It was enough to make her face sting with self-conscious colour and she hastily wriggled her hand free, just as the stewardess came up to offer them a glass of champagne.

'Champagne!' Saskia's eyes widened as she took a sip from the glass Andreas was holding out to her and she gasped as the delicious bubbles exploded against her taste buds.

It had to be the champagne that was making her feel so relaxed and so…so…laid-back, Saskia decided hazily a little later, and when the captain announced that they were coming in to land she was surprised to realise how quickly the time had flown—and how much she had enjoyed the conversation she and Andreas had shared. She was even more surprised to discover how easy it was to slip her hand into the reassuring hold of Andreas's as the plane's wheels hit the tarmac and the pilot applied reverse thrust to slow them down.

'I can either have our driver take you to the family apartment in Athens, where you can rest whilst I see my grandfather, or, if you prefer, I can arrange for him to drive you on a sightseeing tour,' Andreas offered, casually lifting their cases off the luggage carousel.

He was wearing a pair of plain light-coloured trousers and a cool, very fine white cotton short-sleeved shirt, and for some indefinable reason it did odd things to Saskia's normally very sensible female senses to witness the way the muscles hardened in his arms as he swung their cases on to the ground. Very odd things, she acknowledged giddily as the discreet smile of flirtatious invitation she intercepted from a solitary woman traveller caused her instinctively to move possessively closer to him.

What on earth was happening to her? It *must* be the champagne...or the heat...or perhaps both! Yes, that was it, she decided feverishly, grateful to have found a sensible explanation for her unfamiliar behaviour. After all, there was no reason why she should feel possessive about Andreas. Yesterday morning she had hated him...loathed him... In fact she had been dreading her enforced time as his 'fiancée'—and she still was, of course. Of course! It was just that...

Well, having met Athena it was only natural that she should feel *some* sympathy for him. And she had been fascinated by the stories he had told her during the flight—stories which had been told to him by older members of his Greek family and which were a wonderful mix of myth and folklore. And it was a very pleasant experience not to have to struggle with heavy luggage. Normally when she went away she was either with a group of friends or with her grandmother, and...

'Saskia...?'

Guiltily Saskia realised that Andreas was still waiting for an answer to his question.

'Oh, I'd much prefer to see something of the city,' she answered.

'Well, you won't have a lot of time,' Andreas warned her. 'Our pilot will already have filed his flight plan.'

Saskia already knew that they would be flying out to the island in a small plane privately owned by Andreas's grandfather, and what had impressed her far more than Andreas's casual reference to the plane had been his mention of the fact that he himself was qualified to fly.

'Unfortunately I had to give it up. I can't spare the amount of hours now that I believe are needed to keep myself up to speed and in practice, and besides, my insurance company were extremely wary about insuring me,' he'd added ruefully.

'It's this way,' he told her now, placing his hand on her shoulder as he turned her in the right direction.

Out of the corner of her eye Saskia caught a

glimpse of their reflections in a mirrored column and immediately tensed. What was she *doing* leaning against Andreas like that? As though...as though she *liked* being there...as though she was enjoying playing the helpless fragile female to his strong muscular male.

Immediately she pulled away from him and squared her shoulders.

'Athena would have loved to have seen you do that,' he told her sharply, the disapproval clear in his voice.

'We're supposed to be in love, Saskia...remember?'

'Athena isn't here,' she responded quickly.

'No, thank God,' he agreed. 'But we don't know who might accidentally observe us. We're a *couple*—very much in love—newly engaged...and you're about to fly to my home to meet my family. Don't you think it's natural that—?'

'That I should feel nervous and intimidated...worried about whether or not they'll think I'm good enough for you.' Saskia interrupted him angrily, her pride stung by what he was suggesting. 'And what am I supposed to do? Cling desperately and despairingly to you...afraid of their rejection...afraid of *losing* you...just because—'

She stopped as she saw the blank impatient look Andreas was giving her.

'What I was about to say,' he told her grimly, 'was don't you think it's only natural that I should want to hold you close to me and equally that *you* should want that same intimacy? That as lovers we *should* want always to be physically in touch with one another?' He paused. 'And as for what you have just said, I'm a man of thirty-five, long past the age of needing *anyone's* approval of what I do or who I love.'

'But you don't...' Saskia began, and then stopped as she realised what she had been about to say. Andreas hardly needed *her* to tell him that he didn't love her.

'I don't what?' he prompted her, but she shook her head, refusing to answer him.

'So you want to see the Acropolis first?' Andreas checked with Saskia before getting out of the limousine, having first given the driver some instructions in Greek.

'Yes,' Saskia confirmed.

'I have told Spiros to make sure you are at the airport in time for our flight. He will take care of you. I am sorry to have to leave you to your own devices,' Andreas apologised formally, suddenly making Saskia sharply aware of his mixed cultural heritage.

She recognised how at home he looked here, and yet, at the same time, how much he stood out from the other men she could see. He was taller, for one thing, and his skin, whilst tanned, was not as dark, and of course his eyes would always give away his Northern European blood.

Saskia gave a small emotional sigh as she finally turned her back on the Acropolis and started to walk away. She had managed to persuade the driver that she would be perfectly safe on her own, but only after a good deal of insistence, and she had enjoyed her solitude as she had absorbed the aura of the ancient building in awed appreciation.

Now, though, it was time for her to go. She could see the limousine waiting where she had expected, but to her consternation there was no sign of its driver.

There *was* a man standing close to the vehicle, though, white-haired and elderly. Saskia frowned as she recognised that he seemed to be in some distress, one hand pressed against his side as though he was in pain. A brief examination of the street confirmed that it was empty, apart from the old man and herself. Saskia automatically hurried towards him, anxious for his well-being.

'Are you all right?' she asked in concern as she reached him. 'You don't look well.'

To her relief he answered her in English, assuring her, 'It is nothing...the heat—a small pain. I have perhaps walked further than I should...'

Saskia was still anxious. It *was* hot. He did not look well, and there was certainly no way she could possibly leave him on his own, but there was still no sign of her driver or anyone else who might be able to help, and she had no idea how long it would take them to get to the airport.

'It's *very* hot,' she told the old man gently, not wanting to hurt his pride, 'and it can be very tiring to walk in such heat. I have a car...and...and a driver... Perhaps we could give you a lift?' As she spoke she was searching the street anxiously. Where *was* her driver? Andreas would be furious with her if she was late for their flight, but there was no way she could leave without first ensuring that the old man was alright.

'You have a car? This car?' he guessed, gesturing towards the parked limousine.

'Well, it isn't *mine*,' Saskia found herself feeling obliged to tell him. 'It belongs to...to someone I know. Do you live very far away?'

He had stopped holding his side now and she could see that his colour looked healthier and that his breathing was easier.

'You are very kind,' he told her with a smile, 'But I too have a car...and a driver...' His smile broadened and for some reason Saskia felt almost as though he was laughing a little at her.

'You are a very kind girl to worry yourself so much on behalf of an old man.'

There *was* a car parked further down the street, Saskia realised, but it was some distance away.

'Is *that* your car?' she asked him. 'Shall I get the driver?'

'No,' he denied immediately. 'I can walk.'

Without giving him any opportunity to refuse, Saskia went to his side and said gently, 'Perhaps you will allow me to walk with you to it...' Levelly she met and held the look he was giving her.

'Perhaps I should,' he capitulated.

It took longer to reach the car than Saskia had expected, mainly because the old man was plainly in more distress than he wanted to admit. As they reached the car Saskia was relieved to see the driver's door open and the driver get out, immediately hurrying towards them and addressing some words to her companion in fast Greek. The old man was now starting to look very much better, holding himself upright and speaking sternly to the driver.

'He fusses like an old woman,' he complained testily in English to Saskia, adding warmly, 'Thank you, my dear, I am *very* pleased to have met you. But you should not be walking the streets of Athens on your own,' he told her sternly. 'And I shall—' Abruptly he stopped and said something in Greek to his driver, who started to frown and look anxiously up and down the street.

'Yannis will walk back with you to *your* car and wait there with you until your driver returns.'

'Really, there's no need for that,' Saskia protested, but her new-found friend was determinedly insistent.

'There really is no need for you to come with me,' she told the driver once they were out of earshot of the older man. 'I would much rather you stayed with your employer. He looked quite poorly when I saw him in the street.'

To her relief, as she finished speaking she saw that her own driver was getting out of Andreas's car.

'See, there is no need to come any further,' she smiled in relief, and then frowned a little before saying anxiously to him, 'Your employer... It is none of my business I know...but perhaps a visit to a doctor...' She paused uncertainly.

'It is already taken care of,' the driver assured her. 'But he... What do you say? He does not always take anyone's advice...'

His calmness helped to soothe Saskia's concern and ease her conscience about leaving the older man. He was plainly in good hands now, and her own driver was waiting for her.

CHAPTER SIX

SASKIA darted a brief look at Andreas, catching back her gasp of pleasure as she stared out of their plane and down at the blue-green of the Aegean Sea beneath them.

He had been frowning and preoccupied when they had met up at the airport, not even asking her if she had enjoyed her sightseeing trip, and now with every mile that took them closer to his home and family Saskia could feel her tension increasing. It seemed ironic, when she reflected on how she had dreamed of one day spending a holiday in this part of the world, that now that she was actually here she was far too on edge to truly appreciate it.

The starkness of Andreas's expression forced her to ask, more out of politeness than any real concern, she was quick to assure herself, 'Is something wrong? You don't look very happy.'

Immediately Andreas's frown deepened, his gaze sweeping her sharply as he turned to look at her.

'Getting in some practice at playing the devoted fiancée?' he asked her cynically. 'If you're looking for a bonus payment, don't bother.'

Saskia felt a resurgence of her initial hostility towards him.

'Unlike you, I do not evaluate everything I do by how I can best benefit from it,' Saskia shot back furiously. 'I was simply concerned that your meeting hadn't gone very well.'

'*You?* Concerned for *me*? There's only one reason you're here with me, Saskia, and we both know that isn't it.'

What did he expect? Saskia fumed, forcing herself to bite back the angry retort she wanted to make. He had, after all, blackmailed her into being here with him. He was using her for his own ends. He had formed the lowest kind of opinion of her, judged her without allowing her the chance to defend herself or to explain her behaviour, and yet after all that he still seemed to think he could occupy the higher moral ground. Why on earth had she ever felt any sympathy for him? He and Athena deserved one another.

But even as she formed the stubborn angry thought Saskia knew that it wasn't true. She had sensed a deep coldness in Athena, a total lack of regard for any kind of emotion. Andreas might have done and said many things she objected to, but there was a warmly passionate side to him...a *very* passionate side, she acknowledged, trembling a little as she unwillingly remembered the kiss he had given her... Even though it had merely been an act, staged for Athena's benefit he had still made her feel—*connected* at a very deep and personal level. So much so, in fact, that even now, if she were to close her eyes and remember, she could almost feel the hard male pressure of his mouth against her own.

'As a matter of fact my meeting did *not* go well.'

Saskia's eyes opened in surprise as she heard Andreas's abrupt and unexpected admission.

'For a start my grandfather was not there. There

was something else he had to do that was more important, apparently. But unfortunately he did not bother to explain this to me, or to send a message informing me of it until I'd been waiting for him for over half an hour. However, he *had* left instructions that I was to be informed in no uncertain terms that he is not best pleased with me at the moment.'

'Because of me...us?' Saskia hazarded.

'My grandfather knows there is no way I would or could marry a woman I do not love—his own marriage was a love match, as was my parents', even if my mother did have to virtually threaten to elope before she got his approval. When my father died my grandfather admitted how much he admired him. He was a surveyor, and he retained his independence from my grandfather.'

'You must miss him,' Saskia said softly.

'I was fifteen when he died; that was a long time ago. And, unlike you, at least I had the comfort of knowing how much he loved me.'

At first Saskia thought he was being deliberately unkind to her, and instinctively she stiffened in self-defence, but when unexpectedly he covered her folded hands with one of his own she knew that she had misinterpreted his remark.

'The love my grandmother has given me has more than made up for the love I didn't get from my parents,' she told him firmly—and meant it.

His hand was still covering hers...both of hers...and that funny, trembly sensation she had felt inside earlier returned as she looked down at it. Long-fingered, tanned, with well-groomed but not manicured nails, it was very much a man's hand:

large enough to cover both of hers, large enough, too, to hold her securely to him without any visible effort. It was the kind of hand that gave a woman the confidence to know that this man could take care of her and their children. Just as he was the kind of man who would always ensure that his woman and his child were safe and secure.

What on earth was she thinking? Agitatedly Saskia wriggled in her seat, snatching her hands from beneath Andreas's.

'Are you sure this is a good idea?' she asked him slightly breathlessly as she tried to concentrate on the reality of why she was sitting here next to him. 'I mean, if your grandfather already doesn't approve of our engagement…'

It was so long before he replied that Saskia began to think that her question had annoyed him but when he did answer her she recognised that the anger she could see darkening his eyes wasn't directed at her but at Athena.

'Unfortunately Athena claims a blood closeness to my grandfather which he finds flattering. His elder brother, Athena's grandfather, died some years ago and whilst there is no way at all that Athena would allow anyone, least of all my grandfather, to interfere in the way she runs her own financial empire, she flatters and encourages him to the point where his judgement is sometimes not all that it should be. My mother claims that the truth will out, so to speak, and that ultimately my grandfather will see through Athena's machinations.'

'But surely she must realise that you don't want to marry her,' Saskia suggested a little bit uncomfortably. It was so foreign to her own way of behaving to even consider trying to force anyone into a relationship with her that it was hard for her to understand why Athena should be driven to do so.

'Oh, she realises it all right,' Andreas agreed grimly. 'But Athena has never been denied anything she wants, and right now...'

'She wants you,' Saskia concluded for him.

'Yes,' Andreas agreed heavily. 'And, much as I would like to tell her that her desires are not reciprocated, I have to think of my grandfather.'

He stopped speaking as their plane started to lose height, a small smile curling his mouth as he saw Saskia's expression when she looked out of the window down at their destination.

'He can't possibly be intending to put this plane down on that tiny piece of land,' she gasped in disbelief.

'Oh, yes, he can, It's much safer than it looks,' Andreas said reassuringly. 'Look,' he added, directing her attention away from the landing strip and to the breathtaking sprawl of his family villa and the grounds enclosing it.

'Everything is so green,' Saskia told him in bemusement, her eyes widening over the almost perfect oval shape of the small island, the rich green of its gardens and foliage perfectly shown off by the whiteness of its sandy beaches and the wonderful turquoise of the Aegean Sea that lapped them.

'That's because the island has its own plentiful supply of water,' Andreas told her. 'It's far too small to be able to sustain either crops or livestock, which is why it was uninhabited—as you can see it is quite some distance from any of the other islands, the furthest out into the Aegean.'

'It looks perfect,' Saskia breathed. 'Like a pearl drop.'

Andreas laughed, but there was an emotion in his eyes that made Saskia's cheeks flush a little as he told her quietly, 'That was how my grandmother used to describe it.'

Saskia gave a small gasp as the plane suddenly bumped down onto the runway, belatedly realising that Andreas had deliberately distracted her attention away from their imminent landing. He could be so entertaining when he wanted to be, so charming and so easy to be with. A little wistfully she wondered how much difference it would have made to his opinion of her had they met under different circumstances. Then she very firmly pulled her thoughts into order, warning herself that her situation was untenable enough already without making it worse by indulging in ridiculous fantasies and daydreams.

There was a bleak look in Andreas's eyes as he guided Saskia towards the aircraft's exit. There was such a vast contradiction in the way he was perceiving Saskia now and the way he had perceived her the first time he had seen her. For his own emotional peace of mind and security he found himself wishing that she had remained true to his first impression of her. That vulnerability she fought so determinedly and with such pride to conceal touched him in all the ways that a woman of Athena's coldness could never possibly do. Saskia possessed a warmth, a humanity, a womanliness, that his maleness reacted and responded to in the most potentially dangerous way.

Grimly Andreas tried not to allow himself to think about how he had felt when he had kissed her. Initially he had done so purely as an instinctive response to his awareness that Athena was in his apartment—that appalling overpowering scent of hers was instantly recognisable. Quite how she had got hold of a key he had no idea, but he suspected she must have somehow cajoled it from his grandfather. But the kiss he had given Saskia as a means of reinforcing his unavailability to Athena had unexpectedly and unwontedly shown him—*forced* him to acknowledge—something he was still fighting hard to deny.

He didn't *want* to want Saskia. He didn't want it at all, and he certainly didn't want to feel his current desire to protect and reassure her.

Athens had been hot, almost stiflingly so, but here on the island the air had a silky balminess to it that was totally blissful, Saskia decided, shading her eyes from the brilliance of the sun as she reached the ground and looked a little uncertainly at the trio of people waiting to greet them.

Andreas's husky, 'Here you are, darling, you forgot these,' as he handed her a pair of sunglasses threw her into even more confusion, but nowhere near as much as the warm weight of his arm around her as he drew her closer to him and whispered quite audibly, 'Our harsh sunlight is far too strong for those beautiful Celtic eyes of yours.'

Saskia felt her fingers start to tremble as she took the sunglasses from him. They carried a designer logo, she noticed, and were certainly far more expensive than any pair of sunglasses she had ever owned. When Andreas took them back and gently slipped them on for her she discovered that they fitted her perfectly.

'I remembered that we didn't get any in London and I knew you'd need a pair,' he told her quietly, leaning forward to murmur the words into her ear, one arm still around her body and his free hand holding her shoulder as though he would draw her even closer.

To their onlookers they must look very intimate, Saskia recognised, which was no doubt why Andreas had chosen to give them to her in such a manner.

Well, two could play at that game. Without stopping to think about the implications of what she was doing, or to question why she was doing so, Saskia slid her own arm around *his* neck, turning her face up to his as she murmured back, 'Thank you, darling. You really are so thoughtful.'

She had, she recognised on a small spurt of defiant pleasure, surprised him. She could see it in his eyes—and she could see something else as well, something very male and dangerous which made her disengage herself from him hastily and step back. Not that he allowed her to go very far. Somehow he was holding her hand and refusing to let go of it, drawing her towards the small waiting group.

'Mama. This is Saskia...' he announced, introducing Saskia first to the older of the two women.

Warily Saskia studied her, knowing that if she and Andreas were really in love and engaged her heart would be in her mouth as she waited to see whether or not she and Andreas's mother could build a true bond. Physically she looked very much like Athena, although, of course, older. But the similarity ended once Saskia looked into her eyes and saw the warmth there that had been so markedly lacking from Athena's.

There was also a gentleness and sweetness about Andreas's mother, a timidity almost, and intuitively Saskia sensed that she was a woman who, having loved only one man, would never totally cease mourning his loss.

'It's a pleasure to meet you, Mrs Latimer,' Saskia began, but immediately Andreas's mother shook her head chidingly.

'You are going to be my daughter-in-law, Saskia, you must call me something less formal. Helena is my name, or if you wish you may call me Mama, as 'Reas and my daughters do.' As she spoke she leaned forward and placed her hands gently on Saskia's upper arms.

'She is lovely, 'Reas,' she told her son warmly.

'I certainly think so, Mama,' Andreas agreed with a smile.

'I meant inside as well as out,' his mother told him softly.

'And so did I,' Andreas agreed, equally emotionally.

Heavens, but he was a wonderful actor, Saskia acknowledged shakily. If she hadn't known how he really felt about her that look of tender adoration he had given her just now would have...could have... A man like him should know better than to give a vulnerable woman a look like that, she decided indignantly, forgetting for the moment that so far as Andreas was concerned she was anything *but* vulnerable.

'And this is Olympia, my sister,' Andreas continued, turning Saskia towards the younger of the two women. Although she was as darkly Greek as her mother, she too had light coloured eyes and a merry open smile that made Saskia warm instantly to her.

'Heavens, but it's hot down here. Poor Saskia must be melting,' Olympia sympathised.

'You could have waited for us at the villa,' Andreas told her. 'It would have been enough just to have sent a driver with the Land Rover.'

'No, it wouldn't,' Olympia told him starkly, shrugging her shoulders as her mother made a faint sound of protest. She looked anxiously at her, saying, 'Well, he has to know...'

'I have to know what?' Andreas began to frown.

'Athena is here,' his mother told him unhappily. 'She arrived earlier and she...'

'She what?'

'She said that your grandfather had invited her,' his mother continued.

'You know what that means, don't you Andreas?' Olympia interrupted angrily. 'It means that she's bullied Grandfather into saying she could stay. And that's not all...'

'Pia...' her mother began unhappily, but Olympia refused to be silenced.

'She's brought that revolting creep Aristotle with her. She claims that she is right in the middle of an important business deal and that she needs him with her because he's her accountant. If it's so important, how come she had time to be here?' Olympia demanded. 'Oh, but I hate her so. This morning she went on and on about how concerned Grandfather is about the business and how he's been asking her advice because he's worried that you...'

'Pia!' her mother protested again, and this time Andreas's sister did fall silent, but only for a few seconds.

'What I can't understand is why Gramps is so taken in by her,' she burst out, as though unable to contain herself. 'It's obvious what she's doing. She's just trying to get at you, Andreas, because you won't marry her.'

'I'm sorry about this,' Helena Latimer was apologising gently to Saskia. 'It can't be pleasant for you. You haven't met Athena yet, I know—'

'Yes, she has,' Andreas interrupted his mother, explaining when both she and Pia looked at him questioningly, 'Somehow or other she managed to get a key for the London apartment.'

'She's the worst, isn't she?' Pia told Saskia. 'The black widow spider I call her.'

'Pia!' Andreas chided her sharply.

'Mama hasn't told you everything yet,' Pia countered, looking protectively at her mother before continuing, 'Athena has insisted on having the room that Mama had arranged to be prepared for Saskia. It's the one next to your suite—.'

'I tried to stop her, Andreas,' Helena interrupted her daughter unhappily. 'But you know what she's like.'

'She said that Saskia could have the room right down at the end of the corridor. You know, the one we only use as an overspill when absolutely everyone is here. It hasn't even got a proper bed.'

'You'll have to say something to Athena, Andreas.

Make her understand that she can't...that she can't have that room because Saskia will be using it.'

'No, she won't,' Andreas contradicted his mother flatly, sliding his arm very firmly around Saskia, imprisoningly almost, drawing her right into his body so that her face was concealed from view as he told his mother and sister, 'Saskia will be sharing *my* room...and *my* bed...'

Saskia could sense their shock, even though she could not see their faces. *Now* she knew why he was holding her so tightly, preventing anyone else from seeing her expression or hearing the panicky denial she was trying to make but which was muffled against the fine cotton of his shirt.

There was just no way that she was prepared for anything like this. No way that she could ever be prepared for it. But her attempts to tell Andreas were bringing her into even more intimate contact with him as she tried to look up into his face.

His response to her efforts to attract his attention made the situation even worse, because when he bent his head, as though anxious to listen to what she was saying, her lips inadvertently brushed against his jaw.

It must be a combination of heat and shock that was sending that melting liquid sensation of weakness swooshing through her, Saskia decided dizzily. It certainly couldn't be the feel of Andreas's skin against her lips, nor the dangerous gleam she could see in his narrowed eyes as they glittered down into hers. The arm he had around her moved fractionally, so that the hand that had been resting on her waist was now somehow just beneath the curve of her breast, his fingertips splaying against its soft curve and making her...making her...

'Saskia will be sharing your room!' Pia was breathing, verbalising the shock that Saskia herself felt and that she suspected his mother was too embarrassed to voice.

'We *are* engaged...and soon to be married...' Andreas told his sister smoothly, adding in a much rougher, rawer, spine-tinglingly possessive voice, 'Saskia is mine and I intend to make sure that everyone knows it.'

'Especially Aristotle,' Pia guessed. 'I don't know how Athena can endure him,' she continued shuddering. 'He's like a snake, Saskia. All cold and slimy, with horrid little eyes and clammy hands...'

'Athena endures him because of his skill at "creative" accounting,' Andreas informed his sister dryly.

'You mean he's dishonest,' Pia translated pithily.

'You didn't hear that from me,' Andreas warned her as he started to shepherd all three of them towards the waiting Land Rover.

Whilst they had been talking the driver had loaded their luggage, and as he held the door open for his mother, sister and Saskia to get in Saskia heard Andreas asking him about his family, listening interestedly whilst the driver told him with pride about his son who was at university.

'Grandfather was not very pleased at all when Andreas said that he wanted to use the money our father had left him to help pay for the education of our personal household staff,' Pia told Saskia.

'Pia, you aren't being very fair to your grandfather,' her mother objected.

Andreas had done that? Stubbornly Saskia refused to acknowledge that she was impressed by his philanthropy.

Had he really meant what he had said about them sharing a room? He couldn't have done—could he? Personally she didn't care *where* she slept, even if it was a normally unused bedless room, just so long as she occupied it on her own.

'We have both had a long day and I imagine that Saskia is going to want to have a rest before dinner,' Andreas was saying as the Land Rover pulled up in a cool paved courtyard with a central fountain that sent a musical plume of water up into the air to shower back to earth in millions of tiny teardrops.

'I'll make sure everyone knows that you aren't to be disturbed,' his mother responded. 'But perhaps Saskia would like something light to eat and drink…'

Before Saskia could say anything Andreas was answering for her, telling his mother, 'I'll see to that,' before placing his hand beneath Saskia's elbow and telling her in a soft voice in which she suspected only she could hear the underlying threat, 'This way, Saskia…'

CHAPTER SEVEN

'I CAN'T sleep in this room with you!'

Saskia had been able to feel herself trembling as Andreas had whisked her down a confusing maze of corridors. She had known that he must be able to feel her nervousness as well, but somehow she had managed to keep her feelings under control until they were both inside the huge elegant bedroom with the door firmly shut behind them.

Right now, though, she was in no mood to appreciate the cool elegance of her surroundings. Whirling round, she confronted Andreas determinedly. 'No way was *that* part of the deal.'

'The "deal" was that you would act as my fiancée, and that includes doing whatever has to be done to ensure that the act is believable,' he told her angrily.

'I won't sleep here with you,' Saskia protested wildly. 'I don't... I haven't...' She could hardly bear to look at the large king-sized bed as panic filled her, flooding out rationality. She had gone through so much, and now she was hot and tired and very, very afraid. Her emotions threatened to overwhelm her.

Quickly she turned away as she heard Andreas saying, almost mundanely, 'I'm going to have a shower, and if you'll take my advice you'll do the same. Then, when we're both feeling cooler and calmer, we can discuss this whole situation less emotively.'

A shower! With Andreas! Saskia stared at him in mute shocked disbelief. Did he really think that she would...that she could...?

'You can use the bathroom first,' he told her.

First! So he hadn't meant... Relief sagged through her, quickly followed by a furious burst of toxic anger.

'I don't want to use the bathroom at all,' she burst out. 'What I *want* is to be at home. My *own* home, with my own bathroom and my own bedroom. What I want is to be free of this stupid...stupid charade... What I *want*...' She had to stop as her feelings threatened to overwhelm her, but they refused to be contained, spilling out in a furious fierce torrent of angry words. 'How could you let your mother and sister think that you...that we...?' She shook her head, unable to put into words what she wanted to say.

Andreas had no such qualms.

'That we are lovers?' he supplied dramatically for her. 'What else should they think? I'm a man, Saskia, and you and I are supposed to be engaged. And if in reality we were, do you think for one minute that I wouldn't—'

'Want to test the goods before you bought them?' Saskia threw wildly at him. 'Oh, of course, a man like you would be bound to want to do that...to make sure...'

She tensed as she saw the way he was looking at her and the bitter anger in his eyes.

'That kind of comment is typical of a woman like

you,' he ground out. 'Reducing everything to terms of money. Well, let me tell you—'

But Saskia wouldn't let him finish, defending herself sharply instead as she insisted, '*You* were the one who said…'

But Andreas immediately checked her.

'What I said, or rather what I was *trying* to say before you interrupted me,' he told her grittily, 'was that if I genuinely loved you there would be no way I would be able to deny myself—or you—the pleasure of showing that love in the most intimate physical way there is. There would be no way that I could bear to let you out of my sight or my arms, certainly not for the length of a whole night.'

Saskia discovered that she had started to tremble almost violently as his words struck sharply sensitive chords deep within her body that she had not even known existed. Chords that activated a deep core of feminine longing, that brought her dangerously close to the edge of tears she had no idea why she wanted to cry. Panic raced through her veins, flooding out common sense. She could feel her heart thumping frantically with anxiety.

She opened her mouth to tell Andreas that she had changed her mind, that she wanted to go home, that she was not prepared to stay a minute longer, no matter how much he tried to blackmail her into doing so. But her panic didn't stem from any fear of him. No. It was herself she feared now, and the way she was beginning to feel, the thoughts she was beginning to have. She *couldn't* allow herself to feel that way about him. She *couldn't* be attracted to him. He wasn't her type of man at all. She abhorred the way he had treated her, the way he had misjudged her. But the shocking shaft of self-awareness, of longing she had felt as he'd described his desire for the woman he would love wasn't going to be dismissed.

'I can't...' she began, stopping as Andreas held up his hand warningly, silencing her as someone knocked on the door.

Dry-mouthed, Saskia waited whilst he went to open it, watching as their cases were brought in— not by the driver of the Land Rover but by another smaller, older man to whom Andreas was talking in Greek, smiling warmly at him as he did so, and then laughing good-humouredly as the older man looked past him at Saskia herself, before clapping him on the shoulders with a wide, beaming smile.

'What was that all about?' Saskia demanded curiously once he had gone and they were on their own again.

'Stavros was saying that it is high time I had a wife...and that I must lose no time in getting myself a fine boy child,' he added mercilessly.

Saskia could feel herself colouring to the roots of her hair as she looked everywhere but at the king-sized bed in the centre of the room.

Despite the room's air conditioning she felt stifled, unable to breathe...hunted and desperate to escape.

'I'm going to have that shower,' Andreas told her, mundanely breaking into her thoughts, turning away from her as he did so and heading for one of the three doors that opened off the bedroom.

Once he had disappeared Saskia looked at the door to the corridor, longing to have the courage to walk through it and demand that she be flown back immediately to Athens. But if she did she would lose her job—Andreas would make sure of that!

Fiercely Saskia tried to concentrate on something else, *anything* else but the appalling situation she was in. She hated what Andreas was doing to her...what he was making her do. And she hated Andreas himself too...didn't she?

Unable to answer her own question honestly, Saskia studied the view beyond the large patio doors that opened out onto an enclosed courtyard, which itself surrounded a tantalisingly tempting swimming pool complete with its own bubbling spa pool.

Small oases of green plants broke up the paving and the brilliant harshness of the sunlight. Comfortable-looking sun loungers complete with umbrellas offered a lazy way to enjoy the sunshine. The whole scene looked like something out of an exclusive holiday brochure, the kind Saskia had only been able to glance at enviously, knowing such a holiday was way beyond her means. But right now the only place she wanted to be was safe in her own home.

Andreas couldn't really expect her to share a room—never mind a bed—with him. She couldn't do it. She wouldn't...she was so...

'The bathroom's free...'

Saskia froze. She had been so engrossed in her thoughts she hadn't realised that Andreas was in the bedroom with her...standing right behind her, she recognised as she picked up the clean, warm scent of his newly showered body.

'I'll go and sort out something light for you to eat. Dinner won't be for a few hours yet, and if you'll take my advice you'll try to rest for a while. Greeks eat late and go to bed even later.'

'But I thought that we'd be having separate rooms,' Saskia burst out, unable to control her panic any longer. 'I would never have agreed to come here if I'd thought that I'd— No! Don't you dare touch me,' she protested as she felt him moving closer to her, reaching out to her. She wouldn't be able to bear it if he touched her, if he...

Frantically she turned and ran towards the door, but somehow Andreas managed to get there before her, blocking her access to it, taking hold of her, his fingers biting into the soft flesh of her arms.

'What the hell do you think you're doing?' he ground out savagely. 'What exactly is it you're pretending to be so afraid of? This? A woman like you!'

Saskia gasped and shook from head to foot as his arms closed imprisioningly around her and his mouth came down on hers. He was wearing a robe, but as she struggled to break free it was his bare skin she could feel beneath her flaying hands. Warm, damp...hard, his chest roughened by dark hairs. Her hands skittered wildly over his torso, shocked by the intimate unexpected contact with his bare skin, seeking some kind of purchase to thrust him away and finding none.

He was kissing her with an angry passion that made her feel weak, the blood roaring in her head as her brain recognised her inability to deal with the searing experience of so much furiously male arrogant sensuality.

'Stop acting like a novice, an innocent,' Saskia heard him demanding against her mouth. His tongue forced her lips to part for its entry and the hand that was imprisoning her urged her even deeper into the sensual heat of his parted thighs as he leaned back against the door, taking her with him. His free hand was on her body, arrogantly stroking its way up past her waist to the curve of her breast.

Saskia tensed in shock as it cupped her breast, his thumb-pad circling her nipple and somehow enticing it to peak into a shocking bud of delicious wanton pleasure.

She could feel the aroused heat of him like a brand, and beneath her anger she felt a sharp, spiralling stab of female curiosity and excitement...a dangerous surge to conspire with him, to allow her traitorous body to experience even more of the intimacy of their embrace.

Without knowing she had done so she opened her mouth, hesitantly allowing him access to its sweetness, shyly starting to return his kiss and even more shyly allowing her tongue to mesh seductively with his.

'Andreas? Are you in there? It's me, Athena...I need to talk to you.'

Saskia froze as she heard Athena's voice from the other side of the door, but Andreas showed no sign whatsoever of any confusion or embarrassment. Still holding Saskia against him in a grip she could not break, he opened the door and told Athena flatly, 'Not now, Athena. As you can see, Saskia and I are busy.'

'She is with *you*,' Athena snapped angrily, darting Saskia a look of icy venom. 'Why isn't she in her own room?'

'She is,' Andreas returned coolly. 'My room is Saskia's room. My bed...her bed. My body...her...'

'Your grandfather will never allow you to marry her,' Athena breathed, but Andreas was already closing the door, ignoring her insistence that he listen to her.

'Andreas, let me go,' Saskia demanded. She couldn't bear to look at him. Couldn't bear to do anything, least of all think about the way she had responded to him...the way she had encouraged him...

Derisively Andreas watched her.

'Okay, Saskia, that's enough,' he told her. 'I know I told you I wanted you to act like a faithful fiancée, but that does not mean you have to pretend to be an innocent virgin who has never—' Abruptly he stopped, frowning as he mulled over the unwanted suspicions that were striking him as he looked at Saskia's pale face and hunted eyes.

Even though he had let her go she was still shaking, trembling from head to foot, and he could have sworn just now, when he had held her in his arms and kissed her...touched her, that he was the first man to make her feel so...

For a moment he examined what he was thinking, and feeling, and then firmly dismissed his suspicions. There was no way she could be so inexperienced, no way at all. There was enough Greek in him for him to consider that the gift of her virginity, her purity, was one of the greatest gifts a woman could give to the man she loved, but his cultural heritage from his British father and schooling mocked and even deplored such archaic feelings.

Would a woman expect a man to keep himself pure until he met her? No. So why should it be any different for a woman? As a mature man he accepted and respected a woman's right to choose how she dealt with her own sexuality. But he knew too that as a lover, a husband, there would be a deeply, darkly passionate and possessive part of him that yearned to be his beloved's only partner, an ache within him to teach her, show her the delights of sensual love. And right now something about Saskia's reaction to him was sparking off a reaction he was having to fight to control, a response that was pure primitive Greek male. A need!

'I'm not sleeping in this room with you,' Saskia reiterated numbly. 'I'm…'

If she *was* acting then she deserved an Oscar, Andreas decided grimly. But a fiancée who looked terrified at the very thought of being with him was the last thing he needed. He had to calm her down, to calm them both down.

'Come with me,' he commanded, taking hold of her hand and drawing her towards one of the doors that opened off the bedroom.

When he opened it Saskia could see that the room that lay beyond it was furnished as an office, with all the latest technological equipment.

'Will it make you feel any better if I tell you that I intend to sleep in there?' Andreas demanded.

'In there? But it's an office. There's no bed,' Saskia whispered shakily.

'I can bring in one of the sun loungers and sleep on that,' Andreas told her impatiently.

'You mean it...' Saskia was wary, reluctant to trust or believe him.

Andreas nodded his head grimly, wondering why on earth he was allowing his overactive conscience to force him into such a ridiculous situation. He knew there was no way she could possibly be the naïve, frightened innocent she was behaving as though she was.

'But surely someone would notice if you removed a sun bed?' she was asking him uncertainly.

'Only my room opens out onto this pool area. It's my private territory. The main pool which everyone else uses is round the other side of the villa.'

His own private pool. Saskia fought not to be impressed, but obviously she had not fought hard enough, she recognised ruefully as Andreas gave her an impatient look.

'I'm not trying to make a point, Saskia, one-upmanship of that boastful sort is anathema to me. My grandfather may be a millionaire but I most certainly am not.'

It wasn't entirely true, but something about the look in Saskia's eyes made him want to refute any mental criticism she might have that he was some kind of idle playboy, lounging by a swimming pool all day.

'It's just that I happen to like an early-morning swim when I'm here at the villa; my sisters used to claim that I woke them up so I had this pool installed for my own use. Swimming laps helps me to clear my thoughts as well as allowing me to exercise.'

Saskia knew what he was saying, she felt the same about walking. Whenever she was worried about something, or had a problem to mull over, she walked.

As he watched her Andreas asked himself grimly why he was going to so much trouble to calm and reassure her. That frightened heartbeat he had felt thudding so anxiously against his own body just had to have been faked. There was no way it could not have been. Just like that huge-eyed watchfulness.

Saskia bit her lip as she looked away from him. It was obvious that Andreas meant what he said about sleeping in his office, but right now it wasn't their sleeping arrangements that were to the forefront of her mind so much as what was happening during their waking hours—and what she herself had just experienced when he kissed her.

She couldn't have secretly wanted him to kiss her. Surely it was impossible that that could happen without her being consciously aware of it. But what other explanation could there be for the way she had responded to him? her conscience demanded grittily.

'Right,' she could hear Andreas saying dryly, 'now that we've got *that* sorted out I've got some work to do, so why don't you have something to eat and then have a rest?'

'I need to unpack,' Saskia began to protest, but Andreas shook his head.

'One of the maids will do that for you whilst you're resting.'

When he saw her expression he told her softly, 'They work for us, Saskia. They are servants and they work to earn their living just as you and I work to earn ours.'

* * *

'Oh, I'm sorry, I didn't wake you, did I?' Pia said *sotto voce*. 'But it will be dinner time soon and I thought you might appreciate some extra time to get ready.'

As Saskia came fully awake and struggled to sit up in the bed she recognised that her unexpected visitor was Andreas's sister Olympia.

The arcane grin that crossed Pia's face as she added, 'We normally dress down here, not up, but Athena is bound to want to make an impact,' made Saskia warm to her friendliness.

'Where's...?' she began anxiously, but didn't get any further than the first word of her enquiry.

'Where's Andreas?' Pia supplied for her, 'Grandfather telephoned to speak to our mother and then he wanted to have a word with Andreas.' She gave a small shrug. 'He's probably still on the phone, and I have to warn you he isn't in a very good mood.' As she saw the way Saskia's eyes became watchful she hastened to assure her. 'Oh, it isn't you. It's Athena. She's brought her accountant with her and Andreas is furious. He can't stand him. None of us can, but Athena insisted that Grandfather invited Aristotle personally.'

As Pia darted about the room, switching on lamps to illuminate the darkness of the Greek evening, Saskia swung her feet to the floor. She had fallen asleep fully dressed and now she felt grubby and untidy. The thought of having to sit down at a dinner table with Andreas and Athena was not one she was looking forward to, but Pia was right about one thing: she *would* need to make an impact. Andreas would no doubt expect it of her. Still, with her suitcase full of the new clothes he had insisted on buying for her, she had no excuse *not* to do so.

'Maria's already unpacked your cases for you,' Pia informed her. 'I helped her,' she added. 'I love that little black number you've brought with you. It's to die for. Your clothes are gorgeous. Andreas kept coming in and telling me not to make so much noise in case I woke you up.' She pulled another face. 'He's so protective of you.

'Mama and I are so glad that he's met you,' she added more quietly, giving Saskia a look of warm confidence that immediately made her feel horribly guilty. 'We both love him to bits, of course,' she went on, 'and that hardly makes us impartial. But we were beginning to get so afraid that he might just give in to Grandfather and Athena for Grandfather's sake—and we both know he could *never* love her. I suppose he's told you about what she did when he was younger?'

Without waiting for Saskia to say anything Pia continued in a quick burst of flurried words, 'I'm not supposed to know about it really. Lydia, my sister, told me, and swore me to secrecy, but of course it's all right to discuss it with you because Andreas must have told you about it. He was only fifteen at the time—just a boy, really—and she was *so* much older and on the point of getting married. I know the actual age gap in terms of years would be nothing if it had been between two adults, but Andreas wasn't an adult. He was still at school and she… I think it was wonderfully brave and moral of Andreas to refuse to go to bed with her—and do you know something else? I think that although Athena *claims* to love him a part of her really wants to punish him for not letting her—well, you know!'

Athena had tried to *seduce* Andreas when he had still been a schoolboy! Saskia had to fight hard to control both her shock and the distaste Pia's revelations were causing her.

It was true that in terms of years—a mere seven or so—the age gap between them was not large. But for a woman in her twenties to attempt to seduce a boy of fifteen—surely that was almost sexual abuse? A cold shiver touched Saskia's skin, icy fingers spreading a chilling message through her.

Would a woman who was prepared to do something like that allow a mere bogus fiancée to come between her and the man she wanted? And Athena obviously did want Andreas very badly indeed— even if her motivation for doing so was shrouded in secrecy.

Andreas was such a very *male* man it was hard to imagine him in the role of hunted rather than hunter. If ever a man had been designed by nature to be proactive, arrogant and predatory that man was, in Saskia's opinion, Andreas. But there was something so alien to Saskia's own experience in Athena, a coldness, a greed, almost an obsessiveness that Saskia found it hard to relate to her or even think of her in terms of being a member of her own sex.

Her determination to marry Andreas was chillingly formidable.

'Of course, if it wasn't for Grandfather's health there wouldn't be any problem,' Pia was saying ruefully. 'We all know that. Grandfather likes to think that because he works for him Andreas is financially dependent on him, but...' She stopped, shaking her head.

'You are going to wear the black, aren't you? I'm dying to see you in it. You've got the colouring for it. I look so drab in black, although you can bet that Athena will wear it. Whoops!' She grimaced as they both heard male footsteps in the corridor outside the bedroom. 'That will be Andreas, and he'll scalp me if he thinks I'm being a pest.'

Saskia tensed as Andreas came into the room, watching as his glance went from the bed to where she was standing in the corner of the room.

'Pia,' he began ominously, 'I told you...'

'I was awake when she came,' Saskia intervened protectively. She liked Andreas's sister, and if she'd been genuinely in love with him and planning to marry him she knew she would have been delighted to have found a potential friend in this warm-hearted, impulsive woman.

Pia launched herself at Andreas, laughing up into his face as she hugged him and told him triumphantly, 'See? You are wrong, big brother, and you must not be so firm and bossy with me otherwise Saskia will not want to marry you. And now that I have met her I am determined that she will be my sister-in-law. We were just discussing what she is going to wear for dinner,' she added. 'I have warned her that Athena will be dressed to kill!'

'If you don't take yourself off to your own room so that we can *all* get ready, Athena is going to be the only one who is dressed for anything,' Andreas told her dryly.

Kissing his forehead, Pia released him and hurried

to the door, pausing as she opened it to give Saskia an impish grin and remind her, 'Wear the black!'

'I'm sorry,' Andreas apologised after the door had closed behind her. 'I asked her not to disturb you.'

So he hadn't been deceived by her fib, Saskia recognised.

'I don't mind; I like her,' Saskia responded, this time telling him the truth.

'Mmm... Pia's likeability is something I'm afraid she tends to trade on on occasion. As the baby of the family she's a past mistress at getting her own way,' he told Saskia in faint exasperation, before glancing at his watch and informing her, 'You've got half an hour to get ready.'

Saskia took a deep steadying breath. Something about the revelations Pia had made had activated the deep core of sympathy for others that was so much a part of her nature. Somewhere deep inside her a switch had been thrown, a sea change made, and without her knowing quite how it had happened Andreas had undergone a transformation, from her oppressor and a dictator whom she loathed and feared to someone who deserved her championship and help. She had a role which she was now determined she was going to play to the very best of her ability.

'Half an hour,' she repeated in as businesslike a manner as she could. 'Then in that case I should like to use the bathroom first.'

CHAPTER EIGHT

'So, SASKIA, how do you think you will adjust to being a Greek wife—if you and Andreas *do* actually get married?'

Saskia could hear Pia's indrawn gasp of indignation at the way Athena had framed her question, but she refused to allow herself to be intimidated by the other woman. Ever since they had all taken their places at the dinner table Saskia had recognised that Athena was determined to unnerve and upset her as much as she could. However, before she could say anything Andreas was answering the question for her.

'There is no "if" about it Athena,' he told her implacably. 'Saskia *will* become my wife.'

Now it was Saskia's turn to stifle her own potentially betraying gasp of shock, but she couldn't control her instinctive urge to look anxiously across the table at Andreas. What would he do when he ultimately had to back down and admit to Athena that their engagement was over? That was *his* problem and not hers, she tried to remind herself steadily.

Something odd had happened to her somehow; she was convinced of it. Andreas had walked out of the office adjoining 'their' bedroom earlier this evening and come to a standstill in front of her, saying quietly, 'I doubt that any man looking at you now could do anything other than wish that you were his, Saskia.'

She had certainly never had any desire to go on the stage—far from it—and yet from that moment she had felt as though somehow she had stepped into a new persona. Suddenly she had become Andreas's fiancée and, like any woman in love, not only was she proud to be with the man she loved, she also felt very femalely protective of him. The anxiety in her eyes now was *for* him and *because* of him. How would he feel when Athena tauntingly threw the comment he had just made back in his face? How must he have felt when he had first realised, as a boy, just what she wanted from him?

'Wives. I love wives.' Aristotle, Athena's accountant, grinned salaciously, leaning towards Saskia so that he could put his hand on her arm.

Immediately she turned away from him. Saskia fully shared Pia's view of Athena's accountant. Although he was quite tall, the heavy, weighty structure of his torso made him look almost squat. His thick black hair was heavily oiled and the white suit he was wearing over a black shirt, in Saskia's opinion at least, did him no favours. Andreas, on the other hand, looked sexily cool and relaxed in elegantly tailored trousers with a cool white cotton shirt.

If she had privately thought her black dress might be rather over the top she had swiftly realised how right Pia had been to suggest that she wore it once she had seen Athena's outfit.

Her slinky skintight white dress left nothing to the imagination.

'It was designed especially for me,' Saskia had heard her smirking to Andreas. 'And it is made to be worn exactly the way I most love—next to my skin,' she had added, loudly enough for Saskia to overhear. 'Which reminds me. I hope you have warned your fiancée that I like to share your morning swim so she won't be too shocked...' She had turned to Saskia. 'Andreas is like me, he likes to swim best in his skin,' she had told her purringly.

In his skin. Saskia hadn't been able to prevent herself from giving Andreas a brief shocked look which, fortunately, Athena had put down to Saskia's jealousy at the thought of another woman swimming nude with her fiancée.

Whilst Saskia had been digesting this stomach-churning disclosure she had heard Andreas himself replying brusquely, 'I can only recall one occasion on which you attempted to join me in my morning lap session, Athena, and I recall too that I told you then how little I appreciate having my morning peace interrupted.'

'Oh, dear.' Athena had pouted, unabashed. 'Are you afraid that I have said something you didn't want your fiancée to know? But surely, Andreas,' she had murmured huskily, reaching out to place her hand on his arm, 'she *must* realise that a man as attractive as you...as virile as you...will have had other lovers before her...'

Her brazenness had almost taken Saskia's breath away. She could imagine just how she would be feeling right now if Andreas *had* indeed been her fiancée. How jealous and insecure Athena's words would be making her feel. No woman wanted to be reminded of the other women who had shared an intimate relationship with her beloved before her.

But Andreas, it seemed, was completely unfazed

by Athena's revelations. He had simply removed her arm by the expedient of stepping back from her and putting his own arm around Saskia's shoulders. He had drawn her so close to his body that Saskia had known he must be able to feel the fine tremor of reaction she was unable to suppress. A tremor which had increased to a full-flooded convulsion when his lean fingers had started almost absently to caress the smooth ball of her bare shoulder.

'Saskia knows that she is the only woman I have ever loved—the woman I want to spend my life with.'

The more she listened to and watched Athena the more Saskia subscribed to Pia's belief that it wasn't love that was motivating the other woman. Sometimes she looked at Andreas as though she hated him and wanted to totally destroy him.

Aristotle, or 'Ari' as he had told Saskia he preferred to be called, was still trying to engage her attention, but she was deliberately trying to feign a lack of awareness of that fact. There was something about him she found so loathsome that the thought of even the hot damp touch of his hand on her arm made her shudder with distaste. However, good manners forced her to respond to his questions as politely as she could, even when she thought they were intolerable and intrusive. He had already told her that were he Andreas's accountant he would be insisting she sign a prenuptial contract to make sure that if the marriage ended Andreas's money would be safe.

Much to Saskia's surprise Andreas himself had thoroughly confounded her by joining in the conversation and telling Aristotle grimly that he would never ask the woman he loved to sign such an agreement.

'Money is nothing when compared with love,' he had told Aristotle firmly in a deep, implacable voice, his words so obviously genuine that Saskia had found she was holding her breath a little as she listened to him.

Then he had looked at her, and Saskia had remembered just how *they* had met and what he really thought of her, and suddenly she had felt the most bitter taste of despair in her mouth and she had longed to tell him how wrong he was.

At least she had the comfort of knowing that his mother and sister liked her, and Pia had assured her that their elder sister was equally pleased that Andreas had fallen in love, and was looking forward to meeting Saskia when she and her husband and their children came to the island later in the month.

'Lydia's husband is a diplomat, and they are in Brussels at the moment, but she is longing to meet you,' Pia had told her.

She would have hated it if Andreas's close family had *not* liked and welcomed her.

Abruptly Saskia felt her face start to burn. What on earth was she thinking? She was only *playing* the part of Andreas's fiancée. Their engagement was a fiction, a charade...a *lie* created simply to help him escape from the trap that Athena was trying to set for him. What she must not forget was that it was a lie he had tricked and blackmailed her into colluding with.

Aristotle was saying something to her about wanting to show her the villa's gardens. Automatically

Saskia shook her head, her face burning with fresh colour as she saw the way Andreas was watching her, a mixture of anger and warning in his eyes. He couldn't seriously think she would actually *accept* Aristotle's invitation?

'Saskia has had a long day. I think it's time we said our goodnights,' she heard him saying abruptly as he stood up.

Saskia looked quickly round the table. It was obvious from the expressions of everyone else just what interpretation they were putting on Andreas's decision, and Saskia knew that the heat washing her face and throat could only confirm their suspicions.

'Andreas...' she started to protest as he came round to her chair and stood behind her. 'I don't...'

'You're wasting your breath, Saskia.' Pia chuckled. 'Because my dear brother obviously *does*! Oh, you needn't put that lordly expression on for me, brother dear.' She laughed again, before adding mischievously, 'And I wouldn't mind betting that you won't be lapping the pool at dawn...'

'Pia!' her mother protested, pink-cheeked, whilst Athena gave Saskia a look of concentrated hatred.

Hastily Saskia stood up, and then froze as Aristotle did the same, insisting in a thick voice, 'I must claim the privilege of family friend and kiss the new addition to the family goodnight.'

Before Saskia could evade him he was reaching for her, but before he could put his words into action Andreas was standing between them, announcing grimly, 'There is only one man *my* fiancée kisses...'

'If you'll take my advice, you'll keep well away from Aristotle. He has a very unsavoury reputation with women. His ex-wife has accused him of being violent towards her and—'

Saskia turned as she stepped into the bedroom, her anger showing. 'You can't mean what I *think* you mean,' she demanded whilst Andreas closed the door. How could he possibly imagine that she would even contemplate being interested in a man like the accountant? It was an insult she was simply not prepared to tolerate.

'Can't I?' Andreas countered curtly. 'You're here for one reason and one reason only, Saskia. You're here to act as my fiancée. Whilst I can appreciate that, being the woman you are, the temptation to feather your nest a little and do what you so obviously do best must be a strong one, let me warn you now against giving in to it. If you do, in fact…'

If she *did*… Why, she would rather *die* than let a slimeball like Ari come anywhere near her, Saskia reflected furiously. And to think that back there in the dining room she had *actually* felt sympathetic towards Andreas, had actually wanted to *protect* him. Now, though, her anger shocked through her in a fierce, dangerous flood of pride.

'If you want the truth, I find Ari almost as repulsively loathsome as I do you,' she threw bitterly at him.

'You dare to speak of me in the same breath as that reptile? How dare you speak so of me…or to me…?' Andreas demanded, his anger surging to match hers as he reached out to grab hold of her. His eyes smouldered with an intensity of emotion that Saskia could see was threatening to get out of control.

'That man is an animal—worse than an animal. Only last year he narrowly escaped standing on a criminal charge. I cannot understand why Athena tolerates him and I have told her so.'

'Perhaps she wants to make you jealous.'

It was an off-the-cuff remark, full of bravado, but Saskia wished immediately she had not said it when she saw the way the smoulder suddenly became a savage flare of fury.

'*She* does? Or *you* do...? Oh, yes, I saw the way he was looking at you over dinner...touching you...'

'That was nothing to do with me,' Saskia protested, but she could sense that the words hadn't touched him, that something else was fuelling his anger and feeding it, something that was hidden from her but which Andreas himself obviously found intolerable.

'And as for you finding me *loathsome*,' Andreas said through gritted teeth. 'Perhaps it is unchivalrous, *ungentlemanly* of me to say so, but that wasn't loathing I could see in your eyes earlier on today. It wasn't *loathing* I could hear in your voice, *feel* in your body...was it? *Was it?*' he demanded sharply.

Saskia started to tremble.

'I don't know,' she fibbed wildly. 'I can't remember.'

It was, she recognised a few seconds later, the worst possible thing she could have said. Because immediately Andreas pounced, whispering with soft savagery, 'No? Then perhaps I should help you to remember...'

She heard herself starting to protest, but somehow the words were lost—not because Andreas was refusing to listen, but because her lips were refusing to speak.

'So when exactly *was* it that you found me so loathsome Saskia?' Andreas was demanding as he closed both his arms around her, forming them into a prison from which it was impossible for her to escape. 'When I did this...?' His mouth was feathering over hers, teasing and tantalising it, arousing a hot torrent of sensation she didn't want to experience. 'Or when I did *this*...?'

Now his tongue-tip was probing the lips she was trying so desperately to keep firmly closed, stroking them, tracing their soft curves, over and over again, until she could hear herself moaning helplessly as they parted softly for him. But still it seemed he hadn't extracted his pound of flesh, because even this victory wasn't enough for him.

'What? Still no answer...? I wonder why not,' he was taunting her, before adding bitingly, 'Or do I need to wonder at all? You are a woman who is used to giving her body to a man, Saskia, who is used to experiencing pleasure. And right now you want that pleasure from *me*.'

'No,' Saskia moaned in denial, trying to turn her face away from his and to break free of him.

'Yes,' he insisted rawly. '*Yes*. Admit it, Saskia... You *want* me... Your body wants *mine*. It wants the sexual satisfaction it's used to...it aches and craves for.'

A shudder of shock ripped through her as Saskia recognised the truth of what he was saying. She *did* want him, but not in the way he was suggesting. She wanted him as a woman wanted the man she loved, she realised shakily. She wanted him as her lover, not merely as her sexual partner, someone with whom she could find a release for a basic physical need, as he was so cruelly saying. But how could she love him? She *couldn't*... But she *did*.

She had fallen in love with him virtually the moment she had set eyes on him, Saskia acknowledged despairingly, but she had told herself that because of her loyalty to her friend he was out of bounds to her and that she could not, *must* not allow herself to have such feelings, just as she could not allow herself to have them now. Although for very different reasons. Megan was no longer a barrier to her loving Andreas, but Andreas himself and what he thought about her certainly was.

'Let me go, Andreas,' she demanded.

'Not until you have admitted that I am right and that you want me,' Andreas refused. 'Or are you trying to goad me into *proving* to you that I am right?'

Saskia flinched as she felt the suffocating, dangerously toxic mix of fear and excitement explode inside her.

She hesitated whilst she tried to formulate the right response, the only sane, sensible response she could give, and then she realised that she had waited too long as Andreas told her rawly, 'You've pushed me too far, Saskia. I want you, but you already know that, don't you? How could a woman like you *not* know it? You can feel it in my body, can't you?' he demanded. 'Here...'

Helplessly Saskia leaned against him whilst she tried to absorb the shock of having her hand taken and placed so explicitly against the hard, intimate throb of his maleness. If only she could find the strength to drag her hand away, to tell him that she didn't want the intimacy he was forcing on her. But despairingly she knew that she was too weak, that there was no way she could stop herself from aching to use the opportunity he had given her to touch and explore him, to know him…to know his maleness…to—

She gave a small moan as her body started to shake with tremors of desire. Andreas's heart was pounding so savagely that she could feel it almost inside her own body. Earlier in the evening, when he had almost absently caressed the ball of her shoulder—the touch of an established lover for his beloved—she had shuddered in mute delight, but that was nothing to what she was feeling now.

She ached for him, hungered for him, and when she closed her eyes she could see him as Athena had so tauntingly described him—proud and naked as his body sliced the water. She moaned again, a high, sharp sound this time that had Andreas covering her mouth with the hard, hot, demanding pressure of his, the words he was groaning against her lost as his passion sent a kick of shocking voluptuous pleasure searing through her.

Her mouth was properly open beneath his now, her tongue hungry for the sensual melding stroke of his, and the intensity of her own feelings was dizzying and dazzling her.

'You want me… You need me…'

She could feel him mouthing the words and she couldn't deny them, her body, her emotions were saturated with the intensity of a response to him so new to her that she had no defences against it.

Everything else was suddenly forgotten, unimportant. Everything else and every*one* else. All she needed... All she wanted... All she could ever want was here within her reach.

She moaned and trembled as she felt Andreas's hands on her body and over her dress, their touch hard, hungry...excitingly, *dangerously* male. The unfamiliar intimacy of his body against hers was depriving her of the ability to think or to reason properly. There was no place for reason to exist in this new world she was inhabiting anyway.

'I want to see you...watch you whilst I make love to you,' Andreas was saying thickly to her. 'I want *you* to see me... My God, but I can understand *now* just why all those other men fell victim to you. There's something about you, some witchery, some— What's wrong?' he demanded as he felt the abrupt way Saskia had tensed against him in rejection.

Saskia could not bear to look at him.

With those few contemptuous words he had destroyed everything, totally obliterated her wonderful new world and brought her crashing back to her old one. She felt sick to her soul from her own behaviour, her own folly.

'No, no, I don't want *this*,' she protested frantically, pushing Andreas away.

'What the...?' She could hear the anger in his voice, feel it almost, but still he released her.

'If this is some kind of game—' he began to warn her, and then stopped, shaking his head in disbelief.

'My God, I must have been out of my mind anyway, to even contemplate... I suppose that's what too many years of celibacy does for a man,' he threw at her unkindly. 'I never thought I'd be idiotic enough...'

He turned back to her, stopping when Saskia froze.

'You're quite safe,' he told her grimly. 'I'm not going to touch you. There's no way—' He broke off and shook his head again, and then walked abruptly away from her, telling her brusquely, 'I've got some work to do.'

The bedroom was in darkness when Saskia woke up, and at first she didn't know what had woken her. Then she heard it again, the rhythmic sound of someone swimming. The patio doors to the pool area were open, and as she turned her head to look towards them she could see the discreet lights which were illuminating it.

Andreas was swimming... She looked at her watch. It was three o'clock in the morning and Andreas was swimming...tirelessly up and down the pool. Warily she sat up in bed to get a closer look as his powerful crawl took him to the far side of the pool. As he executed his turn Saskia lay down again. She didn't want him to see her watching him.

Beneath the bedclothes she was naked, apart from a tiny pair of briefs. The one thing Andreas had apparently forgotten to buy for her had turned out to be any kind of nightwear. *That* discovery had caused her to remain for nearly fifteen minutes in the locked privacy of the bathroom, agonising over what she should do until she had finally found the courage to open the door and make an undignified bolt for the bed, her body hidden from view by the towel she had wrapped around it. Not that she need have been so concerned. Andreas had remained out of sight in his office.

But he wasn't in his office now. Now he was swimming in the pool.

Beneath the protective cover of the bedclothes Saskia's brain worked feverishly. Should he be swimming alone at night? Was it safe? What if...? Almost the very second that fear formed her ears registered the fact that she could no longer hear the sound of Andreas swimming. Quickly she lowered the bedclothes and looked anxiously towards the pool area. The water was still, calm—and empty of its sole swimmer.

Andreas! Where—? She gripped hold of the bedclothes as she saw him climbing out of the water— totally naked—totally! She tried to drag her recalcitrant gaze away from his body but it was no use; it was refusing to listen to her, refusing to obey her, remaining fixed in hungry female appreciation on the pagan male beauty of Andreas's nakedness.

Surely any woman would have found the sight of Andreas breathtaking, Saskia thought fervently, her gaze devouring the pure sensuality of his back view as he walked across the tiles. His skin shone sleekly, still damp from his swim, and beneath it the muscles moved in a way that had a shockingly disconcerting effect on her *own* body.

Naively Saskia had always previously assumed that there could be little difference in seeing a statue or a painting of a naked man and viewing the real thing, but now she knew how wrong she had been. Perhaps it was her love for him that made the difference, perhaps it was... She gasped as he suddenly turned round. He seemed to be looking right into the bedroom. Could he see her? Did he *know* that she was watching him? She lay perfectly still, praying that he could not do so, unable to bear the humiliation of his mockery if he were to come in to her now. If he were to...

She just managed to suppress the audible sound of her own longing. If he came to her now and held her, touched her, kissed her...*took* her as she was so aching for him to do, it wouldn't be in love but in lust. Was that really what she wanted? she asked herself sternly. No, of course it wasn't, was her helpless response. What she wanted was for Andreas to love her the way she did him.

He was turning away from her now, his body silhouetted by the light. Saskia sucked in her breath sharply, every feminine instinct and desire she possessed flagrantly ignoring her attempts to control them. He looked... He was... He was *perfect* she acknowledged, silently whispering the soft accolade beneath her breath as her eyes rounded and she saw that the male reality of him far, far outreached anything she had ever thought of in her innocent virginal imaginings.

Once again he looked towards the bedroom and Saskia held her breath, praying...hoping...*waiting*... She expelled it on a small rush of sound as he reached down and retrieved his robe, shrugging it on before walking not back to the bedroom and to her but away from it. Where was he going? she wondered. Back to his office?

For what felt like a long time after he had gone Saskia lay where she was, afraid to move, unable to sleep and even more afraid to think. What was the matter with her? How could she possibly love a man who had treated her as Andreas had done, who had blackmailed her, threatened her, refused to allow her to tell him the truth about herself? A man who had the lowest possible opinion of her and yet who, despite that, had still kissed her. How could she? Saskia closed her eyes. She didn't know the answer to that question. All she knew was that her emotions, her heart, her deepest self were crying out—how could she *not* love him?

'Sunbathing? I never thought I'd see the day when you would just laze around,' Pia teased Andreas as she came hurrying out of the villa in the tiniest little bikini Saskia had ever seen and curled up on the vacant sun bed next to where Saskia was lying.

'Saskia didn't have a good night. She needs to rest and I didn't want her overdoing things or lying too long in our strong sun,' Andreas lied unblushingly to his sister.

'Oh, poor you,' Pia immediately sympathised with Saskia as she studied her pale face.

Guiltily Saskia said nothing. After all, she could hardly admit that the reason she was so jaded was because she had spent so many of the night hours when she should have been sleeping thinking about, *fantasising* about the man lying right next to her. In daylight Saskia dared not recall the very personal and intimate nature of her fantasies. She knew that if she did so her face would be as brightly coloured as it was now pale. Mercifully Andreas had put her huge eyes and pale face down to travel tiredness.

'Well, that's one improvement you've made on my brother's lifestyle already, Saskia,' Pia approved with a grin. 'Normally when he comes to the villa we can't get him out of the office. When did Grandfather say he is going to arrive?' she asked Andreas.

'I must say I'm surprised that your grandfather intends to come to the island at all at the moment,' Athena answered for Andreas as she and her accountant came out of the villa to join them.

Saskia's heart sank a little as she saw them. Over breakfast Ari had been so over-fulsome in his praise of her, and so obviously sexually motivated, that she had been glad to escape from him.

As Pia started to frown Athena added maliciously, 'He isn't very happy with you right now, Andreas...'

'My grandfather is never happy with anyone who takes a different view from his,' Andreas told her dryly. 'He has a quick temper and a short fuse and thankfully an even shorter memory—'

Andreas had insisted that Saskia was to lie beneath the protection of a sun umbrella because of her fair skin, but as she watched Athena untying the wrap she was wearing to reveal an even smaller bikini than Pia's, Saskia felt envious of her rich golden tan.

'How uncomfortable you must be lying in the shade,' Athena said, adding bitchily, 'I would *hate* to have such a pale skin. It always looks so...'

'Saskia's skin reminds *me* of the purest alabaster,' Andreas interrupted Athena smoothly.

'Alabaster—oh, but that is so cold.' Athena

smiled, giving Saskia an assessing look. 'Oh, now you are frowning and looking grumpy,' she told Andreas softly, 'and I know *just* the cure for that. Let me put some oil on for you, Andreas, and then...'

Saskia could hardly believe it when she heard herself saying firmly, 'I'll do that for you, darling.' Turning to look at Athena, she added boldly, 'A fiancée's privilege.' And then, ignoring both the frowning look Andreas was giving her and her own shaking hands, she got up off her sun lounger, took the bottle of oil Pia was offering her with an approving smile and walked over to where Andreas was lying.

Very carefully Saskia poured a little of the oil into her cupped hand and then, even more carefully, leaned over Andreas's prone body, making sure as she did so that she stood between his sun bed and the one Athena was reclining on in a pose carefully designed to flaunt to full effect her generous breasts.

Saskia's hair swung over her face as she nervously started to smooth the oil over Andreas shoulders. His skin felt warm and sleek beneath her touch. As sleek as it had looked last night. She paused as her hands began to tremble. Last night! She must *not* think about *that* now. But somehow she found herself doing so; somehow, too, her hands were moving sensually against his skin, stroking, smoothing, even kneading instinctively when she found that his muscles were bunching beneath her touch.

He had been lying on his stomach with his eyes closed, but suddenly they opened and he told her abruptly, 'That's enough. I was about to go for a swim anyway.'

Even so it was still several seconds before he actually got up and walked away from her to the end of the pool, diving in cleanly and then swimming virtually a full length beneath the water before resurfacing and starting to lap the pool with a hard, fast-paced crawl.

Andreas tried to concentrate on what he was doing, to empty his head of any thoughts as he always did when he was swimming. It was his favourite way of relaxing—or at least it had been. Right now the *last* thing he felt was relaxed. Even without closing his eyes he could still remember exactly how it had felt to have Saskia's hands moving over his body, soft, caressing...knowing...

He slid beneath the water, swimming under it as he tried to control his aching body. God, but he wanted her; ached for her; lusted for her. He had *never* felt like this about anyone before, never needed anyone with such an intensity, never been in a situation where he simply could not control himself either physically or emotionally. She *must* know what she was doing to him, a woman of *her* experience...a woman who prowled bars at night looking for a man. Of *course* she must; of course she *did*. And yet...

And yet he couldn't stop himself from contrasting what he knew cerebrally about her with the way she had felt in his arms, the soft, hot sweetness of her kiss, the desire hazing her eyes and the shock which had later replaced it. She had caught him off guard just now, when she had refused to allow Athena to touch him—caught him off guard and filled him with a certain hot male triumph and pride that she should feel so possessive about him. But of course she didn't—did she? She was simply acting, playing out the role he had forced her into.

Andreas frowned. His own mental use of the word 'forced' and the admission which it brought rasped against his conscience like sandpaper. It was wholly out of character for him, against his strongest held beliefs to force anyone to do anything, but he had begun to fear he could find no way out of the present situation without endangering his grandfather's health. What he was offering was an explanation, not an excuse, he warned himself sternly and if he had now discovered that he had merely exchanged one hazard for another which was even more potentially dangerous then he had no one but himself to blame.

Had Saskia seen that betraying surge of his body before he had turned away from her? Athena had. Athena... Andreas's mouth hardened.

At fifteen, and still a schoolboy, he had tried to convince himself that he was mature enough to take over his father's role, strong enough to support and protect his mother and his sisters. But a part of him had still been childish and he had often ended up crying alone at night in his bed, confused and angry and missing his father, wondering furiously why he had had to die.

That period had surely been the worst of his life: the loss of his father and then Athena's attempt to seduce him. Two events which together had propelled him into an adulthood and maturity he had in no way been prepared for.

Athena's desire for him had held none of the classic 'Mrs Robinson' allure. She had been coming on to him for weeks, ever since he had returned home from school for the summer holidays, but he had never dreamed that she was doing anything other than playing some mysterious adult female game that was beyond his ability to comprehend—until the day he had found her in his room—naked!

When she had handed him the vibrator she was stroking herself with, commanding him to use it on her, it had been all he could do not to turn on his heels and run. But boys ran, and he hadn't wanted to be a boy, but a man...the man his father would have wanted him to be, the man his mother and sisters needed him to be.

'I don't think you should be in here, do you?' he had asked her woodenly, avoiding looking at her naked body. 'You are engaged to be married.'

She had laughed at him then, but she hadn't been laughing later, when he had held open his bedroom door and commanded her to leave, warning her that if she didn't he would have no compunction in getting a couple of members of staff to physically remove her.

She had gone, but not immediately, not until she had tried to change his mind.

'You have a man's body,' she had told him angrily. 'But like a fool you have no knowledge of what to do with it. Why won't you let me show you?' she had coaxed. 'What is it you are so afraid of?'

'I'm not afraid,' he had responded stoically, and truthfully. It hadn't been fear that had stopped him from taking advantage of what she was offering but anger and loathing.

But Athena was a woman who couldn't endure to accept that he didn't want her. Tough! Her feelings, if she genuinely had any—which he personally doubted—were her problem. His grandfather was a very different matter, though, and even without the cloud currently hanging over his health, Andreas would have been reluctant to quarrel with him—though he felt that the old man was being both stubborn and difficult. How much of the blame for that lay with Athena and how much with his grandfather's fiercely guarded fear of growing old and the future Andreas could only hazard a guess at.

It was ironic, really, that the means he had adopted to help him overcome his problems should have resulted in causing him even more. An example, perhaps, of the modern-day ethos behind the ancient Greek mythology Saskia had expressed a love of. She might love Greek mythology but she most certainly did not love him. Andreas frowned, not wanting to pursue such a line of thought.

'That is a very pretty little ring you are wearing,' Athena commented disparagingly as she got up off the lounger and came to stand next to Saskia.

They were alone at the poolside, Athena's accountant having gone to make some telephone calls and Pia having left to help her mother, who was preparing for the arrival of her father.

'But an engagement ring is no guarantee of marriage,' Athena continued. 'You look like a sensible girl to me, Saskia. Andreas is a very wealthy and experienced man. Men like him get so easily bored. You must know that yourself. I suspect that the chances of you actually walking down the aisle and marrying Andreas are very limited indeed, and they will become even more slender once Andreas's grandfather arrives. He doesn't want Andreas to marry you. He is very old-fashioned and very Greek. He has other plans for his only grandson and for the future of the business he has built up.'

She paused, watching Saskia calculatingly, and Saskia knew what she was thinking. Athena too had other plans for Andreas's future.

'If you really loved Andreas then surely *he* would be far more important to you than your own feelings. Andreas is devoted to his grandfather. Oh, I know he may not show it, but I can promise you that he is. Think what it would do to him emotionally, not to mention financially, if there were to be a rift between them. Andreas's mother and his sisters are both financially dependent on their grandfather... If he were to banish Andreas from his life then Andreas would be banished from *their* lives as well.'

Athena gave a deep, theatrical sigh and then asked pseudo-gently, 'How long do you think he would continue to want *you* once that had happened? And I can *make* it happen, Saskia...you know that, don't you. His grandfather listens to me. It is because he wants my business to be joined to his, of course. That is the Greek way of doing things.' She bared her teeth and gave Saskia an unkind smile. 'It is *not* the Greek way of doing things for a millionaire to allow his heir to marry a penniless foreigner.

'But let's talk of something more pleasant. There is no reason why we shouldn't come to a mutually happy arrangement—you and I. I *could* sit back and wait for Andreas to leave you, but I will be honest with you. I am approaching the age when it may become less easy for me to give Andreas the sons he will want. So, to make it easy for us both, I have a proposition to put to you. I am willing to pay you *one million pounds* to remove you from Andreas's life—permanently.'

Saskia could feel the blood draining out of her face as shock hit her. Somehow she managed to drag herself into a sitting position on the sun lounger and then to stand up, so that she and Athena were face to face.

'Money can't buy love,' she told her fiercely. 'And it can't buy me. Not one million pounds, not one hundred million pounds! *No* amount.' Tears stung her eyes and she told herself that shock had put them there. 'If at any time Andreas wants to end our engagement then that is his prerogative, but—'

'You're a fool—do you know that?' Athena breathed, her whole face contorted with fury and malice. 'Do you really think Andreas meant what he said about not insisting on a prenuptial agreement? Ha! His grandfather will *make* him have you sign one, and when Andreas grows tired of you, as he undoubtedly will, you will get *nothing*...not even any child he may have given you. Greek men do not give up their children. Greek *families* do not give up their heirs.'

Saskia didn't want to hear any more. Without even bothering to pick up her wrap she started to walk towards the house, only just managing to prevent herself from breaking into a run.

As Saskia reached the house Pia was coming out of it through the open patio door.

'Saskia...' she began in concern, but Saskia shook

her head, knowing she was in no fit state to talk to her—to her or indeed to anyone. She felt degraded by what Athena had said to her, degraded and angry. How dared Athena believe that her love was for sale...that *money* mattered more to her than Andreas...that she would *ever*...? Abruptly Saskia stopped. What was she *thinking*? She turned round and went back outside, heading not for the pool area but beyond it...to the island and the pathway along the cliffs. She needed to be on her own.

The full irony of what had happened was only just beginning to sink in. She had agreed to come to the island only because Andreas had blackmailed her into doing so and because she couldn't afford to lose the income from her job. Yet when she was offered what amounted to financial security for life, not just for herself but more importantly for her beloved grandmother, as well as an immediate escape from her intolerable situation, she turned both down.

Angrily Pia started to hurry towards where Athena was lying sunning herself. After what she had just overheard there was no way she was not going to tell Athena what she thought of her. How dared she treat Saskia like that, trying to bribe her into leaving Andreas?

Andreas!

Pia came to an abrupt halt. Perhaps she ought to tell her brother what Athena had been up to and let him deal with her. Saskia had looked so dreadfully upset, and no wonder. Reluctantly Pia listened to the inner voice warning her that Andreas would not thank her for pre-empting his right to be the one to confront Athena. Turning on her heel, she walked back inside the villa in search of Andreas.

CHAPTER NINE

LESS than a third of the way along the path that circumnavigated the island Saskia stopped walking and turned round. She couldn't go on; she had had enough. Loving Andreas—being so close to him every day in one sense and yet with such an unbridgeable gap between them in all the senses that really mattered—was more than she could cope with. Her love for him, her longing for him, was tearing her apart.

Slowly she started to walk back to the villa. She had no idea what she was going to do—throw herself on Andreas's mercy and beg him to release her from their 'agreement'? There was no point in trying to tell him what Athena had done. He was hardly likely to believe her, not with his opinion of her, and besides, she didn't want him to know. If he did...once he did... Andreas was no fool, he was an astute, sharp-minded businessman, it wouldn't take him long to guess what had happened, how she felt, and that was something she could not endure.

Once she reached the villa Saskia went straight to 'her' room which, thankfully, was empty. The maid had been in and the bed was freshly made. Quickly removing her swimsuit, she went to have a shower.

'Andreas,' Athena purred seductively as she saw him coming out of his grandfather's office.

'Not now, Athena.' Andreas cut her short. He had spent the best part of the last couple of hours trying to come to terms with feelings he had never expected to have, never mind *wanted* to have, and now that he had come to a decision he was anxious to act on it without any delay, especially from Athena.

It was no use trying to hide the truth from himself any longer.

He had fallen in love with Saskia. How? Why? When? To his exasperation no amount of analytical self-probing on his part had been able to produce any kind of logical answers to such questions. All his heart, his body, his emotions, his very soul kept insisting over and over again was they wanted her; loved her; craved and needed her. If the logical-thinking part of him that was already fighting a desperate rearguard action should dare to argue, then his emotions would see to it that his life was no longer worth living.

But look at what she *is* he had tried to remind himself. But his emotions had refused to listen. He loved her as she was, past errors of judgement and all. Errors of *judgement*? Picking up men in bars...coming as near as dammit to selling herself to them—if not for money then certainly for the pseudo-love they had offered her.

It wasn't her fault, his heart had protested in loving defence. She had been deprived of her father's love as a child. She was simply trying to compensate for that. With love, *his* love, she could be made whole again. She would forget her past and so would he. What mattered was the here and now and the future they would share…a future which meant nothing to him without her in it.

And so it had continued, on and on, when he was supposed to be working. In the end he had had no option other than to give in, and now he was on his way to find Saskia to tell her…ask her…to beg her if necessary.

'Is Saskia still outside?' he asked Athena, impatient to tell Saskia how he felt.

Athena's eyes narrowed. She knew that look in a man's eyes, and to see it now, in the eyes of the only man she wanted, was not to be tolerated. If Saskia couldn't be induced to leave Andreas then *he* must reject her, and Athena knew exactly how to make *that* happen.

'Oh…' Immediately she faked a look of concern, 'Didn't you know? She's gone for a walk…with Ari. I know you won't like me saying this, Andreas, but—well, we all know how much Ari likes women, and Saskia *has* been making it rather obvious that she reciprocates… Not whilst you're around, of course…'

'Andreas—' Pia tried to stop him several minutes later but he refused to stop or listen.

'Not now Pia, whatever it is…' he said brusquely, before striding down the corridor towards his suite.

Goodness, but he looked angry, Pia reflected as she watched his departing back. Well, what she had to tell him wasn't going to lighten his bad mood, but he would have to be told. She knew that.

Andreas could hear the sound of the shower running as he walked into the bedroom and slammed the door behind him.

'Saskia?' he demanded, striding towards the bathroom and pulling open the door.

Saskia blanched as she saw him. She had just that second stepped out of the shower and wrapped a towel around her damp body—thank goodness.

'Why are you having a shower?' Andreas demanded suspiciously.

Saskia stared at him nonplussed.

'I've just been for a walk and it was hot and...'

Andreas could feel the shock of his jealousy jolt right through his body, exploding inside him, almost a physical pain. It furnished him with some very vivid and very sexual images of just why Saskia might want to cool down. Like any man in love, he couldn't bear the thought of his beloved in the arms of someone else, and he reacted predictably.

Taking hold of her, his fingers gripping painfully into the delicate flesh of her upper arms, he gritted jealously, 'You just couldn't wait, could you? Where did he take you?'

'He...?' Saskia started to protest, confused by both his words and his actions. 'What on earth...?'

But Andreas wasn't listening.

'Was it out in the open, where anyone could have seen you? Is *that* what you like, Saskia...demeaning yourself so completely that...? But of course you do. I already know that, don't I? You *want* to be treated badly, to be used and then discarded like a... Well, then, if that's the way you like it then let's see if *I* can come up to your expectations, shall we? If I can give you what you so obviously want.'

He was a man no longer in control of what he was doing, wanting passionately to stamp his possession on her—body and soul—to make her his and wipe from her memory all thoughts of any other man!

What on earth had happened to turn Andreas from the cool, remote man she was familiar with into the raw explosion of male fury and passion she was facing now? Saskia wondered in bemusement. It was passion she could sense most strongly, she recognised dizzily. It emanated from him like a heat haze, drawing her into its danger and excitement, melting, burning away her own protective caution.

Wasn't this secretly what a part of her had *wanted* to happen? For him to look at her as he was doing now, with the fierce, elemental need of a man no longer able to fight off his own desire.

Somehow, seeing Andreas so close to losing control allowed her to give full reign to her own feelings and longings.

'You're mine,' Andreas was telling her rawly as he pulled her hard against his body. 'Mine, Saskia... And what is mine I mean to have full measure of,' he added thickly.

Saskia could feel her skin starting to quiver responsively where he was touching it. He slid his hands oh, so deliberately up her bare arm and over her shoulder, his fingertips caressing the nape of her neck. Blissfully she arched her spine, offering herself up to his touch, feeling the quiver-raising goose-bumps on her skin moving deeper, growing stronger, as they became a pulse that echoed and then drove her heartbeat.

'Kiss me, Andreas...'

Had she actually said that? Demanded it in that

unfamiliar husky little voice that sounded so sexy and made Andreas's eyes glitter even more hotly?

'Oh, I can promise you that I'm going to do far more than just kiss you,' Andreas assured her as his hands very deliberately removed the towel from her body. 'Far, far more,' he repeated sensually, before adding, 'But if a kiss is what you want...'

His hands were spread against her collarbone and her throat, his thumbs massaging her fragile bones, his lips brushing just the merest tantalising breath of heat against the pulse that raced so frantically beneath her skin.

'Where exactly is it you want me to kiss you, Saskia?' he was asking her. 'Here...? Here...? Here..?'

As his mouth moved tantalisingly over her throat and then her jaw, covering every inch of her face but her lips, Saskia heard herself start to moan softly with longing until, unable to endure any more of his delicious torment, she put her hand against his face and turned his mouth to hers, exhaling in a soft swoon of relief as she finally tasted the hard warmth she had been aching for.

'Andreas... Andreas...' She could hear herself whispering his name as she slid her fingers into his hair and clasped his head, probing the hard outline of his lips with small, frantic thrusts of her tongue-tip.

Over her shoulder Andreas caught sight of their entwined reflections in the mirror. Saskia's naked back view was as perfectly sculpted as that of any classical statue, but her body was composed of living, breathing flesh, and just the feel of her sweetly firm breasts pressing against him, never mind what the dedicated assault of her honey tongue was doing to him, totally obliterated everything but the way he felt about her.

Against the delicate pallor of her Celtic skin his hands looked shockingly male and dark as he caressed her, held her, moulded her so close to his body that he could taste her small gasp of sensual pleasure as she felt his arousal. His clothes were a hindrance he no longer wanted, but he couldn't make the time to remove them until he had punished that sexily tormenting tongue of hers for the way it was destroying his self-control.

He felt the deep, racking shudder of pleasure that ran right through her body as he opened his mouth on hers, taking into his domain full control of their kiss and of her.

Saskia gasped and trembled, yielding the sweet intimacy of her mouth and the soft-fleshed nakedness of her body to Andreas's dominance. What was happening between them was surely the pinnacle of her whole life, the reason she had been born. Here, in Andreas's arms, love and desire were coming together for her in the most perfect way possible.

Saskia had forgotten what she had been going to tell him, why it was so imperative for her to leave. *This* was what she had wanted to happen from the very first second she had set eyes on him.

Unable to bring himself to break the intoxicating sensuality of their shared kiss, Andreas picked Saskia up and carried her over to the bed. Whatever she had been before no longer mattered. From now on she would be his.

The heavy natural linen curtains Saskia had closed over the large windows before taking her shower diffused the strong sunlight outside, bathing the room in a softly muted glow that turned her fair skin almost ethereally translucent. As he laid her on the bed Andreas gave in to the temptation to caress the taut quivering peak of one breast with his lips, savouring it in a slow, careful exploration which made Saskia's whole body shake with sharply intense arousal.

'No, I don't want to rush this,' Andreas denied to her, his voice thick, almost cracking over the words as he refused the frantic pleas of her writhing body. 'I want to take my time and savour everything!' he emphasised as his hand caressed the breast he had just been suckling, his thumb tip etching unbearably erotic circles around the sensitively receptive nub of flesh.

'I want you so much,' Saskia whispered achingly. 'I want you...' She stopped, her eyes clouding with a mixture of anxiety and uncertainty as she heard her own voice and briefly recognised her own danger.

It was too late. Andreas had heard her. Pausing in the act of removing his clothes, he leaned over her, bracing himself so that the muscles in his arms corded tautly, capturing her awed gaze whilst he asked her rawly, 'Where do you want me, Saskia? Tell me... Show me...'

But he already knew the answer to his question because he had already lifted his hand from the bed and brushed his knuckles in the gentlest of touches the full length of the centre of her body, letting it come to rest palm-down against the soft swelling of her most intimate heart.

'You haven't answered my question, Saskia,' he reminded her softly, as his fingertips drew delicate circles of pleasure against her, so jaw-clenching desirable that Saskia thought she might actually faint from the heat and intensity of the longing they were arousing.

'Tell me...tell me what you want,' Andreas was insisting, spacing each word between kisses so ravishingly tender that Saskia felt as though she was melting.

In the cocoon of her own private world he had become for Saskia the lodestone that drew her, the focus of everything she was experiencing, of everything she was and ever wanted to be, the centre of her world.

'I want you,' she responded feverishly to him. 'I want you, Andreas. I...' She shuddered, unable to say any more because Andreas was kissing her, sealing her mouth with a kiss that was a hot, passionate brand of possession. As he wrapped his arms around her Saskia clung to him shyly, stroking the side of his face.

'Look at me,' he demanded.

Hesitatingly she did so, the melting, soft, languorous longing of her gaze entrapped by the hot, fierce glitter of his.

Very slowly and tenderly he began to caress her. Saskia felt as though her whole body was going to dissolve with her longing for him, her need of him. She reached out to touch his bare shoulder, his arm, and made a helpless little sound of taut female need against his throat as she pressed her lips to it.

Beneath his hands her body softened and responded magically, welcomingly, as though his touch was a special key. But *he* was the key to what she was feeling, Saskia acknowledged hazily, lost fathoms—oceans—deep in her love for him.

'There isn't going to be much time...I want you too much,' he told her almost bluntly, softening the words with another hotly passionate kiss that made her hips lift achingly against him whilst her whole body writhed in longing for him.

'Next time we can take things more slowly,' Andreas gasped harshly against her breast, his voice and actions revealing his increasing need.

Next time... Saskia felt as though she might die from happiness. 'Next time' meant that he shared her feelings, that he felt the same way as she did.

It seemed to Saskia almost as though the air between them throbbed with the intensity of their shared passion, with the way their bodies synchronised together with a perfection surely only given to true lovers.

Each sigh, each gasp, each heartbeat served only to bind her closer to him, emotionally as well as physically, until she was captive to him and her desire, her love, was laid as bare to him as her quivering body.

When he finally whispered to her, 'Now, Saskia... Oh, God, now!' she knew her body had given him its most eager assent before her lips could even begin to frame the words she wanted to say. Automatically she was already wrapping the slim length of her legs around his waist, raising up to meet him, to feel him. She heard him cry out as he entered her, a sound of both torment and triumph, and then he was filling her with his own unique intimate, heavy warmth, and her body, pausing only to tense briefly in sweetly virginal shock, welcomed each ever deepening thrust of him within her.

Andreas felt her body's unexpected resistance, his brain and his emotions even registered their shock at what it meant, but his body refused to react to that knowledge. It loved the hot snug fit of her around him, holding and caressing him, urging him to forget what he had just experienced and to satisfy the age-old demand her femaleness was making on his maleness. Deeper, harder, stronger, until you reach the deepest heart of me, each delicately soft contraction of her flesh around his urged him. Deeper, stronger, surer, until you are *there*. Yes, *there…there…*

Andreas felt as though his heart and lungs might burst as he drove them both to the place where they could finally fly free.

Saskia cried out in softly sweet awe and relish as she experienced for herself what true completion was…what it truly meant to be a woman, completely fulfilled, elevated to a place, a state…an emotion so piercingly intense that it filled her eyes with hot, happy exhausted tears.

Someone was trembling… Was it her…or was it both of them? She had heard Andreas groan in those final unbelievable seconds before he had wrapped his arms securely around her and then sent them both hurtling into infinity, calling out her name in a way that had made her tingle with raw emotion.

As he fought to regain control of his breathing, and himself, Andreas looked down at Saskia.

She was crying, huge silent tears. Of pain? Because of *him*...because he had...?

Even now his thoughts skidded away from the reality, the truth that his brain was trying to impose on him. She couldn't have been a virgin... It was impossible.

But his self-anger and guilt told him that it wasn't, and she had been. Unforgivably, he had hurt her and made her cry, selfishly taking his pleasure from her at the price of her innocence, so unable to control what he felt for her that he had not been able to stop when he knew that he should have done.

Sickened by his own behaviour, he pulled away from her.

'Andreas...' Saskia reached out towards him uncertainly. Why was he withdrawing from her? Why wasn't he holding her, caressing her...*loving* and reassuring her?

'What is it...what is wrong?' she begged him.

'Do you really need to ask?' Andreas responded tersely. 'Why didn't you tell me...*stop* me...?'

The anger in his voice was driving away the sweet mist of her joy and replacing it with anxiety and despair. It was obvious to her now that what had been so wonderful, so perfect, so *unique* for her had been nowhere near the same kind of experience for Andreas.

Andreas was furious with himself for not somehow having had the insight to know. She had been a virgin, and he, damn him, had practically forced himself on her... He was disgusted with himself, his pride scorched not just by his actions but his complete misreading of her.

'You *should* have stopped me,' he repeated as he got off the bed and went into the bathroom, returning with a towel wrapped around his naked body and his robe, which he handed to Saskia, and sitting down on the bed, turning away from her as she tried to put it on.

What would he say if she were to tell him that the last thing she had wanted was for him to stop? Saskia wondered wretchedly. Her hands were shaking so much she could hardly pull the robe on, never mind fasten it, and when Andreas turned to look at her he gave an impatient, irritated sigh and pushed her hands out of the way, pulling it on properly for her.

'You aren't safe to be let out alone. You realise that, don't you?' he exploded savagely. 'Even if *I* hadn't, Aristotle—'

'Aristotle!' Saskia picked his name up with loathing in her voice and in her eyes. She shuddered, and told him fiercely, 'No—never... He's loathsome and...'

'But you went for a walk with him...'

'No, I didn't,' Saskia protested.

'Athena said you'd gone for a walk,' Andreas insisted, but Saskia wouldn't let him finish.

'Yes, I did...on my own. There were things I wanted...' She stopped, lowering her head and looking away from him. Then she told him in a tear-filled voice, 'I want to go home, Andreas. I can't...'

He knew what she was saying; of course he did, Andreas acknowledged—and why! Of *course* she wanted to get away from him after what he had done...the way he had...

'You should have told me.' He stopped her sharply. 'If I'd known that you were a virgin...'

He might be concerned about taking her virginity but he obviously had no compunction at all about breaking her heart, Saskia decided angrily. For her the loss of her emotional virginity was something that hurt far more—and would continue to hurt.

How could she have been stupid enough to think he felt the same way about her as she did about him? She must have been crazy...*had* been crazy, she recognised grimly. Crazy with love for him!

'I thought...' she heard him saying, but now it was her turn not to allow him to finish.

'I know what you thought,' she cut in with sharp asperity. 'You've already made it very plain *what* you thought of me, Andreas. You thought I was some cheap, silly woman throwing herself at you because of your money. And when I tried to explain you wouldn't let me. You *wanted* to believe the worst of me. I suppose that Greek male pride of yours wouldn't allow you to acknowledge that you might just possibly be wrong...'

Andreas looked at her. His jealousy had led to this...had led to his unforgivably appalling treatment of her. He ached to be able to take her in his arms, to kiss away the traces of tears still on her face, to hold her and whisper to her how much he loved her, how much he wanted to protect her and care for her...how much he wished he could wipe away the wrong he had done her, the pain he had caused her... He ached too, if he was honest, to lie her down on the bed beside him, to remove the robe she was wearing and to kiss every silky inch of her adorable body, to tell her how he felt about her, to show her too. But of course he could do no such thing...not now...

To keep his mind off what he was feeling...off the way he wanted her, he told her gruffly, 'Explain to me now.'

For a moment Saskia was tempted to refuse, but what was the point? She *would* tell him, and then she would tell him that she intended to leave—but she certainly wouldn't tell him why.

Just for an irrational silly female heartbeat of time she ached for him to reach for her, to stop hurting her with words she did not want to hear and to caress and kiss her until her poor deluded heart believed once again that he loved her as she did him.

But thankfully she had enough instinct for self-preservation left to stop herself from telling him so. Instead she began to explain about Megan and Mark and Lorraine.

'She made you do *what*?' Andreas demanded angrily.

She was hesitantly explaining about Lorraine, and her insistence that Saskia make herself look more sexy, when, after a brief rap on the door, Pia burst in and told them, 'Grandfather has arrived. He wants to see both of you.'

'I'd better get dressed,' Saskia mumbled self-consciously.

Pia seemed oblivious to her embarrassment, adding urgently, 'Oh, and Andreas, there's something I want to talk to you about...before you see Grandfather.'

'If you're going to ask for an advance on your

allowance,' Saskia heard Andreas saying hardily to Pia as he walked with her to the door, allowing Saskia to make her own escape to the bathroom, 'you haven't picked a very good time.'

CHAPTER TEN

SASKIA glared reprovingly at the reflection glowing back at her from the bedroom mirror. Her own reflection. The reflection of a woman whose body had enjoyed in full measure every nuance of sensual satisfaction and was proud to proclaim that fact to the world.

That was *not* how she wanted to look when she confronted Andreas's grandfather—the man who was ultimately responsible for her being here...the man who did not think she was good enough for his grandson...the man who preferred to see him marry Athena. Neither did she want *Andreas* to see her like this.

Why on earth couldn't her idiotic body see beyond the delicious fulfilment it was currently basking in and instead think ahead to the loneliness and pain her emotions already knew were lying in store?

Andreas had returned to their room very briefly after Pia's interruption, showering and dressing quickly and then informing her that, although his grandfather was insisting that he wanted to meet her as soon as possible, there were certain matters he needed to discuss with him in private first.

'It won't take very long,' he had told her grimly, before striding out of the room without giving her a chance to tell him that right now, for her own sanity and safety, she wanted to get as far away from him as fast as she could.

Soon, now, he would be coming back for her, to take her and introduce her formally to his grandfather.

Saskia pulled an angry face at her still glowing reflection. She looked, she admitted angrily, the perfect picture of a woman in love. Even her eyes had a new sparkle, a certain glint that said she was hugging to herself a wonderful, special secret.

She had tried over and over again to tell her love-crazed body just what the real situation was, but it simply refused to listen. And so now... She gave a nervous start as she heard the bedroom door opening...

Andreas took a deep breath before reaching out for the bedroom door handle and grasping it firmly.

Pia had been so incensed, so protective and angry on Saskia's behalf, that it had taken her several minutes to become calm enough to spill out in a way that made sense the conversation she had overheard between Athena and Saskia.

'Athena actually tried to bribe Saskia to leave you. She promised her a million pounds if she did. Of course Saskia refused, but I don't see why Athena should be allowed to get away with such insulting and...and offensive behaviour. Grandfather should be told what she's really like—and if you aren't prepared to tell him...' she had threatened darkly.

'Andreas?' she had demanded when he made no response, obviously puzzled at his lack of reaction, but Andreas had still been trying to come to terms with the 'insulting' and 'offensive' behaviour *he* had already inflicted on Saskia. Now, to learn what Athena had done and how nobly Saskia had behaved made him feel... How *could* he have been so wrong about her, so judgemental and...and biased?

A tiny inner voice told him that he already knew the answer. Right from the first second he had set eyes on her there had been something—a sharp warning thrill of sensation and, even more dangerously, of emotion—which he had instantly tried to suppress. His infernal pride had resented the fact that he could fall in love with a woman who was so obvious, and because he had listened to his pride, and not his heart, he had witlessly destroyed something that could have been the most wonderful, the most *precious* part of his life. Unless... Unless Saskia could be persuaded to give him a second chance...

But, whether or not she would allow him the chance to prove his love for her, there was something that *had* to be done, a reparation that *had* to be made. He was Greek enough to think that Saskia should bear his name well before there was any chance of the world knowing that she might bear his child. She had given him her innocence and in exchange he would give her his protection, whether or not she wanted it.

He had told his grandfather exactly what he planned to do, adding truthfully that Saskia was far more important to him than wealth and position and even the love and respect of his grandfather himself.

He had even been tempted to refuse to allow his grandfather to meet her, rather than subject Saskia to any possible hurt or upset, but there was no way he wanted his grandfather to think that he was hiding Saskia from him because he feared she would not be good enough for him. Not good enough! She was *too* good, *too* wonderful...*too* precious...

His final act before heading back to the bedroom had been to tell Athena to leave the island immediately.

'Don't bother to try and persuade my grandfather to allow you to stay. He won't,' he had warned her truthfully.

Now he hesitated before going into the bedroom. He could see Saskia standing waiting for him, and his heart rocked on a huge surge of longing and love for her.

She looked as radiant as a bride, her eyes sparkling, her mouth curved in a smile that was a cross between pure joy and a certain secret, newly discovered womanliness. She looked...

She looked like a woman who had just left the arms and the bed of the man she loved.

But the moment she saw him her expression changed; her eyes became shadowed, her body tense and wary.

Helplessly Andreas closed his eyes, swamped by a wave of love and guilt. He longed more than anything right now to close the door on the rest of the world, to take her in his arms and hold her there for ever whilst he begged for her forgiveness and for the opportunity to spend the rest of his life showing her how much he loved her.

But he had his responsibilities, and primarily, right now, he had to fulfil the promise he had just made to his grandfather that he would introduce Saskia to him.

For his grandfather's sake he trusted that the older man would remember the promise *he* had made that he would treat Saskia gently.

As Andreas crossed the room and took hold of her

hand Saskia shrank back from him, terrified of betraying her feelings, knowing that she was trembling from head to foot simply because of the warmth of his hand clasping hers.

She knew that he was bound to make some irritated, impatient comment about the role she was supposed to be playing, but instead he simply released her hand and told her in a low voice, 'I'm sorry to have put you through this my...Saskia...'

'It's what you brought me here for,' Saskia reminded him brutally, not daring to look at him. Surely she must be imagining that raw note of remorse in his voice.

As they left the room the pretty little maid who looked after it came in, and Andreas paused to say something to her in Greek before following Saskia into the corridor.

It was only natural in the circumstances, Saskia knew, that Andreas should take hold of her hand again and close the distance between them, so that when they walked into the cool, simply furnished room that gave out onto the main patio area they did so with every outward appearance of a couple deeply in love. But what was surely less natural, and almost certainly unwise, was the sense of warmth and security that she got from being so close to him.

To try and distract herself from the effect Andreas's proximity was having on her, Saskia looked to where his sister and mother were standing talking to an elderly white-haired man Saskia knew must be Andreas's grandfather.

As they walked towards him he started to turn round, and Saskia could hear Andreas saying formally, 'Grandfather, I'd like to introduce Saskia to you.'

But Saskia had stopped listening, her attention focused instead on the familiar features of the man now facing her. He was the same man she had seen in the street in Athens, the man who had seemed so unwell and whom she had been so concerned about. He didn't look ill now though. He was smiling broadly at them both, coming forward to clasp Saskia's free hand in both of his in a grip heart-rockingly similar to that of his grandson.

'There is no need to introduce her to me, 'Reas.' He laughed. 'Your beautiful fiancée and I have already met.'

Saskia could see how much he was enjoying the shocking effect of his announcement on his family. He was obviously a man who liked to feel he was in control of things...people...who liked to challenge and surprise them. But where that trait in Andreas had angered her, in his grandfather she found it almost endearing.

'You and Saskia have already met?' Andreas was repeating, frowning heavily as he looked from his grandfather to Saskia.

'Yes. In Athens,' his grandfather confirmed before Saskia could say anything. 'She was very kind to an old man, and very concerned for him too. My driver told me that you had expressed your concern for my health to him,' he told Saskia in a broadly smiling aside. 'And I have to confess I did find that walk in the heat plus the wait I had for you to return from the Acropolis a trifle...uncomfortable. But not, I suspect, as uncomfortable as Andreas was, arriving at my office to discover that I had cancelled our meeting,' he added with a chuckle.

'You didn't really think I'd allow my only grandson to marry a woman I knew nothing about, did you?' he asked Andreas with a little swagger that made her hide a small smile. He was so very Greek, so very macho. She knew she should be annoyed, but he was so pleased with himself that she didn't have the heart to be cross.

Andreas, though, as it soon became obvious, was not so easily appeased.

'You decided to check up on Saskia—?' he thundered, giving his grandfather a hard look.

'You have definitely made a good choice, Andreas,' his grandfather interrupted him. 'She is charming...and kind. Not many young women would have taken the time to look after an old man who was a stranger to them. I had to meet her for myself, Andreas. I know you, and—'

'What you have done is an insult to her,' Andreas cut him off coldly, whilst Saskia stared at him in astonishment. Andreas defending and protecting *her*? What was this? And then, abruptly, she remembered that he was simply acting out a role...the role of a loving protective fiancé.

'And let me tell you this, Grandfather,' Andreas was continuing. 'Whether you approve of Saskia or not makes no difference to me. I *love* her, and I always will, and there are no threats, no bribes, no blandishments you can offer that could in any way change that.'

There was a brief pause before the older man nodded his head.

'Good,' he announced. 'I'm glad to hear it. A woman like Saskia deserves to be the focus of her husband's heart and life. She reminds me very much of my Elisabeth,' he added, his eyes suddenly misty. 'She had that same kindness, that same concern for others.' Suddenly he started to frown as he caught sight of Saskia's ring.

'What is *that* she is wearing?' he demanded. 'It is not fit for a Demetrios bride. I'm surprised at you, Andreas...a paltry plain solitaire. She shall have my Elisabeth's ring, and—'

'No.' The harshness in Andreas's voice made Saskia tense. Was he going to tell his grandfather that it was all a lie? Was the thought of Saskia wearing something as sacred to their family as his dead grandmother's ring too much for him to endure?

'No,' he continued. 'If Saskia wants a different ring then she shall choose one herself. For now I want her to wear the one *I* chose for her. A diamond as pure and shiningly beautiful as she is herself.'

Saskia could see Andreas's mother's and sister's jaws dropping, as was her own at such an unexpectedly tender and almost poetic declaration.

Ridiculously tears blurred her eyes as she looked down at the solitaire. It *was* beautiful. She thought so every time she put it on. But for her to treasure such a ring it would have to be given with love. It was the commitment it was given with that made it of such value to a woman in love, not its financial worth.

But Andreas's grandfather was brushing aside such irrelevancies, and demanding jovially, 'Very well, but what I want to know now is when you plan to get married. I can't live for ever, Andreas, and if I am to see your sons...'

'Grandfather...' Andreas began warningly.

Later, after a celebratory lunch and rather more vintage champagne than had perhaps been wise, Saskia made her way with solemn concentration back to her room. Andreas was with her, as befitted a loving and protective fiancé.

Outside the room Andreas touched her lightly on her arm, so that she was forced to stop and look at him.

'I'm sorry about what happened in Athens,' he told her, his brusqueness giving way to anger as he added, 'My grandfather had no right to subject you to—'

'In his shoes you would have done exactly the same thing,' Saskia interrupted him quietly, immediately leaping to his grandfather's defence. 'It's a perfectly natural reaction. I can remember still the way my grandmother reacted the first time I went out on a date.' She laughed, and then stopped as she saw that Andreas was shaking his head.

'Of course she would be protective of you,' he agreed flatly. 'But didn't my grandfather realise the danger you could have been in? What if he had mistimed his "accidental" meeting with you? You were alone in an unfamiliar city. He had countermanded my instructions to your driver by telling him to keep out of sight until he saw him return to his own car.'

'It was broad daylight, Andreas,' Saskia pointed out calmly. But she could see that Andreas wasn't going to be appeased. 'Well, at least your grandfather won't be trying to convince you that you should marry Athena anymore,' she offered placatingly as they walked into the bedroom. She came to an abrupt halt as she saw the new cases Andreas had bought her for their trip in the middle of the bedroom floor. 'What...?' she began unsteadily but Andreas didn't let her finish.

'I told Maria to pack for both of us. We're booked onto the first flight in the morning for Heathrow.'

'We're leaving?'

Even as she spoke Saskia knew that showing her shock was a giveaway piece of folly. Of course they were leaving. After all, there was no need for Andreas to keep her here any more. His grandfather had made it very plain during lunch that Athena would no longer be welcome beneath his roof.

'We don't have any option,' Andreas replied flatly. 'You heard my grandfather. Now that he's been given a clean bill of health he's itching to find something to occupy him. Organising our wedding and turning it into something between a lavish extravaganza worthy of a glossy magazine and a chance to gather as many of his business cronies under one roof as he can isn't going to be an opportunity he'll want to miss out on. And my mother and sister will be just as bad.' He started to scowl. 'Designer outfits, a wedding dress that could take months to make, plans to extend the villa so that it can accommodate the children my mother and my grandfather are so determined we're going to have...'

Greedily Saskia drank in every word. The mental image he was creating for her, the blissful pictures he was painting were becoming more alluring with every word he said. Mistily she allowed herself to dream about what she knew to be impossible—and then Andreas's next words sent her into shocked freefall.

'We need to get married immediately. We just don't have the time for that kind of delay. Not after... If you are already carrying my child then...'

'What are you saying?' Saskia protested, white-faced. 'You can't be serious. We *can't* get married just because...'

'Just because what?' Andreas challenged her bitterly. 'Because you were a virgin, an innocent who had never known a man before? I...I am Greek, Saskia, and there is no way I would *ever* abandon any child I had fathered. Under the circumstances there is nothing else we *can* do.'

'You're only half-Greek,' Saskia heard herself reminding him dizzily, before adding, 'And anyway I may not even be pregnant. In fact I'm sure I'm not.'

Andreas gave her a dry, almost withering look.

'And you're an expert on such things, of course. You, a woman who hasn't even...'

'They say you don't always...not the first time...' Saskia told him lamely, but she could see from his face that he had as little faith in that particular old wives' tale as she did herself.

'I don't want this, Andreas,' she insisted, trying another tack. Her voice and her body had both begun to shake with shock at what Andreas intended.

'Even if I am to...to have a child...these days that doesn't mean... I could bring it up by myself...'

'What on?' he challenged her. 'Not the one million pounds you turned down from Athena, obviously.'

Saskia's eyes looked bewildered at the way he'd slipped the thrust up under her guard.

'A child needs more than money. Much, much more,' she defended herself quickly. How did he know about Athena's offer to her? Athena herself wouldn't have told him. 'A child needs love,' she continued.

'Do you think *I* don't know that?' Andreas shot back. 'After all, surely I am far better placed to know it than you, Saskia. I had the love of both my parents as a child, and I can promise you I would *never* allow a child of mine to grow up without my love.'

He stopped abruptly as he heard the quick indrawn gasp of pain she had given, his eyes darkening with remorse.

'Saskia, my beloved heart, I am so sorry. I didn't mean to hurt you, just to make you understand that I could no more walk away from our child than I can from you.'

Saskia stared at him, unable to speak, to move, to breathe as she listened to the raw fervency of his declaration. He was acting. He had to be. He *didn't* love her. She *knew* that. And somehow hearing him say to her the words she so much ached to hear whilst knowing they were lies filled her with more anguish than she could bear.

Tugging frantically at the ring he had given her, she started to pull it off, her eyes dark with anger, sparkling with tears of pride and pain whilst Andreas watched her as he had been watching her all through lunch, and then afterwards when the wine she had drunk had relaxed her.

'I felt so angry when Athena offered Saskia that money,' Pia had told him passionately. 'And so proud of her. She loves you so much. I used to think that no one could ever be good enough for you, my wonderful brother, but now I know I was wrong. She loves you every bit as much as you deserve to be loved, as I one day want to love the man I marry...'

'She is perfect for you, darling,' his mother had whispered to him.

'She is a beautiful young woman with an even more beautiful heart,' his grandfather had said emotionally.

There had been one unguarded moment after lunch, when his grandfather had been teasing her about something and she had turned to him, as though seeking his protection. The look in her eyes had made him ache to snatch her up and carry her away somewhere he could have her all to himself and create that look over and over again.

Finally she managed to pull the ring off, holding it out to him she told him, head held high, 'There is no way I would ever marry a man who does not love me.'

Andreas closed his eyes, replayed the words to make sure he hadn't misheard them, and then opened his eyes again and walked purposefully towards her. He was about to take the biggest gamble he had ever taken in his entire life. If he lost he would lose everything. If he won...

He took a deep breath and asked Saskia softly, 'Shouldn't that be you wouldn't ever marry a man you did not love?'

Saskia froze, her face going white and then a soft, deepening shade of pink.

'I...that was what I meant,' she began, and then stopped as panic overwhelmed her. 'I can't marry you, Andreas,' she protested as he closed the distance between them, masterfully sweeping her up into his arms.

'And I won't let you go, Saskia,' he told her in a low, throbbing voice.

'Because of what happened...because there might be a baby?' she guessed, but the words had to be mumbled because Andreas was holding her so tightly, his lips brushing irresistibly tender kisses against her throat and then her jaw, moving closer and closer to her mouth.

'Because of that,' he agreed, whispering the words against her lips. 'And this...and you...'

'Me?' Saskia started to squeak, but Andreas wouldn't let her.

Cupping her face instead, he looked down into her eyes, his own grave with pain, heavy with remorse, hot with love and desire, as he begged her, 'Please give me a chance to show you how things could be between us, Saskia. To show you how good it could be, how good it *will* be...'

'What are you trying to say?' Saskia demanded dizzily.

Still cupping her face, Andreas told her, 'I'm trying to say with words what my emotions, my heart, my soul and my body have already told you, my beloved heart, my adored, precious love. Surely you must have guessed, felt how it was for me when we made love?'

Lifting her head so that she could look into his eyes, search them to see if she actually dared believe what she was hearing, Saskia felt her heart starting to thud in a heady mixture of joy and excitement. No man could possibly fake the way Andreas was looking at her, and if that wasn't enough his body was giving her a very distinct and intimate message of its own. Unable to help herself Saskia started to blush a little as she felt her own body respond to Andreas's arousal.

'I...I thought that must just be sex,' she told him bravely.

'What have I said?' she demanded in bewilderment when Andreas started to laugh.

'My dearest love,' he told her, still laughing, 'if I hadn't already had incontrovertible proof of your innocence, that remark would have furnished me with it. *Any* woman who had experienced "just sex" would have known immediately that—' He stopped and smiled down at her, tenderly kissing her before telling her gruffly.

'No. Why should I bother to explain? After all, there's never going to be any way that you will know what it is to have "just sex". You and I, Saskia, will be making love, sharing love, giving one another love for all our lives.'

'Oh, Andreas,' Saskia whispered deliriously as he pulled her firmly into his arms.

'No, Andreas, we can't,' she protested five minutes later as he carried her towards the bed and started to undress her.

'All my clean clothes are packed...I won't have anything to wear...and...'

'Good,' Andreas informed her without the remotest hint of remorse. 'I can't think of anything I want more right now than to have you naked in my bed with no means of escape.'

'Mmm... That's funny,' Saskia told him impishly. 'I was thinking exactly the same thing myself!'

EPILOGUE

'WELL, your grandfather may not have got his own way over our wedding, but he certainly wasn't going to allow us to have a quiet family christening!' Saskia laughed with Andreas as they both surveyed the huge crowd of people filling the recently completed and refurbished 'special occasions' suite at the group's flagship British hotel.

'Mmm... Are you sure that Robert will be okay with him?' Andreas asked anxiously as he focused with fatherly concern on the other side of the room, where his grandfather was proudly showing off his three-month-old great-grandson to his friends and business cronies.

'Well, as your grandfather keeps on reminding us, he's held far more babies than you or I in his time,' Saskia said, laughing.

'Maybe, but none of them has been *our* son,' Andreas returned promptly, adding, 'I think I'd better go and retrieve him, Sas. He looks as though he might be starting to get fretful, and he never finished that last feed...'

'Talk about doting fathers,' Pia murmured to Saskia as they both watched Andreas hurrying proprietorially towards his son. 'I always knew that Andreas would be a good father, mind you...'

Saskia smiled at her as she watched her husband expertly holding their son—born nine months and one day exactly after their quiet wedding, tactfully arriving three weeks after his predicted birth date. But of course only she and Andreas knew *that*...just as only they knew as yet that by the time he reached his first birthday he would have a brother or a sister.

'Isn't that a bit too soon?' Andreas had protested when she had first told him her suspicions, and Saskia had blushed and then laughed, remembering, as she was sure Andreas was as well, that *she* had been the one to initiate their first lovemaking after Robert's birth.

Andreas was the most wonderful father, and an even more wonderful husband and lover. Saskia gave a small sigh, a look darkening her eyes that Andreas immediately recognised.

If his mother was surprised to be suddenly handed her grandson whilst Andreas insisted that there was something he needed to discuss with his wife in private, she gave no sign of it, going instead to join Saskia's grandmother, with whom she had already formed a close bond.

'Andreas! No, we *can't*,' Saskia protested as Andreas led her to the most luxurious of the hotel's refurbished bedrooms and locked the door.

'Why not?' he teased her. 'We own the hotel and we are married—and right now I want you so much.'

'Mmm... Andreas...' Saskia sighed as his lips found the exquisitely tender cord in her throat that always and unfailingly responded to the sweet torment of his lips.

'Mmm... Andreas...what?' he mouthed against her skin.

But Saskia didn't make any verbal response, instead pulling his head down towards her own, her mouth opening sweetly beneath his.

'I knew the first moment I set eyes on you that you were a wanton woman.' Andreas laughed tenderly. '*My* wanton woman…'

Award-winning author **Anne McAllister** was once given a blueprint for happiness that included a nice, literate husband, a ramshackle Victorian house, a horde of mischievous children, a bunch of big friendly dogs, and a life spent writing stories about tall dark handsome heroes. 'Where do I sign up?' she asked, and promptly did. Lots of years later, she's happy to report, the blueprint was a success. She's always happy to share the latest news with readers at her website: www.annemcallister.com and welcomes their letters there or at P.O. Box 3904, Bozeman, Montana 59772 USA (SAE appreciated).

**Look out for Anne McAllister's latest sexy and compelling title:
IN McGILLIVRAY'S BED
Coming in October 2004, in Modern Romance™!**

THE PLAYBOY AND THE NANNY
by
Anne McAllister

CHAPTER ONE

NIKOS COSTANIDES needed a woman.

Not just any woman, either. He needed a babe. Luxuriously blonde. Definitely sultry. Naturally brash. And the blowsier the better.

It wouldn't hurt if she wore a skintight leopard-spotted dress, either, he thought with a ghost of a smile. But he wasn't going to hold out for that, he decided as he tucked the telephone under his chin and punched in the number. A close approximation would do just fine.

"Debbie's Dollies Escort Service," a voice purred moments later on the other end of the line.

Nikos grinned. If the woman who came was as promising as the voice on the phone, he'd be out of here by sundown. "I'd like the services of one of your escorts this afternoon."

"Certainly, sir," the voice purred. "Whatever your heart desires."

What his heart desired was to be five thousand miles away from his father's Long Island mansion, but he knew that wasn't what the woman on the phone had in mind. Still, she would be helping him get there, so he gave the receptionist an idea of the sort of escort he wanted.

"A flagrant sort of woman?" she said doubtfully when he'd finished.

"In your face," Nikos agreed cheerfully. "Over the top. Definitely not subtle. You know what I mean?"

"Er, well," the receptionist said, though she still

sounded a little doubtful. Then her business sense won out. "I'm sure we have just the woman. I'll send her right out."

Nikos gave the receptionist the address. "I'm in the caretaker's cottage behind the main house. There's a party going on by the pool, but it's perfectly all right if she comes straight up the main drive and walks right past them."

Nikos looked out at the group of party-goers on the patio behind the main house—particularly at his stubborn, strait-laced father, who was carrying a footstool for Julietta, his very pregnant young wife—and flexed his shoulders in anticipation. The weight of his confinement eased slightly. It wouldn't be long now and the shackles would be completely gone.

"Yes, sir. I'll tell her. And I'm sure she'll do just what you want her to, Mr. Costanides," the receptionist assured him.

"Yes," Nikos agreed with a purr of satisfaction in his own voice. "I'm sure she will."

It was actually closer to forty-five minutes before he heard the knock on the cottage door. It was a short rap. Brisk and no-nonsense. Not especially sultry. But then it was probably hard to sound sultry in a knock.

No matter. Maybe the gardener had stopped her when she came up the drive, suspecting she was lost. She would hardly look like one of the guests coming to his stepmother's baby shower! Nikos grinned again and finished stuffing the last of his gear into a duffel bag, the better to be ready when his father threw him out.

If he'd been able to drive, he'd have been gone long before this. But a car accident following a shouting match with his father a month ago had left him with a cast on his leg that limited his mobility. It had given his father the chance he wanted—to nail Nikos down until he could badger him into working for Costanides International.

Not on your life, Nikos thought now, as he thought every time the subject came up. There would be six feet of snow in hell first.

He hauled himself out of his chair to go answer the door, thinking that if, in fact, old Thomas the gardener had stopped the floozie, it would be that much better. He would be one more person shocked by Nikos's disrespectful behavior, one more voice telling Stavros that his elder son was irredeemable, one more reason to throw the blackguard out.

To be honest, though, Nikos doubted it. After thirty years in the employment of the Costanides family, Thomas was unlikely to be shocked by anything any of them did.

It didn't matter in any case. It was his father he wanted to shock, his father he wanted to anger, not the long-suffering Thomas. It was even too bad he would horrify all those women fawning and fluttering around his gorgeous young stepmother, but that was just tough. And anyway, they'd probably love tittering and gossiping about it.

Nikos was used to being the subject of titters and gossip. He'd cultivated it once he found out how it infuriated his old man. And if people didn't have anything better to do than fret about other's supposed peccadillos, it wasn't his problem.

Still, occasional glances out the window while he'd waited for his buxom lady had proved that his audience was going to be considerably larger than he'd expected when he made the call. At least fifty of the Hamptons' best-dressed, wealthiest women were laughing and chattering on the deck around the pool as Julietta opened a pile of gaily wrapped baby gifts. Julietta's friend, Deanne, who was giving his stepmother the baby shower, must have invited the whole damn county!

Pink and blue balloons, tethered to the light poles for the occasion, bobbed in the soft summer breeze. Streamers of pink and blue ribbon fluttered from the roof of the new gazebo. He'd seen them preparing for it all morning. He'd gritted his teeth then.

Now he gritted them again as he crutched his way slowly to the door. But this time it wasn't precisely a grimace, more like a feral grin. Then, dressed only in a towel and the cast on his leg, Nikos opened the door.

She wasn't a babe.

She wasn't even blonde—or not very. Her hair was brown, but not dark, a sort of deep honey color, long and pulled back into a plait at the nape of her neck, not blowsy at all. She didn't look very sultry, either, though she had the biggest blue-green eyes he'd ever seen. Even with her big wide eyes, though, she looked prim, proper and barely more than a schoolgirl in her plain navy blue skirt and a scoop-necked shirt. It wasn't a very deeply scooped neck either, he noted with considerable irritation.

She had a good bosom on her, though, he'd give her that.

Still, if this was what Debbie's Dollies thought qualified as "in your face," he didn't think they'd be in business very long. His audience was going to have to use a lot of imagination.

Nikos glanced toward the group on the deck to see if they'd even noticed her arrival, since it hadn't been nearly as spectacular as he'd hoped. Almost none of the women was paying attention.

But—Nikos smiled to himself—his father was.

The old man looked definitely curious. He stood just a little apart from the women, his body turned toward the group sitting around the table where his wife was still opening gifts. But his gaze—and his attention—were focused toward the cottage.

Good.

It would have been better, of course, if she'd been blowsy and brash, but at least she was a woman—and as such she would suffice.

Maybe her schtick was the prim schoolmarm façade that became all the more sexy by contrast once she let her hair down. Looking her over, Nikos could see where that act might have possibilities.

Too bad he wasn't going to get to test it out.

He pasted his best macho shark grin on his face. "It's about time," he reproved her, though his face spoke only eager anticipation. "But at least you got here."

She opened her mouth, but he didn't give her a chance to speak. "Come and show me what's under that prissy look, sweetheart." And, so saying, he reached out, hauled her into his arms and kissed her.

Past her ear he saw his father's jaw drop. The old man's eyes bugged. If he'd been closer, Nikos would have bet he could've seen his father's mustache quiver.

He wanted to cheer. Instead he pressed his advantage, wrapping his arms around the woman and, because upon touch she turned out to be far more tempting than he'd expected, he thrust his tongue past her parted lips as he molded her body to his.

For just a moment it was a stiff, resisting body. A

body that exactly mirrored the starchy persona she was playing.

And then, almost imperceptibly, she changed. The starch went out of her. The ice melted. She drew a sweet, astonished breath—as astonished as the one Nikos himself was drawing because, by God, yes, there was fire here!

And then she bit him!

Nikos yelped. He jerked back and swiped the side of his hand across his mouth. There was blood on it. She'd *bitten* him!

"What the hell—?" He glared at her. "You won't get very many jobs if you behave that way, lady!"

"Getting kissed like that isn't part of any job I want!"

"Kissing's extra, then?" Nikos asked, annoyed. "You'll have sex with me, but you won't kiss me?"

Her face flamed. "I'll do no such thing! What do you think—?"

"I think you're carrying the prissy librarian act too damn far!" She was going to spoil the whole thing. Nobody—least of all his father!—was going to believe he was flaunting a high-priced prostitute, if his high-priced prostitute kept on behaving like a nun.

And she didn't need to think she was going to get paid if she kept her prissiness up, either!

"Librarian act?" the woman sputtered.

"Some men might find it sexy, sweetheart. I don't." He shot a quick glance in the direction of the pool. There were several onlookers now, including his old man who was actually looking poleaxed. Maybe all was not lost.

Nikos reached out a hand and snagged hers. "Come on."

She tried to jerk away from him, twisting sideways. But clutching both crutches under one arm, he slid the other around her, making them look even cozier as he wrestled her inside.

With one leg in a cast and his arm still healing from the sprain, he was barely strong enough to hold her. And, once the door was shut and he was leaning against it, he let her go at once and shut his eyes.

Damn it! The toll of even limited exertion was still more than he could handle. He still wasn't used to it. He'd barely done more than eat, sleep and argue with his father in the two weeks he'd been out of the hospital. Damn. He hated this weakness. His head was beginning to throb again, too. It did almost every time he tried to focus on anything too long.

"What do you think you're doing?" his sexy librarian raged at him now. "Open this door. I want to leave. Now!"

"No."

Her blue-green eyes widened. "What do you mean, no?"

"Just what I said." Nikos sucked in a harsh breath. "You were hired. You're here, and by God you're going to stay. Sit down."

She didn't. She backed up. Damn it! If his father came down to see what was going on, he'd know it wasn't what Nikos wanted him to think. She was fully clothed and perfectly visible through the window.

"Damn it all. I said, sit down!" Nikos barked.

She shook her head. "I can't. I have to leave. I must have got the wrong place."

"No. It's the right place. Relax, damn it. How the hell did you get into this line of work?" he muttered.

She straightened up and glared at him. "I'm very good at my job."

She sure didn't look like it. But maybe she was—once she got out of her no-nonsense clothes.

There had sure been heat in that kiss they'd shared. It was a shame he wasn't going to be able to enjoy this encounter the way it was meant to be enjoyed.

"Well, you'll have to show me another time," he drawled.

She wrapped her arms across her breasts. "I don't intend to show you anything. I don't even know who you are! But you have to let me go!"

You have to shut up! Before his head exploded. "Sit down!" Nikos bellowed.

The force of his voice seemed to plop her right into the chair. She glared up at him.

"Not there." Nikos sighed wearily. "He can see you there. Sit on the couch."

She didn't move. "He who? What are you talking about?"

Nikos didn't answer. He just stood, teeth gritted, and looked from her to the couch expectantly. He didn't move away from the door either. Couldn't if he wanted to remain upright. God, his head hurt!

"I don't know why you're doing this," she muttered ungraciously. But at last she got up and moved to the couch.

"Thank you," Nikos said tightly. He waited until she was settled, then lowered himself gingerly into the armchair across from her. He adjusted the towel. She looked at it, the color rising in her cheeks. Quickly she glanced away, her gaze going toward the door again.

"Don't even think about it."

She looked at him, startled, but she didn't try it.

And thank God for that, because the truth was, he didn't think he had the strength to stop her.

Fortunately she didn't move. She sat right where she was, hands folded in her lap like some proper Sunday school teacher, looking at him with a combination of wariness and expectancy. There was nothing sultry or seductive about her—except the way she'd kissed him.

"You haven't been doing this long, have you?"

"Four years."

"Four years?" He couldn't imagine.

"I started while I was working on my master's degree. I have excellent qualifications. I'm very good at what I do," she told him firmly. "I have references."

Nikos bit back a grin. "I'd like to see them."

Her eyes flashed green fire at him. "I don't have to show them to the likes of you! I don't understand why you're keeping me here," she said fretfully. "I must have made a mistake and got the wrong cottage. Please! I need to talk to Mr. Costanides."

Nikos stuck his casted leg out in front of him and settled back into the chair. "You're talking to him."

"You're not Mr. Costanides! I've met Mr. Costanides! He's much older. He has a mustache. He's—"

Nikos sat bolt upright. *She'd met his father?* Bloody hell!

He couldn't believe it. The old man might have had his profligate tendencies over the years, but Nikos had never thought they'd ever extended to bringing home women of the evening! Stavros had always had too much respect for family. That was, in fact, precisely why Nikos was throwing this woman in the old man's face now.

"Who are you?" he demanded.

"My name is Mari Lewis," she said stiffly.

Which meant precisely nothing. "The dolly?" he prompted.

"Dolly?" Her brow furrowed. "No. What dolly? I'm the nanny."

The *nanny?*

Nikos gaped. And then, replaying the whole scene in his mind, he began to understand what had happened. And with understanding came not consternation, but an even greater satisfaction. An unbelievable satisfaction. The grin spread all over his face.

He'd kissed the new nanny? He'd swaggered out dressed in only a towel and, before his father's eyes, had swept his half-brother, Alex's, brand-new nanny off her feet?

No wonder the old man was looking apoplectic.

It was even better than he'd dared hope!

No matter how badly he wanted to strongarm Nikos into the company, Stavros would never let him stay here after he'd sullied darling Alexander's new nanny.

Let him stay, hell! Rigid, strait-laced Stavros would throw his philandering firstborn out on his ear!

He might even go so far as to make his secondborn his heir. And why not?

As far as Nikos could see, Alexander, the four-year-old result of his father's second marriage, was the center of the old man's universe, anyway. Alexander was the sun around which Stavros Costanides spun, the darling doted-upon child that his elder son had never been—which didn't bother Nikos a bit.

In fact it made him feel a little sorry for the kid.

Not that he'd ever had much to do with the boy. He barely even knew his half-brother. Stavros did his best to keep his younger son away from his disreputable older one.

He'd never exactly told Nikos to stay away, had never come right out and said Nikos was a bad influence on the boy, but Nikos didn't have to be told.

Nothing he did had ever pleased the old man.

He'd long ago stopped trying to. It was a hell of a lot more interesting—and rewarding—to be the thorn in Stavros Costanides's side. As long as he could leave when things got unbearable.

Since the accident Nikos hadn't been able to leave. As if the cast wasn't impediment enough, the head injury he'd received in the car accident required him to be on medication. He couldn't drive until he was through with it. And Stavros wasn't allowing anyone else to drive him.

"You're keeping me prisoner!" Nikos had accused him.

"I am looking out for your well-being," his father had replied. "Besides," he'd added scornfully, "it's not as if you have any pressing demands on your time. Work, for example?" A bitter smile had touched Stavros's features. "God forbid."

Nikos hadn't replied. There was no point. Stavros had long ago decided that he was a good-for-nothing. It was Nikos's greatest joy to do his best to confirm his father's estimation.

"It's time you settled down," his father had gone on implacably. "Until you are able to drive away under your own power, you will stay here."

And there was no arguing with him. No going around him. No convincing anybody to spirit him away. He was stuck until he could drive—with his father and his father's notion of how things ought to be done.

It was exactly what his father had been angling for. It had been the subject of their quarrel right before

Nikos's accident. It had been the subject of the quarrel they'd had last week.

Stavros had come to the cottage to try to badger Nikos into studying the company prospectus. "Learn about your inheritance," he'd demanded.

"I know all about my inheritance," Nikos had retorted bitterly, and he'd tossed the prospectus aside.

"I'll shape you up if it's the last thing I do," his father had vowed, glowering down at Nikos who had stared insolently back.

Nikos's jaw tightened. "I'd like to see you try!"

"Would you?" Stavros went very quiet. "Fine. Count on it." He'd turned on his heel and stalked out. The door shut quietly, ominously, behind him.

Nikos had ignored it, ignored *him*. He'd been enormously pleased that, for the last five days, the old man had been avoiding him completely. So he wasn't counting on Stavros being able to "shape him up."

He was counting on getting out of here—away from his father, away from all the demands and distrust, away from the bitterness and the battles and the disappointment they'd been to each other for all of Nikos's thirty-two years. He didn't need it, God knew.

Let Alex have it—all of it—and the grief that went with it.

He looked at the woman sitting primly on the sofa now. She did look like a nanny. Or a nun.

Poor Alex.

She must have impeccable credentials, Nikos thought. He paused and corrected himself—must *have had* impeccable credentials. His father wouldn't have picked anyone less worthy than Mary Poppins to look after the likes of master Alex.

"Sorry about that," he said with a repentance he didn't feel. In fact, he was still grinning.

She wasn't. "It's not funny. I have a reputation to uphold. Standards to maintain."

"I wouldn't give you a nickel for your reputation now, sweetheart," Nikos said cheerfully. "Or your standards."

"Mr. Costanides will be upset."

"I devoutly hope so." He wondered if the old man was even now bearing down on the cottage, determined to rescue Mary Poppins from his grip.

"He expected me at three. It's important for me to arrive on time," she said. "To be punctual. To be fair. To be strict. Mr. Costanides says his son needs that."

Did he? Nikos didn't know Alex well enough to say. Certainly the kid wasn't as headstrong as he'd been.

"Punctual. Fair. Strict. You must be a regular paragon. I'm sure you'll impress the hell out of him," he said lazily. "What other virtues do you have?"

"I don't use profanity," she said.

Ah, so she could sting when she wanted to. Nikos grinned. "Little brat getting out of hand? Don't want him turning out like his big brother, do we?"

The nanny looked perplexed. "Big brother? Are there *two* children? Mr. Costanides didn't mention a brother."

"I'm not surprised," Nikos said drily.

"But, yes," Miss Mari Lewis went on quite sincerely, "he did say Nikos had been giving him some problems."

"*What?*"

His yelp caused her to jump. But instead of answering him, she folded her hands in her lap, pressed her lips together, and looked like he'd have to torture the information out of her.

"What did you say?" Nikos demanded again.

She gave a quick determined shake of her head. "I shouldn't have said anything. Not about the child—or his behavior. It's indiscreet. Improper. It's entirely between me and my employer."

But Nikos wasn't listening to her babbling. "The boy," he demanded, hobbling close, glowering down at her. "What did you call him?"

Mari Lewis blinked at him like some near-sighted owl, but he wasn't ruffling her feathers. She lifted her chin, as if to tell him he wasn't going to intimidate her. Then, "Nikos," she said, exactly as he'd thought she had.

His teeth came together with a snap. "No."

"Yes."

"No," he said again. "His name is Alexander."

"No," she replied just as firmly, "it's not."

She reached down and picked her bag up and pulled out a contract. She held it out toward him. "See for yourself. It says right there. His name is Nikos. I might have got the wrong cottage, but I have not got the wrong child!"

Yes, she damned well had!

But, from his father's standpoint, obviously, no, she had not.

The old man hadn't been apoplectic at all. He might have been a little astonished when Nikos had hauled Mary Poppins into his arms and kissed her, but ultimately he would have been amused—and justified.

His son's flagrant disregard for propriety, his inappropriate kissing of a total stranger would have only underscored Stavros's notion that he had done the right thing.

The old rogue had hired a nanny to straighten him out!

Far from running down here to rescue her, the old man was probably standing up on the deck now, congratulating himself—and laughing his fool head off.

Nikos's teeth came together with a snap. His headache returned with a vengeance. He dropped his head back and shut his eyes, his mind whirling furiously. And furious was the operative word.

"I'll shape you up if it's the last thing I do." His father's words came back to haunt him. To mock him. To humiliate him.

It was Stavros Costanides, down to the ground.

"Mr....er...I'm sorry, I don't know your name—" the very proper nanny's voice broke into his bitter reverie "—but you really do have to let me go. I have to find the right cottage. I have to—"

Nikos opened his eyes and glared at her.

She blinked again, but met his gaze determinedly.

Just how determined was she? He couldn't imagine. He could bet, though. And he was willing to bet he could run her off in less than twenty-four hours.

A corner of his mouth tipped up slightly. Did the old man think he was just going to roll over and give up his wicked ways without a fight?

Well, if he did, he'd vastly underestimated his older son.

Whatever he was paying Miss Mari Lewis, it had better be a bundle. She was damned well going to earn it.

"You don't have the wrong cottage," Nikos told her.

"But you said—" She looked around, puzzled. "But...where's Nikos?"

He smiled. It was a hard smile. There was nothing pleasant about it. "I'm Nikos."

She gaped at him.

"Welcome to your new job, Ms. Lewis. Apparently my father has hired you to babysit me."

He was obviously a madman.

But he was the most stunningly handsome madman she'd ever seen. He had dark brown eyes and tousled black hair, a lean face with high cheekbones and a wicked-looking dimple just to one side of his mouth that deepened when he gave her that bitter smile of his.

And he kissed like—

Mari didn't want to think about what he kissed like! She'd never been kissed like that in her life!

A lesser woman—*many* lesser women, she was sure— would have fallen panting at his feet.

Mari Lewis was made of sterner stuff.

She had a job to fulfill, a reputation to uphold, a magazine ad and article to live up to, and a pair of lovable, impractical, dangerously gullible aunts to support.

And despite the fact that her heart was still hammering and her head was still spinning and her lips were still tingling, she needed to find Stavros Costanides. And she needed to do it fast.

But how? When Mr. Whoever-he-was was sitting next to the door, looking as if he would pounce on her if she made a move in that direction.

"Look, Mr...." She paused.

"Costanides," he said helpfully. He smiled again. The same humorless smile he'd smiled before. However heart-stopping it was, his smile wasn't meant to be friendly. It wasn't even, she was fairly sure, meant to be attractive. Unfortunately it was. The dimple deepened again.

She wanted to touch it. To touch him. Again. *Help!*

Determinedly Mari looked away and forced herself to say in a level tone, "Mr. Costanides, then. I don't know why you're doing this, but—"

"You'd do better wondering why my father is doing this."

"Your father?"

"The well-known despot, Stavros Costanides. You know? Older than me. Mustache." He parroted back her description. "The man who hired you."

"To take care of his little boy."

"To take care of Nikos," her fully-grown, very masculine nemesis agreed. He poked his chest. "Me."

"But that's ridiculous!"

"You're telling me," he muttered. His smile faded and suddenly he rubbed fiercely at his forehead. "Damn."

Mari frowned. Maybe he wasn't totally mad, after all, she thought. Maybe he was suffering from concussion— a head injury that made him think he was someone else. He certainly looked as if he'd recently done battle with something formidable—and lost.

His left leg was in a cast; he held one arm close to his body, as if he was protecting his ribs; he had a fresh scar on his jaw, and his very handsome face still showed the lingering signs of bruising beneath the left eye and temple.

"Are you all right?" she asked quickly.

He lifted his gaze to meet hers. "Would you be?"

The very bleakness of his tone startled her. It also stopped her cold, having the effect that his words hadn't had. It made her think that he wasn't talking only about his physical condition at all.

It made her worry that he might be telling her the

truth. Mari swallowed. Pushed the notion away. Tried not to think about it.

Stavros Costanides had hired her to be a nanny to his son. His little boy! She knew he had a little boy. She'd glimpsed a picture of him on the credenza in Stavros's office.

"Is that Nikos?" she'd asked him.

He'd smiled a proud papa smile and had picked up the picture, saying proudly, "That's my son."

Nikos, she'd thought.

But he hadn't actually said, "That's my son, Nikos," she realized now. He'd just agreed, "That's my son."

And the devilishly handsome man sitting across from her now was...?

"You're Nikos?" she asked faintly. "You're not... kidding?"

Deep brown eyes met hers. Slowly he shook his head. "I'm not kidding."

Outside in the distance Mari could hear the gabble of cheerful women. Overhead a jet engine droned. A bird twittered.

"But...but it doesn't make sense. I mean, why would he—?" she faltered. "You're not—" She broke off. "I understood he had a four-year-old. He showed me a picture of a four-year-old!" She gave him an accusing look.

"He does have a four-year-old. My half-brother. Alexander."

"Then it's obviously a mistake."

"It's not a mistake."

"But—"

"It's his way of making a point. He thinks I'm wasting my life. He thinks I don't take things seriously enough, that I haven't accepted my responsibilities as heir to his damned empire, that I'm shirking my duty to follow in his footsteps as the eldest son.'' His tone became more and more bitter as he spoke. His dark eyes flashed, and it was all Mari could do not to flinch under his gaze.

She didn't, because as a nanny she knew that the slightest crack in her armor could do her in. *Don't let them intimidate you,* was the cardinal rule of dealing with one's charges.

One of her charges?

She wasn't seriously thinking she was this man's nanny, was she?

It was a joke. Any minute now Stavros Costanides would come along to say he'd made his point and they would all laugh about it—though this particular son might laugh a little harshly—and then she would get her real job as nanny to Alexander.

Wouldn't she?

Oh, heavens, she'd better! She *had* to have a job. She couldn't *not* have a job!

Aunt Emmaline and Aunt Bett would be out on the street if she didn't keep this job. It had been a godsend when Stavros Costanides had called her two days ago and wanted to hire her.

"I read about you in a magazine my wife gets," he told her. "You're the woman who could make Little Lord Fauntleroy out of a Katzenjammer Kid?"

Mari remembered laughing a little self-consciously. "The writer might have been exaggerating a little," she allowed, recalling the article that had appeared in last month's issue of an upscale magazine for parents. The article had been subtitled *"Mari's not Mary, But This Nanny Could Make That Poppins Woman Take a Back*

Seat'' and it raved about Mari's ability to deal with problem kids. "I was nanny to her nephew for two years."

"He was a handful?"

"Oh, yes."

"My son is, too."

His four-year-old, she'd thought.

The more fool she.

It certainly explained the bonus offer he'd made her when she'd met him at his office yesterday afternoon. He'd detailed his son's stubbornness, his reluctance to toe the line, his determined rebellion in the face of parental authority.

"I thought I could handle it myself," he'd said gruffly. "Now I don't think so. But I need it done. If you bring him up to scratch at the end of six months— if you *last* six months—I'll give you a hundred thousand dollars bonus."

Mari had gaped at him.

And then, steepling his hands on his desk, and looking at her over the tops of his fingers, he'd said, "And if you quit before six months are up, you owe me ten."

"Ten?"

"Thousand dollars."

To him it was chicken feed. To her, in her family's straitened circumstances, it was more than she could promise.

But she wouldn't *have* to give him ten thousand dollars, she'd reminded herself—if she didn't quit. She wouldn't quit. She knew she *couldn't* quit!

"All right," she'd agreed.

"He must have been kidding," she said hopefully now to the dark brooding man who sat and watched as all these thoughts flitted across her face.

Slowly, deliberately, Nikos Costanides shook his head. "No."

"But—"

"He's hired you to reform me."

Mari wanted to deny it. She couldn't. She had the awful sinking feeling that it was true.

"I can't—"

"You bet your sweet tail you can't!" he said harshly. "So just march yourself up to the house and tell him the joke is on him."

"What do you mean?"

"I mean, go tell him you're not going to play. That whatever he's paying you, it's not enough. That there's no way on earth he can con you into staying."

Ah, but there was. There was that enormous white elephant of a house her aunts owned—their pride and joy, their legacy from their profligate father. It ate money. They couldn't give it up.

"Where would we go, dear?" Aunt Em's frail voice echoed in her ears. "We've always lived here."

"Can't put Em in one of those homes," Aunt Bett said over and over. "It'd kill her."

Probably, Mari acknowledged, it would. Aunt Em had a bad heart. It wouldn't feel any better if she learned about Aunt Bett's disastrous attempt to bail them out by playing the ponies, either.

Actually having to leave their home would likely kill them both. And Mari could see that they didn't have to leave it—she could even see that the gambling debt was paid and the house had new struts, new paint and a new roof—*if* she managed to keep this job and earn Stavros Costanides' bonus.

"No," she said. "I can't."

Nikos Costanides scowled at her. "Why the hell not?"

"Because I need the job."

"What did he offer you?"

Mari blinked. "What?"

"Obviously he offered you a bundle," Nikos said impatiently. "Fine. I'll offer you more to leave."

It was tempting. Terribly tempting. She wanted to take it. And yet—

She shook her head. "I can't."

He glared at her. "What do you mean, you can't?"

She knotted her fingers. "My reputation is at stake."

"What?" He looked thunderous.

"I have a professional reputation, as I said before." She felt her cheeks warm and, certain that he could see how flimsy that excuse was, she felt compelled to add, "Not the sort you imagined, but such as it is, it's important to me."

His jaw clenched. Their eyes battled.

Mari's heart beat faster, her pulses raced. She felt like a racehorse in the home stretch, given its head. "All you have to do is shape up," she reminded him a little breathlessly.

"Like hell. I'll be damned if I'll knuckle under to his threats!"

"Yes, well—" She took a careful shallow breath, then shrugged lightly. "Maybe you can't."

A nerve in his temple pulsed. He shoved a hand through disheveled dark hair. His eyes narrowed. "You're saying you're staying, Ms. Lewis?"

Say no, she told herself. *Walk out. To hell with your reputation, your aunts, the hundred thousand dollars, the way he kisses! Where's your common sense?*

She didn't know. She only knew that something had

happened when Nikos Costanides kissed her. She had been kissed before. Heavens, she'd even been *engaged* before. But when Ward had kissed her it had been pleasant, warm, and in a few seconds, gone.

Even now the imprint of Nikos's mouth was still on hers. The taste of him was a part of her, reaching into her. And somewhere deep inside it was as if a fundamental answering chord responded.

She hadn't known such a response existed. She wanted desperately—perhaps foolishly—to know more.

Sanity—despite her reputation, her aunts, the money—told her to say no. It was foolish. It was insane to agree to be nanny to a grown man for any reason or any amount of money.

Mari was practical. Mari was sensible. Mari was grounded.

"People who are grounded have never flown," her free spirit uncle Arthur always said with a twinkle and a hint of challenge in his eye.

She took a deep breath and said, "Yes."

CHAPTER TWO

SHE had lost her mind.

A twenty-nine-year-old virgin who'd never felt the slightest tingle—not even from the kiss of the man she'd been engaged to for three years—had no business taking on a man who looked like he ate nuns for breakfast!

But she'd committed herself.

Mari didn't see that she had any choice.

It wasn't just the fact that she'd given her word—even if Stavros Costanides had fudged a little bit on his. It wasn't just that it was a matter of honor. And pride. And integrity. And the fact that she *was* good at what she did.

It was that recently she'd felt incomplete. Unfinished. Inadequate somehow.

At least Ward had certainly thought she was!

"You want to know why I'm breaking it off?" her fiancé Ward Bishop had said last month when he'd come to tell her he'd had second thoughts about marrying her. "It's because you're a cold fish, Mari. I want to make love and you talk about the weather. I touch your breasts and you grab my hands. I kiss you and you don't respond."

"You mean I don't tear your clothes off—or mine," Mari had retorted scathingly, hurt beyond reason at her fiancé's outspoken words.

"You don't even unbutton them," Ward snarled.

Later he'd apologized, had said he'd never meant to be so blunt. "You're a fine person, Mari," he'd said in a conciliatory, unctuous manner that made her want to wipe the floor with him. "It's not your fault. You just aren't...passionate."

"I don't remember *you* burning down any buildings either!" Mari retorted, stung.

"Not with you I haven't," he'd agreed readily enough. Which she supposed meant that he and the new love of his life, Shelley—the twenty-three-year-old he was dumping her for—were setting whole forests on fire!

Well, fine. Let him. Let him have Shelley! Let them burn up the world!

She didn't care. Much.

But, as little as she wanted to admit it, long after Ward had gone his accusation still hurt. It hurt thinking there was something wrong with her, that other people had something she was lacking, some fire deep within that God had apparently forgotten to build.

And then this afternoon, completely unexpectedly, totally out of the blue, something had happened—something deep, strong, *passionate*. And all she could think was that God apparently hadn't forgotten to build the fire at all.

It just wasn't Ward who'd been given the match!

But...*Nikos Costanides?* A—

"How old are you?" she asked a glaring Nikos as she came back into the cottage with her luggage.

"Thirty-two," he growled as he watched her come in with her luggage.

A thirty-two-year-old Greek playboy? Because she had no doubt now that a mindless frivolous playboy was exactly what he was.

Mari shook her head. What *could* God have been thinking about?

Nikos apparently wondered the same thing. He was

sitting right where she had left him, scowling at her. While she'd been out finding Thomas the gardener, he had put on a pair of white shorts, and she supposed that was some concession. Still, he looked very adult, very masculine and very intimidating as he again sprawled bare-chested in the chair, watching like a sulky child as Thomas, laden down with suitcases, followed her in.

"How old are you?" he asked insolently.

She lifted her chin. "Twenty-nine."

"You don't kiss like you're twenty-nine."

Mari felt her cheeks flush. The feelings of inadequacy reared their head again. She wondered if that meant Nikos hadn't felt what she'd felt.

At his impertinent words Thomas made a disapproving noise in his throat, and Mari knew she should be feeling more embarrassed than she was, but in fact she was mostly curious. *Hadn't he?* She looked at Nikos closely.

Immediately his gaze shifted away.

Yes! He *had* felt it! Mari felt a twinge of triumph. Hugging herself inwardly, inadequacy vanquished for the moment, Mari said to Thomas as blithely as she could manage, "Don't mind him. He's just sulking."

"I am *not* sulking!"

His outrage made Mari hide another smile. "You can take them through here," she said to Thomas, ignoring Nikos. She started toward the hallway that led away from the small living room, then looked back. "I presume that's where the bedrooms are?" she said over her shoulder.

Nikos grunted something. His dark gaze was brooding as he looked at her again.

"*Did* he kiss you, miss?" Thomas asked worriedly.

"Oh, yes." She tried to sound blithe, matter-of-fact

and indifferent, not at all as if, by doing so, he had turned her world upside down.

"She's not any good at it," Nikos said loudly.

"I can see why your father thinks you need a nanny," Mari said pleasantly. "Someone needs to teach you how to behave."

Then she sailed out of the room and down the hallway. A strategic exit after having the last word was always a nanny's strength.

"A nanny?" Thomas's eyes goggled.

"Mr. Costanides has a strange sense of humor apparently," Mari said. It was all she was going to say.

"Didn't know he *had* a sense of humor," Thomas mumbled. Then, "Which room, miss?"

Behind her Nikos called, "She can sleep with me."

"Mr. Nikos!" Thomas was clearly scandalized.

"She loves it when I talk dirty." Nikos's voice followed them.

Thomas sputtered.

"Children act up when they think we're watching, Thomas," she said firmly. "I advise you to ignore him. Come along. I'll find my own room."

Down the short hallway beyond the small living room and kitchen, Mari found three bedrooms. The biggest, with a view overlooking the garden, was clearly the one Nikos was inhabiting. The king-size bed was unmade. There was a laptop computer and a lot of boating magazines scattered on the desk. *The better to choose his next yacht from*, Mari thought.

The room itself was actually very Spartan-looking, done in whites and tans and browns with just a hint of black. Somber. Harsh.

Rather like its occupant, Mari thought.

"Like my bed?" Nikos called. "It's plenty big enough to share."

She ignored him. She tried to ignore the bed, too. But the thought of sharing it with Nikos was astonishingly vivid. She could imagine him naked against those white sheets, could envision herself, equally naked, tangling with him—

Oh, girl, stop this! She'd never had such blatant fantasies in her life!

She wondered if it had something to do with the squid her Aunt Em had fixed for lunch. Was squid an aphrodisiac?

She turned and hurried out of the room.

The bedroom across from Nikos's was equipped as an office, but with a daybed instead of a sofa or pair of chairs. It didn't look as if anyone was using it at the moment. No big surprise there. If Stavros imagined that Nikos needed "shaping up," it wouldn't be because he was a workaholic!

She could have stayed in this room, but somehow Mari didn't want to be that close to Nikos Costanides— whether because she thought he might get the wrong idea, or whether she didn't trust herself, she wasn't sure.

Fortunately there was a third bedroom along the back of the house. It was a long narrow room that seemed to have been converted from a sleeping porch and was more casually decorated than the rest of the house. Airy and sunlit, with balloon curtains done in white eyelet, it was soft and romantic. Soothing, not passionate.

Just as well, Mari thought. She was curious. Not suicidal.

"Put my things here, will you, Thomas?" She went over to the window and looked out. Beyond the main house she could see the beginning of the dunes that dipped toward the Atlantic. Now, in the silence, she could hear the sounds of the waves.

"Miss?"

She turned to see that Thomas had set down her cases and now stood looking at her. He had a slight smile on his face. "I just wanted you to know, miss...he isn't as bad as he says."

"He couldn't be," Mari agreed drily.

Thomas's bare hint of a smile turned into a real one. He almost chuckled. "He'll try, though."

"It...should be interesting," Mari agreed. "Tell me, Thomas. Did you know about this? That Mr. Costanides was setting us up, I mean?"

Thomas hesitated a moment, then said, "No, but, I'm not surprised. It's no secret Mr. Costanides is worried—about Mr. Nikos, about the future of his company. He's getting older. He's had one heart attack. He wants time with Mrs. Costanides and the children. So he wants Mr. Nikos to take over. But," he added, "only if he does it the way Mr. Costanides wants."

Which was the situation in a nutshell. "And why am I sure that Nikos has his own mind?" she asked wryly.

Thomas smiled again. "Because he's his father's son." Thomas shook his head. "Mr. Costanides doesn't always handle Mr. Nikos very well."

"And he thought hiring a *nanny* would help?"

"I'm not sure he thinks anything will help at this point," Thomas said bluntly. "But this, at least, he hasn't tried."

That would make two of them.

"He won't hurt you, miss," Thomas said quickly. "He teases, that's all. If he gives you trouble, you call me. I'll come whip him into shape for you." He grinned. "Mr. Nikos listens to me."

"But not to his father." It wasn't a question.

Thomas shook his head adamantly. "Never. Mr. Costanides never talks to Mr. Nikos, come to that. Just yells. And demands." He gave a shake of his head, then brightened and looked at her. "You can fix that."

"Sounds like it's been broken for a very long time."

Thomas hesitated, then gave a small nod. "They're good men, though. Both of them."

"Then what's the problem? *Why* don't they listen to each other? *Why* don't they talk to each other?" She needed a place to start. Some clue as to what dynamic existed between them.

Thomas lifted broad shoulders. "You got to ask Mr. Nikos or Mr. Costanides about that." His warm brown eyes met hers. He reached out a hand and squeezed hers briefly. "I wish you luck, miss."

Mari thought she was going to need it.

The knock on the door was quick and staccato. Seven taps, the last two separated from the first ones in brisk, cheerful fashion.

Obviously the old man—pleased with himself and coming to gloat.

"Door's open," Nikos growled.

A second later it was, and a seductively stacked blonde in a revealing leopard-spotted dress sashayed in. "Nikos?" she purred, her eyes lighting up at the sight of him.

Oh, hell. He'd forgotten about her!

But a second later he grinned with unholy glee at the thought of what his father must be thinking now—and how gloriously shockable the Mary Poppins clone was going to be!

He pushed himself forward in the chair and held out a hand. "Come here, sweetheart," he drawled.

Debbie's Dolly shut the door behind her, then moved toward him, unbuttoning the top two buttons of her very low-cut blouse as she came. "Aw, did you hurt yourself, darlin'?" she murmured, taking in the yellowing bruises on his face. "Let me kiss it and make it better." She bent over him, giving him a good glimpse of a pair of her more outstanding assets as she did so.

"I wouldn't if I were you," said a firm female voice from the hallway.

The blonde jerked back.

Mari Lewis stood in the doorway to the living room, a stern look in her eyes. The blonde, eyes like saucers, looked quickly from Mari to him.

Nikos didn't move, just watched, fascinated, as Mari gave the blonde what looked like an affable smile, and said almost pleasantly, "Or what happened to him could happen to you."

The blonde looked beyond Nikos's bruises to his taped ribs and casted leg and gulped. Then her eyes narrowed. "Who are you?"

"His nanny."

"What?"

"I'm Nikos's nanny." Mari Lewis repeated the words as if they made perfect sense, and she said them with such forcefulness that Nikos found himself admiring her. For a second.

Right before annoyance set in.

He could sense the blonde beginning to retreat. "Don't mind her," he said, reaching out a hand and snagging hers, drawing her close. "Ms. Lewis is just a frustrated spinster my father's wished on me. She won't bother us."

"Won't I?" Mari said, and once again, though her expression was perfectly pleasant, her tone was like steel.

He didn't think it was a question even though it sounded like it. But he was damned if he was going to let some governess bully him!

"Of course not," he said. "Because if you leave," he told the blonde, though he slanted a gaze Mari's way, "she knows I'll have to kiss her again instead."

"Again?" the blonde echoed nervously. She tugged her hand out of his and stepped back, looking from Nikos to Mari, an increasingly worried expression on her face. "I...think maybe you should settle this between yourselves," she said quickly, edging toward the door.

"Excellent idea," Mari said, moving toward her.

"Terrible idea," Nikos disagreed. Didn't Debbie's Dollies have any backbone? "Come back here."

"Keep right on going," Mari suggested, herding the blonde ahead like a sheepdog nipping at the heels of a ewe. "Thomas, would you show Miss...Miss...?"

"Truffles," the blonde supplied nervously.

"Would you show Miss...Truffles the way out, please?" Mari said quite pleasantly, though Nikos was sure he could hear a hint of a smile when she said the ridiculous name. He gritted his teeth. Surely even a blonde with very little brain could have thought of a better moniker than that!

"And give her something for coming all this way," Mari added.

"You stay right here," Nikos commanded. But the blonde wasn't listening to him. She fumbled to open the door. Mari opened it for her.

"He doesn't need to give me anything. We have his credit card number," the blonde said nervously.

"You're not charging me! You didn't do any—"

"We're supposed to charge whether or not they—" Truffles-the-blonde apologized to Mari. She wasn't even looking at him! "For the, um, er...house-call, y'know?" she said a little desperately.

"Of course." Mari nodded sagely. "Makes perfect sense."

"The hell it does!" Nikos shoved himself up, trying to get out of the chair. "You can't give my money away like that!"

She turned and gave him a blithe smile. "I didn't. You did."

"Come along, miss," Thomas said smoothly, taking the blonde by the arm. He gave Nikos a hard level look over his shoulder and a slow despairing shake of his head as he steered the woman down the path. "You should be ashamed of yourself."

Nikos wasn't sure if Thomas meant the blonde or him, but judging from the look on the old gardener's face he had a pretty good idea.

The door shut. The silence was deafening.

Used to prevailing in arguments about bedtime, homework and when to allow a friend to sleep over, Mari found it a little difficult to pretend that she commonly vanquished women of the evening—as Aunt Bett called them—in the course of her work.

It's not much different than a sleepover, she told herself firmly, then rolled her eyes.

Surreptitiously she wiped damp palms on the sides of her navy skirt and drew several steadying breaths before she shut the door after Thomas and Miss—she still smiled as she thought the name—*Truffles*, and turned to face the ire of Nikos Costanides head on.

Big mistake.

The sizzle she'd felt from his kiss seemed to arc right across the room and hit her between the eyes. He was slumped back into his chair again, glaring at her, looking for all the world like a sulky child who'd just had his treat taken away, and she could feel her palms dampen and her mouth dry out. There was some deep primitive response going on inside her, too, that she didn't really want to focus on.

'Hormones, dear,' her Aunt Bett would have said, as if it was the most natural thing in the world. And doubtless Uncle Arthur would have winked at her.

Well, now was *not* the time for hormones!

No matter how curious she was, she couldn't simply jump a man she didn't know. A man she probably didn't even *want* to know!

What, she wondered, were you supposed to do if these suddenly wide-awake and raring-to-go hormones aimed you at entirely the *wrong* man?

Go slow, she cautioned herself. *Learn as much as you can about the phenomenon.* Then, once she understood it better, she could transfer the feeling to someone more suitable than Nikos Costanides.

Right now the thought of what he and Miss Truffles would be doing if she *hadn't* arrived set a blush on Mari's cheeks. Was that why he'd been so eager? she wondered with sudden dismay. Had he been primed for any woman, and simply let it all out for her?

Now there was food for thought.

She slanted a glance at him again, wondering just what sort of man he was. Surely he didn't routinely hire "women of the evening" and parade them past his father and family!

If he did, it was no wonder his father was out of patience with him.

"You don't look like you'd have to hire that sort of thing," she said now.

Nikos blinked. Then, "I don't," he said flatly.

"Then why—?"

He plucked irritably at the fabric on the arm of the chair. "Think about it," he growled at last.

Mari tried. She thought about everything that had happened since she'd knocked on the door, expecting Stavros Costanides and his four-year-old son and getting a virile man clad only in a bath towel instead. A virile man in a bath towel who'd said, "About time," and then hauled her into his arms and *kissed* her!

She hurried past that part of the memory before it could affect her equilibrium again. But as soon as she did, she had to back up and go over it again, because somehow she suspected it was the key.

Obviously he'd mistaken her for Miss Truffles. But why was he waiting to *kiss* Miss Truffles? It wasn't as if he knew the woman, for heaven's sake!

Mari was sure he'd never seen her before in his life. Anyway, even in Mari's non-existent experience, a man didn't lie in wait to kiss a woman he hired by the hour.

Unless, perhaps, he was doing it for effect.

Effect. On whom?

She remembered the gathering at the poolside. There had been a lot of women, a few children. And his father.

She remembered seeing him there, starting to go over to talk to him, but then him shaking his head and waving her on. Waiting. Watching.

For Nikos to open the door. To meet his *nanny*. To blow sky-high?

Perhaps. Or maybe to be amenable then to another

"discussion" with his father. Yes, she was willing to believe that was what Stavros had been doing.

And Nikos?

She suspected that, for all their differences, he was his father's son.

"What were you trying to prove?" she asked.

"I wasn't trying to prove anything. I was trying to get him to damned well throw me out!"

"Ah." *Flaunt the hooker in front of the family and watch Daddy take action.* She understood now. But... "He's keeping you prisoner?"

Nikos lifted the cast. "I can't drive. As soon as I can, I'm out of here."

"I see." She did. Sort of. She wondered what Stavros was playing at, hiring her, then. Nikos was certainly not going to be wearing the cast another six months.

"I doubt it," he said flatly. "He's a manipulator."

"And you're not?"

He frowned. "I'm only doing this in response to what he's done. He doesn't have to keep me here."

"He started it, in other words?"

The frown deepened. "You make it sound like two little kids fighting."

"I see some similarity," Mari pointed out.

"You don't see a damn thing."

"Well, I'm sure you'll enlighten me."

"I don't want anything to do with you."

Mari wasn't entirely sure she wanted anything to do with him, either. If she hadn't felt what she'd felt when they'd kissed, she would have been running the other way.

"Why are you staying?" Nikos demanded.

"I gave my word."

"He as much as lied to you!"

"I know that." Mari shrugged. "I'm not going to play on his level."

"You're going to reform me instead?" he said cynically.

I wish, Mari thought. She ran her tongue over her lips. "I'm going to stay here because that's what I've been hired to do. I'm going to try to help because that's my job. What happens between your father and you—well, I'll do my best."

"It won't be good enough," Nikos said. Then almost to himself he added, "It never is."

Mari, caught by his words, wanted to ask what he meant, but he hauled himself to his feet and crutched past her toward his bedroom. "I have a headache. I'm going to sleep. Do whatever the hell you want. Just go away and leave me alone."

She left him alone.

She went looking for his father. She had plenty of questions that only Stavros Costanides could answer.

He wasn't with his wife and her shower guests. Julietta waved a hand toward the house. "He took Alex in a little while ago. He's probably in his office by now. It's on the second floor. Go right on up. I think he's expecting you." As she said this last with a completely straight face, Mari merely thanked her and headed toward the house.

"'I think he's expecting you'," she muttered under her breath. "I'll bet."

Stavros was sitting at his desk, the phone to his ear, when she appeared in the doorway. When he saw her, he smiled and beckoned her in.

Mari didn't smile back. She entered the office, but she didn't take the seat he indicated. She had no intention of sitting down and putting herself at an even greater disadvantage.

"Tell Adrianos to get right on it," Stavros said into the phone. "That's right. As quick as he can." This last was almost a bark. Then he hung up and turned a thousand-watt smile on her. "Ah, Miss Lewis, you've come to chat."

"Not quite."

"You can't quit," he reminded her. "You signed the contact."

"I know that. What I don't know is what you expect me to do! If you intended to annoy and humiliate your son, I think you succeeded. Beyond that, I'm at a loss."

"He was annoyed? Good. Humiliated? It serves him right. He has done plenty to humiliate me. And I want exactly what I said that I wanted. He is a problem. I want him not to be."

"He's thirty-two years old!"

"And he needs to grow up. He is lazy. He will not work in the company. He would prefer to be sailing his boat. Dancing attendance on unsuitable women. Creating gossip. Irritating *me*." He fixed her with a charming, conspiratorial smile. "I want it to stop."

His smile was, in its way, as handsome as his son's. But Mari felt no sizzle, only annoyance. "He won't cooperate, Mr. Costanides."

He lifted a brow. "And always your charges cooperate, Miss Lewis?" His tone was deceptively mild.

"Not always," she admitted.

"So you have ways...yes?" He looked hopeful. He made it sound like she tortured them into behaving properly.

"I teach by love and care and example," she said with an edge to her voice.

He nodded. "Just so." He steepled his hands on his desk and regarded her complacently over the top of them. "I should like to you love and care for Nikos."

A frisson of primal fear skittered down her spine. Perhaps it was because he'd used the words *love* and *Nikos* in such close proximity—even though Mari knew he didn't mean *that* kind of love!

She paced to the far end of his office and turned, with her hands on her hips. "And you think that will work?" she demanded finally, when he just looked at her expectantly.

"My dear Miss Lewis, you yourself *assured* me it would work."

"But—"

But there was nothing to say to that because, in fact, she had. And it *had* worked—with all her other charges. But this was different!

"He's not a child!" she argued.

"No, he is not. But I lost him when he was a child. I think I have to start there to get him back."

It was the first real honest remark she thought he'd made. Mari took a seat in the chair she'd been avoiding. "Why, Mr. Costanides?" She leaned her elbows on her knees and rested her chin in her palm so she could look at him as she asked quietly, "Why now?"

For a moment Stavros Costanides stared off out the window toward the beach and the ocean beyond. It was a beautiful view, but Mari didn't think he was seeing it. What *was* he seeing? Nikos? As a child? And himself? A young father? His expression grew almost pained for a moment. Then he seemed to recollect himself. His jaw tightened and he looked back at her as he admitted almost grudgingly, "I need him now."

"You didn't before?" she pressed.

He gave an irritable wave of his hand. "We don't talk about 'before.' Before is over. It is now that matters. Now and the future."

Mari didn't believe that. He'd said himself that what was happening now was a result of what had gone before. But obviously he wasn't willing to talk about it.

Stavros picked up a silver pen and tapped it on the desk, watching the movement it made for a long moment before he continued his explanation. "I want to slow down. I work too hard. Too many years too hard. I am getting old. Sixty, you know? I don't have so many years left. Two years ago I had a heart attack. Not bad, you understand. But it scares me a little. I will not live forever. I want to spend time with my wife. My children." He raised his gaze to meet hers. "You understand?"

"Children?" Mari said archly.

Stavros's mouth pressed into a thin line for a second, as he absorbed the hit, then he nodded to acknowledge it. "My *little* children. They need a father."

"And Nikos doesn't?"

"Nikos is an adult, for all that he acts like an irresponsible idiot!"

And I wonder why that is? Mari said silently. But she just waited for Stavros to continue.

"I keep my company, though," he said. "I built it!" These last three words were spoken with the most emotion she'd heard from him. "From nothing I built it. Almost thirty-five years I have invested in it. It is my life, my legacy! I won't see it wasted." His eyes met hers again, dark and fierce. "I don't let Nikos waste it!"

"You think he would?" Mari didn't know anything about that possibility.

Stavros made a spitting sound. "Bah. Why wouldn't

he?" He picked up a folder from his desk and shoved it at her. "See for yourself!"

Mari took the folder automatically. It was at least an inch thick, filled, she could see, with copies of newspaper clippings. Headlines like *"Greek Playboy Turns Heiress's Head"* and *"Nick the Hunk Bares All"* blared out at her. She shut the folder with a snap.

"You see? He knows nothing! He cares nothing! He respects nothing!" Stavros's dark complexion was a deep shade of red. He aimed the pen at her. "That is what I want you to fix."

Helping children become emotionally healthy was something she was pretty good at. Keeping an adult man from running amok in the scandal sheets and driving a family business into the ground was not exactly in the same league.

"I'm not sure..." she began hesitantly.

"*I* am sure." The pen leveled on her again. "You will teach him to respect."

It was on the tip of Mari's tongue to tell him that respect was earned, not taught, but she didn't think he wanted to hear it.

Stavros tapped the pen irritably on the desktop. "He is smart. He is clever. He could do well if he wanted to. But he has to understand the business, the work I do. He won't. He behaves like a fool. Then he wants to take over just like that." He snapped his fingers. "'I can do it,' he says. 'Trust me,' he says. 'You want me to take over? Step down, I will take over,' he says. *Never! I* never started at the top!"

Fire blazed in Stavros's eyes. And then, as it ebbed, he got once more that faraway look, and Mari imagined that he was remembering that time thirty-five or so years ago when Costanides International had been no more than a dream. For a long moment neither of them spoke.

Then Stavros seemed to collect himself and he went on firmly, "Even so, I don't want to cut him out. He is my son. But," he added with heavy emphasis, "he is no longer my only son. I have another. Maybe I will have two others. If Nikos wants to take over, to be part of Costanides International, he must learn!"

To do it my way, Mari finished for him silently.

"I can't teach him anything about your business, Mr. Costanides."

"*I* teach him that," he said emphatically. "You teach him how to listen, to do what I say!"

"To respect," Mari said quietly, inevitably.

Stavros poked the pen-point into the blotter on his desk. "Exactly. Yes." He gave a nod of dismissal. "Go now."

Just like his son, he had a way of ending things. Mari got to her feet and started for the door.

"Miss Lewis?"

She turned back.

He pointed at her again with the silver pen, fixing her where she stood. "And you start with no more kisses. Understood?"

Nikos rolled over on his bed and pushed back the curtain, watching Mari Lewis return from the main house and wondering how in heaven's name he'd ever mistaken her for one of Debbie's Dollies. He must have overdosed on his pain medication.

With her pinned up hair and her white blouse and navy blue skirt, she really did look like some damn librarian—or a convent schoolgirl.

Still, for all that she resembled a refugee from *The*

Sound of Music, she sure didn't *kiss* like a convent schoolgirl!

Or, if she did, he'd better start taking another look at convents.

He waited, watched her...and wondered if she'd let him have another soon.

From the look on her face, he didn't think it likely. And yet—

She'd wanted it. He would swear she'd wanted it. He would swear she'd wanted *him*!

Who was the real Mari Lewis under that schoolgirl disguise? Whoever she was, she was wasted on little kids!

He hadn't been lying about his headache. It was better now, but he wasn't getting up and going to look for her. If she wanted to talk to him, she could come in here. He folded his arms under his head and waited.

He didn't have to wait long. In a moment there was a tap on the door.

"Come to share my bed?" he asked her.

"Not now," she said.

He blinked and shoved himself up against the headboard. *Not now?*

When? he wanted to ask her.

But she didn't even seem to be thinking about that. She came just inside the door and said, "There's not much love lost between you, is there?"

"Not much," Nikos agreed. "Did he spell it all out for you? His demands and my bad behavior?"

She hesitated. "He...dropped some hints."

"I'll fill you in, if you'd like."

She rubbed her forehead. "No, thanks."

"I could save us both some headaches if you'd just drive me to the airport."

"I can't do that."

"Why not?"

"I don't think that's in the plan."

"Screw his plans," Nikos said sharply. "If I didn't have this damn cast I'd be out of here so fast his head would spin."

"And give up your inheritance?"

He frowned. "What the hell do you mean by that?" *Now what was the old man up to?*

"That's what he's threatening. You don't play ball his way, do what he wants, and the company goes to Alex and the new baby."

"Let it, then!" Nikos exploded.

"He doesn't want it to. He'd rather you take over."

"But he won't let me."

"He will if—"

"I do it *his* way. No thanks."

"According to him, you need to understand how the business works."

"I *know* how businesses work!"

Mari's brows went straight up beneath the fringe of hair across her forehead. Nikos said something rude under his breath. If he shocked Miss Goody Two Shoes, he didn't care.

"I gather you don't agree you need to know."

"I don't agree I need to know."

"Then prove it," she suggested mildly, "by listening to him and showing him."

"Why the hell doesn't *he* listen to *me*?"

"I don't know," she said calmly. "I'll ask him sometime."

Nikos muttered again. "Don't bother!" He gave a dismissive wave of his hand, but she didn't move. She stood with her back to the door as if she was terrified of him, and yet oddly he didn't think she was.

"What are you waiting for?" he demanded gruffly. "Another invitation?" He patted the sheet next to him and was pleased to see the color on her face deepen.

"I'll be in the kitchen if you want me," she said, and fled, pulling the door shut behind her.

"I won't want you, sweetheart," Nikos said, but his harsh voice was only loud enough for his own ears. "Unless it's in my bed."

A vision of Mari Lewis's slender curves and ample bosom naked and delectable floated through his mind. Out of her proper clothes and with her long hair unbound, she would be something! Better than what-was-her-name—*Truffles!*—oh, God, yes.

Was he crazy? He was fantasizing about a *nanny*!

His nanny! It was almost kinky.

It had obviously been too damn long since he'd had a woman in his arms.

Mari had made a career of coping with children in trauma. She was used to coming into their lives at moments of crisis—when a parent died or a marriage shattered or a long string of broken promises left them without trust or hope.

Better than all the king's horses and all the king's men, Mari Lewis was a master at putting them together again. She gave them hope, taught them to trust themselves first and then to judge others. It was hard work. It was more than hard work—it was exhausting work at times.

But it was ever so rewarding to know she'd made a difference.

She'd believed she could make just such a difference to Nikos Costanides—when she'd believed he was four!

And now?

Well, he certainly wasn't four, and the trauma, whatever it was, went a lot deeper. But that didn't make him any less needy. She could almost see the need crying out from deep inside him.

Oh, yes. That's definitely what you're interested in, she jeered at herself.

Well, okay. She wasn't only interested in his pain and his miserable childhood. She was also interested in Nikos as a man.

But the man was a product of his upbringing, wasn't he? And it was her job to deal with that.

She knew without giving it a thought what his reaction would be. *Forget it.* She was sure he'd said it plenty of times. *I don't need that son-of-a-bitch!* She could almost hear him say those words, too.

But why?

What had happened between Nikos and his father to bring them to this?

The folder Stavros had given her sat on the desk in her bedroom. She had put it there the moment she'd returned. She hadn't picked it up. She didn't want to pick it up.

She wanted to get to know Nikos for herself.

And then what?

Put the family back together again. Of course.

And?

And nothing, she told herself sharply. She was doing her job, that was all.

And what about the kiss? What about the sizzle?

Did Mary Poppins ever have to think about things like that?

CHAPTER THREE

THE phone rang at three a.m.

Mari, startled out of a restless sleep, wasn't even sure where she was for a moment. When she finally remembered, it wasn't an improvement. Was Stavros Costanides doing a bed-check? she wondered.

She groped for the phone on her bedside table. But when she picked it up, she discovered that Nikos was already on the line.

And so was a soft-voiced woman with a British accent. "Ah, Nikos," she said, "I got you up."

"Again," Mari heard Nikos growl sleepily. "You never let me get a full night's sleep, Claudia."

The woman on the other end of the line giggled.

Hastily Mari slammed the phone down. She shouldn't have been surprised. She *wasn't* surprised. Annoyed was more like it.

Annoyed because she'd been awakened. Not because Nikos Costanides had another woman! Mari rolled over and punched her pillow, then settled her head down again. She didn't care. She had no reason to care.

Only the memory of his kiss. And that incredible sizzle.

She hard-boiled his egg. She burned his toast. She had to start over with both before she got them the way she always fixed them. And then she carried them on a tray to his bedroom and tapped on the door.

If he'd been four, she'd have walked in.

She wasn't walking in on *this* Nikos Costanides.

"Come in," he growled.

She pushed the door open and pasted a bright good-morning smile on her face. A good thing, too, because if she'd waited to try to do it until she'd actually confronted him, ruffled and sleepy, sprawled in his bed with the sheet barely pulled over the most private parts of him, she doubted if she could have made her muscles work.

As it was, she managed to swallow and that was about it.

"Come to cuddle?" he drawled, and gave her what was undoubtedly one of his better playboy leers.

She remembered Thomas saying he liked to tease, and knew that she was the butt of this particular joke. She wondered what he would do if she said yes!

Not that she was going to! she reminded herself smartly. Curiosity killed the cat, after all. Who was to say she was immune?

It was enough to know that whatever spark had existed between her and Nikos Costanides, it had lasted to live another day.

"I've brought you some breakfast," she said, crossing the room and setting the tray on the table.

He stared at it. "Boiled egg and toast fingers?" He sounded incredulous.

"I can fix oatmeal if you'd like."

"Being a nanny entails fixing breakfast?"

"Generally, yes. Especially since we're, um…on our own down here." She wasn't sure she wanted to call attention to that, but since it was obvious, she didn't suppose it made any difference. He wasn't dim.

"I see. And then what do you do? Teach me my numbers? Help my tie my shoes?"

"I do whatever needs to be done," Mari said. "Manners, in this case, I should think."

A grin slashed across his dark features. "Ouch." But he shoved himself up further to get in position to take the tray. The duvet covering him slipped another inch or so, and Mari's eyes shifted in that direction. The look Nikos gave her was silently amused.

She prayed he wouldn't comment, though. It was one thing to acknowledge "sizzle." It was another to want to rip the covers off him and study his naked form!

Just how she knew he was naked under that duvet, she didn't want to think. She couldn't recall *ever* thinking about Ward's state of dress or undress, even when she'd brought him breakfast in bed during his occasional weekend visits to The Folly, her aunts' old Victorian house.

"No coffee?" Nikos asked hopefully as she set the tray on his lap. "Or am I getting cocoa instead?"

"I...I'll get you some coffee," Mari said quickly. "Anything else?"

He raised one dark brow. "You?"

She fled.

With her hair pulled back into a ponytail and no makeup on her face, Mari Lewis still looked like a bit player in *Sister Act* when she carried that boiled egg and those ridiculous toast fingers into his room. At least she was dressed more informally in a pair of slacks and a scoop-neck rose-colored T-shirt.

To match her rose-colored glasses, Nikos thought as he picked up his fork and poked at the egg. He hadn't had a boiled egg in years. His mother was the last person to ever make him a boiled egg, and he thought he must have been about ten at the time.

He felt about ten right now. Stubborn and cranky and up to no good.

He stabbed the egg. His stomach growled. *Damn it.* He gritted his teeth, feeling betrayed by his body as well as by everything else. He set down his fork. Glared at the egg. Glared at the toast. Glared at the door through which Mari Lewis had departed.

His stomach growled again. Reluctantly, irritably, he picked up his fork and took a bite.

The egg was good. The toast was crisp and golden, lightly buttered. Perfection. *Hell!* He ate them both in moments.

His only solace was that Mari Lewis appeared equally astonished at the empty tray when she came back with the coffee.

"Would you like another?" she asked. "I didn't give you very much. I'm used to cooking for smaller appetites."

He was tempted to say something smart, but she hadn't spoken mockingly, so he didn't either. Actually, the egg and toast had hit the spot. His father's cook, Alana, who had sent down meals, did an excellent job, but she tended to make exotic things that very pregnant women had cravings for and their very wealthy husbands felt inclined to indulge.

Nikos didn't mind the meals she sent down—it was better than having to fix his own—but there was something oddly comforting about the stupid boiled egg and toast.

It was a nice thing to eat when you felt like hell.

He felt like hell.

He hadn't slept much last night. Being thwarted never did much for his ability to get a good night's sleep. And his father's latest salvo had made him fume and toss and turn for hours. And just when he'd finally got to sleep Claudia had called.

He'd spent an hour on the phone with her. And after that he hadn't been able to sleep. Consequently, his headache, which on normal days stayed pretty controllable, was already nagging at his temples. He couldn't do much for it. But his stomach was another matter.

"I wouldn't mind another egg," he allowed now.

"Or two?" Mari Lewis asked.

He hesitated. Then, "Two," he agreed gruffly. "And some more toast," he added as she turned back toward the kitchen. "I would have expected you to do toy soldier toast men actually," he gibed.

"I do," she said, "for good little boys."

He stuck out his tongue at her.

She laughed.

Her whole face lit up when she laughed. Her blue-green eyes sparkled and the few freckles on her cheeks seemed almost to dance, and her mouth looked more kissable than ever. Nikos felt a very strong urge to do just that. And he would—the next time she got close enough.

"Two pieces of toast," he answered her. "Please."

The word came out unbidden, though it didn't surprise him really. He was generally more polite than he'd been to Mari Lewis. Not that she didn't deserve a little shortness, as agent of his father's misplaced behavior modification program!

She grinned delightedly, as if she'd won a round, and he frowned fiercely at her. It didn't stop her smiling. And he had to wait until she'd gone into the other room to close his eyes and rub his aching head.

His eyes were still closed a few minutes later when she returned.

"Here you go." A clean dish materialized in front of him with two more perfectly done boiled eggs. Beside it, with a flourish, she set a plate of toast fingers—cut like toy soldiers.

Nikos goggled at them, then at her.

Mari Lewis smiled impishly at him. "You said please," she said, before darting out of his reach.

Damn, but he wanted to kiss her!

"Is he a nice little boy, darling?" Aunt Emmaline asked.

And how am I supposed to answer that? Mari wondered. She bent her bare toes over the rung of the kitchen stool and glanced over her shoulder toward the bedroom where she'd left Nikos and his toast and eggs minutes before. *Fine as long as he stayed right where he was,* she thought. But she glanced over her shoulder every few seconds, it seemed, to make sure he did. She'd had the definite impression that if he'd been able to, he would have grabbed her when she'd brought him that toast and eggs.

And then what would he have done? she wondered. *Kissed her?*

There was that possibility. *And that's bad?*

Of course it was. There was Claudia, after all.

Whoa! Wait just a minute. You aren't angling to marry him, only to kiss him, to discover the extent of your own passion. Well, in that case...

But even so, she thought she needed a little more time, a little more space, a little more preparation. She didn't want to be caught off-guard the way she had been the first time.

"Mari? Are you there? Do we have a bad connection? I asked you about Nikos."

"He's, um...fine," she fumbled. "Most of the time."

"Not as badly behaved as you'd feared?"

"Different than I'd feared." That was certainly the truth!

"But you can handle him," Aunt Em said with her perennial confidence. "Did you say his father was a widower?"

Aunt Em was always on the lookout for Ward's replacement. She'd never thought he was good enough for her niece. After Shelley, Mari had no trouble agreeing with her.

"His father is remarried," she explained. "And the little boy's name is Alex."

"Alex?" This was Aunt Bett on the extension. "I thought you said his name was Nikos."

"I thought it was. I...was mistaken." But she wasn't about to make the mistake of telling her aunts anything about the true nature of her job! They fussed about her enough. One word about the real Nikos Costanides and the fussing would reach a new level altogether.

"I get Thursday off." She changed the subject. "I'll be around to see you then." Their house on Orient Point was about an hour's drive from the Costanides place.

"Will you be bringing Alex?" Aunt Em asked eagerly.

"No," Mari said. "Days off imply just that, Aunt Em. I don't have to bring him."

"Bring whom? Where?" a masculine voice said right behind her.

Mari jumped a foot. She jerked around to see Nikos leaning on his crutches and regarding her with amusement from the hallway. Damn it! How could he walk so soundlessly when he was using a cast and crutches, for heaven's sake?

She put her hand over the receiver. "This is a private conversation!"

"It's a pack of lies," he said genially. "Who're you talking to?"

"It is not!" Mari defended herself.

"Is that the little boy's father?" Aunt Em asked. "What a nice strong voice he has."

Mari removed her hand, since it wasn't doing any good anyway. "Isn't it?" Mari said. Then to Nikos, she hissed, "None of your business. Go away."

"If I'm your business, you're mine, sweetheart. Give me the phone. I'll tell the truth."

"No!" She had no intention of giving him the phone and letting him talk to her aunts! She should have waited to call them. But she'd promised them that she would call once she got settled in. They had known she wouldn't call the first night, but they did worry, so she wanted to let them know all was well—even if it wasn't!

Nikos cocked his head and grinned coaxingly. "Please?" He said the word mockingly, and she wished she'd never given him those damned toy soldier toast fingers!

"I have to go now," she said quickly to her aunts. "He's misbehaving."

"Begin as you mean to go on," Aunt Em advised.

"Spare the rod, spoil the child," Aunt Bett intoned.

"Oh, yes," Mari agreed. "I'll call you later." She hung up and stood to face him. He wasn't more than four inches taller than she was, yet he seemed so much bigger. And so very...male. She ran her tongue over her lips.

Nikos didn't stop grinning. "Misbehaving, am I?"

"Badly," Mari affirmed. "My aunt thinks I should take a switch to you."

He lifted a brow. "Kinky, is she?"

Mari felt her cheeks flame. "She's a very proper eighty-one-year-old lady with strict ideas of how children should be raised."

Nikos still grinned. "I'd like to meet her."

"Not on your life! Have you finished with your breakfast?"

"Yes. But I couldn't manage the tray and the crutches."

"You don't need to bring it in. I'll come and get it. You should stay in bed."

"I'm not that much of an invalid."

"Perhaps not. But you didn't get much sleep, did you?"

He frowned. "How did you know that?"

"I heard the phone. I picked it up and—" She stopped, not wanting to admit hearing the lilting English voice of the woman who'd called him.

"Oh, Claudia." A sort of wry smile touched his face. "She thinks I've got insomnia so she never cares when she calls."

So Claudia was his girlfriend. It must be a pretty intense relationship if she felt free enough to call him at any hour of the day or night. "And Claudia is...?" she ventured, hoping that he would expand on that.

"Important," he said firmly. "Whenever she calls, you get me, understand?"

Mari blinked at the firmness of his tone. She swallowed, then nodded her head. "Of course."

"Even if I'm in the shower. *Especially* if I'm in the shower." A grin flashed across his face.

Mari felt her cheeks turning red. How dare he come on to *her* when he was talking about another woman!

The phone rang just then and she said frostily, "In

this case, I won't need to get you at all." And she brushed past him to go get the tray, leaving him to answer it.

"Costanides," Nikos growled into the receiver. There was a second's pause, then, "Go to hell," he said to whoever was on the other end, and slammed the receiver down.

"Not Claudia?" Mari asked over her shoulder.

"Your esteemed employer," he said through his teeth.

The phone rang again.

Nikos ignored it. It rang again. And again. "I'm not answering it." He fitted his crutches beneath his arms and hobbled away from the phone. "He's your boss, not mine."

Mari stared at him, then at the phone. She didn't much want to answer it, either. She didn't want to hear any more lectures from Stavros on respect. And she didn't need him looking over her shoulder every second. She didn't particularly want to answer the phone in front of Nikos, either. But she knew Stavros well enough to know that he'd keep right on ringing until someone answered it.

She stalked over and snatched it up. "Yes?"

"Ah, Miss Lewis," Stavros's unmistakable Greek-accented English rasped in her ear. "And how are things today?"

Mari's teeth came together. "They *were* fine."

She saw Nikos stiffen and stop at her tone. He turned to look at her.

"He is behaving badly already?" Stavros's voice became angry. "I did not think—! He has always been good to women! Despite everything else, he has shown *them* respect! But to you he is—!"

"He's fine, Mr. Costanides," Mari cut in. "But I can't

focus on him if you're calling me all the time. I need time with him. Alone. Without your interference.''

There was stunned silence on the other end of the line.

Nikos broke into a grin. Mari glared at him.

"Respect is—"

"Respect is something that takes time to develop, Mr. Costanides," she said as evenly as she could. "Especially when you've wasted opportunities to develop it over the years."

"I—"

"I appreciate your concern. But please, let me do my job."

"Yes, yes. Your job. You— "

"I need you to give us space. Time."

"Privacy," Nikos murmured with a wicked grin on his face.

Mari turned her back on him. "You reward his worst behaviour, Mr. Costanides. If you constantly check up on us and fuss about every little thing…"

"Fuss? *I?* Fuss?" Stavros sounded outraged.

"Get upset," Mari corrected herself. Clearly the self-concept of a sixty-year-old Greek patriarch did not include "fussing." "I appreciate your concern, Mr. Costanides, but I really must handle Nikos on my own."

Over her shoulder, she could hear the soft sound of Nikos applauding. She stiffened her back, and her resolve not to turn around and look at him.

"I only try to help," Stavros said, wounded.

"Then give me the space I need. And silent support."

"Silent?"

"Silent," Mari repeated firmly.

She got silence. She wasn't sure about the support. But finally, about the time she thought she was listening to dead air, Stavros said worriedly, "He is treating you all right?"

"He is treating me fine." That was, if she ignored his more flagrantly teasing remarks, he was treating her fine.

"You're sure?"

"I'm positive, Mr. Costanides." She wanted to hang up. She wanted to say, *Oh, for heaven's sake, leave me alone.*

She didn't, because she knew if she did, he would be over here in five minutes, sticking his nose in, making things fifty times worse. She had no idea if she could do what he wanted or not. But she knew quite well *he* couldn't do it with his methods. If he had been able to, he'd have managed it years ago.

"You will call if you need me?"

"Certainly."

"You don't take disrespect?"

"Of course not."

He made a harumphing sound, one that said he wasn't *quite* convinced, but... "Very well, Miss Lewis. I give you space."

"Thank you, Mr. Costanides." She started to hang up.

"We will see you at lunchtime."

"We won't be here at lunchtime."

"Not here? But—"

"Nikos and I need time together. Alone," Mari said as quietly as she could, all the while moving as far away from the man standing in the hall behind her as she could.

Obviously, from the gleeful, "Hear, hear," coming from Nikos, she hadn't moved far enough. She turned and glared.

Nikos grinned unrepentantly.

"I have to go, Mr. Costanides. There are matters here that need my attention."

"Nikos? Is he—?"

"Goodbye, Mr. Costanides. I'll call you in a few days."

"Days?" she heard him begin to sputter, but she didn't stop to listen to anymore. She hung up. She faced Nikos and dared him to tease her now.

He regarded her solemnly. The grin he'd been wearing had vanished when she put the receiver down, and his brows hiked up beneath the fringe of disheveled dark hair that straggled across his forehead.

"Whoa," he said, and he sounded not sarcastic or teasing, but almost respectful. "Guess you told him."

"I said what had to be said."

"And what no one else has ever dared say before," Nikos said drily.

"You appear to have told him a few less than palatable things over the years," Mari pointed out. "I can't believe I'm the first person to thwart him."

"Maybe not. But you might be the first one he's listened to."

"We don't know that he's listened yet, do we?" Mari said, a little apprehensive that Stavros might at this very moment be striding across the grass that separated the big house from Nikos's small cottage.

As if he'd read her mind, Nikos crutched his way over to the window and tipped the blind aside so he could look up at his father's house. "Nobody coming," he said. "And no cannons being aimed in our direction."

Mari managed a smile. "That's good news, I suppose." She felt a little weak in the knees now that the conversation was over.

"So, where are we going?" Nikos asked.

"What?"

"You told him we weren't going to be here at lunchtime," he reminded her. "I wondered where we were going to be."

"Oh. Right." She smiled a little guiltily. "I don't know. I just knew that putting the two of you together right now wasn't going to accomplish anything."

"It would make him mad." Nikos didn't look as if that would dismay him at all.

"Which is not what I want to do, even if you do," Mari said sharply. "But I suppose you're right. We should go somewhere. Would you like to go for a drive?"

Nikos smiled and shifted on his crutches, stretching slightly. It ought to have looked as if he was adjusting something that annoyed him, instead it seemed to her a decidedly sexy stretch. He was still bare-chested, which gave her quite a lot of uncovered masculine flesh to study. But when he stretched his shorts dropped another inch and she got even more!

"I'd like that very much." And it sounded less as if he'd said the words and more as if he'd actually *purred* them!

She'd stuck up for him!

He couldn't believe it. In his entire life, only one person had ever stuck up for Nikos with his father—his mother.

Like a lioness protecting her cub, Angelika Costanides had fought with her husband again and again—rejecting his father's seemingly endless demands that he change schools, move to Greece, study at a particular university, take certain courses, work in the family business, marry the right woman.

"He is not you!" Angelika said over and over. "Let him alone!"

"He needs to know! To learn!" Stavros countered.

And his mother always replied heavily, "He'll know. He'll learn all he needs to soon enough."

By that time in the conversation, there was always such a wealth of pain in her voice that Nikos wanted to slam in and break it up, to throw his father out, to comfort his mother's anguish.

Always he waited, impotently and furiously, until his father nodded his head and said in a cold remote voice, "Just as you wish, Angelika," and disappeared out of their lives once again.

And then she would turn to Nikos, pacing and fuming in his wake, and say, "He is your father. You must respect that."

"I don't respect *him*," he told his mother every time.

"Ah, Nikos." She put her hand on his arm and he allowed her to drag him into a gentle embrace. At first he had been small enough to press his face into her breasts. But at the last he could rest his chin on the top of her head. He would feel her shake her head gently and say words he never understood. "Poor Stavros. He can't help it. He tries."

As far as Nikos could see, the old man didn't try at all. Except to cause hurt and pain to his wife—a woman who had given him everything she had in terms of both worldly wealth and womanly devotion for her whole life.

It had been an arranged marriage, Nikos knew that. He supposed that was why his father didn't care. Stavros had married her, Nikos was sure, for the money that her family had. He'd never really cared about the woman who'd come with it. They hadn't lived together since Nikos was eight years old.

And yet he knew, despite their separation, that his mother had always loved her husband. She would never let Nikos speak badly of him. She never said a bad thing herself. She just looked sad. And lonely. And she'd been alone—except for her son—when she'd died of a heart attack six years ago.

The death of his mother was the most painful loss Nikos had ever experienced. He'd been grief-stricken, missing her terribly, devastated by her loss, even though intellectually he should have been prepared.

For over a year he'd known she had a bad heart. She hadn't wanted to tell him, but eventually she couldn't hide it anymore. She was too pale, too weak to pretend. For some time after he'd settled in Britain, he didn't see her as often as he would have liked. She hadn't minded.

"You have your life," she'd said. "You must do what you must do."

She'd never made the demands his father had. It had been a shock, then, to come flying in for a visit and find her much paler than he remembered her. During their visit, she'd tired easily, too. He'd asked what was wrong; she'd dismissed it. He'd let her get away with it then. Perhaps, he thought, it was only the result of the bronchitis she'd had in the winter. But he came back a month later and she'd been no better. She was worse.

That was when she'd had to tell him. He had believed it. He'd done everything he could to get her to find a cardiologist who could help her.

"I've done all I can," she assured him. "There is nothing left."

Nothing but coming back as often as he could. He flew in nearly every weekend that last year. He spent the last month of her life with her.

He'd never seen Stavros there.

So his father's claim to grief—the old man had wept beside her grave, for heaven's sake—had seemed like just so much false emotion to Nikos.

"Where were you when she was alive?" he'd demanded harshly before they even left the cemetery.

And if his father had still looked ashen, Nikos didn't care. The old man was a good actor! He couldn't fool the young man who'd been by his mother's side for twenty-six years when his father had been everywhere else but home.

And as far as Nikos was concerned, Stavros had proved it a year later when he'd married Julietta, a woman young enough to be his daughter!

All Nikos could say about that was that his old man had good taste. Hell, yes, Julietta was lovely! So lovely that Nikos himself had actually dated her a few times.

But she'd been too prim and proper and too "old line Greek" for him. She was controlled by her family much the same way his mother had been controlled.

He supposed she had her family to thank for her ridiculous marriage to his father, too!

Though, he had to admit, you wouldn't know it to look at them. What a devoted little family they'd become—Stavros, Julietta, and their own little Alexander. Smiling, happy. Hugging and talking and laughing together. A perfect little threesome. And now they had a new baby on the way.

Nikos gritted his teeth whenever he stopped to think about his father's new happy little brood.

He knew he shouldn't begrudge Stavros the joy of his second marriage—however insane it might be. And when he was feeling sane and sober and sensible, Nikos wished them all well.

He even occasionally found himself hoping that the

old man did for Alexander what he'd never done for his older son. Because it would be good for Alexander to know his father cared about him—*not* because it would be good for the old man.

He didn't give a rat's ass about his old man—or his company.

And he wasn't about to shape up because a pretty little nanny told him to!

She was a pretty little nanny, though, Nikos thought. And she *had* taken his part this morning. Not to mention the way she kissed.

Going for a drive with her might be the best thing that had happened to him in a long while!

Going out for a drive with him was not the brightest idea she'd ever had. The confines of a car were bound to make her even more aware of him. As if she weren't aware enough already!

But she didn't see that she had any choice. If she wanted to make an effort to do her job—to help foster a real reconciliation between Nikos and his father—she was going to have to keep Stavros at arm's length.

That she could—and would—do.

The trouble was going to be keeping Nikos at arm's length as well.

It was interesting how *aware* she was of him. Her reactions were nothing like the ones she'd had to Ward and every other man she'd ever dated—not that she'd dated a vast number, of course.

Maybe she'd only dated duds.

Nikos wasn't a dud. The trouble was, he was likely to be far more man than she could handle.

"Just say no, darling," she remembered Aunt Em advising her on the subject of boys and temptation.

Up until now that had been no problem. But up until yesterday she'd never kissed Nikos.

It was like playing with fire. Attractive. Tempting. Fun. Dangerous.

Children shouldn't do it. But Mari was an adult. She needed to know how to deal with fire—how to test it, fan it, encourage it, control it.

With Nikos Costanides?

She was out of her blinking mind!

She was waiting by the pool with Julietta and Alex when he finished showering, got dressed and was ready to go. He had made an effort and put on a pair of bleached canvas trousers and a dark red T-shirt in honor of the occasion. It was the first time since he'd come from the hospital that he'd bothered to put on more than a pair of ragged cut-offs or faded shorts.

Or a towel. He remembered yesterday with a smile.

His father always looked like he'd just stepped off Savile Row—even when he was "relaxing."

"You must convey a responsible image," he had said more times than Nikos wanted to count.

A "responsible image" was the last thing Nikos wanted to convey—especially when the old man was around. He had made a habit of dressing down for years. But today, for the lovely nanny, who kissed like a dream and had stuck up for him, he made a small effort. After all it was his father he was annoyed at, not her.

Whether Mari appreciated his sartorial elegance was not immediately apparent. She was talking to Julietta. He stopped, realizing that he'd have to weather Julietta's knowing smiles and inane remarks if he made his way up there. She would undoubtedly think his father saddling him with a nanny was just "too funny for words."

To someone else it probably was. Nikos set his teeth, prepared to endure the encounter. After all, he'd endured far worse.

But he didn't need to, for as soon as Mari saw him coming, she said goodbye to Julietta and hurried toward him.

Another point for the nanny. Nikos leaned on his crutches and waited for her, breathing a sigh of relief.

"Sorry," she said a little breathlessly. "I didn't mean to keep you waiting. I just wanted to see how Julietta was feeling." She had dressed for the occasion, too, in a pair of chambray slacks and a scoop-necked bright turquoise shirt. It wasn't quite the librarian garb she'd had on yesterday, but it was hardly a sexy outfit. So why was he so damned aware of her?

Because she looked as eager and well-scrubbed as a schoolgirl? Because he made it a habit to toy with innocents? Because he wanted a ride up the coast and nothing more.

No, no, and no again.

He studied her hair, which she had clamped in a barrette at the nape of her neck. It was as anchored down as she was—and yet it loosened a little and blew in the wind. Would *she* loosen? Would she let her hair down for him?

She didn't look like it. But God, had she ever kissed like it.

Remembering, trying to figure it out, Nikos limped toward the garage on his crutches and Mari walked alongside him.

"What's wrong?" she asked at his frown of concentration.

"Why don't you wear it down?"

She blinked at him. "What?"

"Your hair. It hates being confined like that."

She smiled. "You can tell, can you?"

"Yes. Absolutely. Here." He reached out a hand and deftly loosed it from the barrette she wore.

"Nikos!" She reached back and grabbed it out of his hand.

He let her have the barrette, much more interested in running a hand over her hair. It glinted in the sunlight, the deep honey color shot through with gold. It was as soft and heavy as he'd imagined it would be. He smiled.

She caught his hand and pulled it away from her hair. "No," she said.

"No?" He tried turning her hand in his, but she held on.

"No," she repeated. "You can't do that."

"I just did," he reminded her.

"But I didn't want you to."

His gaze narrowed. "You did, too."

A hint of red touched her cheeks. She shook her head. "I didn't."

He just looked at her.

Her gaze slid away. "I shouldn't," she qualified gruffly after a moment.

A corner of Nikos's mouth quirked at her honesty. "A nanny never lies?"

Her color deepened. "I try not to." She refused to look at him, keeping her eyes cast down. She reminded him for all the world of Maria, the misbehaving postulant in *The Sound of Music* that his mother had taken him to see when he was a child.

He wanted to argue with her. He wanted to tell her he was teasing, that it was no more than play between men and women, and that it would lead them exactly where they wanted to go.

It wasn't like he was grabbing her and throwing her down on the grass and having his way with her, for heaven's sake! It wasn't as if he'd taken her in broad daylight and kissed her senseless! It wasn't—

He stopped. He remembered.

He remembered yesterday. Julietta and all her friends had been up by the pool and Nikos had come out the door, wearing only a towel. And he'd taken Mari into his arms and kissed her. Deeply. Hungrily. Possessively. Senselessly.

He shut his eyes. When he opened them again, she was still standing there, eyes downcast, unmoving.

He sighed. "Turn around."

She flicked a quick glance up at him. "What?"

He took hold of her shoulder gently and turned her. "Turn around."

She must have realized what he was doing then, for she turned. She stood with her back to him. And Nikos, leaning heavily against his crutches, took hold of that golden honeyed shank of hair and pulled it back into his hand. Then, because he couldn't quite behave perfectly, he combed his fingers through it for just a moment. Finally, though, reluctantly, but firmly, he fastened the barrette into place once more.

"There." He let his hands drop.

Mari turned back to face him and the smile she gave him was almost worth it. "Thank you, Nikos." She looked like Maria-the-nun again.

He shut his eyes. *Ah, Mari Lewis, what am I going to do with you?*

CHAPTER FOUR

MARI didn't know what she would have done if he hadn't given her back the barrette.

It was one thing to draw the line with a four-year-old. It was something else entirely to have to put down limits with a man the tabloids called Nick the Hunk. There was no real way she could count on them being honored—except by an appeal to respect.

And she feared it was much too early for that. Besides, according to Stavros, Nikos knew nothing about respect.

So why had he given her back the barrette?

Of course he'd taken his own sweet time about it, turning her and touching her and combing his fingers through her hair and sending a whole raftload of sizzles through her. But he'd done what she asked.

She had sizzle—and she had control. She gave a small skip of sheer satisfaction.

She could do this. She *could!*

Nikos pressed a remote garage door opener as they approached the building, and by the time they arrived, the door had rolled up to reveal four gleaming cars.

"Take your pick," he said, "since you're going to be driving."

Mari looked them over and swallowed hard. Like Nikos, they were all out of her league. Big and shiny and dangerous or small and sleek and lethal. And every one worth far more than she would make in a year.

"How about taking mine? I know how to drive it."

73

Nikos grinned. "The principles are the same no matter what the car."

"I don't think—"

"You want me to be brave and grow up willing to try new things, don't you?" Nikos asked, his dark eyes glinting with wicked humor and challenge.

Mari groaned. "That is tripe."

Nikos laughed delightedly. "I bet you don't say that to all your charges."

She shook her head, sighing, but still smiling. "Just the ones old enough to understand."

"Right. Then, how about this?" The smile on his face vanished. "I respect your ability to do it." The humor had faded from his eyes, but the challenge didn't. He regarded her intently.

It was called being hoist by your own petard, and she knew it. "Damn," she murmured.

Nikos made a disapproving sound.

Mari swallowed a smile. "Drat," she amended sulkily. Then, in the face of his grin, she sucked in her breath and nodded. She would try it. She could call it another exercise in control.

Nikos beamed. "So, what's your choice? New and stuffy? New and stodgy? New and fast or—" and here he drew her around to see a low, sleek hunter green Jaguar convertible "—or old and fast and classy as hell."

It was clear which one he wanted her to pick.

Mari had never driven a car like the Jaguar in her life. She had a seven-year-old compact car with a dented front right fender. Her aunts favored large American sedans of a certain vintage that resembled a cross between gun boats and land barges to Mari.

"Safety first," Aunt Em always said.

This car was anything but. Mari gave a last longing thought toward her small serviceable car, her staid predictable cold fish life, and drew a deep breath.

"Old and fast and classy as hell," she said.

She didn't drive like Maria-the-nun.

Oh, granted, she'd taken it slow at first, moving up the drive with the speed of a sailboat caught in a calm. But then she'd got through town and hit the open road and, slowly but surely, her foot went down on the accelerator and the car speeded up. In a matter of minutes, it was like the wind had risen, and far from being becalmed now they were moving swiftly.

Nikos felt as if he'd been let out of prison.

His eyes opened wider. His heart beat more easily. For the first time since the accident, he could breathe.

Since he'd been confined at the cottage, he hadn't made any effort to hobble up to the pool or over to the beach. Any ventures out ran the risk of another confrontation with Stavros. His head already ached enough without that. So he'd stayed in. He had enough to keep him busy, though his father would never believe it. He'd even assured himself it was all right, that he would be fine until he got the damned cast off and finished the medication. He hadn't realized until now just how badly he'd needed to get out.

At midweek the traffic was less than on the weekends, and as they drove further out on the coast toward Montauk, it got even thinner. He breathed deeper, then glanced over to see how Mari was doing.

She was smiling, her earlier white-knuckled grip relaxed.

"How you doing?"

She laughed. "I feel like I've got a hundred wild horses at the end of a very thin rein."

"More like two hundred and sixty-five."

"Yikes." She shot him a horrified look.

"You'll feel better if you're part of the elements," he told her. "Pull over."

"What?"

"Stop on the shoulder up there." He directed her to the gravel alongside the roadway. When she stopped, Nikos moved to get out. It wasn't easy. He cursed his inability to negotiate cramped spaces with his cast and ribs, but finally he got out of the car, then started to put the top down.

"What are you doing?" Mari yelped.

"Putting you in the elements," Nikos said.

"I don't—"

"You'll love it," he said firmly, and gave her an encouraging grin.

She got out and put her hands on her hips. "If I argue, you'll tell me I should be setting an example for you so that you're willing to try new experiences."

His grin widened. "You're catching on. Here. Help me with this."

If she hadn't, he didn't know if he'd have been able to manage by himself. But after a moment's hesitation, she did, and within moments they had the top down.

"Now," he said, "you'll get the feel of things."

"Literally," Mari said drily. But she didn't look unhappy.

They got underway slowly again, but as the breeze caught her hair and lifted it, tugging it from the confines of the barrette and doing what he'd wanted to do, she flexed her fingers on the steering wheel and they didn't look so white-knuckled any longer. A few more miles per hour and she lifted her chin, letting the wind caress her face. She smiled.

"Terrible, isn't it?" he shouted at her over the wind.

"Awful." But she flashed him a brilliant smile.

He lay his arm along the back of the seat just behind her. Her honey-colored hair blew across his hand. He let his fingers tangle in it. "Amazing what those new experiences will do."

She stuck out her tongue at him.

Oh, very good. Way to go. There's a good example you're setting, Mari Lewis, she chastised herself. *Just stick your tongue out and get right down to his level.*

But she couldn't keep a stern demeanor, not even when she knew she ought to. She was enjoying this too much.

Stavros would be appalled. He would think she'd been taken over by the enemy!

It wasn't true, Mari told herself.

She was in control. She had never had so much speed and power under her command before. It was a little terrifying. And exhilarating as all get out!

And if Stavros asked, she could say she was simply trying to understand the world the way Nikos saw it. It helped to try to put herself in the shoes of the child. If she saw life the way the child saw it, she usually had a better idea of how to help them deal with.

She didn't know, of course, if the same thing applied to thirty-two-year-olds called Nick the Hunk. But she assured herself that it must.

And the Jaguar was marvelous regardless!

She was glad he'd virtually dared her to drive it. It was so different from driving any car she'd ever driven before. Like he was so different from any man she'd kissed before. She had thought she would just go to Amagansett and turn around, but when they got there, she didn't want to stop. So she kept right on, heading toward Montauk.

There she basically ran out of road, and that was when she finally slowed down. "Do you want to go back yet or would you like to stop and get something to eat?"

"Lunch sounds good." Nikos said. He was smiling, too. It was a heady experience just looking at him. Even with his fading bruises and battered face, he looked vibrant, alive—and even more dangerous than the Jaguar.

But the danger wasn't scary, even though perhaps it ought to have been. On the contrary, Mari found herself intrigued by it, enticed, eager to know it—to know *him*—better.

Purely professionally, of course.

Oh, yes. Sure. Drat, but she wished she were better at lying to herself.

Nikos directed her to a small café near the beach. It was off the beaten track and clearly wasn't frequented by tourists. But when Nikos opened the door, he got a profuse welcome.

"Hey, Nick, honey! How are you? We heard about your accident!" The waitress, a buxom woman in her fifties hurried over, gushing motherly concern. "What happened?"

"Just a little run-in with a tree," Nikos said easily.

"You sure?" The woman looked worried. "There was a picture in the paper. It looked mighty bad. You sit down here. Rollie, Nikos is here!" she hollered toward the kitchen.

A stout, fiftyish man in jeans and a white shirt poked his head out. "Hey, Nick! How ya doin'?"

Nikos shrugged. "Better. Fine now."

The man called Rollie looked him up and down. "Don't look fine." Then he eyed Mari and a speculative grin touched his mouth. "Well, some things do." He waggled his eyebrows at Nikos.

"She's a friend of my father's."

Rollie laughed. "Yeah, sure. You're just saying that 'cause you don't want Nita to be jealous."

Nita, Mari gathered, was the waitress. She was a good twenty years older than Nick, but she clearly found him as intriguing as Mari did, which should not have surprised her. Nikos Costanides was the sort of man *all* women would notice.

Would his kisses make them all sizzle? Mari wondered.

"Sit down, friend of Nikos's father," Rollie said now. "What'll you have?"

Mari glanced around. There didn't appear to be any menus, just a blackboard with the daily specials written on it. "What's good?" she asked Nikos.

"All the fish. Fresh daily."

"A codfish sandwich, then," she said. "And iced tea."

"Same for me," Nikos told the waitress. "But I'd like a beer."

"Sure thing, sweetheart," she replied. "You gonna sit in here or out there?" There was a patio with half a dozen tables alongside the café, sheltered from the offshore breeze. Nikos looked at Mari.

"Outside, please," she said.

They went outside, and Mari took a seat at a table overlooking the beach. There were two other couples and a large family already out there, talking and laughing and eating. A couple of children were squabbling over some French fries. A golden retriever sat on the other side of the patio railing, looking hopeful as sandwiches were consumed. Nikos settled carefully into the chair opposite her, and propped his crutches against the railing.

"What a wonderful place," Mari said.

"It is," he agreed.

"There's a place a little bit like it near where my aunts live on Orient Point."

Nikos's brows went up. "Were you raised around here?"

"On the north shore."

"I was, too. Part of the time anyway," he said. "My mother lived near Greenport."

Mari knew that quite a lot of Greek-American families had homes or summer homes in that area of Long Island. She hadn't expected that Nikos's family would have, though. She'd have imagined they would go back to Greece when they weren't in New York City. "Was your mother from the U.S., then?"

He shook his head. "No. From Greece."

"Then why—?"

"Because my father was from here. And even after he never came around anymore, she wouldn't leave him. God knows why," he added harshly.

There were half a dozen landmines in those few words, and Mari knew it. She picked her way carefully. "Your parents weren't...together?"

"You mean the old man didn't tell you he ditched my mother?"

"I understood she had died."

"Six years ago. But he left her long before that."

Long before? "How old were you?"

"Eight."

Old enough to miss his father dreadfully. Her own

father had died when she was only a few years older, and it had been terrible. How much worse it would be, she thought, to lose a father and know he was still alive—just not with you.

She began to understand a bit of the estrangement between Stavros Costanides and his son.

"You stayed with your mother?"

"Yes." A muscle in his jaw ticked and he looked away, deliberately turning his attention to the golden retriever. He snapped his fingers and, when the dog came over, scratched him behind the ears. He didn't look at Mari again. "What about you?" he asked her after a moment. "How did you end up working for my old man?"

"He saw an article in a magazine," Mari said. She felt a little self-conscious bringing it up. It had been mostly hype, but there had been a core of truth to it. "It made me sound like the answer to the troubled parent's prayer."

"Are you?" Now he was looking at her. And the steadiness of his gaze was even more unnerving than the question.

"I try. Mostly I succeed."

"You think you're going to succeed with me?"

"I'm going to try," she said.

He shook his head. "Waste of time."

"You don't know."

"I *do* know, sweetheart. The old man and I have spent too many years at odds to patch things up now."

"But—"

"We have. It's hopeless. And in a week I'll have the cast off and I'll be gone."

"A week?" How on earth was she going to do anything in a week?

"A week. I have places to go, people to see. And no interest in staying here at all."

Anita the waitress appeared just then with their sandwiches. "Lola was asking about you just the other day, Nick," she told him as she set his plate down.

"How is Lola? Tell her hi." He took a bite of his sandwich. "Tell her I miss her."

"And Lucy. You know Lucy. She'd follow you to the moon."

Nikos's smile widened. "Lucy, too."

When Anita left Mari looked at him speculatively. "So many women, so little time?"

Now his grin flashed her way. "Something like that."

Mari couldn't believe the stab of annoyance she felt. Was this possessiveness? Jealousy?

Surely not.

She didn't even know the man! She certainly had no claim on him. Just because she'd kissed him, been kissed *by* him—

She tried to shove the feeling away. Tried to remind herself how inappropriate it was—how inappropriate *he* was!

Just because she'd reacted to him sexually, she had no right to be jealous of his interest in other women.

He certainly wouldn't be interested in her!

And if the memory of that folder Stavros had pressed on her, and Anita's passing references to other women didn't convince her, ten minutes later the aforementioned Lucy showed up in person.

Of course Mari didn't know it was Lucy when a woman in her very early twenties, a dark-haired vivacious beauty, shouted, "Nicky!" when she spied him on the patio and practically leaped the railing to get to him.

"Hey, Lucy! How's it going?" He didn't rise, just held out a hand to her.

She swooped down, kissing him on the mouth, then stepped back and said,

"Oh, Nicky, darling! Your poor face. And your leg! Are you all right?"

He gave the same dismissive answer to her that he had given the waitress. And Mari had to give him grudging credit for not taking advantage of all the sympathy he could have elicited from them. "No big deal. I'm fine," he assured Lucy when she continued to gush and fret.

"But—"

"Don't worry about me," he told her firmly.

"I can't help it." Lucy's lower lip went out. "You matter to me." The look she gave him was equal parts possessiveness and adoration. The one she gave Mari was meant in no uncertain terms to tell her that Nikos was taken.

"Who's she?" Lucy asked Nikos, jerking her head in Mari's direction.

"A friend," Nikos said.

Mari noticed that he didn't add *of my father's* this time. Was he using her as a buffer, then? Interesting thought.

"Mari Lewis," he said, introducing them. "Lucy Ferrante."

"Hello," Mari said genially, holding out a hand.

Lucy nodded. "Hi." Then she turned right back to Nikos. "Why didn't you call me? I'd have come to visit you."

"They wouldn't let me have visitors at the hospital."

"After then?"

"I'm staying at my father's."

"I would have come there."

Nikos didn't reply to that. He changed the subject, asked Lucy about her brothers, what each one was doing this summer, then about her parents. Lucy answered, but at every pass she tried to turn the conversation back to coming to visit Nikos.

He didn't take her up on it, but he didn't rebuff her either. He was a master when it came to dealing with women, Mari decided.

By the time Lucy left ten minutes later, prompted by the honking of a horn that belonged, she said, to her brother's Jeep, she was convinced that it was her idea not to come and see Nikos.

"It would wear you out, I know," she said, patting his arm. "You'll tell me when you're feeling well enough?"

"Of course."

"See you soon?" A hand lingered on his shoulder.

Nikos slanted a grin up at her. "Very soon," he promised.

"Nice to have met you," Mari said, though she was quite sure Lucy didn't even remember she was there.

"Oh. Yeah. You, too," Lucy said. "Take good care of yourself, Nicky." She ruffled Nikos's hair and, after another impatient beep, took off on a run.

"Nicky?"

A corner of Nikos's mouth tipped up. "We go back a long way."

"You must have changed her diapers then," Mari said tartly.

"Jealous?"

She felt her face flame and she scowled at him. "Hardly."

He grinned knowingly, but he didn't comment, and

Mari was oddly relieved when he kept his gaze on Lucy and said, "She's a good kid."

"I'm sure she wouldn't appreciate hearing you say so. She wants to 'matter.'"

He shrugged. "She does matter."

"Not the way she'd like to."

He settled back in his chair and looked at her. "Should I tell her to get lost, then?"

"I didn't mean that," Mari said quickly. "Actually," she admitted after a moment, "I think you handled it very well."

"What's this? The Mari Lewis Seal of Approval? I've finally done something right?"

"I'm sure you do a lot right," Mari said. "I'm sure you aren't all those things the papers—" She broke off, embarrassed.

"You've been doing a little research, have you?" Nikos asked. "Did you do it on your own or did the old man provide the reading material?"

Mari hesitated. "Your father gave me them," she said finally. "I haven't read them."

"Go ahead," he said gruffly. "Read your fill."

"I don't want to."

He stared at her, his dark eyes hard and angry and disbelieving. Then he shoved his chair back, got awkwardly to his feet and tossed some bills on the table. "Let's go."

Silently Mari followed him, wondering what she should have done, what she should have said.

He was standing by the car, waiting for her because she had the keys. She moved to unlock the door and he didn't step back. Instead he caught her arm and drew her hard against him.

Her eyes jerked open wide as their bodies came in contact. "Nikos!"

"You want this," he told her. "You've been asking for it!"

And he lowered his mouth to hers.

So much for control.

What on earth had she been thinking? How could she have for one minute allowed herself to believe that she could manage what happened when Nikos Costanides touched his lips to hers?

She couldn't. It was as plain and simple as that.

One touch, one taste, and all the good sense and best intentions in the world went right out of her head. She was putty in his hands.

And if she hadn't had one flickering instant's memory of Anita, of Lucy, of Lola, of the lilting Claudia and heaven knew how many other women, there was no telling what a fool she might have made of herself.

They'd driven back to the cottage in silence. She put the car in the garage and handed him back the keys without a word. She didn't look him in the eye. She couldn't.

She would see mockery. Amusement. A playboy's knowing leer.

She hurried back to the house and shut herself in her bedroom.

How was she going to survive this? Nanny to a thirty-two-year-old ladies' man? *Oh, Mari, you fool!*

The first thing she saw was the folder Stavros had given her.

She shouldn't read it. She shouldn't look at anything that might color her view of his older son. It wasn't professional.

And kissing him was?

She glanced sideways at the folder, then curled her fingers into a fist.

The phone rang. She picked it up.

But so had Nikos. It was Claudia again. "Didn't get you up this time, did I?" she said on a voice soft with laughter.

Mari hung up and reached for the folder. The articles all told her what she knew already: that Nikos Costanides was a shallow, irresponsible playboy.

It was the one thing upon which nine out of ten gossip columnists agreed...

CHAPTER FIVE

MARI had never read a lot of tabloid journalism, but she had the notion that very little of it ought to be believed. Still, if even a tenth of what she read was credible, Nikos Costanides was one of the world's sexiest men—with an insatiable appetite for the world's sexiest women.

There didn't seem to be a single actress, model or female recording artist under the age of forty that he hadn't had a fling with. And if those were the ones worthy of being written about, how many hundreds had he bedded who were not?

Heavens.

She read until far into the night. And finally she shoved the folder onto the table unfinished. There was, perhaps, too much punishment here even for her.

She switched off the light and rolled onto her side and told herself not to think about it—about *him*.

Of course she thought about it. She went to sleep and *dreamed* about it. She must have awakened half a dozen times from dreams—or nightmares—in which Nikos kissed, caressed or otherwise touched some of the world's most gorgeous women.

She woke up cranky and out of sorts. Who could blame her? She'd never had dreams like these when she'd been anyone else's nanny!

She tried telling herself that the articles were meaningless—pure hype designed to sell the newspapers or magazines that ran them.

But even if she managed some of the time, Nikos seemed determined to prove that they were true.

Certainly over the next few days he seemed to take great pleasure in flaunting risqué, not-so-*sotto-voce* conversations with a variety of women on the telephone.

There was, of course, the ubiquitous Claudia, still calling at all hours of the day and night. But there were others besides Claudia. In fact, every time Mari came into the living room he was talking or listening to someone of the female persuasion.

Sometimes he was jotting notes on paper and Mari thought he was actually talking business—though she couldn't imagine what because according to the articles he was an unemployed member of the idle rich. But just when she had that notion, he said something like, "Aw, sweetheart, I love it when you say things like that," or, "Oh, pussycat..."

The blatantly seductive tone of his voice set her teeth right on edge. It was as if he was flaunting them in front of her.

Well, fine. Let him.

It wasn't as if she was really interested in him. Not at all. As far as she was concerned, he was just a piece of evidence—living proof, as it were, that she was capable of passion.

He didn't seem capable of anything beyond seductive phone conversations and interminable computer games. Every time he disappeared into his room, talking to Claudia or one of the other women in his life, he seemed to end up sitting on his bed with the laptop, scowling in concentration.

"What a productive existence," Mari jibed, when she brought him lunch one afternoon.

"Huh?" He looked at her, distracted, then rubbed his

eyes, and gave her a bleary ironic smile. "A man's gotta do what a man's gotta do."

And a woman—*this woman*—had merely to survive. She could do that, she assured herself. He was giving her *no* reason to look twice at him. And once he had gone, and she was free of the Costanides men, she could set to work finding the right man to focus her newly discovered passion on.

In the meantime, though, because it was what she was here for, she felt obliged to try to create some sort of rapport between Nikos and his father.

"Talk to him," she urged him. "Listen to him."

But Nikos didn't want to talk, and he didn't want to listen—to her or his father. He turned his back, shrugged her off, ignored her words.

"I'm not interested," he said.

"You are," she argued. She'd seen the look on his face whenever he looked up toward the main house and, especially, when he caught glimpses of Stavros out by the pool with his wife and little boy.

Nikos might think he didn't care, but it was as plain as day that he cared a great deal.

But, "Leave me alone," he said whenever she brought it up.

"I have a headache," he said, almost as often. And, rubbing his temple, he retreated to his room.

Mari thought the headaches might go away if Claudia's interminable middle-of-the-night phone calls went away.

"Doesn't that woman ever sleep?" she groused after four days of being awakened at three o'clock in the morning.

Bleary-eyed and clearly in pain, Nikos shrugged.

"She needs me," he said. And he didn't seem to mind. In fact, sometimes Mari heard him calling her!

But this time when the phone rang again, it was someone Nikos called Briana, with a seductive teasing tone that reminded Mari again what a two-timing bastard he was. She gnashed her teeth as, cradling the receiver against his ear, Nikos disappeared into the bedroom.

She should have been glad. After all, she reminded herself, there was no way she could entertain the notion that he was worthy of her interest when he was totally consumed with half the other women on the planet. He must have a little black book the size of the Manhattan phone directory.

"Do you ever date the same woman twice?" she asked him the next night. She didn't want to pretend interest, but the question was out before she could stop it.

He leaned back in his chair and smiled one of his blatantly sexy smiles, though his eyes were still bloodshot from being up most of the night again, and his continual rubbing of his eyes and his temples indicated another headache. "If they're worth it," he said with that easy, teasing smile of his. She could almost hear the smoulder in his voice.

"Is that your way of finding the perfect woman to settle down with?" She knew her tone was sharp, but she couldn't seem to stop that either.

"I'm not settling down. Ever." The seductiveness was gone. Now his tone was just as sharp as hers.

Surprise, surprise. "Too many women in the world to limit yourself to just one?"

"Exactly." He bit the end of the word off, then shoved himself out of his chair. "And I have to go call one now." He started to hobble toward his bedroom.

"It's a little early for Claudia, isn't it?" she asked his back.

"This is Briana," he said without turning. Then, mockingly, he added, "Are you keeping score?"

When the phone rang at a little past three, Mari ignored it. She knew who it was. She had no desire to hear the lovely Claudia again this morning. She rolled over, punched her pillow and said silently to Nikos, *I hope you have the damnedest big headache in the world.*

When it rang again, she said, *Take your time, why don't you?*

And when it shrilled yet again, she yanked the pillow over her head and thought dire thoughts about him and the insomniac Claudia.

Finally, after five rings, it stopped. *About time,* Mari thought. She settled on the pillow again, banishing all thoughts of Nikos bare-legged and bare-chested, having sleepy nocturnal conversations with other women.

There was a tap on her door.

Disoriented, she rolled over, thinking she'd imagined it. Then it came again. "Mari?"

The door opened. Nikos poked his head in. "Do me a favor." His voice sounded rough and edged with pain.

Mari scrambled out of bed and grabbed her robe and pulled it on in the darkness. "Are you all right?"

"Yeah. Just a headache."

"Another one," she growled.

"I'll be fine. But I need to read some figures and I can't seem to focus."

"Figures?" What? They did math problems in the middle of the night? Whatever happened to verbal lovemaking? Or, for that matter, counting sheep?

"Will you help or not?" He was impatient now.

"Lead on." Shaking her head, she wrapped the robe around her and knotted the tie as she followed him out the door.

He was heading back toward his bedroom as fast as his crutches could take him. By the time she got there, she could just make out his form on his bed. He was lying flat on his back, an arm over his eyes. Beside him lay the phone and the laptop computer.

Nikos kept his arm across his eyes, but gestured toward the computer with his other hand. "Read the figures on that screen into the phone."

Into the phone? Claudia wanted *Mari* to read her a bunch of numbers? What were they doing, comparing Jezzball scores?

"Just sit down, for God's sake," Nikos muttered, and reached out for her hand, pulling her down onto the bed.

Mari sat, but she edged away from him, then fiddled with the angle of the screen, trying to see what numbers he was talking about. There appeared to be a whole row, none of which made any sense to her.

"Hello?" she said tentatively into the phone.

"Hello." A very masculine, albeit British voice startled her in reply. "Brian Jenkin here. I gather Nikos is under the weather at the moment. Don't blame him, he's been working flat out. So if you could just read me the specifications, please?"

Working flat out? Nikos?

She shot Nikos a curious hard stare, but he still had his hand over his eyes. And Brian Jenkin—*Briana?* she wondered. No, it couldn't be! But still—

"Er, yes." Mari fumbled once more with the screen, then slowly, haltingly read down the list of numbers. *M* equaled some number or other. Other letters equaling other amounts. The word *volume* cropped up a lot. It made no sense to her, but, it seemed to satisfy Brian Jenkin.

"Sounds great. Tell him I'll talk to Carruthers and see if this will fly. Or sail, I suppose I should say," Brian said jovially. "Does he want to talk to Carruthers himself?"

Mari relayed the question to Nikos.

"No."

Brian said, "I heard him. That's it, then. Tell him I'll ring back as soon as I've had a word with Carruthers. Thanks a lot." He hung up the phone.

Mari sat with the receiver in her hand, feeling somewhat at sea herself. She looked at the computer screen, at Nikos. She remembered the myriad phone calls, the middle-of-the-night conversations, the soft, seductive, suddenly highly suspicious *"Ah, Briana"*'s breathed into the phone. Her teeth clamped together. A muscle in her temple ticked.

She took a careful measured breath. "He says he'll call you as soon as he's talked to Carruthers."

Nikos grunted. "Thanks."

"How long has this been going on?"

He ran his tongue over his top lip. "Started a few hours ago." His voice was barely more than a whisper.

"I don't mean the headache," Mari said sharply.

He winced. But he didn't answer.

"Briana?" she said sweetly.

The wince became a grimace. Still he didn't talk.

"Who's Claudia?"

He let out a weary exhalation of air. "My secretary."

"Not the one who keeps your little black book straight." Somehow she was sure of that.

"No."

"Who's Brian?" Mari said.

"A friend."

"And business partner," Mari prompted him.

Nikos sighed. "That, too."

"So this playboy thing is an act." It wasn't even a question.

He moved his arm and opened his eyes. "It's not an act," he protested.

"No, I suppose some of it wasn't." She would allow him that much. "You couldn't have possibly conned the world's freest press into reporting a hundred sightings of you and the world's most gorgeous women if there was no kernel of truth. But there's more to you than Nick the Hunk, isn't there?"

"I never said there wasn't."

"You did your damnedest to give that impression."

"It's none of your business what I do."

"Nor your father's?"

"Especially not his!" Nikos propped himself up on his elbows and glared at her. "He never gave a damn about me. He only wants me to do what he tells me to do!"

"And what do you really do?"

There was a pause. "Design boats. And ships."

Mari's eyes grew as big as dinner plates. "*That's* what I was reading to Brian?"

"You were reading conversions for some tankage we had to adjust. Brian is the on-site coordinator. In Cornwall. That's where we're based."

"The three a.m. phone calls?"

Nikos grimaced. "It's eight in Cornwall. He works on his time—and when he needs me, I do, too."

"This is a...big business?"

"Yes." And somehow that wasn't a surprise, either.

"Have you been doing it long?"

"Why? Do you want references? Want me to design you a ship?" he snapped. "I'm out of your price range."

"Undoubtedly. But I'm still curious. Why would you bother to keep a perfectly respectable career hidden?"

His jaw tightened. "Because I choose to."

"You want to be thought of as a playboy."

"I never said I was a playboy."

"But—"

"And you're not telling the old man about this."

"But he'd— "

"*No!*" His fingers tightened so hard around her wrist that she thought he would cut off the circulation. Experimentally she wiggled her fingers. It seemed to make him aware of the pressure he was exerting. He dropped her hand. "Sorry. But I don't want you to tell him." Dark, pain-filled eyes bored into hers.

Mari nodded slowly. "I won't."

He sank back and shut his eyes again. His chest heaved slightly, then he breathed more easily.

"You're a naval architect?" Mari asked after a moment. "How did that happen?" It wasn't something a person just fell into.

"I always messed about in boats. Goes with the genes, I suppose." His mouth twisted bitterly. "Costanides men have been involved with boats in one way or another as long as anyone can remember. I had a boat when I was a kid. Sailing was my...salvation." His face relaxed a little in reflection. "I liked drawing them, designing them, too—as well as sailing them." He shrugged. "Nobody tried to tell me how to do that."

"Nobody like Stavros?"

"He was very big at trying to tell me what to do. Wanted me to do things his way. Work in his business. Study what he told me to."

And he wouldn't have gone along with any of it, she could see that. A boy like Nikos, whose father had left him, would never respect that father enough to do what he wanted.

"'Go to Greece,' he said. 'Or go to Harvard,'" Nikos went on. "'Learn the old family way. Learn the new Harvard Business School way.' I wasn't interested. I didn't want Greece or Harvard. I went to Glasgow."

"Scotland?"

"They taught what I wanted to learn."

"Naval architecture."

"Yes. But he didn't know that. He never asked. He just said that if I didn't do what he wanted, he wouldn't foot the bills. I could waste my life as far as he was concerned." He opened his eyes and looked at her again. "So as far as he is concerned, I have."

And Mari knew that was the whole reason for Nikos's playboy façade right there.

If Stavros didn't care enough to find out who his son really was, if he only thought of Nikos as an extension of him, Nikos would solve the problem his own way. A typically in-your-face Costanides way. *Let the old man think I'm wasting my life. Let him fret. Let him stew. He doesn't want me, I don't want him.*

"And that was that?"

"Not quite. He demanded that I come work for him in the summer—to learn the business, not because he wanted me around. I went, even though I didn't want to, because my mother asked me to. 'You'll get to know each other better,' she told me." Nikos gave a bitter laugh. "I never saw him. He put me in some damned smelly warehouse in Athens one year, and the next he stuck me in an airless office building in the Bronx where I spent eight hours a day filling out forms. The next year

I had a chance to work on a design project. I wanted to do that. He threw some nonsense at me about only wanting to play, never wanting to work." His fists clenched around the sheet and he had to consciously loosen his fingers.

"And that's when you decided to let him think what he wanted."

"He already thought what he wanted. He always has." He shut his eyes and sighed. "So now you know."

Mari sat quietly, studying the complex man lying just inches from her. She saw the sexy playboy, the intense designer, the hurt child. They were all there, tangled up inside one tough, hard-edged man.

She sighed softly, too. "Now I know."

He'd blown his cover.

He remembered that the minute he opened his eyes and saw the computer back on the desk where it belonged and not in the bed where he seemed to have had it most of the time over the past few days.

He sighed and rubbed a hand over his eyes. They were what had finally betrayed him. All the hours squinting at the screen had done exactly what the doctor had told him they would do.

"Strain and stress will cause you headaches. Head injuries take time to heal," he'd said the last time Nikos went in, complaining. "Give it a rest."

But he couldn't give it a rest when work needed to be done.

Finally, though, he couldn't even focus on the work he'd done. When Brian had called, needing the answers, he'd needed them right then. There was no time for Nikos to say he'd call back in a few hours when the lines sorted themselves out and the numbers made sense again.

So he'd had to get Mari to read them. And of course Mari knew she wasn't reading the scores of some computer game.

Now what?

He didn't know. He dared hope she wouldn't tell his father, though he supposed it wouldn't matter much if she did. The pleasure he'd got out of convincing the old man that his oldest son was a worthless, lazy ladies' man had waned some time ago.

Now keeping up the façade was just a matter of principle.

The phone rang, and he noticed that it was out of reach as well. He sighed and started to haul himself up to get it, but it stopped ringing almost at once. If he was very quiet, he could hear Mari talking in the living room.

To Stavros?

Maybe. He didn't care.

To her aunts? Possibly. He wondered about them. Were they like her? She'd told him a few days ago that they raised her after her parents had died. That explained a lot of her more nunlike tendencies. He'd said that just to watch her blush, and he'd been gratified when she had.

"I had other influences in my life, too," she'd told him seriously. "My uncle Arthur was a dancing instructor. He had quite a way with the ladies. Though he was not," she'd added, "quite as proficient as you."

He wondered what she thought about his proficiency now.

She knew who Claudia was. She knew that all those phone calls from "Briana" were really Brian with business problems. There had been women who had called him over the past few days. Lucy had called. So had her sister, Lola. But not as many as he'd made it seem. He'd played it up, teased them, made sure Mari had heard.

So she'd think what his father thought. So she'd cross him off as a hopeless womanizer.

And now?

Now there was a light tap and door opened a crack. Mari peeked in. "Oh, you are awake. Good. Brian's on the phone. He wants you to know that Carruthers is pleased." There was a hint of a smile on her face. "For the moment," she added with an almost impish grin.

Seeing it, Nikos permitted a hint of a smile to touch his lips. Something in him seemed to loosen, to lighten. Not only because he'd satisfied Carruthers, though that was certainly worth celebrating.

Mari knew. He'd thought he would be sorry.

Instead he was relieved.

She was out of her depth, out of her league, over her head.

It would have been better by far if he'd been the womanizing playboy he'd pretended to be.

It had made sense to fight her attraction to a man who had a woman in every port. It hadn't been easy to resist Nikos Costanides's charm when she'd been sure he laid it on so freely, but it had been easier than it was now.

He *did* lay it on freely, she reminded herself. Even naval architects with clients and demands and a secretary named Claudia could be charming! *Remember Nita, and Lucy, and all those women in the magazines and newspaper?*

But that wasn't the *real* Nikos. Or certainly not the *whole* Nikos. That was the public Nikos—the one he had created to irritate his father.

That was the Nikos who had kissed her the first day when she'd knocked on his door. She understood that. And she could resist him. She had been resisting him since she'd been here.

The question was, which Nikos had kissed her beside the car the day they'd gone to Montauk?

There hadn't been any photographers there then. There hadn't been any journalists. Not even any interested witnesses. It had happened just between the two of them.

She and...*which Nikos?*

She tried to tell herself it didn't really matter. *Whichever* Nikos it was, she couldn't handle him. Didn't *want* to handle him. It was her passion she needed to develop and control—not the man who'd inspired it. Passion was a transferrable commodity.

At least she told herself that. And hoped.

She should have run.

She didn't have the chance.

She took the call from Brian and received his misplaced congratulations—as if *she'd* had anything to do with their success beyond reading the numbers on the screen. Then she went to see if Nikos could talk to him.

He had fallen asleep soon after they'd hung up the phone after talking to Brian in the middle of the night. She'd got some pain medication down him, then wordlessly rubbed his temples and the back of his neck, trying to ease what strain she could.

She hadn't known if it would help, but when she'd quit before he fell asleep, he'd muttered, "Don't stop," and so she'd started again.

When at last he had gone to sleep, she'd slipped out of the room to her own. But not before she'd stood and looked at him, traced his features, softened only slightly by sleep, and remembered the feel of his lips on hers.

The feel—the passion—she would do her damnedest to transfer to another man. A safer man.

The memory of Nikos—well, she just wanted that for herself.

Now she waited until he finished talking to Brian, then she said, "I'll turn in my notice."

He frowned. "What? Why?"

"You obviously don't need 'shaping up.' And I..." She didn't think there was any way she could tell him the rest.

In any case, he didn't give her the chance. He said, "No."

"What do you mean, no? That's what you've wanted all along! To get rid of me, to turn your back on your father—"

"I still don't give a damn about my father," he said. "But I don't want you to go."

Her foolish heart leapt for just a moment. Then she steeled herself against any such feelings. "Why?"

"Because I could use your help for one thing. Brian and I have been working on designs for a shipper. It's a big contract. Not just in terms of money, but in terms of reputation. For the company, not me. I'm a pretty silent partner. Brian deals with the customers, does the on-site stuff, and I stay at home, take the specs he gives me and work on the actual design. Some people are easier to please than others. Some people let you do it your way as long as you give them what they want. The guy we're working with now has a mind of his own. And he changes it frequently as you've seen," Nikos added grimly. "I've been trying to accommodate all his suggestions and all the things he says he needs. And every time I get them figured out, they change again. That's why all the phone calls. We've got other customers, too, though. Other designs that need to be worked on. And I don't have time to field all Brian's calls and read him stuff when I should be working on other projects. *Anyone* can read him the stuff I've come up with."

"Me," Mari translated, trying not to feel deflated. After all, she didn't *want* him to want her, did she?

Nikos nodded. "Yes. Can you type?"

"Of course."

"Even better."

"But—" Mari shook her head. "I work for your father."

"So go right ahead. Look." Nikos leaned forward earnestly. "He tricked you into this, right? I don't know what he did to make you stay, but he must have done something so that you couldn't—or wouldn't—walk the minute you realized you weren't dealing with a four-year-old. Right again?" He waited for her reluctant nod. "So, fine. You stay, you're fulfilling your obligation to him."

"I'm not teach—"

"Not teaching me respect?" His gaze narrowed. "I have a lot of respect for people who earn it, Mari Lewis."

Yes, she supposed he did.

"It wouldn't be honest."

"There's nothing to stop you *trying* to teach me to respect him," Nikos pointed out, though his smile told her it was damned unlikely that her efforts would bear fruit. "I'll pay you."

"I'm already being paid. I can't take your money."

"Give the old man his back when we're done."

"And when would that be?"

"When I get my cast off I'm leaving. I told you that. I'll go to Cornwall where Brian is. That's where we build—in a shipyard in Falmouth. Then Brian will be able to get at me in a zone where it's daytime for both of us."

"A few days, in other words?" Was she terrible to be considering it? Did she have any real choice?

Nikos dipped his dark head. "As you say. A few days."

"And you won't...you won't..." Instinctively and unintentionally she pressed her hand against her mouth again. She could remember the touch of his mouth as if it had just been there.

"Kiss you?" Nikos finished for her. "Only if you want me to." A hint of the wickedest grin in the world touched his mouth. Then, quite suddenly, it faded and the look on his face became serious. "*Do* you want me to?"

She shook her head vehemently, then abruptly she stopped at the realization that there was one part of her that *did* want him doing it again.

Honesty, she always told the children she cared for, was the best policy. For the first time she really doubted that. But the habit was deeply ingrained. "I liked it when you kissed me," she admitted, not looking at him. "And I liked kissing you, but—"

"But kissing for you has to do with love and marriage and commitment?" He said the words almost harshly.

Mari nodded. She slanted a glance in his direction. The look on his face was unreadable. His dark eyes were hooded. One of his fists was white-knuckled as he gripped a handful of the sheet.

"It doesn't mean that for me," he told her.

"It could—" Oh, heavens! What was she saying?

He shook his head. "No. I won't let it. I don't want it!"

And she did.

A corner of Nikos's mouth lifted in rueful acknowledgement of their quandary. Then he pressed his lips together. "I have, despite what the tabloids might say, a certain amount of self-control. And I really could use your help until I get this cast off. If you change your mind," he added hopefully, "you feel free to tell me. But if that's the way you want it, Mari Lewis, I won't be kissing you again."

CHAPTER SIX

So she stayed.

And if her conscience bothered her whenever Stavros rang up to demand a report, she took solace in the fact that she could tell him quite honestly that she and Nikos were getting along, that he was talking to her, that they seemed to be on the same wavelength.

This last might have been stretching it a bit. But over the next three days she really did find herself getting attuned to Nikos's work habits and thought patterns.

Maybe it was an instinctive rapport that grew up between them because she had grown up sailing boats, too. She didn't know the first thing about tankage and impact resistance, and some kind of density or other that seemed to be giving him headaches figuratively as well as literally, but these were *boats* he was talking about, figuring about, worrying about—even in the abstract—and as such she was interested.

Or maybe she was just interested in him.

She discounted that, of course. She didn't want to think about the chemistry that existed between herself and Nikos Costanides! If he could put it aside for the best interests of his business, so could *she!*

That's what she told herself. For the most part, that's what she did.

But the awareness was still there.

Sometimes, to get away from it, she would leave him working and go up to the pool and swim or play with Alexander and talk to Julietta, who was seven months into a difficult pregnancy and was happy to have someone else to talk to and to chase Alexander around.

She did her best to avoid Stavros. For all his obtuseness when it came to dealing with his son, he was surprisingly astute in other ways. She thought he might well manage to worm some hint of Nikos's occupation out of her. Especially because she would have really liked to tell him.

"I don't see why you won't tell him," she said to Nikos more than once. "It would make all the difference."

"Yes," Nikos agreed drily, "it would."

Which, she understood from the silence that followed, was exactly why he wasn't. It was a matter of pride. And if Stavros was a proud, stubborn man, Nikos had more pride than anyone she knew.

So Mari didn't say a word. Even though she was working for Stavros, her allegiance was to his son. It would have been that way even if Nikos were really four years old. Though the parent footed the bills, a nanny's first commitment was to the child.

Even if the child was thirty-two!

They worked well together. That was the good news. The bad news, as far as Mari was concerned, was that, now that he felt no need to hide his career from her, she liked him even more.

She saw the serious, dedicated side of Nikos Costanides that he kept well hidden from his father and the rest of the world. She saw the way he tackled the problems Brian called with and spent hours, literally, working them out, trying first one thing and then another. He was dedicated, tenacious, determined.

Everything she admired in a man.

Except that he wanted nothing to do with commitment. And therefore, realistically, he wanted nothing to do with her.

That didn't stop him looking at her, though. It didn't stop the leisurely wander of his gaze when they were working together. It didn't stop him licking his lips sometimes or sighing and shaking his head.

She knew what he was thinking!

If the truth was known, she was thinking it, too!

But she had to resist. Getting involved with Nikos Costanides would be a one-way trip to misery. He didn't want what she wanted. He wanted to make love, not really love.

And so sometimes, when the wanting got too obvious and her own good intentions got particularly feeble, she took herself off to the pool.

The breeze off the ocean kept things cool most of the day, and the water kept Alexander occupied when he didn't have a friend over to play.

Mari thought Julietta could have used some help at this point in her pregnancy. But Julietta was as stubborn as the rest of the Costanides family. "Angelika raised Nikos by herself," she'd told Mari early in their acquaintance. "Stavros thought it was a good thing."

Mari was surprised that Julietta, and Stavros for that matter, measured the way to raise a child by the way Nikos had been raised, but she had merely nodded and smiled. "Well, if you ever need a little rest, give me a call," she'd said. "I'm sure Nikos won't mind sparing me for a while."

Exactly what Stavros had told his wife about her living with Nikos, Mari was never sure. And Julietta never said. She seemed to take it for granted that Mari was there to help Nikos. That she'd been a nanny seemed beside the point, and Mari had never spelled it out for her.

This afternoon Julietta was resting on a chaise longue and Alexander was playing alone in the shallow end of the pool when Mari walked up to join them.

"Is Nikos taking another nap?" Julietta asked when Mari got close enough to talk.

"He doesn't need me right now." Mari didn't want to lie and she wasn't about to say that Nikos was on the phone arguing with Brian. The variable Mr. Carruthers had handed down some more modifications this morning, after Nikos had worked most of yesterday trying to accommodate the last set.

This time when Brian called, he had blown sky-high.

Mari did her best to soothe him, but he wasn't in the mood for soothing. "There's only one thing that would soothe me," he told her sharply—and the way his gaze drifted down her body, she didn't have to ask what it was.

"You said you wouldn't even kiss—" she began.

"I know what I said," Nikos retorted between clenched teeth. "So if you don't want me going back on my word, get out of here now and leave me to this."

Mari left.

"I'm soooo bored," Julietta said now. "I feel like a beached whale or a pregnant hippo." She rubbed her distended abdomen and sighed.

"Maybe it would be good for you to go in the pool. The water could help you support the baby."

"Maybe," Julietta agreed. "But I can't as long as it's just me here with Alex. He tries to be careful, but he forgets he can't leap on me these days."

"I'll go in with you."

Julietta's eyes lit up with gratitude. "Oh, would you

mind? That would be wonderful." She eased her ungainly body to a sitting position and, with Mari's help, hauled herself to her feet. "I'm so swollen," she said, craning her neck to look down in an effort to see her feet and ankles. "Much more this time than with Alex."

"Every baby's different, they say." Mari took her arm so Julietta wouldn't slip on the wet tiles.

"Well, I'll be glad to get this one out of me and on its way." Julietta made a face. "Alex, at least, was a winter baby." She smiled at her dark-haired son, who was jumping up and down in the water in eagerness as he watched her come down the steps into the pool.

"Are you comin' swimming with me, Mommy?" Alex was bouncing on his toes.

"How about if Mommy swims on her own and you swim alongside with me," Mari suggested.

Alex looked at her warily. He wasn't exactly shy with other people, but he was definitely reserved, as if he was going to do some serious study before he made up his mind about anyone. A lot like his brother, Mari thought.

She'd told Nikos yesterday at dinner how much his half-brother was like him.

"Don't tell the old man that," Nikos had said promptly. Then his face had split in a grin. "On second thought, do. It'll drive him nuts."

In fact, Mari didn't know how Stavros would react to the idea. She knew he was deeply devoted to his little son. She suspected he was equally devoted to the older one—but had no idea how to show it. He couldn't play catch with Nikos or throw him up in the air or give him rides on his shoulders in the pool.

Had he ever done any of those things with Nikos? she wondered. But one look at Nikos's hard closed expression, and she had known better than to ask.

"What do you say?" she asked Alex now. "Shall we swim alongside your mom?"

He chewed on his fingernail. "Mmm. Yeah, I guess. Or we could race her!"

Mari slipped down into the water. "Come here, then."

She felt Alex's small eager hands grip her shoulders, and she put her hands behind her, giving him a boost so that he could wrap his legs around her torso and his arms across her neck. "Okay. Here we go. Watch out, Mom." She grinned at Julietta, by this time submerged till only her head and shoulders were out of the water. "Better get going or we'll catch you."

"Oh, you will, will you?" Julietta began a lazy breaststroke toward the far end of the pool. Mari started after her.

At first Alex was content just to ride. But as his mother got further ahead, the Costanides competitive spirit won out.

"C'mon, Mari!" he yelled, kicking her like a pony. "Catch her!" He wriggled and bounced, digging his heels even harder into her sides as if that would make her go faster. It slowed her down and they began to fall behind.

"No!" he wailed in dismay. "We're gonna *lose!*"

Then Julietta, bless her, slowed a little, and Mari and Alex surged past.

"We won! Mari an' me won!" Alex crowed.

"Oh, good for you!" Julietta beamed at her son. "Thank you," she mouthed to Mari.

"My pleasure," Mari mouthed back. Then she said, "Come on, Alex. Let's swim back to the other end and you can show me how well you swim on your own."

Alex went with her eagerly, not kicking this time. "You're living with Nikos."

"I'm helping him," Mari corrected him, but she supposed from the boy's point of view, he was right, too.

"He's my brother."

"I know."

Alex made swishy fish movements with his hands. "He doesn't like me."

Mari looked at him, startled. "He doesn't? How do you know that."

Alex lifted narrow shoulders. "He doesn't talk to me. He just walks away. An' he never smiles."

"I think he has important things on his mind," Mari said.

"Maybe." But he didn't sound convinced. He sounded forlorn. Mari wondered if Nikos knew that Alex noticed—and cared.

She gave the boy's small hand a squeeze. "I think Nikos likes you, Alex. But he hasn't had a lot of experience with little boys."

"How come? He used to be one," Alex said.

Out of the mouths of babes. "Well, yes, but that was a long time ago. Sometimes when they grow up, big boys forget."

"Maybe it's 'cause he hit his head. Nikos had a accident, you know. He was hurt bad. My daddy said he might die."

"Your daddy told *you* that?"

Alex ducked his head. "I was listenin'. He said it to my mom."

"I think your daddy was really worried about Nikos right after the accident," Mari said carefully. "But he doesn't have to worry now, and neither do you. Nikos didn't die then, and he's not going to die now."

"You sure?" Alex's brown eyes, so like his brother's, searched hers.

Mari gave the little boy a hug. "I'm sure."

Julietta thanked her again profusely when she came out of the pool. "I know other mothers cope wonderfully well without any help at all," she said ruefully. "But I have been so tired these last couple of weeks. And now that Stavros is gone…"

"Stavros is gone?"

"He had to go to Athens," Julietta explained. "He'll be home next week."

By next week, Nikos would be out of his cast and gone. Mari wondered if Stavros realized that. She wondered what he'd say to her when he came back and found Nikos had left.

"He works so hard," Julietta said. "He ought to slow down. He had a heart attack two years ago, you know. I…hope you can convince Nikos to come back into the firm. It would be so much better."

For Stavros, Mari wanted to say.

And for Nikos?

She didn't know.

"Alex thinks you don't like him," she told Nikos that night.

He was lying on the bed with his eyes shut. He'd been working all afternoon with some CAD program that was going to save his business and ruin his head, he told Mari. She forced another dose of the pain medication down him. "Rest," she commanded.

"I can't. Not until I tell Carruthers what I think of him," he muttered.

"I'll do that for you. Lie down and dictate."

He flashed a grin at her. "To you, sweetheart? I'd be delighted."

Mari flushed. "You promised not to do that!"

"No. I promised not to kiss you. I didn't say I wouldn't flirt."

So to change the subject, she told him what Alex had said.

Nikos lifted one brow. "Don't like him? I never have anything to do with him."

"I think that's the whole point. He'd like to have something to do with you."

"Tell that to the old man. He makes damn good and sure Alex is never around when I am. Doesn't want me contaminating him."

"Oh, I doubt that."

But Nikos didn't, it was clear.

The next morning she went back to the big house to see if perhaps she could give Julietta a break and, incidentally, find out what Stavros's second wife thought.

Julietta was feeling a little better this morning, and she suggested they walk down to the beach. They did, and while Alex played in the sand Mari brought the subject up. "Nikos says Stavros won't permit Alex to come to the cottage."

Julietta pursed her lips. "I think 'won't permit' is a little strong."

"But he does discourage Alex from going down to see Nikos?"

Julietta scooped up a handful of sand and let it trickle through her fingers. "I think he's afraid that Nikos's resentment will hurt Alex."

"Nikos resents his father, not Alex."

"Yes. And I wouldn't blame him, I guess. Stavros wasn't the father to Nikos that he has been to Alex. He had to work so hard back then,'' she explained earnestly. "To make the business a success, to justify his marriage.''

Mari's brows drew together at this last. "What do you mean, to justify his marriage?"

"Angelika was the daughter of a very wealthy family, and she was supposed to marry someone else. She was *promised* by her father to someone else. But she loved Stavros, and her father finally gave in." Julietta sighed and shook her head. "I think Stavros always felt he *had* to be a success so he could prove he was worthy of her."

Mari digested that. She had assumed that the marriage was arranged. She hadn't assumed that Angelika had loved Stavros. Not at first anyway. Later—well, Nikos had agreed she'd loved him then.

When she went back to the cottage, she tried to ask Nikos about it. But he wouldn't discuss his father and mother in the same breath.

"Worthy of her?" He nearly spat. "He *wasn't* worthy of her!"

And that was that.

The phone rang then.

"Damn it! Doesn't Brian ever sleep?" Nikos muttered.

"I'll get it," Mari said. But it wasn't Brian at all. It was her aunt Em.

"We've missed you, dear. Are you coming this week? Are you bringing little Nikos?"

"It's my day off," Mari protested. And he wasn't *little* Nikos! Nor was she about to bring him!

"But we love to meet your little charges," Aunt Em said wistfully. "You know how lonely we get out here now that Bett doesn't drive anymore."

"Well, I—"

"We'd watch him," her aunt assured her. "You could have your rest."

"I don't need rest exactly, but—"

"His parents wouldn't approve?"

Mari hesitated. There was no way, of course, that she was taking Nikos out there. But maybe she could take Alex. It would be good for Julietta to have a little time to herself. And it would be equally good for her aunts. And she really didn't need a day off that badly.

"I'll see," she said. "But remember, his name is Alex, not Nikos."

When she hung up, Mari turned back to Nikos. "It was my aunt. Tomorrow's my day off," she explained, "and they'd like me to come. I thought maybe I could take Alex with me..."

A grin quirked his mouth. "Not me?"

Mari shook her head. "Definitely not you."

He managed to look crestfallen. Then he grinned. "Pity. I'd like to meet the women who raised you."

"And I *wouldn't* like them to meet you."

"You don't think I've behaved myself this week?"

"Of course you have. Sort of," she qualified. "But..."

"I think we've done very well." He grimaced. "And it hasn't been easy."

Mari's eyes widened. She felt a hint of color bloom on her cheeks. He was still interested, then? In spite of not wanting to be?

"Good thing I'm leaving," he said.

"What?" She felt her whole body tense. "When?"

"Tomorrow. I'm getting the cast off in the afternoon."

"Tomorrow?" He'd never said that! Had never even mentioned it!

"The nurse called this morning while you were at the beach. Said they had a cancellation. Wondered if I wanted it. I said yes. Twenty-four more hours and I'll be gone."

And not a moment too soon.

He'd had all he could do these past few days to keep his hands off Mari Lewis. It was all well and good to say he wasn't going to kiss her again, to tell her he was keeping his hands off unless she invited him to do otherwise, of course, to tell himself that he was doing the sane, sensible thing—hell, even *honorable*—by keeping their relationship on a completely professional footing.

It was something else again to get to sleep at night.

He didn't *want* to be sleeping at night. He wanted to be in bed with Mari Lewis doing what God intended men and women to do—and enjoying every minute of it.

Instead he was tossing and turning in his wide empty bed, alone, with visions of ship's tanks and Mari Lewis chasing each other through his brain. It had been like that every night since she'd been here. It was no wonder his damned head ached!

His head wasn't the only thing either.

And watching Mari Lewis nibble on a strand of her hair, watching her tip her head and lick her lips when she was tasting dinner, watching her sashay down the hall wearing that stupid robe that simply accentuated all her curves, was making it worse.

He needed relief. He needed out.

So this morning he'd called the doctor and asked for his earliest appointment. The sooner he was free of the cast, the sooner he would be free of a lot of things that ailed him.

Tomorrow, he promised himself.

Less than twenty-four hours and he would be in Cornwall, sorting out Brian, taking on Carruthers face-to-face, getting his life back.

Mostly he would be free of his father—and Mari Lewis.

Julietta was thrilled at Mari's suggestion that she take Alex to visit her aunts. "If you wouldn't mind," she added hesitantly. "I know you're supposed to be with Nikos."

"Nikos has a doctor's appointment," Mari said. "And he arranged for Thomas to take him." He'd informed her of that this morning.

"But I'd—" But she hadn't finished her sentence. If he didn't want her accompanying him, he didn't want her. And that was that. She wasn't going to beg.

Something in her expression must have said that because Nikos grimaced slightly. "It's better this way," he said.

"So we'll say goodbye now," Mari replied after a moment.

"Yes."

Their eyes met. He reached out a hand and took one of hers. It was a touch she'd longed for, but until his fingers wrapped hers, she hadn't realized just how much. She tried to fight the feeling, but it was useless.

"Bye," she said softly. She flicked a glance up at him, but couldn't hold it.

"Bye." But he didn't let her hand go. He squeezed it lightly, his fingers tightening over hers, linking them for just a moment. Then, "Mari?"

She blinked and managed to meet his gaze.

He tipped his head, a corner of his mouth lifted. "How about just one...for the road?"

She should have said no. *Of course she should have said no.*

She didn't. She couldn't. One for the road. One to remember him by. One kiss by the real Nikos Costanides.

She ran her tongue lightly over her lips and gave a quick almost jerky nod of her head. Then she lifted her face, offering her mouth. Bracing herself.

"It won't hurt," he whispered as he loosed her hand and brought his up to cup the back of her neck and hold her. Then he touched his lips to hers.

His kiss was warm, gentle. Tender. It wasn't at all like the first kiss he'd given her. It was everything like the second. It taught her as nothing else could exactly which Nikos Costanides had been kissing her that day. It made her feel alive, eager, hungry. It spoke of longing and desire and passion.

And she answered with longing and desire and passion of her own. She answered with her heart. And she heard a harsh aching sound come from somewhere deep inside him.

Then he stepped back, breathing heavily, raggedly, and just looked at her.

Mari looked back.

Then he said roughly, "Go on."

And she went. But she went knowing he was wrong. He'd said it wouldn't hurt.

It did.

Taking Alex to visit her aunts was the best thing she could have done.

He was all eyes and ears. Bouncing. Talkative. Eager.

She had once thought there was nothing as distracting as a four-year-old when it came to keeping you from thinking about anything else but him.

That was the case with Alex. And a good thing, too.

If she hadn't had Alex to deal with, she'd have thought too much about Nikos. As it was, she had no time.

"Look! A sailboat!" He pointed one out on the horizon. "Do your aunts got a sailboat?"

"A small one."

Alex looked at her with shining eyes. "Can we go sailing? Please, Mari! Please?"

At the sight of his eager face, she understood all too well how some parents got sucked into promising more than they could deliver. "We'll see."

Aunt Em and Aunt Bett wouldn't be up to going sailing. But maybe she could make time, after she'd paid the bills and finished talking to the bank manager. She'd always loved to sail. Uncle Arthur used to call it "her passion." Once upon a time she'd thought that sailing was all she had a passion for. Before Nikos.

Everything she did that day seemed to come back to Nikos.

She was almost grateful for the bills to pay, and the nagging credit manager to placate, and the books to go over. Except the rows of figures reminded her of Nikos. And the little boy following her aunts around and chattering reminded her of Nikos. And the sight of the sea reminded her of Nikos. And—

There was no end to her thoughts of Nikos.

It was almost a relief to finish the bills and have Alex come into the dining room with a plate of the cookies he and the aunts had made, begging her, "Can we go sailing now?"

"Yes," Mari said. "Let's." She could use the exercise. Perhaps it would *exorcise* the man in her mind. At least she and Nikos had never gone sailing.

"Nikos has a sailboat," Alex told her as he skipped alongside her down to the dock. "He's a *good* sailor. My daddy says so. They used to go sailing when Nikos was little."

That was interesting. He'd never mentioned sailing with his father at all. "Do you sail with your daddy?"

Alex shook his head. "Nope. He only goed with Nikos. But maybe if I knew something, he'd take me," he added, brightening just a bit.

So Mari taught him how to cast off, how to put up the sail. She took him out on the water and, catching a cross wind, pointed the boat toward the house, then put Alex's hand on the tiller.

"Here," she said, "aim for Aunt Em on the dock."

"M-me aim? Me sail." His eyes went round and wide as he looked at Mari. He held the tiller in a death grip.

"You. Easy there," Mari said. "Yes, like that." She kept her hand near his as they moved quickly toward where Aunt Em stood, watching. Alex, his arm almost rigid with his determination to do it right, reminded her of Nikos when he was hunched over his figures, trying to get them perfect.

Don't, she admonished herself. *Don't think about him.*

She tried not to. When they got close to the dock, she said, "All right. My turn," and she tacked and brought the boat around so they were headed toward the point. "Your turn again."

Eagerly Alex took hold once more and, catching his tongue between his lips, he pointed the boat in the direction she indicated. This time he relaxed a little, eased up on his grip, actually breathed a couple of times. The first time she thought he hadn't!

"Good job," she said. "Wonderful. I think you're a born sailor, Alex."

"Do you?" he asked eagerly, and the grin he gave her was Nikos when all his figures were perfect.

They didn't stay out long. Short and sweet, Mari believed, was the best way to teach anybody anything. *"Leave 'em wanting more,"* Aunt Bett had always said. It was clear that Alex still wanted more when she tacked once more and said, "Enough for now. Back to Aunt Em."

"Awwww," Alex moaned. Then, "I can come again, can't I?" he pleaded.

"I hope so," Mari said. Though exactly where she would be standing with regard to the Costanides family after Nikos left today remained to be seen.

Maybe, she thought, Stavros would keep her on to help with Alex while Julietta took care of their new baby. Certainly Julietta's desire to take care of her own children was admirable, but where was the harm in having a little help?

And if she stayed on to help care for Alex, perhaps she would see Nikos.

Ah, Mari, don't even think about it.

"Didja see us?" Alex asked, almost leaping out of the boat when they reached the dock where Aunt Em and Aunt Bett waited. "Didja see me sailing?"

"Indeed we did. You did very well." Aunt Em gave him a hug.

"My, yes. You're a natural sailor, I would say," Aunt Bett concurred.

Alex beamed. "That's what Mari said."

"Well, Mari's right. Now come along and let's see

what a natural you are in the kitchen. You can help me peel potatoes for supper."

Alex looked at her wide-eyed. "Me?"

"Of course, dear." Aunt Bett held out a hand to him. "All good sailors peel potatoes."

Alex went off with them, an aunt on either hand, and left Mari to finish with the boat. She lowered the sail and took it off, then began to fold it, trying not to dream about staying on with Alex, about maybe seeing Nikos again.

It would be far better, she knew, if she *never* saw him again!

"Mari!"

She jerked and spun around, startled. *"Nikos?"* Here? Indeed he was.

As if her foolish longing had conjured him up, he was limping down the steps toward her. He no longer had a cast on. He no longer used crutches. But he probably should have, because he was moving so fast and so precariously that he looked as if he might fall over.

Mari hurried toward him. "I thought you'd left!"

"I was leaving. But Julietta was having contractions. I've taken her to the hospital!"

CHAPTER SEVEN

HE SHOULD never have stopped at the house.

If he hadn't, he wouldn't have known. He wouldn't have seen Julietta's white face, wouldn't have heard the panicky quaver in her voice when she told him she was having contractions, that she thought she was having the baby.

"You can't be!" he'd said, as if he could somehow stop it just by command. As if he'd been able to command anything to do his bidding of late.

"I am," Julietta said miserably. "They've been getting worse all day."

"Did you call the doctor?"

She shook her head. "I didn't think it was going to happen. I'm not due for two months."

"Tell that to the kid," Nikos said harshly. "Come on. Get on the couch. Lie down."

He took her arm and steered her in that direction. It wasn't easy. He didn't have good balance since they'd taken the cast off. He had an orthopedic shoe contraption that made him feel like he was stumbling every time he took a step. He *really* felt like he was stumbling now.

What the hell was he supposed to do with his pregnant *stepmother,* for heaven's sake? Getting involved with his father's new family was the last thing he wanted to do.

"Where's the old man?" he'd asked harshly.

"Stavros is in Athens," Julietta said faintly. She put her feet up on the couch and looked up at him as if he could somehow conjure up her husband.

"Figures," Nikos snapped. Stavros was never around when he was needed. That, at least, hadn't changed. "Have you called him?"

"I can't...f-find him."

"What do you mean, you can't find him?"

"He was having some sort of top-flight meeting with a company he's thinking of buying. He said it was all hush-hush. He didn't tell me where he was going to be."

"Of all the idiotic—" Words failed him.

"Oh, Nikos!" She wrapped her arms around her middle. "Here it comes again."

Nikos swore. Then he called the doctor. Then he called the hospital. The doctor said he'd meet her there. The hospital said to bring her right in.

"Me?" Nikos said.

Who else?

It wasn't his job. It was Stavros's job! But Stavros was halfway around the world.

"Poor Stavros," Julietta murmured as he bundled her into his car. "It'll be just like last time."

Nikos didn't know what the hell she meant by that. Had the old man been on the other side of the earth when Alex was born, too?

He got her to the hospital in record time. He handed her over to the nurses and turned to go. "I'll call Adrianos and see if he can find the old man," he said.

She nodded weakly. "And Alex. You have to tell Alex."

Nikos gaped at her. "Me?"

"You're his brother."

Nice of someone to remember that. Nikos scowled. "Where is he?" he asked at the very moment he remembered. "Is he still with Mari Lewis?" he asked, knowing what the answer would be.

Julietta nodded. She gave him the aunts' address.

He shook his head. "I'll leave a note at the house. I've got a plane to catch."

Julietta caught his hand. She looked up at him with eyes as big as the moon. "Don't let it be for him like it was for you, Nikos," she begged. "Please!"

Like it was for him? He didn't know what she was talking about.

"Go to him. Bring him to me!" Her nails were digging into his wrist.

"The old man—"

"I'm not your father, Nikos! And I'm not asking you for him! I'm asking for me. And for Alex. Please."

The doctor appeared just then, his competent, soothing professional smile in place. "Well, let's see if this little one is serious, Julietta," he said.

Julietta didn't even look at him. She only looked at Nikos. "Please."

So he went to Mari's aunts'.

He saw Mari down at the dock before he made it to the house. The minute he saw her, he felt better, as if he wasn't carrying the world on his shoulders anymore. Or if he was, at least he wasn't carrying it alone.

Mari was here. She would share it with him.

"Julietta?" she said now, her own flushed cheeks paling at his news.

"She wants Alex."

"Of course. I'll get him." She started to run toward the house. "We'll be right with you."

"I can't stay. I've got a plane to catch. I just came to tell you."

She turned. "To tell me?" she echoed. "And that's all?"

He didn't like the look on her face. It asked for things he didn't want to give. He shrugged irritably. "She's not *my* wife."

"Alex is *your* brother."

"Interesting how everybody's remembering that now," Nikos said bitterly.

"What?" Mari looked confused. And he didn't really have the right to say that to her. She'd always remembered. She'd tried to get him to care, to be involved earlier.

He jammed his hands into the pockets of his jeans. "Never mind," he muttered.

Just then the sound of running footsteps approached them. "Mari! Time for sup—" Alex stopped dead at the sight of his brother. "Nikos?"

"Hi, Alex."

The little boy looked from Mari to Nikos and back again, confusion and wariness in his face. Nikos didn't want to see it. He didn't want to see the flicker of hope there, either. It reminded him too forcibly of his own continually thwarted hopes as a child. But that was about his father, he reminded himself. Fathers were far more consequential than brothers—and half-brothers, at that.

But Alex's father was half a world away, and unlikely to be of much use even if he'd been there.

Damn it.

Nikos turned to the little boy. "Listen, Alex," he said quietly, "I came to get you. Your mother needs you. She had to go to the hospital."

"Hospital?" Alex looked at Mari.

"She's been having a few contractions," Mari said. "You know? Remember when she'd let you put your hand on her tummy to feel it get all hard and tight?"

Alex nodded. "How come she has to go to the hospital for that?"

"Well, if it starts happening regularly it might mean she's going to have the baby. It was sort of a surprise, having them now, so she wants you to come see her, just in case she has to stay and have the baby."

"Now?"

"Now," Mari said.

"What about supper?"

"Aunt Em can put our supper in some dishes and we can bring it along. We can eat back at your house after we see your mommy. We'll have a picnic."

Alex's eyes lit up. "Really?"

Mari smiled. "Yes. Run on up and tell Aunt Em we have to go."

Nikos listened to the whole exchange with awe. She seemed to know exactly what to say, the right note to strike. She didn't make Alex promises she couldn't—or wouldn't—keep. She didn't play down any fears he might have, but she offered him support, friendship.

"Where were you when *I* was growing up?" Nikos muttered.

"Too young to be any use at all," Mari said. She started toward the house after Alex. Nikos followed, curious still to see these aunts of hers.

When he'd met them, he had a good idea how Mari came to be the way she was. They were warm and welcoming, caring and kind. They told him what a handsome fellow he was, and how much Alex resembled him, and wasn't it funny that his name was Nikos.

"You know," Aunt Em confided, "Mari thought she was supposed to be nanny to a Nikos!" She smiled gleefully. "Imagine, being nanny to you."

"Imagine," Nikos echoed faintly. Mari pretended not

to hear. He could see that her cheeks were red, though, as she gathered up the containers as Aunt Bett filled them.

"We really need to be going," she said, herding Alex toward the door. "Say thank you, Alex."

"Thank you," he parroted. But then he turned and gave each of her aunts a big hug. "Thank you for the cookies 'n' for playin' cards 'n' for letting me go in your sailboat. C'n I come again?"

"Of course, darling," Aunt Em said.

"By all means. A born sailor like you should have lots of sailboat rides," Aunt Bett said, then slanted a glance at Nikos. "And bring your brother with you next time."

Mari bustled in, gave them each a kiss, then grabbed Alex's hand, and with the containers in the other arm, hurried out to the car.

Nikos started toward the Jag.

"I'll follow you," Mari said. "And don't expect me to keep up if you drive fast." She turned to Alex. "You'll make sure he drives slow enough for me, won't you?"

The little boy looked at her, speechless.

So did the big one. "Now wait a minute," Nikos began.

But Mari nailed him with a look. "I'm sure Alex would prefer a ride in a great car like yours to an old clunker like mine." She went around and opened the passenger door of the Jag. "Come on, Alex."

"Just a damn—"

"A-hem!"

Nikos scowled at her, but he shut his mouth.

The frost in her glare turned to a sweet smile. "It's

the best idea,'' she said lightly, but Nikos heard the underlying firmness in her voice.

"Fine," he muttered. "See you there."

The Jag had always seemed just right for two. When one of them was a pretty woman it almost seemed too big. When one of them was Alex, it wasn't nearly large enough. The child seemed to be sitting right on top of him!

Nikos drove fast, but not too fast, through the narrow back roads between the north and south forks of Long Island. Behind him he could see Mari's headlights in his rearview mirror.

Next to him, Alex sat unmoving, neck craned to see out the windshield. Only when the hospital came in sight did Nikos hear a sound out of him, and it wasn't a word so much as a tiny desperate gasp for air.

Instinctively Nikos reached over and put his large hand over one of Alex's small ones. Little fingers curled around his, tight. They hung on.

Nikos glanced down. Alex was still staring straight ahead, teeth biting down on his lower lip. Nikos pulled into a parking place and cut the engine, then gave Alex's hand a squeeze.

The boy turned his head and looked at Nikos with big worried eyes. "I want my daddy," he whispered.

Nikos's throat tightened. His teeth clenched. He had consciously to ease the muscles in his jaw. "I know," he said hoarsely. "But your dad isn't here right now. Mari and I are, though. We'll come with you if you want."

He didn't know why he was saying that! Well, yes, actually he did. He was saying it because they were words he'd needed to hear when he was a child when his own mother had been taken to the hospital and—

He couldn't remember. Until this moment he hadn't even remembered that his mother had gone to the hospital. Now he did. He remembered the long corridors. The odd metallic sounds. The hushed voices. He remembered sitting there alone, with people walking past him, talking around him, over him. Forgetting him.

It was as if he wasn't even there.

But he was. It was his father who hadn't been.

Just the way he wasn't here now. Nikos got out of the car and went around, taking Alex's hand in his. "Come on," he said. No one was going to do to Alex what they'd done to him.

Mari didn't know what had happened between Nikos and Alex on the trip from her aunts' to the hospital. All she knew was that, when she got out of her car in the lot and went to meet them, something had changed.

Nikos wasn't completely different. He wasn't embracing the whole notion of being involved with Stavros and his family, but something had happened. It was obvious in the way he stood next to Alex, almost protectively. She heard it in the firm voice with which he spoke to the hospital staff, and in the gentle reassurance with which he took the boy down the hall to see his mother.

This was the Nikos that Stavros had always wanted and feared didn't exist. This was a responsible, capable, caring man taking charge.

Mari didn't say a word. She just stood back and watched. She went with them down to see Julietta because Nikos's expression included her when he said, "We want to see Mrs. Costanides." She did talk to Julietta, calmly and optimistically, because in his stepmother's hospital room, Nikos didn't say much.

But he was there. He held Alex's hand while Mari talked to Julietta. He stood back next to Mari and waited while Alex went up to his mother's bed. Julietta touched her son's face and kissed him. She talked in a low, soft voice to him, explaining that the baby might be coming early and she had to wait here and see.

"Can I stay, too?" Alex wanted to know.

Julietta smiled. "There's only one bed in here. And Mari says she'll spend the night with you at home. That will be better than staying here. And then tomorrow we'll know if the baby is coming or not. If not, I can come home. Okay?"

Alex nibbled on his lip for a minute, then nodded. "I guess," he said, then looked back over his shoulder. "Is Nikos coming, too?"

Standing beside him, Mari could almost feel Nikos stiffen at the little boy's words. A fierce tension seemed almost to emanate from him. But it wasn't an angry tension. It was more like an intense very personal vibration. A sort of force field. Magnetic. Almost without realizing it, Mari drew closer.

Their arms brushed against each other. She felt Nikos's fingers grip hers. His hand was cold and damp, the clasp of his hand hard. She rubbed her thumb across his knuckle.

"Are you, Nikos?" Alex persisted.

"If you want me to." The words seemed dragged up from Nikos's toes.

Alex nodded solemnly. "I do."

It shouldn't have reminded Mari of a wedding. It was a four year old boy and his much older brother. But there was a sense of something sacramental about it. A vow. A promise.

She gave Nikos's hand a gentle squeeze and got a death grip in return.

"Nikos?" Julietta raised her voice, and Nikos's gaze jerked up to meet hers. His stepmother smiled mistily at him. "Thank you."

He was out of his flaming mind.

He shouldn't be here! *Couldn't* be here. Never in a million years would have believed he was here in his father's house, waiting while Alex put on his pajamas and got ready for bed.

But even as he thought it, he knew there was nowhere else he could possibly be.

And Mari knew it, too.

She watched him as carefully as she'd been watching Alex—as if she really was his nanny, concerned for his welfare above all else.

After they'd talked to Julietta, whom they left resting, Nikos had taken Alex back out to the car, while Mari stayed on a few minutes longer at Julietta's request, getting an earful of the things Alex didn't need to hear. But only a few minutes later she hurried to meet them by the car, cheerful smile in place as she said, "All set for that picnic, you two?"

Alex, who had been yawning and holding Nikos's hand silently, brightened at once and answered for both of them. "Yep. I'm starved."

Mari didn't even bother to warm the dinner, just served it cold to the three of them as they sat on a cloth spread on the deck overlooking the pool. Nikos looked at it doubtfully, but didn't say anything. Mari seemed to know what she was doing. And she proved it again because by serving it cold she got at least half a meal down Alex before he fell fast asleep on a chaise by the pool.

"You knew he was fading," Nikos said.

"There are signs. He's had a hard day. You have, too," she added. "How's your head? And your leg? I haven't even had time to ask."

Nikos shrugged. "They're all right." He picked up his jacket and put it over the sleeping boy.

"It was...kind of you to stay."

His mouth twisted wryly. "That's me, kind."

"Don't disparage yourself," Mari said sharply. "I know how hard it was for you."

No, you don't, he wanted to say. But, oddly, he felt as if she really did know. As if she had been there with him all day, feeling what he felt, sharing his pain, halving it. "Yeah," he said, his voice low. He stared out across the pool, a turquoise gem, glowing from its underwater light.

He didn't let himself look at her. If he did, he would see her mouth and remember her kisses. He would see her hair and remember its softness. He would see her body and remember its response.

His own was responding even now.

He shoved himself awkwardly to his feet and bent to pick up the sleeping child. "I'll carry Alex in. Get his bed ready, will you?"

Mari scrambled up as well and hurried into the house ahead of him. He gave her a good headstart. He stood there on the deck by the pool, the warm weight of his small brother in his arms, and tried to divorce himself from the moment.

Think about Cornwall, he told himself. *Think about Brian and Claudia, about Carruthers, about the life you want.*

But tonight he wanted something else. Something he couldn't have. Something he wouldn't let himself have.

And tomorrow? He prayed he wouldn't want it tomorrow.

And if he did?

He wouldn't let himself think about that.

"She wants me to *what?*"

"Don't shout. You'll wake Alex," Mari warned him. They were in the living room of the main house. Nikos had just put Alex in his bed and stood there looking down at his little brother for a long moment. Then, resolutely, he'd turned away, heading back for the living room, determined to get out now, before he did something he'd regret.

And now here Mari was, telling him to do the one thing in the world he'd regret even more!

"Call Stavros? You're crazy!" He fumed. He paced. He glared. "You don't mean it?"

"Julietta means it. She asked me to ask you."

"She didn't ask me herself!"

"Because she felt awkward."

"*This* is awkward!"

"I know that. But it has to be done. Someone has to call him."

Nikos would have liked to have called his father every name in the book! How the hell could the old man go off and leave his wife when she was this close to having his child?

"*You* call him," he suggested.

Mari shook her head. "I don't think anyone would pay any attention to me. They'd pay attention to you."

"Pay attention to Nikos, his no-good playboy son?" Nikos sneered.

"Maybe not. But they'd pay attention to Nikos, the responsible man I saw take over at the hospital."

Nikos growled. He muttered. Mari didn't say anything else. He wished she would! It was easier to argue with someone than to argue with himself—especially when he was losing!

"He deserves not to be here," he snapped at her. "If he doesn't have the sense to stay when she needs him, he *deserves* to miss it."

"But does Julietta deserve not to have his support?"

Damn her! Damn her gentle logic! Damn her quiet confidence that he would come around and do the right thing!

He didn't *want* to do the right thing! He wanted Stavros to suffer.

But he didn't want Julietta to suffer. It wasn't her fault. And it wasn't Alex's fault. And the last thing Alex had murmured as Nikos had put him in bed was, "Night, Da…"

"Oh, hell! All right."

Nikos snatched the phone off the hook and stalked out of the room. He'd find the old man if he had to fly to Athens and knock down the Parthenon to get to him.

It just about came to that.

It was early morning in Athens and very late that night in New York when Nikos finally bullied his way through enough flunkies to get to Adrianos, one of his father's top aides.

"What's your business with him?" they all asked.

"None of yours," Nikos snapped over and over.

He wasn't telling any of them. No one but the old man. He didn't care if it took forever. The blistering he gave Adrianos brought his father, at last, to the phone.

Stavros was indignant. "Ah, Nikos, to what do I owe the pleasure of your phone call?" His tone was acidic. "Is the nanny being too hard on you?"

Nikos let his sarcasm pass. "Your wife's in the hospital," he said flatly. "Get your ass home."

There.

He'd done everything they'd asked of him. He'd taken Julietta to the hospital. He'd brought Alex to see her. He'd eaten a picnic with his brother. He'd put him to bed. He'd gritted his teeth and spent three hours tracking down his father. The old man was on his way home.

Nikos was out of here.

What more could anyone ask?

"What do you mean, I have to pick him up?" He stared at Mari, horrified. Furious. "I'm not going to get him! Let Thomas go get him."

"It's Thomas's day off," she reminded him gently.

"Then he can take a cab."

"He can't take a cab."

"He can afford it!"

"It's not a matter of affording it. It's that he needs someone to meet him."

"Not me!"

"He sounded shattered when he called from London. He—"

"He damned well ought to be!" Nikos was giving no quarter.

"I agree. But even he needs support," Mari went on firmly. "He needs his family there now." She looked at him. "You."

They glared at each other. Nikos raked his fingers through his hair. "*You* go get him then."

"I'm not family. And—" she forestalled his protest "—I need to stay with Alex. He didn't sleep well. He came to me in the middle of the night. He was tired from excitement after yesterday. Now he's tired from stress. He needs routine."

Nikos opened his mouth to argue with that, then shut it again. He couldn't argue because he knew it was true. He jammed his hands in the pockets of his trousers and scowled out the window at the sea. He didn't *want* to go get his father! Not for anything—or anyone—on earth.

"Mari?" a small voice came from the hallway. Alex stood there with a stranglehold on his rabbit.

Mari smiled. "Ah, there you are! Good morning, Alex."

"Morning," he said, then his gaze went straight to Nikos. He smiled shyly. "Hi," he said softly.

Nikos raked his fingers through his hair. "Hi," he said to his brother, his voice ragged even though he managed to give Alex a smile. Then he let out a harsh breath and looked at Mari. "All right," he said. "You win."

CHAPTER EIGHT

THE man who got off the airplane that afternoon didn't even look like his father.

If the gray-faced old man making his way into the terminal hadn't said, "Nikos?" in a shocked tone, Nikos might have let him walk on by.

Stavros seemed to have aged twenty years in the space of the week since he'd left. And he was clearly astonished to see Nikos there waiting for him.

"Believe me, I wouldn't be here," Nikos said before his father could comment, "if there had been anybody else."

"Is she...?" Stavros couldn't even get the words out. He groped for something to hang onto, and Nikos, without thinking, caught his father's arm to support him.

"She's holding her own," he said gruffly. "The contractions have stopped. I called the hospital before I came this morning."

"Thank God." The faintest color reappeared in Stavros's complexion. He swallowed and a tremor seemed to run through him. But then he straightened and pulled himself together.

Nikos let go of his arm. "Come on. Let's get going."

The drive to East Hampton took two and a half hours. They made it in silence except for his father's questions about Alex right after they left JFK.

"How is he? Is he all right?"

Nikos's jaw tightened. He didn't take his eyes off the road, but he didn't feel as if he could see it at all. For a long minute he couldn't answer. He couldn't get words past the thickening in his throat. At last he nodded, and when he could speak, he said harshly, "Mari has him. She's good at what she does."

The look Stavros gave him was a hard and assessing look.

Nikos didn't care. Let the old man think whatever he wanted. Let him *wonder* whatever he wanted. Nikos deliberately flexed his fingers on the steering wheel and drove on.

If Stavros had more questions, he didn't ask them. He did pull out a cellular phone once and call the hospital. His relief at being allowed to speak directly to Julietta was profound.

"Ah, *agape mou!* Julietta, my love, how do you feel?"

Nikos's teeth clenched. *Don't play the devoted husband in front of me, old man.* He didn't want to hear it! He didn't even really believe it.

But though he began by doubting his father's sincerity, once the niceties were dealt with, and Stavros would customarily have lapsed into his normal curt, businesslike manner, with Julietta he was not curt or businesslike at all. His tone was soft, his questions gentle. This loving man, this agonized husband was Stavros Costanides?

This was his father?

Nikos's hands strangled the steering wheel. He stepped down harder on the accelerator. His leg hurt from the continued demands of driving. He wanted to stretch it. Ease it. *Kick something.* Someone.

He thought he might explode.

They continued in silence. Nikos drove straight to the hospital. It wasn't until he'd pulled up out front and said,

"I'll take your gear to your place," that his father spoke again.

Stavros sighed just slightly and looked down at his hands before he turned his gaze to meet his son's. "Nikos," he said. His voice was as gentle as Nikos had ever heard it when speaking his name.

He looked away.

"Nikos," his father said again, and didn't move to get out until Nikos had looked back at him. "Thank you."

"I didn't want his damned thanks!" Nikos was prowling the length of the patio overlooking the pool where Mari was sitting and watching while Alex paddled in the shallow water. She'd seen Nikos coming and had sent her own prayer of thanks winging heavenward.

She'd had visions of him dropping Stavros off at the hospital, then taking straight off for London, figuring he'd done more than enough, and washing his hands of the whole mess.

But he was here. Limping. Irritable. Irascible. Annoyed. But *here*. And Mari breathed a sigh of relief.

"I know," she said softly now. "But keep your voice down or Alex will hear."

Nikos scowled, but he stopped fuming, and he stopped muttering. He stood, instead, just watching his brother play. There was a gentleness on his face, when he watched Alex, that Mari never saw there any other time.

"He's very like you," she said.

Nikos grunted. "More than you know."

She cocked her head to look at him, wanting him to continue, praying that he would.

"I've been where he is," was all he said.

"Nikos?" Alex stopped jumping in the water and looked up at his brother. "Can you come swimmin'?"

Nikos started to shake his head, to say no. Then he stopped. He glanced at his watch. "For a little while. I have a plane to catch."

"A plane?" Mari felt a sinking feeling in her stomach.

"Cornwall. Brian. My work. Remember?" Nikos said.

"Yes, but—"

"I'm not going to stay here. They don't need me!"

Mari thought they did, but she didn't think an argument would convince him. She just looked at him sadly.

Nikos didn't look at her at all. "How about going down to the ocean?" he said to Alex.

His little brother beamed. "Oh, yeah!" He started scrambling out of the pool.

Nikos took Alex down to the ocean. Mari didn't go with them. There were things that needed to be done here. And someone needed to stay around to take the calls if Stavros rang. Or Brian, for that matter, she thought glumly.

She glanced toward the beach. Nikos and Alex were standing on the shore, side by side. Nikos seemed to be talking, then Alex looked up and answered. Then they stood there again. Just as she was about to turn and go into the house, she saw Alex reach out and touch his brother's hand. She saw Nikos wrap his bigger hand around his brother's small one.

The two of them stepped closer together.

It was odd the way he felt bonded with Alex.

Or maybe it wasn't odd. The two of them shared a common parent. A pretty unfortunate tie, as far as Nikos could see. But no one else shared it. And as much as he personally would have liked to have washed his hands of his father, he couldn't quite do it yet.

Not until he'd told Alex what no one had ever told him.

It was easier somehow in the ocean. The ocean had always seemed to Nikos, ever since his childhood, to be his home. It was easier to understand than the people he'd lived with—his loving, doting, supportive mother, who let herself be hurt by a man not worthy of her love; his hard, unyielding father, who demanded so much and gave so little. Nikos loved the former, despised the latter—and understood neither.

It was easier to be by himself on the ocean. Sailing had been his salvation. Swimming had been his joy. Just sitting by the water had soothed him when the various sides of his world had seemed at odds with each other.

Until now he'd gone there alone. No—once at least he'd come close to bringing someone else. Mari—the day they'd gone to Montauk.

He'd barely known her then, but somehow he'd sensed that she would love it the way he did. Watching her drive his car had taught him that. It was the same feeling—being small and yet taking on something powerful, harnessing the power and making it your own.

He'd done it with the sea. Mari had done it with his Jaguar. Yesterday she'd taken Alex to sail, to share that love with him. Alex had told him about it while they'd walked down to the sea together.

"We sailed," he'd told Nikos. "Fast!" His eyes were bright. "Mari let me hold the rudder."

"Tiller," Nikos corrected gently.

"Yeah, that. We went soooo fast!" Alex had given a little hop. "I never been so fast. We're gonna do it again.

We're gonna go to her aunts' and go sailing again. Do you want to go, Nikos?" He'd looked up at his brother, his eyes shining. "I wish you would go, Nikos."

And Nikos had smiled. "Yeah, Alex. I'd like that."

Alex's trust made it easier to tell him—to say the words he needed to say, that Alex, even if he didn't know it yet, needed to hear.

They were together, out in the ocean, far enough out so that Nikos was holding Alex in his arms while they bobbed up and down as the swells pushed toward the shore. "Alex, if you ever...need, um...if you ever need...anyone—" he couldn't say *me* "—if you ever need anyone...for anything...you can always call me. Always."

Alex, who had been bouncing against his chest, seemed to sense Nikos's sudden seriousness. He stopped and looked. Their eyes, on a level this once, locked. It was like looking into a mirror, Nikos thought.

For a long moment Alex didn't say anything, and Nikos wondered if he understood, or if he was too young...if what he remembered—the desolation, the loneliness, the anguish—were his alone. A projection, nothing more.

And then Alex bumped his forehead against Nikos's. "Good." And then he giggled and nipped Nikos's nose.

Mari met them coming up from the beach.

They were running, but Nikos was lagging a little behind, letting Alex take the lead. They were laughing. They looked like father and son. At least, Mari thought, they were acting like brothers.

And a good thing, too.

She hurried on, needing to reach them, to tell them.

"Mari! I catched a wave!" Alex yelled. "Me an' Nikos rode a wave!" He lunged forward and threw his small wet arms around her legs.

Mari caught him, hugged him close, but her eyes raised to meet Nikos's.

"What's up?" He arrived just as wet and a whole lot more desirable than his little brother. His dark eyes searched her face.

She mustered a smile. "Do you want the good news or the bad news first? The good news is they've got the labor stopped and Julietta is resting comfortably. The bad news is...your father had a heart attack."

CHAPTER NINE

ON SUNDAY, Julietta, worried but stable, came home.

Brian, worried, called almost hourly about Carruthers—who to Nikos's way of thinking was definitely *un*stable—and his latest revisions of the boat they were building for him.

Stavros, out of danger and stable for the moment, was still in the hospital where he was the doctors' problem. Nikos was glad. Anyway, there was nothing he could do for the old man.

"You'll be fine. Just fine," he told Mari firmly Sunday evening as they sat in the living room of the little cottage where they had brought Alex for the night so that Julietta could get some rest. "Everything's under control. And for you actually," he went on cheerfully, "things couldn't be better."

Mari looked at him doubtfully. "Oh, really?"

"Sure," he said, not looking at her. He *couldn't* look at her, hadn't been able to do more than glance at her since he'd thought he was home free only to be thrown back into her company again. It was too tempting. *She* was too tempting. And she needed somebody far better than him. "They *need* a nanny," he told her now. "And you're the best. You've proved it. You've saved their necks over the past few days."

"Not just me!" she exclaimed. "You—"

He cut her off. "You wondered what you were going to do when I left? Now you know. The old man will be eating out of your hand just for being here and taking over. He'll give you whatever you want." It was true. All of it. The only bad part was, if she was working for his father, sometime, somehow, he would probably see her again.

"So it's perfect." He forged on. "And it's fine for me, too. I was here when you...when you needed me. And now I'd be in the way if I stayed. Besides, I can do my work better there."

He still didn't look at her. But he made the mistake of looking at Alex, playing cars on the floor, instead.

Alex looked up at him, dark eyes serious. "But *I* need you here, Nikos," he said.

It felt like they were playing house.

Like Mari was the mommy and Nikos was the daddy and Alex was the little boy. There was, of course, this underlying strain in Nikos that Mari couldn't pretend she didn't see. But at least she didn't think Alex saw it.

And Alex, of course, was the reason he stayed.

She knew it was for Alex, not for her. But she couldn't help herself—she was glad he was there. At some point she had quit lying to herself about it being the passion that was important. Certainly passion was important.

But Nikos was more important.

She loved him.

She wasn't sure when she stopped lying to herself about that, too. She thought it might have been when he went to get Stavros at the airport, even though she knew it was hard. She thought perhaps it was when she saw him with Alex on the shore, hand in hand. But she knew for sure when Alex looked up at him and said, "I need you here, Nikos," and he stayed.

She knew it was hard. She knew he hurt. She wanted to heal him.

She wasn't sure how.

She thought he was avoiding her, but it didn't seem like he was angry at her. More like she made him nervous.

She asked him why.

He looked at her like she'd grown antlers on her head. "Why the hell do you think?" They were sitting on the beach, watching Alex build a sandcastle. Or rather *Nikos* was watching Alex build a sandcastle. Mari was watching Nikos. She had been all day.

He'd looked at her once—just after breakfast. And, catching her eye, he'd looked abruptly away. He had studiously avoided looking her way ever since. He'd tried to discourage her from coming with him and Alex to the beach.

"It will give you a break," he'd said.

But Alex had wanted her to come. "She hasn't seen me body surf," he'd told Nikos.

"You're not missing much," Nikos had said under his breath so only Mari could hear.

But Alex had pleaded and Mari had wanted to go anyway, so she'd come.

But Nikos hadn't looked at her. Still.

"You act like you're mad at me. Like you don't want me here. Don't you?" she asked him bluntly.

He looked at her then, his dark eyes fathomless. "I want you in my bed." His jaw bunched tightly. His fist curled over a handful of sand.

Mari burned under the intensity of his gaze. And knew she wanted it, too. She swallowed. She ran her tongue over salty parched lips. "So do I," she said.

His eyes widened. He gave a hard quick shake of his head. "Don't say things like that."

"It's true."

"Even if it is, don't say things like that!" He shoved himself up and limped down the beach toward his brother.

Mari pulled her knees up to her chest and wrapped her arms around them. She watched him drop down on the sand next to Alex. She saw their two dark heads bent over the castle. Alex look her way, waved, beckoned her. Nikos said something to him, distracted his attention.

Oh, Nikos. I love you. Mari rested her head against her knees. *I would show you. I would sleep with you.*

But Nikos wouldn't sleep with her!

Did that mean he loved her, too?

He was a fool.

She'd virtually offered him her body. And he'd said no!

He needed to get out of here!

Regardless of what he'd promised Alex, he needed to leave. To get his own life back. At the very least, he needed to get out of here tonight. To stop playing house with Mari.

It would be fine if "playing house" extended to the bedroom. But he couldn't *let* it extend to the bedroom!

So he needed some other woman's bedroom. Some other woman's arms. Some other woman who could make him forget all about Mari Lewis's sweet face, her curvy body, her luscious mouth.

A man could be celibate just so long.

Nikos was way past that!

He waited until Julietta had retired to her room, until Alex had gone to bed, until there was just Mari and himself—and then he grabbed his jacket and headed for the door.

"Nikos?" She looked up from where she was sitting in the den. She had her shoes off and her feet tucked up under her. Her hair was loose, framing her face, making him focus on it—on her mouth.

"What?" he said harshly, still moving toward the door.

"Do you have work to do? Did Brian call? Do you want some help?"

"No. I don't need help. Or not that kind anyway! I need—" he glared at her "—damn it all, you *know* what I need!"

And he slammed out.

He could find it in East Hampton. He could go into a bar and meet some lonely woman, someone who wanted just one night and nothing more. There were plenty of women like that—refugees from the city, come out to the Hamptons for a little R&R.

It wouldn't be a problem. No problem at all.

He'd have his pick, he was sure.

The trouble was, he discovered, after four bars and four times that many likely women, he found something wrong with all of them. This one was too forward, that one was too tall. This one was a redhead. That one was blonde.

None of them had a sunny smile and an infectious giggle. None of them had lips begging to be kissed. At least not by him.

They'd have been willing—if he had.

He couldn't do it.

Damn it to hell!

What was the matter with him?

Maybe he needed a celebrity. Maybe all his days as

a globe-trotting playboy had spoiled him. Maybe he needed a photographer and notoriety to spark his interest.

But in the fifth bar he found a model he'd dated once or twice, one he'd been photographed with on several occasions. Where Karla went, photographers went—so if that was his problem, Karla could fix it.

And Karla was clearly willing.

But Nikos said, "I can't," when she asked him back to the house she was renting for the week.

"Can't?" Karla looked at him, astonished. He doubted very many men said no.

"I...have to get back," he said. "My brother..." *Oh, good,* he berated himself, *start dragging Alex up as an excuse.* "I can't," he said again.

Karla's brows lifted. "Brother?"

Nikos shook his head. He wasn't going into that. "I'll...see you around."

"Of course, darling," Karla said. She pursed her lips for a kiss.

Nikos ducked in, but turned his head at the last moment. His lips grazed her cheek.

She looked at him, eyes as big as soup bowls. But Nikos couldn't explain. He didn't understand himself. He just knew he had to get out of there.

He got into the Jaguar and drove. And drove.

He drove for hours, it seemed—along one back road after another. From one side of the island to the other. At two in the morning he found himself sitting in the Jag overlooking the dock by Mari's aunts' house.

Damn, he thought. *Oh, hell.*

Damn, she thought. *Oh, hell.*

She thought a few other unprintable things over the

next few hours. She couldn't decide if she was more furious or more hurt.

She knew, of course, what he was doing. He was out bedding another woman. Having sex with another woman. She refused to say *making love* with another woman. She was sure that love had nothing to do with it—unless it was because he was running scared from his love of her.

Did he love her?

Or was that merely wishful thinking? Had she gone beyond Mary Poppins, right into a Pollyanna approach to life?

Mari sat in the dark on the deck and tried to sort things out. It wasn't easy. For a long time after Julietta's light had gone out and Alex had long since gone to sleep, she'd paced the house and the grounds.

How dare Nikos just up and leave like that? How dare he imply that it was somehow her fault?

She hadn't refused him, for heaven's sake! In fact— and she blushed as she recalled it—this afternoon she had frankly admitted she wanted to go to bed with him, too!

But had he taken her up on it?

No. He'd acted like she'd said something wrong! Like she was Eve, holding out the apple that would damn him!

Mari would like to damn him right now.

She jumped to her feet and began to prowl again, turning every once in a while to glare down the drive toward the road in the direction he'd gone. Where was he? Who was he with?

It didn't bear thinking about!

She should have gone to sleep hours ago. She couldn't. She'd tried about midnight. She'd put on a pair of sleep shorts and a T-shirt, and she'd gone to bed. But she couldn't sleep. She'd tossed and turned and thought of Nikos.

Nikos the traitor.

Nikos. In bed with another woman.

There had been no use staying in bed trying to sleep when thoughts like that played havoc with her mind. She got back up. She went outside. She went up to the big house and checked on Julietta and on Alex. All was well.

She went back outside.

The night was still and almost moonless. There was no light but that since she'd shut off the pool light hours ago. There was no wind either—except the searing awful wind of pain that blew through her when she thought about Nikos with someone else. She needed to do something—to work off the feelings that buffeted her.

A sail would have been wonderful. But it was the middle of the night and she had no boat.

A swim, then. The ocean always helped. If she couldn't be on it, she could be *in* it. But she knew better than to do that, too. She wouldn't swim alone in the ocean. Not when no one knew where she had gone.

But she could swim in the pool.

And so she did. She shed her shorts and shirt and dove straight in. Who was there to see, after all?

Nikos?

Hardly. And if he were there, he would turn his back!

She swam long and hard. Lap after lap. Back and forth. On and on. As if swimming would purge her need, cleanse her soul, calm her emotions.

It tired her out. Her heart beat from the exertion. Her pulses raced from the effort expended. But the need was still there when she finally glided to the deep end, crossed her arms on the tiles and rested her chin on them.

The need was still there. Not even dulled. Sharper, if anything, because it was the strongest feeling in her. Passion.

Once she'd marvelled at it, had been amazed to feel it. Now it was her constant companion. Since she'd met Nikos, it wouldn't leave her alone.

He would, though. He had.

He was with someone else.

Slowly Mari hauled herself out of the water. She stood naked on the tiles, dripping, letting the night air dry her. She wrung the water out of her hair and combed it back with her fingers.

And then headlights came around the curve of the long drive and caught her full force. She stopped, frozen.

The car stopped, too. Jerked to a halt with an instant's screech of the brakes.

Then Mari reached for her clothes, snatched them up and tried to pull them on, hopping toward the house as she did so. *Damn! Oh, damn!*

And then Nikos was out of the car, limping towards her as fast as he could.

She almost made it into the house. She had her shorts on, had the T-shirt almost over her head. And he caught up with her, turned her in his arms, and lowered his mouth to hers.

She should have fought him. He hadn't wanted her! He'd turned his back on her, gone to someone else!

She tried to fight him. But he held her fast, wrapped his arms around her, pressed her wet body to his.

"God, Mari! What you do to me!" He gasped the words against her mouth. He ground his body against hers, showing her all too clearly that, whoever he'd been with, his desire for her had not slackened.

She pushed at him. "Go away! You don't want me! You wanted—"

"I want you! How could you think I don't! You're killing me."

"You left!"

"Because I *shouldn't* want you!"

Their bodies were tangling as they spoke. He kissed her mouth, her cheeks, her eyes. He threaded his fingers through her hair, tugging lightly, tipping her head back to give him greater access. He kissed her neck, her jaw, her ears.

"You went to someone else!"

"I didn't."

"Don't lie."

"I'm not lying. I wanted to. I needed to! I couldn't." He sounded disgusted with himself.

Mari pushed him back and tried to see his expression. It was too dark. She could only hear his labored breathing, feel the hardness of his body, the grip of his fingers on her arms. "Is that true?" she asked quietly.

She heard him swallow. She felt the shudder that ran through him when he exhaled sharply. "It's true."

"You were going to." It wasn't a question.

"Yes. Of course I was. You want forever. I'm not offering forever. So how could I use you?"

"Use?"

"That's what it would be," he said harshly.

"No." She didn't believe that. No matter what he thought he was doing, she was sure he wasn't capable of using her. And she wouldn't be using him. Once she might have—not to make love with, but to learn about her capacity for passion. But this had only peripherally to do with passion. It had only to do with him.

"What do you mean, no?" Nikos rasped.

"I love you," she told him.

He stopped dead. Didn't speak. Didn't move. Didn't even seem to breathe. Then, "No, you don't," he said.

She touched his lips. "I do." She remembered Alex saying those same words and her thinking it sounded like a wedding promise. It sounded like a vow when she said it now, too.

Nikos must have thought so, too, for he pulled abruptly away. He turned his back. He bent his head and hunched his shoulders as if weighed down by some great burden. Then he tipped his head back and threw back his shoulders and stared at the sky as if the answers were there.

The answers, Mari could have told him, weren't anywhere out there. They were inside him.

"I'm not promising forever," he said finally, turning his head toward her. His voice was rough—with need and tension and, perhaps, something else. There was no harshness, though. It was as if he was warning her.

Mari understood.

She reached out a hand and touched his arm. A tremor went through him. She ran her hand down his arm to touch his fingers. She wrapped her own around them. For a long moment he didn't move, as if he was giving her one last chance to back out.

But Mari wasn't backing out.

She was going to love Nikos Costanides—and she was going in head—and heart—first.

He'd thought she was a mirage. An illusion.

He'd thought that one whiskey he'd downed had gone straight to his brain, making him see things that weren't there.

That wasn't really Mari Lewis *naked* on the poolside, was it?

He'd slammed on the brakes, staring in disbelief until he saw her move. She'd reached for her clothes, grabbed them, and started toward the house.

And he knew he wasn't going to let her get that far.

He hadn't. He'd caught her. He'd kissed her. He'd allowed her to feel the feverish need he had for her.

He had wanted her desperately. He *still* wanted her.

He didn't want her to love him.

Why in God's name had she said that she loved him?

"Don't," he'd begged her. *"How could I use you?"* he'd asked her. *I'm not promising forever,* he'd warned.

But it hadn't done any good.

She'd taken his hand. She'd touched his face. She'd put her arms around him and let him feel the beat of her heart.

He couldn't say no any longer. A man could only take just so much.

He took Mari to the cottage, to his room. To his bed.

She went willingly, eagerly even. She sat on the bed and watched while he fumbled to get out of his clothes. His hands were shaking, and finally, with a small smile, she'd said, "Let me. I'm good at this."

For a second he scowled, thinking she meant she'd undressed a lot of men. But then he realized she was talking about undoing buttons and zippers. She was a nanny. It was her stock-in-trade.

She was the sexiest nanny he'd ever seen. The sexiest *woman*. It was all he could do to stand still and let her undo the buttons of his shirt and slide it off, ease down the zipper of his trousers and skim them down his legs. She dropped to her knees to do it. Her wet hair brushed against him. Through his shorts he could feel her. His teeth came together. His shut his eyes. His fingers curled into fists.

He stepped out of the shorts, reached for her, pulled her up against him, and fell back, carrying her with him onto the bed.

God, it felt good, having her body covering his like this. He'd dreamed about Mari Lewis in his bed since the first day he'd seen her. He'd tried not to think of her except as fully-clothed and poring over computer screens full of tankage volumes or playing with Alex on the floor. And during the daylight hours he hadn't done too badly.

The nights his unconscious had taken over, weaving fantasies that drove him wild. One of them had them lying together, Mari on top of him, her weight warm and wonderful, a prelude to her body taking him in.

This Mari was cool, her skin still fresh from her swim in the night air. But the longer she lay atop him, the warmer they became. The heat grew between them—the heat of desire, of need.

Of love, he knew Mari would say.

He couldn't say it. He could feel it, though. He slid his hands down her back, caught his thumbs beneath the elastic of her shorts and tugged them off. Her skin was so smooth, so slick, so soft. So cool. So warm. So hot.

He couldn't get enough of her.

And Mari's touch, as eager and frantic as his, said she felt the same way about him.

Of course she did. She loved him.

He didn't let himself think about that. It was a burden he couldn't carry. It was a promise he couldn't make.

"It's all right," she whispered, as if she knew. And he supposed she might because he had stopped just then.

His hands had ceased their stroking. His body had tensed, holding back.

"It's all right."

It wasn't. But he couldn't help it. He needed her now. He'd warned her. She knew what she was getting. All he could give. Not what she wanted, but what he was capable of.

"Come to me, Nikos." She beckoned. She rolled off him and drew him down upon her. Her hands played down the length of his spine, making him arch against her as they reached his buttocks. They stripped off his own shorts.

He made a sound deep in his throat. A hungry sound. A needy sound. He needed *her,* and it was with great anticipation that he settled between her legs, both of them naked at last.

He wanted to make it good for her. If he couldn't give her forever, he could at least give her the joy of the moment. And so he set about doing just that. But it wasn't only joy for her. He, too, was caught up in what was happening between them.

And when she drew him into her, even though he felt her body's resistance, he could not stop.

"It's all right," she said again because, he understood, she did not want him to stop. She wanted him— all of him. She gave him all of herself.

What was this intimacy they were sharing? How was it different than any other coupling he had ever shared?

Because it was. He knew that from the moment he was inside her.

It was touch. There was always touch. It was friction. But there was always that, too. It was fire, burning hot and strong and vital. But it was also something more.

Intimacy with Mari gave him something he'd never

come close to experiencing with any other woman. He couldn't describe it. Had no words.

Passion? Yes, but...

Desire? Of course, and...

Love?

That, he was sure, was what Mari was calling it. Maybe...maybe it was. He didn't know. Didn't care. It overcame him before he could define it. It drew him in, encircled him, tied him down...

And freed him at the same time.

And when he felt her body shiver around his, when he felt her pulse with release and heard her gasp, "Oh!" as if she'd never experienced anything like this, he knew exactly how she felt.

He felt the same way.

Lost. And suddenly—in her embrace—found.

The phone woke them.

Nikos rolled away from Mari long enough to squint at the bedside clock before answering it. Almost four. He supposed he should be glad that Brian had given them a little more time.

"Whowizit?" Mari mumbled. She rolled with him, keeping him in her embrace. "Brian? C'rruthers?"

"Who else?" Nikos muttered. He didn't want to wake up. Didn't want the real world intruding on what he and Mari had shared. They'd had too little time as it was. He wanted more. Not much. A few hours. He wanted to love her just one more time.

"Can't you give me one night's peace?" he barked into the phone.

There was a long pause.

Then Julietta's wavering voice said, "Nikos? Is Mari with you? I...looked for her. I don't want to bother you. I'm sorry, but I think this is it. This time I really am in labor."

CHAPTER TEN

THERE was no time to be embarrassed.

Mari had to throw on one of Nikos's long-tailed shirts and hurry to the house. There, in the bedroom she'd been using since Julietta had gone to the hospital the first time, she hurriedly dressed and then, despairing of getting a comb through her damp, hopelessly tangled hair, she loped down the hall to find Julietta huddled in her bed.

"They're four minutes apart and they're strong." Julietta's eyes were wide with dark smudges beneath. There was a waver in her voice, too, but it was stronger than it had been at the hospital before. And she didn't look panicky, just nervous. "The doctor said the more time, the better. I hope this is enough."

"It's enough," Mari said, and prayed that she was right.

Moments later Nikos came in. He wore clean jeans and an open-necked blue shirt, which wasn't entirely tucked in. Still, he looked far more put together than Mari knew she did. Having one's hair combed was indeed a help.

"Ready?" he asked Julietta.

She nodded toward the small suitcase by the dresser. "All packed. I just...need to go in and see Alex."

"You're going to wake him?" Nikos frowned.

Julietta shook her head. "Just see him." Holding her abdomen, she trundled into Alex's room and bent over him for just a moment. Her hand touched his hair and he stirred slightly, but didn't wake. Then awkwardly she leaned down and dropped a kiss on his cheek. She looked at Mari, standing in the door to the hallway. "All set now."

Mari stepped out of the way. Nikos, who had put her case in the car, was just coming back in. He looked at Mari, his face whisker-shadowed and haggard, a hint of desperation in his eyes. Mari thought she knew what the desperation was about. He'd just realized that one of them was going to have to go to the hospital with Julietta. One of them might even have to coach her through her labor and delivery. One of them was going to have to tell Stavros. And one of them was going to get to stay home with Alex.

She knew what he expected her to say. She was, after all, the logical one to stay home. She was the nanny.

But she was *his* nanny. And in this case there was no deliberation at all. She had to do what was best for her charge. And in this case it was letting him stay with Alex. It was, if the truth were known, best for Alex, too.

They were brothers. They needed each other.

Later, when Alex was awake, when he could be a buffer between Nikos and the pain, that would be soon enough for them to come to the hospital.

She held out a hand to him. His was cold and clammy. She gave it a squeeze. "You stay," she said. "I'll go."

Something flickered in his eyes. Something relaxed in his body. His fingers returned the squeeze and he nodded. "We'll come later."

Julietta looked at the two of them and smiled right before another contraction hit. Then she said, "We'd better be going."

"A girl?" Alex looked doubtful when Nikos gave him the news several hours later. Julietta's labor had been quick. The baby was small, but apparently strong.

"Mother and daughter are doing well," Mari had called and told him a while ago. "You have a sister."

A sister. A dainty dark-haired child who would grow up to knock men's socks off, Nikos had no doubt. He supposed that meant he would have to be vigilant, protecting her from rakes and scoundrels. From men like him.

Men who took and didn't give.

But, some voice inside him argued, he hadn't taken from Mari last night. She had given—and he had received. It was the most beautiful gift he'd ever had. That was certain. He would cherish it the rest of his life.

He would cherish her.

But he wouldn't marry her. He didn't dare.

"Girls aren't bad," he said now, his voice a little rough. And at Alex's still dubious look, he ruffled the boy's hair. "You'll see."

Alex hopped around the kitchen, having finished the bowl of cereal Nikos had given him. "When? Can we go soon?"

"Soon," Nikos promised. "Just let me clean up here."

In fact it took a little longer than he thought. He had two phone calls, one from Claudia about regular business matters and another more desperate one from Brian a little later. He took some notes and promised to get right on it.

"Do that," Brian said. "And when the hell are you coming back? You're out of the cast now, aren't you?"

"Yeah. It's just...I've been needed here."

"Well, you're needed here, too, old man. I thought you weren't going to let your father run you."

"He's not. It has nothing to do with him."

"Whatever you say," Brian said. But Nikos didn't need much imagination to hear the skepticism in his voice.

He hung up rather more forcefully than necessary, then turned to Alex. "Come on. Let's go to the hospital."

She was a dainty dark-haired child. Just over five pounds, with a red mottled face and the longest eyelashes he'd ever seen.

"She looks sort of like a monkey," Alex whispered to him nervously, out of Julietta's hearing.

She did, in fact. But, "She'll grow out of it," Nikos assured him.

"Did I look like a monkey?" Alex asked.

"I didn't see you when you were a baby," Nikos admitted.

"How come?"

"I was...out of the country." And wouldn't have been willing to come and see this new half-brother even if he hadn't been. Though of course he didn't tell Alex that.

He'd considered Alex's birth more of his father's folly. It wasn't enough that he marry a trophy wife young enough to be his daughter! Then the old man had to go and get her with child. Nikos had been furious when he'd found out.

Now he didn't know what he felt.

Not fury certainly. Somewhere over the course of his stay in the cottage he'd seen real affection between his father and Julietta. As hard as it was to fathom, they actually acted like they loved each other. If he hadn't believed it before, he certainly did after seeing Stavros's white face when he got off the plane that afternoon and then overhearing his father's conversation with his wife.

That was no man talking to a trophy. That was a man in love.

But if seeing that his father really cared for Julietta had reconciled Nikos to his father's second marriage, it hadn't stopped the hurt.

What about his own mother? If Stavros actually had the capacity to love, why hadn't he loved *her?*

Of course Nikos wouldn't ask.

He hadn't seen his father since right after the old man's heart attack. Seeing Stavros with tubes and bags and monitors all around him had made Nikos ill. He'd felt himself get light-headed and, though assured by the nurse that his father was holding his own, Nikos couldn't stay.

"Better if I don't," he'd told Mari when she asked the next day if he was coming to the hospital with them. "Give him another one just to see me there."

She hadn't argued with him, which pretty much proved she felt the same way. She came back later and told him that things were looking good.

"He's stable. It was a mild attack, and his being in the hospital when it happened helped a lot."

Every day he'd improved—or so Nikos heard. He never went back.

Today, of course, he did. When Mari called and said the baby had been born, that Georgiana Elizabeth Costanides was alive and well and snuggled in her mother's arms, he'd known great relief. He'd been glad to take Alex, to stand outside the nursery and hold the little boy up so they could both look at the child in the pink blanket-lined bassinette.

"What do you think of your sister?"

The quiet, raspy Greek-accented voice behind Nikos almost caused him to drop Alex. He turned, holding the boy like a shield.

"Papa!" Alex crowed, and wriggled to get down, to run and embrace the man who leaned on a walker and looked at them both.

Reluctantly, slowly, Nikos let him down, then watched as the boy skirted the walker, then slowed down and carefully put his arms around his father's legs. One of Stavros's hands left the walker to touch Alex's hair, to stroke its softness. His gaze dropped, too. And then he raised it again.

"Nikos?"

There was something hard and huge in Nikos's throat. It took him a moment to get the word past it, but finally he managed. "Congratulations."

And then he turned away.

Mari found him at the far end of the parking lot.

He was standing with his back to the hospital, staring off into space, but she doubted if he was seeing anything.

She had witnessed the encounter between him and his father from the end of the hall. She'd seen the emotions as they had flickered across his face one by one. Surprise. Hurt. Need. Resignation. And then she'd seen him turn and walk away.

She'd wanted to run after him then. But she'd had to wait to be sure that Stavros could manage Alex. And by the time she'd finally got father and younger son settled in and visiting in Julietta's room, Nikos was long gone.

"Sit down," Stavros had commanded her when she moved restlessly about.

But Mari couldn't. She prowled the hallway, went to the waiting room, then came back. Even then she couldn't settle. In desperation she looked out the window—and that's when she saw him.

"I've got to go," she said. And, not caring what any of them thought, she hurried out.

"Mari?" she heard Julietta's concerned voice follow her.

"Miss Lewis!" Stavros's peremptory tone clearly expected her to stop.

But Mari didn't stop. Not until she was within ten feet of Nikos, facing his back. Then she did. She stopped, panicked.

It was practically the first time she'd spoken to him since they'd made love. They'd shared a few necessary sentences since—but none had to do with what had happened between them.

Now didn't seem exactly like the time to talk, either. But maybe it was time for something other than talk. Sometimes, she told the parents she worked with, talk didn't say what needed to be said.

Now, Mari suspected, was one of those times.

So, gearing up her courage, unsure what kind of a reception she was going to get, she came up behind him. "Nikos?"

He stiffened, then turned slowly, his eyes meeting hers. It was all still there—the hurt, the confusion, the pain, the resignation. But, for just an instant, she saw something else—something more. Something, she dared think, for her.

She opened her arms and stepped forward, sliding them around him, pressing against him. She didn't kiss him. She only held him. *I love you,* she told him silently—with her arms and her body and her warmth. This wasn't the passion she'd found with Nikos from the first moment. This was something deeper and something far more precious.

It was love.

She felt a tremor run through him. He stood stone-still. A statue. Not even breathing. And then she felt the weight as he laid his head against her hair. His arms came around her, too. His hands locked against her back, holding them together. He drew a long shuddering breath. First one, then another.

"I love you." She said the words now. She pulled back just a little, enough to look up into his eyes. "I love you," she repeated.

His gaze dropped for a moment, then lifted to meet hers again. "I know," he said, his voice ragged. "I know you do."

He made a reservation for London that afternoon. He would leave the following morning. He told Mari what he'd done that afternoon when she brought Alex home for dinner.

"You're leaving?" She stared at him in disbelief.

He hardened his heart against it. It was better this way, he assured himself. Yes, she loved him. But that didn't matter. When had love ever brought anything but pain? Look what it had done to his mother, after all.

He didn't want to hurt her the way his father had hurt his mother. He was sparing Mari pain.

If he was honest, of course, he had to admit he was sparing himself pain, too.

"I need to get back," he said implacably, ignoring the expression on her face. "I have a life there. A job. It's where I belong. I only stayed because of Alex. You know that. But Alex will be all right now. The baby's here. Julietta's fine. In a few days even Stavros will be home. No one will need me." He was glad Alex was playing in the other room. At least this time his little brother couldn't contradict him.

And Mari wouldn't. He knew that.

He knew, despite the pain he saw in her eyes, that she would let him go. It was the right thing for both of them. She could do far better than him. Ultimately she would understand that.

And he?

He would be fine. *He would be fine.* He would say it until it came true.

"I'm going in the morning," he told her. "I have to go."

He wouldn't do it. She didn't believe him.

He *couldn't* walk away from her so easily, she told herself. He couldn't just turn his back. He loved her, too! She knew he did.

But she couldn't insist. It was for him to say the words. They would mean nothing if she had to drag them out of him.

Say it, she begged silently. *Say you love me.*

But he didn't say anything at all.

He would see reason, Mari told herself. She pasted on as cheerful a smile as she could manage and, after supper, took Alex back to the hospital to see his parents and his new baby sister. They brought helium balloons, one for each, and Alex carried them proudly to each room.

They took Georgiana's to the nursery first. While Alex watched, the nurse tied the pink and silver foil bobbing heart to her bassinette.

"So she can see it when she looks up," Alex explained to Mari. He studied his sister through the glass.

"She is looking better," he decided. "The first time I saw her, she looked pretty much like a monkey."

Mari hid a smile. "She'll get better," she promised.

Alex nodded sagely. "That's what Nikos says."

Mari couldn't count the number of times over the last few days that Alex had quoted his brother. Nikos was clearly a hero in the little boy's eyes. Alex would miss Nikos. He couldn't leave Alex, could he?

They took Julietta her balloon next. Alex's mother was very much herself now that she'd had some rest and was past the stress of labor. She looked much more relaxed today. And she was thrilled with the balloon Alex gave her, tying it to the rail at the foot of her bed, saying, "So I can see it all the time."

"Just like Georgie," he said happily, hopping from one foot to the other. "Mari 'n' me brought Georgie one, too. An' this one's for my daddy." He jiggled the one with the happy face on it.

"Wonderful," Julietta said. "He'll be so happy to get it. Georgiana and I are going to get to come home tomorrow, and Daddy's going to have to stay here all alone."

"How come?" Alex asked.

"Because he needs a few more days' rest," Julietta told him.

Alex's lower lip jutted out. "But he's okay?" he insisted.

Julietta patted the bed and Alex scrambled up next to her, snuggling in. "He's okay, darling. He'll be fine." She gave him a quick hug. The bedside phone rang and she picked it up. Her eyes lit up.

"He's right here," she said. "Yes. Good idea. Are you sure you can walk that far? All right then." She hung up. "That was Daddy," she told Alex. "He's coming to visit, and he wants to know if you'll meet him by the nursery. You can take him his balloon."

Alex beamed and hopped off the bed, running to the door.

"Walk," his mother called after him.

He slowed, but not much.

Julietta smiled. "He's going to keep things lively," she said, shaking her head. "I wish you were going to be staying to help me with him."

Mari felt as if the bottom had dropped out of her stomach. "I'm not?" She shouldn't have said the words. They weren't professional. If Julietta didn't want her, she had no right to question it.

Julietta's brow furrowed. "Well, I assumed you'd be going with Nikos when he goes...wherever he goes. We saw you two," she added, with a tip of her head toward the window, "when you were in the parking lot. We thought..."

Yes, Mari had thought, too. Or maybe *hoped* was the truer word.

Now she shook her head. "No. Nikos is leaving. Tomorrow morning."

"What!"

Mari shrugged. "He has to go."

"You love him." Julietta had no doubt about that. Of course, she'd seen them together and, during the last few days of her pregnancy, she'd had nothing to do but watch—and think.

Mari knew there was no point in denying it. "He's still leaving," she said.

"He loves you, too."

She wouldn't argue that, either, though she suspected Nikos might. "I don't think he wants to love anyone." She looked at Julietta, tried to smile, to sound brave and determined, but there was such compassion and commiseration in Julietta's eyes that Mari couldn't look for long. Her gaze slid away.

"Oh, Nikos," Julietta murmured sadly. She shook her head and looked at Mari again. "Oh, my dear."

A smart woman in possession of the common sense God gave her would not have spent the night in Nikos Costanides's bed.

Mari was a smart woman with a lot of common sense. She didn't go to Nikos. But she couldn't say no when he came to her.

Alex had fallen asleep on the way home from the hospital. He'd bounced out to the car, chattering animatedly about how much his daddy liked the balloon and how good it was going to be to have his mother and Georgie home tomorrow.

"An' pretty soon my daddy, too," he'd said happily. "And then we'll all be together."

And the next thing she knew he was sound asleep in the seat. She parked close to the house and was carrying him up the walk when Nikos opened the door.

Wordlessly he came and lifted Alex from her arms. He carried the little boy with the ease of a father as he strode along the hallway to his brother's bedroom and put Alex into his bed.

Mari took the child's shoes off, then covered him with the duvet, leaving his shorts and T-shirt on. If he woke later she could get him into pajamas, but she didn't think he would. It had been a busy day. He was tired. She bent and kissed him, then stepped back.

Nikos dropped down to his knees by the bed and looked at his little brother. One hand came out and smoothed Alex's hair. A knuckle brushed his petal-soft cheek. Then Nikos, too, pressed a light kiss on his forehead, and got up and followed Mari out of the room.

It was his goodbye to his brother, and she knew it.

If she'd had any hope that he would stay, she lost it then. If he couldn't face Alex and tell him he was leaving, if he couldn't look his brother in the eye and say goodbye, then she knew he was really and truly going.

Maybe that was why she let him come to her that night. So she'd have one more memory to drag out in a lifetime of regret. She hadn't had long with Nikos Costanides. She needed all the memories she could get.

She dared to hope that he needed them, too. His desperation as they made love told her without his having to say anything that he did. If their first night's loving had been strong and urgent and powerful, it was nothing compared to this one.

It was all those things—and gentle besides. His touches were tender, his kisses urgent. His hands made her whimper and reach for him and writhe. She did her share of loving him, too. She had a lifetime of love to teach him in just one night. She molded his face with her hands, memorizing the strong cheekbones, the firm line of his jaw, the sharpness of his nose. She studied his lips, traced them with her fingertip and then her tongue. She kissed his lashes, ran her fingers through his hair, kissed his chest, his navel, let her mouth dip below.

He sucked in a ragged breath and dragged her up the length of his body. "Enough," he muttered as he fitted them together.

But though they loved all night, Mari never got enough.

She didn't think Nikos did, either. His hands were still stroking her, petting her, holding her, as his body spooned around her and they slept.

* * *

She was asleep when he left.

It was all right not to wake her and say goodbye. They'd said goodbye all night long. They'd loved…and loved…and loved. Words couldn't have said anything more.

It was better this way.

Better this way. The words echoed in his mind, a mantra that he said over and over, all the way to the airport. He was doing what he wanted to do. What he needed to do. What was better for her—and for him. He was doing the right thing.

Still, once he got to the airport, he wanted to get on his way! He didn't understand why they had to make him be there two hours before the international flight. Once he was there, he was ready to go. If he was leaving, he wanted to be gone, damn it, gone.

He paced the terminal, scowled out the window, slumped in a chair, then got back up, irritated, distracted, and stared out the window some more.

"Nikos?" The voice was low, raspy, familiar, Greek. Totally out of place.

He spun around.

His father stood right behind him, leaning on a cane, breathing in short shallow breaths, his forehead damp from exertion, his face pale.

"What the hell—?" Nikos shook his head. "What are you doing here? You're supposed to be in the hospital!"

"I checked myself out."

"Why? Do you have a death wish, for God's sake!" Nikos grabbed his father's arm and towed him to a chair and sat him down. He didn't sit down beside him. He stood, glowering, his own heart beating double time.

"Sit," Stavros commanded. He patted the chair next to him.

"I don't want to sit. I'm going to be sitting for six hours!"

Stavros looked up, straight into Nikos's eyes. "Sit."

A muscle ticked in Nikos's temple. He ground his teeth. He rocked back on his heels. He glared at his father. He sat.

"Good." Stavros nodded and took a slow breath. "I come to tell you a story."

"A story?" Nikos was incredulous. "You checked yourself out of the hospital and drove two and a half hours to tell me a story?"

"Thomas drove," Stavros admitted. "I tell you a story."

"So tell me, damn it! Then go home and get back to bed. You're going to die if you don't! You don't want to die. You've got little kids to take care of."

"You would take care of them," Stavros said confidently. He looked at Nikos, his expression almost serene.

Nikos's jaw worked. "You're so sure of that, are you?"

"I am." A faint smile touched Stavros's face. "I saw you with Alex."

Nikos looked away. "He's a good kid," he muttered.

"He is like his brother was."

"*Was* being the operative word."

"Is," Stavros corrected himself.

Nikos looked at him sharply. "Revising your opinion, are you?"

"Yes." There was no apology. Just a statement of fact. He wouldn't have been Stavros, of course, if he had said he was sorry. Still, Nikos felt a small stab of satisfaction.

"I tell you the story," Stavros said. He looked straight ahead out the window, watching planes on the runway while he spoke. "It is about a young man with big ideas. It is about a woman he fell in love with. It is about me—and your mother."

Nikos stared. He didn't speak. He wasn't sure he heard correctly. Was his father saying that he'd loved Angelika?

"The marriage was arranged," he protested.

"Agreed to. Not arranged," Stavros said. "She was to marry someone else. Someone of her own class and background. Not a young upstart like me. A *real* Greek. Not an immigrant who left his country behind. That is what her father said." The older man shook his head. "I comfort myself sometimes thinking that it wouldn't have been any different if she'd married him. But I don't know."

"What the hell are you talking about?" None of this made any sense to Nikos. "Are you saying you took her away from another man?"

"I loved her," Stavros said simply. "She loved me. She would not marry him. She refused. She wanted me, she told her father. She wouldn't marry anyone else. Angelika could be very persuasive," he added ruefully.

"I know."

Nikos knew, too. His mother had always been able to bend him to her will. Not by force but by the warmth and sweetness of her character. But that his father had *loved* her? He didn't know what to think.

"It was a wonderful marriage," Stavros went on, his voice almost dreamy all at once as he stared off into space, seeing, Nikos guessed, the early years of his life with Angelika. "We worked hard together. We played together. We loved each other. And what we had was in two years made better by the arrival of a son." Here he flickered back to the present long enough to look over at that son. "A perfect son." Stavros smiled a little sadly.

His father had thought he was perfect? Well, maybe once he had...a long, long time ago.

"I took you everywhere," he said to Nikos. "To work. To the beach. To sail. You loved to sail."

Nikos didn't remember loving to sail—not with his father anyway. He didn't recall ever sailing with his father. He remembered sitting in the boat, waiting... waiting... He must have been very small.

Yes, he did remember it now. How eager he had been. How much he had waited for the afternoon to come when his father would be back from a trip so they could go sailing again. Again? Something flickered through his mind. Vague displaced memories. The feel of the wind in his face, of the list of the boat, of his father's strong arm around his narrow shoulders. Yes, they had gone sailing...until...

"We were best friends once," Stavros continued. "And all your mother and I could think was how wonderful it would be to have more children like you. So she got pregnant again. And she lost that child. A miscarriage. These things happen, the doctor said. We tried again. And again. More miscarriages. She was in bed a lot. Do you remember? She used to read to you in her bed."

Nikos remembered. He hadn't known why she was in bed. She was "resting," she always told him.

"Come keep me company for a little while," she would say. And she would read to him.

"She needed you there," his father said. "You were the bright spot in her day. So I didn't take you with me so much anymore. Sometimes, though, I took you sailing. I remember the last time. You were five. We had planned it for a week, maybe more. I'd had to go to Athens and I was looking forward to coming home to your mother, who was expecting again, and to you. And when I got there, she was being rushed to the hospital. Another miscarriage. And of course I went with her, not to you. You never forgave me for that." He smiled a little. "You wouldn't listen when I tried to explain. You ran out of the room."

Nikos wanted to deny it. He couldn't. He remembered the waiting. He'd been waiting forever for his father to come. "Soon," his mother would say. "Soon he will come." And then, "Tomorrow." And then, "In a few hours." White-faced, she said then, "Nikos, run get Mrs. Agnostopolis next door." He had.

Then he'd gone down to the dock to wait for his father.

But his father had never come.

And he hadn't listened. He'd been angry. Furious. "You promised," he'd yelled. And then he'd run. He remembered it now as if it were yesterday. And he remembered, too, that he'd never gone sailing with his father again.

"I was a child," he said gruffly, looking away, watching as another child went limp as its mother tried to get it to walk toward the gate.

"You were a child," Stavros agreed. "I should have made you listen. I thought you would come around. I had other things on my mind. Your mother. Her health. My business. It was necessary to work very hard just then. I wanted to prove to your mother's father that I was worthy of her, you see."

Nikos wasn't sure he saw at all. But he didn't run this time. He sat still. He wanted to know. He had so many questions.

"If you loved her, why did you leave?" He tried to make his voice sound casual, as if he was inquiring about the weather. But even he could hear the anguish in it. His jaw locked. He looked away.

Stavros sighed. "Because I was a fool. 'One last time,' she said to me. 'I want to try to have a baby one last time.' You were almost eight. She wanted you to have a brother or a sister. She knew how much I wanted more children. She wanted them herself. 'Please,' she begged me. And—" he shook his head "—I said yes. Our miracle, she called it when she not only got pregnant, but *stayed* pregnant. She was very careful. *I* was very careful. I didn't go near her for fear of making her miscarry. She was doing very well. So well that I took a chance and went to Athens for a meeting. A weekend, I promised her. It was necessary for a merger. She wasn't due for two months. All was well." His voice faded. He stared at his hands which lay loosely in his lap. His shoulders sagged. He looked like a very old man.

Nikos waited for him to say it, even though he thought he knew. He remembered Julietta's words, *Poor Stavros. It'll be just like last time.* Only now Nikos understood what she meant.

"She hemorrhaged. There was something wrong with the placenta, a ridge in it or something. The baby was finally big enough and active enough to kick a piece of it loose. She went into labor the night I left. I didn't get back until after the baby was born."

"And died?" Nikos whispered. It shouldn't have been a question. He knew.

His father nodded. "Stillborn. Too small. A breech birth. She almost died. I would never have forgiven myself if she had died!" He looked at his son, and for the first time Nikos saw clearly the anguish in his father's eyes.

For a long time, neither of them spoke. Nikos tried to remember that time. He didn't remember for sure knowing that his mother was even pregnant. Surely he would have realized!

"She told you she was getting chubby, not that she was expecting a baby," Stavros said, answering the question that Nikos didn't ask. "She didn't want you to know in case it didn't happen. Now I think she was wrong. But then I said nothing. After all, she knew you better than I did."

Or thought she did, Nikos realized. His mother would have thought she was doing the right thing, not getting his hopes up, not wanting him to be disappointed. Protecting him.

"I had made plenty of mistakes up until then," Stavros went on, "but after that I made the worst of all." He folded his hands and looked straight at Nikos. His eyes were like burnt holes in his ashen face. "I still loved your mother, but I couldn't make love to her. If I did, I knew she would insist on trying again. So I stayed away from her. From you. I moved out. I thought I was protecting her. I was determined to be a martyr to my love—to do the right thing." He smiled with wry bitterness. And then his gaze dropped. "I didn't realize what I was doing by turning my back on her. I failed her. I failed you."

Beyond the glass a jet engine thrummed. Inside the terminal a loud speaker called for passengers to approach the gate. A baby cried.

And Nikos swallowed hard, blinked rapidly, and fought his own tears. He wouldn't cry. He *wouldn't!*

And he didn't, until a tear trickled down Stavros's

cheek first, and the old man reached out and pulled Nikos into his arms. Then the tears came, pressed into Stavros's shoulder as his father murmured the Greek words that Nikos had long forgotten. "Ah, my son. I love you, my son."

He was gone.

She awakened and, without even opening her eyes, Mari knew he wasn't there. The bed felt cold and empty. She felt lost.

She tried to tell herself it would be all right. *Of course it would be all right!* She would survive. Other people had survived broken hearts.

But she didn't see how.

She got up, took a shower, washed her hair, put on a fresh sundress, even made an effort with a little makeup. *Look happy, you'll feel happy,* Aunt Em always said.

Not this time, Em. Sorry, Mari thought.

But she tried. And she told herself she would have made it through the morning without crying if Alex hadn't demanded to know where Nikos was, and when she tried to say nonchalantly that he'd had to leave, Alex had burst into tears.

"He said he'd be here!" the little boy wailed. "He said if I needed him, he'd stay!"

"He was here when you needed him," Mari soothed him, pulling him into her lap and holding him close. But pressing her face against Alex's hair, rocking him in her arms, reminded her too much of Nikos—too much of what she had lost. Her tears fell, too.

And, seeing them, Alex had said fiercely, "I *hate* him!"

"No, darling, you love him," Mari said. "That's why you're so hurt."

She understood the emotion, though. She felt it herself. Hate and love all mixed up. The Costanides family ought to patent it, she thought wryly. They do it so often and so well. Now they'd done it to her, too.

She made her escape when Julietta and Georgiana came home. She let herself out the sliding door and headed across the grass toward the dunes and the beach.

It was family time, she told herself. She shouldn't intrude. A wise nanny knew when to step in—and when to step out. This was a time to step away, to let Julietta and the children bond. In a few days Stavros would be with them and they would be a family, the family he had always wanted.

Of course he wouldn't have Nikos to run his business. But she thought perhaps he had a better understanding of his older son now—even though she didn't think he knew yet that Nikos was a well-respected naval architect. He knew enough. He'd seen enough of his older son with his younger one.

Mission accomplished. More or less.

So she could leave. Soon. And the sooner the better.

She would stay for a little while because Julietta would need some help for a few weeks to get back on her feet and get her bearings. But it wouldn't be long until the other woman was capable of handling both children easily, the way she wanted to, raising them herself.

And then Mari would go.

She'd accomplished her own mission, too. She would have enough money to save her aunts' house and provide for their future, that was certain. She would get a good set of references. She was sure Stavros would provide that.

And she would have memories.

Memories of Nikos.

She dropped down just below the crest of one of the small dunes and sat, arms wrapped around her drawn up legs, and indulged herself in memories of Nikos.

The wicked grin. The plaster cast. The stubborn jaw. The dancing eyes. The faraway look. The menacing scowl. The man who had taught her the meaning of love. The man she would never forget.

The breeze blew her hair around her face. She scraped it back. It kicked up sand dervishes. It trickled down the back of her neck.

She reached up and hand and swiped at it, trying to stop it. It kept trickling. She turned—and saw a pair of bare feet. Looked up into Nikos's dark eyes. The wicked grin flashed for just an instant. Then he dropped the handful of sand he'd been pouring down her neck and squatted on the sand beside her.

She looked at him, wide-eyed, astonished. *What was he doing here?* He'd left. Gone back to Cornwall.

"The old man made me stay," he said.

She'd thought her eyes couldn't get any wider. Now they almost popped right out of her head. "What are you talking about?"

"The old man," Nikos said impatiently. "My father. Remember him?" He slanted her an ironic smile.

"What do you mean, he made you stay? Your father's in the hospital!"

"No. He tracked me down at JFK."

"What? How could he? He's under doctor's orders to—"

"I haven't met a doctor yet who could make my old man do a damn thing he didn't want to do. And in this case he was determined. I thought he was bull-headed before, trying to run my life.'' Nikos laughed wryly. ''I hadn't seen anything yet.''

Mari could barely fathom this. ''He went after you all the way to the airport? Why? To make you come back?''

''He wanted to tell me a story,'' Nikos said. The wry grin faded from his face and he settled on the sand next to her. He funneled a handful from one hand to the other, watching the flow, not her. ''Wanted to tell me about him—and my mother. About the past. About a lot of things we should have talked about a long time ago.''

Mari bit her tongue. She didn't dare say it.

Nikos said it for her. He slanted her a glance and said, ''You're entitled. Go ahead. Say *I told you so.*''

Mari shook her head wordlessly. She couldn't seem to say anything at all.

''I understand now,'' Nikos went on. He was looking at the sand again. ''I understand him.''

Mari hugged her knees a little bit tighter. The weight she'd felt lifting earlier at the very sight of him began almost imperceptibly to press down again. She tried to fight it. Told herself she ought to be glad. She *was* glad that Nikos and his father had sorted things out. She was glad he'd come to tell her, to allow her that ''I told you so'' she wouldn't say. But—

She wanted more. And she wasn't going to get it.

''He's still Stavros, though,'' Nikos went on. ''After he told me why he did what he did, he told me not to do it, too.''

Mari didn't speak. She held her breath.

''He said, 'Don't be your father's son, Nikos.''' Nikos managed a passable imitation of his father's raspy voice. '''Don't be a martyr to your love,' he said. 'You're a fool if you do.'''

He looked at her then, and Mari thought she finally

understood what it meant to have your heart in your eyes. It was the way Nikos was looking at her. He swallowed.

"I don't want to go back to Cornwall without you. I don't want to go anywhere without you. I love you. I want to marry you. And you can be damned sure," he added with a sound somewhere between a laugh and a sob, "that I'm not just saying this because my father told me to!"

She said yes.

He wouldn't have blamed her if she hadn't. He wouldn't have blamed her if she'd told him she didn't ever want to see him again.

But he was glad she hadn't.

He'd laughed and rolled her in the sand the minute she said yes, she'd marry him, and that she loved him, too.

She made him laugh a lot over the next months. She made him cry once, too.

It was the day she'd told him she was expecting their child.

"A baby?" Of course he shouldn't have been surprised. They certainly did enough of what was required for her to get in that state.

But somehow, even after taking care of Alex and Georgiana until he was an old pro at this big-brother business, Nikos had never thought of himself as a father. It made him a little nervous and oddly misty-eyed.

"You should not worry," his father said. "You will have plenty of time to worry when this baby is born and making you crazy." The old man's eyes twinkled. His color was better these days. His heart was stronger. "I want to see you be a father," he said to his oldest son.

"He wants to see me make a hash of it," Nikos grumbled to Mari.

She wrapped her arms around him, barely able to link them behind his back because her belly was so round. "I don't believe it."

"I do," Nikos muttered. But he couldn't help smiling when he thought of his father doting on three children. He could see in the old man the young man who had wanted lots of babies. He would have been good with them, Nikos thought.

Mari agreed. Then she pressed her hand to her abdomen. "And it won't be long now."

In the end, she was stronger and braver than he was; Nikos had no doubt. When he saw what Mari went through in her labor, he understood more than ever his father's pain and his mother's love.

"Never again," he told Mari fervently after, when she lay in bed, the tiny blue-swaddled bundle in her arms. "It was awful. You could have died!"

"I was fine," Mari said, holding out her free arm to him. "*You* were the one who fainted!"

"I knew it," Stavros said, coming into the room with Julietta behind him, smiling as well. Stavros went to Mari and gave her a gentle kiss. He touched the baby's cheek lightly.

Then he turned and embraced Nikos, and the two of them grinned at each other like fools. "What have I been saying? I always knew you were your father's son!"

Sara Craven was born in South Devon, and grew up surrounded by books, in a house by the sea. After leaving grammar school she worked as a local journalist, covering everything from flower shows to murders. She started writing for Mills & Boon® in 1975. Apart from writing, her passions include films, music, cooking and eating in good restaurants. She now lives in Somerset. Sara Craven has appeared as a contestant on the Channel Four game show *Fifteen to One* and is also the winner of the 1997 Mastermind of Great Britain championship.

**Watch out for more passionate reads from
Sara Craven
in Modern Romance™!**

THE TYCOON'S MISTRESS

by

Sara Craven

CHAPTER ONE

CRESSIDA FIELDING turned her Fiat between the two stone pillars and drummed it up the long, curving drive to the house.

She brought the car to a halt on the wide gravel sweep outside the main entrance and sat for a moment, her hands still tensely gripping the steering wheel, staring up at the house.

The journey from the hospital had seemed endless, through all the narrow, winding lanes with the glare of the evening sun in her eyes, but she'd have gladly faced it again rather than the situation that now awaited her.

Her mind was still full of the image of her father in the intensive care unit, his skin grey under the bright lights and his bulky body strangely shrunken.

Lips tightening, Cressida shook herself mentally. She was not going to think like that. Her father's heart attack had been severe, but he was now making good progress. And when his condition was sufficiently stable, the surgeons would operate. And he would be fine again—in health at least.

And if it was up to her to ensure that he had a life to come back to, then—so be it.

With a sudden lift of the heart, she noticed her uncle's Range Rover was parked by the rhododendrons. At least she wasn't going to be alone.

As she went up the short flight of steps the front door opened to reveal the anxious figure of the housekeeper.

'Oh, Miss Cressy.' The older woman's relief was obvious. 'You're here at last.'

'Yes, Berry, dear.' Cressida put a comforting hand on Mrs Berryman's arm. 'I'm back.' She paused in the hall, looking round at the closed doors. She drew a deep breath. 'Is Sir Robert in the drawing room?'

'Yes, Miss Cressy. And Lady Kenny's with him. A tower of strength he's been. I don't know what I'd have done without them.' She paused. 'Can I bring you anything?'

'Some coffee, perhaps—and a few sandwiches, please. I couldn't eat on the plane.'

She watched Berry hurry away, then, with a sigh, walked across the hall. For a moment she halted, staring at herself in the big mirror which hung above the pretty crescent-shaped antique table.

She was a cool lady. Her boss said it with admiration, her friends with rueful smiles, and would-be lovers with exasperation bordering on hostility.

It was a persona she'd carefully and deliberately constructed. That she believed in.

But tonight there were cracks in the façade. Shadows of strain under the long-lashed grey-green eyes. Lines of tension tautening the self-contained mouth and emphasising the classic cheekbones.

It was the first time she'd had the chance to take a good look at herself, and the emotional roller-coaster of the past few weeks had left its mark.

Her clothes were creased from travel, and her pale blonde hair seemed to be sticking to her scalp, she thought, grimacing as she ran her fingers through it. She stopped for one deep, calming breath, then went into the drawing room.

She halted for a moment, assimilating with shock the

over-stuffed sofas, with their heavy brocade covers, and matching drapes, which managed to be expensive and charmless at the same time—all new since her last visit.

The lovely old Persian rugs had been replaced by a white fitted carpet, and there were gilt and crystal chandeliers instead of the graceful lamps she remembered, and mirrors everywhere.

It all looked like a stage setting, which had probably been exactly the intention, with Eloise playing the leading part—the nearest she'd ever come to it in her entire career. Only she'd quit before the end of the run...

Sir Robert, perched uneasily on the edge of a chair amid all this splendour, sprang to his feet with open relief when he saw Cressida.

'My dear child. This is a bad business.' He hugged her awkwardly. 'I still can't believe it.'

'Nor can I.' Cressida shook her head as she bent to kiss her aunt. 'Has there been any word from Eloise?'

'None,' Sir Robert said shortly. 'And we shouldn't expect any. She practically ransacked the house before she left.' He frowned. 'Berry says she's taken all your mother's jewellery, my dear.'

'Dad gave it to her when they were married,' Cressida reminded him evenly. 'She was entitled. And as least we're rid of her.'

'But at a terrible price.' Sir Robert pursed his lips. 'Of course, I could never understand what James saw in her.'

'Which makes you quite unique, darling,' his wife told him drily, drawing Cressida down to sit beside her. 'Eloise was a very beautiful, very sexy young woman and she took my unfortunate brother by storm. He was besotted by her from the moment they met, and probably still is.'

'Good God, Barbara, she's ruined him—she and her—paramour.'

'That's the trouble with love,' Cressida said slowly. 'It blinds you—drives you crazy…'

I never understood before, she thought painfully. But I do now. Oh, God, I do now…

She pulled herself together and looked at her uncle. 'Is it really true? It's not just some terrible mistake?'

Sir Robert shook his head soberly. 'The mistake was your father's, I'm afraid. It seems he met this Caravas man when he and Eloise were in Barbados two years ago. He claimed to be a financial adviser, produced adequate credentials, and gave them a few bits of advice which were perfectly sound.' His mouth tightened. 'I think they call it salting the mine.'

'When did he first mention the Paradise Grove development?'

'Several months later,' her uncle said grimly. 'They happened to run into him at the ballet, it seems, except there was nothing random about the encounter. There were a couple of other meetings—dinner, an evening at Glyndebourne which he paid for—then he started talking about this exclusive hotel and leisure complex, and what an investment opportunity it was. He said it would make them millionaires many times over, but only a really high investment would bring a high return.'

Cressy drew a painful breath. 'So Dad put all his money into it? And remortgaged this house? Everything?'

Sir Robert's nod was heavy. 'If only James had told me what he was planning, I might have been able to talk him out of it. But by the time I found out what was troubling him, it was too late.'

'And, of course, it was a sting.' Cressy looked down

at her clasped hands. Her voice was level. 'Paradise Grove was a mangrove swamp in the middle of nowhere. No one was ever going to build anything there.'

'Yes. But it was clever. I've seen the plans—the architects' drawings—the documentation. Including the apparent government licences and permissions. It all looked very professional—very official.'

'Like all the best confidence tricks.' Cressy shook her head. 'And the clever Mr Caravas? When did he and Eloise get together?'

'I imagine quite early on. There's no doubt she pushed James into the scheme for all she was worth. And now she and Caravas have completely vanished. The police say that they'll have new identities and the money safely laundered into a numbered account somewhere. Their plans were carefully made.' He paused. 'Your father wasn't the only victim, of course.'

Cressy closed her eyes. She said, 'How on earth could Dad have taken such an appalling risk?'

Sir Robert cleared his throat. 'My dear, he was always a gambler. That was part of his success in business. But he'd had some stockmarket losses, and—other problems. He saw it as a way of ensuring his long-term security in one big deal. He's never taken kindly to retirement. He wanted to be a key player again.' He paused. 'Quite apart from the personal pressure.'

'Yes,' Cressida said bitterly. 'And now I have to see if there's anything that can be saved from this ghastly mess.' She looked around her. 'I suppose this house will have to go.'

'It seems so,' Barbara Kenny said unhappily. 'I doubt if James will have much left apart from his company pension.'

Cressy nodded, her face set. 'I've brought my laptop

down with me. Tomorrow I'll start looking—finding out how bad things really are.'

There was a tap on the door and Mrs Berryman came in with a tray. The scent of the coffee, and the sight of the pile of ham sandwiches, the plate of home-made shortbread and the rich Dundee cake accompanying them, reminded Cressy how long it was since she'd eaten.

She said warmly, 'Berry—that looks wonderful.'

'You look as if you need it.' The housekeeper's glance was searching as well as affectionate. 'You've lost weight.'

'Berry's right,' her aunt commented when they were alone again. 'You are thinner.'

Cressy was pouring coffee. 'I expect it's an illusion created by my Greek suntan. Although I did do a lot of walking while I was out there.' *And swimming. And dancing...*

'My dear, I'm so sorry that your holiday had to be interrupted like this,' Sir Robert said heavily. 'But I felt you had to be told—even before James collapsed.'

Cressy forced a smile. 'It was time I came back anyway.' Her mouth tightened. 'You can have—too much of a good thing.' She handed round the coffee and offered the plate of sandwiches. 'I'd have been here sooner, but of course it's the height of the holiday season and I couldn't get a flight straight away. I had to spend a whole day in Athens.'

It had been a nervy, edgy day—a day she'd spent looking behind her constantly to see if she was being followed. She'd joined a guided tour of the Acropolis, mingled with the crowds in the Plaka, done everything she could to lose herself in sheer numbers. And all the time she had been waiting—waiting for a hand on her shoulder—a voice speaking her name...

'Cressy, I worry about you,' Lady Kenny said forthrightly. 'You don't have enough fun. You shouldn't have your nose stuck to a computer screen all the time, solving other people's tax problems. You should find yourself a young man. Start living.'

'I like my job,' Cressy said mildly. 'And if by "living" you mean I should be swept away by some grand passion, I think we've seen enough of that in this family.' Her face hardened. 'Watching my father make a fool of himself over someone as worthless as Eloise taught me a valuable lesson. I've seen at first hand the damage that sex can do.'

'He was lonely for a long time,' her aunt said quietly. 'Your mother's death hit him hard. And Eloise was very clever—very manipulative. Don't be too hard on him, darling.'

'No,' Cressy said with sudden bitterness. 'I've no right to judge anybody. It's all too easy to succumb to that particular madness.' *As I know now.*

For a moment she saw a cobalt sea and a strip of dazzling white sand, fringed with rocks as bleached as bones. And she saw dark eyes with laughter in their depths that glittered at her from a face of sculpted bronze. Laughter, she thought, that could, in an instant, change to hunger...

Suddenly breathless, she drove that particular image back into the recesses of her memory and slammed the door on it.

She would not think of him, she told herself savagely. She could not...

She saw her aunt and uncle looking faintly surprised, and went on hurriedly, 'But I shouldn't have let my dislike of Eloise keep me away. Maybe if I'd been around I could have done something. Persuaded Dad, somehow, that Paradise Grove was a scam. And he might not be in Intensive Care now,' she added, biting her lip hard as tears stung her eyes.

Sir Robert patted her shoulder. 'Cressy, you're the last person who could possibly be blamed for all this. And the doctor told me that James's heart attack could have happened at any time. He had warning signs over a year ago. But he wanted to pretend he was still young and strong.'

'For Eloise,' Cressy said bitterly. 'Oh, why did he have to meet her?'

Lady Kenny said gently, 'Sometimes fate works in strange ways, Cressy.' She paused. 'I've prepared a room at our house if you'd like to come back and stay. You shouldn't be on your own at a time like this.'

'It's sweet of you,' Cressy said gratefully. 'But I must remain here. I told the hospital it was where I'd be. And I shan't be alone with Berry to look after me.'

'Ah, yes.' Sir Robert sighed. 'I'm afraid Berry may be another casualty of this debacle.'

'Oh, surely not,' Cressy said in swift distress. 'She's always been part of this family.' One change that Eloise had not been allowed to make, she added silently.

Sir Robert finished his coffee and put down his cup.

'My dear.' His tone was sober. 'I think you must accept that nothing is ever going to be the same again.'

He was right, Cressy thought as she stood on the steps an hour later, waving her aunt and uncle an approximation of a cheerful goodbye.

Everything had changed quite momentously. Beginning with herself.

She shook herself mentally as she went back into the house.

She had to forget about those days of golden, sunlit madness on Myros, and how near she too had come to making a disastrous mistake.

That urgent summons back to England, although devastating, had been in another way a lifeline, dragging her back to reality. Waking her from the dangerous seductive dream which had enthralled her and could have led her to total ruin.

A holiday romance—that was all it had been. As trivial and tawdry as these things always were, with a handsome Greek on one side and a bored tourist on the other. Just for a while she'd allowed herself to indulge a risky fantasy, and then real life had intervened, just in time, returning her to sanity.

For a moment she found herself wondering what would have happened if her uncle's message had not been waiting at the hotel. If she'd actually called Draco's bluff and gone back to Myros…

She stopped herself right there. Speculation of that kind was forbidden territory now. Myros, and all that had happened there, was in the past, where it belonged. A memory that one day, in years to come, she might take out, dust down and smile over.

The memory of desire and being desired…

But not now. And maybe not ever, she thought, straightening her shoulders.

Now she had to look to the immediate future, and its problems. She'd have an early night, and tomorrow she would start to sift through the wreckage, see if anything could be salvaged.

And tonight, she told herself with determination, she would sleep without dreaming.

* * *

But that was more easily said than done. Cressida's night was restless. She woke several times, her body damp with perspiration, haunted by images that left no trace in her memory. Nothing that she could rationalise, and then dismiss.

Perhaps it was simply coming back to this house, where she'd been a stranger for so long, and finding herself in her old room again. The past playing tricks with her unconscious mind.

At least this room hadn't undergone the high-priced makeover inflicted on the rest of the house.

Eloise had been determined to erase every trace of her predecessor, Cressy thought, more with sorrow than with anger. And no expense had been spared in the process—which could explain how James Fielding might have found himself strapped for cash and been tempted to recklessness.

Although, in fairness, this wasn't the first time her father had sailed close to the wind. Only this time his instinct for disaster seemed to have deserted him.

But that, she thought, can happen to the best of us.

She pushed back the covers and got out of bed, wandering across to the window. Light was just beginning to stain the eastern sky, and the cool morning air made her shiver in her thin cotton nightgown and reach for a robe.

She'd never needed one in Greece, she thought. The nights had been too hot except in the hotel, which had had air-conditioning. Each evening the chambermaid had arranged her flimsy confection of silk and lace in a fan shape on the bed, with a rose on the bodice and a hand-made chocolate on the pillow.

Later, in the taverna on Myros, she'd slept naked, kicking away even the thin sheet to the foot of the bed, her body grateful for the faint breeze sighing from the Aegean sea through the open window.

Moving quietly, she went downstairs to the kitchen and made herself a pot of coffee which she carried to the study.

She'd brought in the computer and set it up the night before, and if she couldn't sleep then she might as well start work. Begin to probe the real extent of the financial disaster facing her father.

Because it could be faced. She was convinced of that. James Fielding was a survivor. He would get over this heart attack, and the ensuing operation, and take up his life again. And somehow she had to salvage something from the wreckage—make sure there was something to give him hope.

She'd done some preliminary calculations of her own on the plane, partly to prevent herself thinking of other things, she realised, her mouth twisting, and had worked out how much she could afford to contribute. But the outlook was bleak. Even if she sold her London flat, and worked from this house, she'd struggle to pay the new mortgage.

Besides, she wasn't sure whether she could endure to live under this roof again for any length of time. There were too many bad memories.

Cressida had been a teenager, still mourning her mother, when she had learned of her father's decision to remarry. And her sense of shock, almost betrayal, had doubled when she'd discovered his choice of wife.

Looking back, she could see that she'd responded intolerantly to the newcomer, staring at her with resentful eyes.

Eloise had been a bit-part actress, her chief claim to fame as hostess on a second-rate TV quiz show. She was tall and full-breasted, her lips permanently set in a beguiling pout, her violet eyes wide, almost childlike.

Until she was crossed, Cressida thought wryly. And then they would narrow like a rattlesnake's.

As they'd done when she first met her new stepdaughter. The hostility had not been one-sided by any means. Eloise had made it plain that she had little time for other women, and especially for a young girl just beginning to blossom out of gawkiness, although there was no way Cressy could ever have rivalled her voluptuous charms.

Chalk and cheese, Cressy thought with sadness. And I was just a nuisance, someone to be sidelined, if not totally ignored.

And even when, urged by her father, she'd tried a few awkward overtures, she'd found herself completely rebuffed. Eventually she had acquired a reputation for being 'tricky', if not downright difficult. And James Fielding, unable to see he was being manipulated, had made his displeasure known to his daughter, creating a rift that had widened slowly but surely over the years.

Cressida had soon realised she was no longer welcome in her own home. Even at Christmas Eloise had usually organised a ski-ing holiday for her husband and herself.

'Darling,' she'd said coaxingly when the first one was mooted. 'Cressida doesn't want to spend her vacations with a couple of old fogies. She has her own friends. Her own life.' Her steely gaze had fixed her stepdaughter. 'Isn't that right?'

It had been easier to swallow her hurt and bewilderment and agree. She *had* had friends she could go to, and Uncle Robert and Aunt Barbara had always been there for her, their comfortable, untidy house a second home.

For a long time Cressida had convinced herself that the scales would eventually fall from her father's eyes and that he'd see Eloise's greed and self-absorption. But it had never happened. He'd been carried away by his passion for her—a passion that she had been careful to feed.

As for Eloise herself, Cressida was sure she'd looked at James Fielding and seen only a successful businessman, with a settled background and an attractive Georgian house not too far from London.

What she hadn't understood was that James's company had struggled to recover from the big recession of the eighties, or that James himself had faltered more than once as chairman, and was being encouraged to take early retirement.

Eloise had been too busy entertaining, enjoying weekend parties with amusing people, and being seen in all the right places.

Even after James's actual retirement she'd seen no need to scale down their style of living or their expenditure.

Alec Caravas had been a younger man with a foolproof scheme for making them both instantly wealthy. Cressida could see how easily Eloise would have been seduced.

After all, she thought, I was planning to give up my job, my lifestyle, my independence. I shouldn't judge anyone else.

Her own meetings with her father over the past two years had been mainly confined to lunches in London, with the conversation constrained.

Perhaps I should have made more of an effort,

Cressida thought as she drank her coffee. Perhaps I should have played the hypocrite and pretended to like her. Even looked for her good points. Told myself that, whatever my personal feelings, she loved Dad and was making him happy.

Only, I never believed that. I just didn't want to be proved right quite so comprehensively.

She sighed, and turned resolutely to the computer screen. It was little use rehashing the past, she told herself forcibly. She had to try and salvage something from the present to ensure her father had a future.

She worked steadily for a couple of hours, but found little to comfort her.

Her father's company pension was indeed all that was left. All his other assets had been liquidised to make him a major shareholder in Paradise Grove. And he'd borrowed heavily too.

If he recovered from his heart attack, it would be to find himself insolvent, she realised unhappily.

His whole way of life would have to be downsized. She'd have to rent a larger flat, she thought, or even a house. Make a home for him—and Berry, who'd be needed more than ever. But how could she afford it?

I won't worry about that now, she told herself, glancing at her watch.

It was time she took a shower and dressed, and got over to the hospital again.

As she pushed back her chair, she noticed for the first time the small icon at the bottom of the screen indicating there was an e-mail message for her.

Someone else believes in an early start, Cressida thought wryly, as she clicked on to the little envelope and watched the message scroll down.

I am waiting for you.

The words were brief, almost laconic, but they had the power to make her stiffen in shock and disbelief.

She twisted suddenly in her chair, staring over her shoulder with frightened eyes.

The room was empty. And yet she felt Draco's presence as surely as if he was standing behind her, his hand touching her shoulder.

She said, 'No,' and again, more fiercely, '*No*. It's not true. It can't be…'

And heard the raw panic that shook her voice.

CHAPTER TWO

THERE was a rational explanation. There had to be.

Someone, somewhere, must be playing a trick on her, and had accidentally scored a bullseye.

All the way to the hospital Cressy kept telling herself feverishly that this was the way it had to be. That it must be one of her colleagues...

Except that they were all under the impression that she was still sunning herself on an island in the Aegean. She hadn't told anyone from work that she was back.

And, anyway, the message was too pointed—too personal to have come from anyone else but Draco. Wasn't it?

But how the hell did a Greek fisherman with one small, shabby boat and a half-built house manage to gain access to a computer, let alone have the technical know-how to send electronic mail halfway across Europe?

It made no sense.

Besides, he only knew my first name, she reminded herself with bewilderment. He can't possibly have traced me with that alone.

Her mind was still going round in ever decreasing circles as she went up in the lift to the Intensive Care Unit. But she steadied herself when the sister in charge met her with the good news that her father's condition had greatly improved.

'He's asleep at the moment, but you may sit with him.' Calm eyes looked squarely into Cressida's. 'You can be relied on not to make emotional scenes, Miss Fielding? He really doesn't need that kind of disturbance.'

'Of course not.' Cressy said steadily. 'I just want him to get better.'

She fetched some coffee from the machine in the corridor, then quietly took up her vigil, forcing herself to composure. She couldn't afford to send out any negative vibrations.

And she hadn't time to worry about mysterious e-mail messages or who might have generated them. Her father was her priority now, and nothing else could be allowed to matter.

That worrying grey tinge seemed to have gone from James Fielding's face. He looked more his old self again, she thought, surreptitiously crossing her fingers.

If he continued to make good progress he could soon be moved to a private room, she told herself. The premiums on his private health insurance had been allowed to lapse, but she would pay.

She said under her breath. 'I'll look after you, Daddy—whatever it takes. I'll make sure you're all right.'

He woke up once, gave her a faint smile, and fell asleep again. But it was enough.

Apart from the hum of the various machines, the unit was quite peaceful. And very hot, Cressy thought, undoing another button on her cream cotton shirt.

Almost as hot as it had been in Greece.

For a moment she could feel the beat of the sun on her head, see its dazzle on the water and hear the slap of the small waves against the bow of the caique as it took her to Myros.

* * *

Myros...

She noticed it the day she arrived, when she walked across the cool marble floor of her hotel bedroom, out on to the balcony, and looked across the sparkle of the sea at the indigo smudge on the horizon.

As she tipped the porter who'd brought up her luggage, she asked, 'What is that island?'

'That, *thespinis*, is Myros.'

'*Myros.*' She repeated the name softly under her breath.

She stayed where she was, fingers lightly splayed on the balustrade, lifting her face to the sun, listening to the distant wash of the sea and the rasp of the cicadas in the vast gardens below.

She could feel the worries and tensions of the past months sliding away from her.

She thought, with bewilderment and growing content, I really need this holiday. I didn't realize it, but Martin was quite right.

Her work was always meticulous, but she'd made a couple of mistakes in the last few weeks. Nothing too dire, and nothing that couldn't be swiftly put right without inconvenience to the client, but disturbing just the same.

Martin had looked at her over his glasses. 'When was the last time you took a break, Cress? And I don't mean Christmas and the usual Bank Holidays. I mean a real, live, away-from-it-all, lie-in-the-sun break. The sort that ordinary people have.'

'I have time off,' she had said. 'Last time I decorated my sitting room at the flat.'

'Exactly.' He'd sat back in his chair, his gaze inflexible. 'So you take the rest of the afternoon off, you visit a travel agent and you book yourself at least three weeks of total relaxation in some bit of the Mediterranean. Then get yourself some sun cream and a selection of pulp fiction and go. And that's an order,' he had added as Cressy had begun to protest pressure of work.

She'd obeyed mutinously, agreeing to the travel company's first suggestion of an all-inclusive trip to the latest in the Hellenic Imperial hotel chain.

'They're all the last word in luxury,' the travel clerk had enthused. 'And there's a full programme of sport and entertainment on offer. This one only opened recently, which is why there are still a few rooms available.'

'Anything,' Cressy had said, and had put down her gold card.

She might have arrived under protest, but she couldn't pretend she wasn't impressed.

For the first few days she simply relaxed under an umbrella on one of the sun terraces, swam in each of the three pools, had a couple of tennis lessons, and tried her hand, gingerly, at windsurfing. She also sampled all of the restaurants on the complex.

For once the brochure had spoken nothing but the truth, she thought wryly. The Hellenic Imperial was the height of opulence. The service was excellent, and no element of comfort had been overlooked.

But by the end of the first week Cressy was beginning to feel that it was all too perfect.

Most of the other guests seemed perfectly content to stay on the complex and be waited on hand and foot, but Cressy was restless. She rented a car, and took in the sights. The island's capital, with its harbour full of glamorous yachts and its sophisticated shopping facilities, left her cold. She much preferred driving up throat-tightening mountain roads to see a church with famous frescoes, sampling dark, spicy wine in a local vineyard, or drinking tiny cups of thick, sweet coffee in *kafeneions* in remote villages.

But, more and more, she found herself looking across the glittering sapphire of the Aegean and wondering exactly what lay there on the horizon.

One morning, when she was changing some money at Reception, she said casually, 'How do I get to Myros?'

The clerk could not have looked more astonished if she'd asked what time the next space ship left for the moon.

'Myros, *thespinis*?' he repeated carefully.

Cressy nodded. 'It's not that far away. I presume there's a ferry.'

He pursed his lips. 'There are boats,' he said discouragingly. 'But tourists do not go there, Kyria Fielding.'

'Why not?'

He shrugged. 'Because everything they want is here,' he returned with unshakeable logic.

'Nevertheless,' Cressy said equably, biting back a smile, 'I'd like to know where the boats leave from.'

The clerk looked almost distressed. 'You don't like this hotel, *thespinis*? You find it lacking in some way?'

'Not at all,' she assured him. 'I'd just like a change.'

'But there is nothing on Myros, *kyria*. It has no hotels, no facilities. It is a place for farmers and fishermen.'

'It sounds perfect,' Cressy said, and left him in mid-protest.

She was aware of curious glances as she sat in the bow of the caique watching Myros turn from an indistinct blur into a tall, mountainous ridge, the lower slopes softened by patches of greenery. She was without question the only foreigner on the boat, and the skipper, who looked like an amiable pirate, had initially demurred over accepting her fare.

As the caique traversed the shoreline, Cressy saw long stretches of pale sand, sheltered by jagged rocks.

The fishermen and the farmers have been lucky so far, she thought. Because this place looks ripe for exploitation to me.

The harbour was only tiny, with no smart boats among the battered caiques. Row upon row of small white houses seemed to be tumbling headlong towards the narrow waterfront where fishing nets were spread to dry.

Somewhere a church bell was ringing, its sound cool and sonorous in the hot, shimmering air.

Cressy found her heart clenching in sudden excitement and pleasure.

Her canvas beach bag slung over her shoulder, she scrambled ashore.

There was a sprinkling of tavernas and coffee shops on the harbourside, most of them frequented by elderly men playing a very fast and intense form of backgammon.

Cressy chose a table under an awning at the largest, waiting while the proprietor, a stocky man in jeans and a white shirt, finished hosing down the flagstones.

'Thespinis?' His smile was cordial enough, but the black eyes were shrewdly assessing.

Cressy asked for an iced Coke, and, when he brought it, enquired if there was anywhere she could hire a car.

The smile broadened regretfully. The only vehicles on Myros, she was told, were Jeeps and pick-up trucks, and none were for rent. The roads, the *kyria* must understand, were not good.

Well, I knew they didn't cater for tourists, Cressy reminded herself philosophically. But it was a setback.

She said, 'I saw beaches, *kyrie*. Can I reach them on foot?'

He nodded. 'It is possible, *thespinis*. Our finest beach is only a kilometre from here.' He paused thoughtfully, fingering his heavy black moustache. 'But there is a better way.' From a storeroom at the back of the taverna, he produced an ancient bicycle. 'It belonged to my sister,' he explained. 'But she is in Athens.'

'And you'll lend it to me?' Cressy raised her eyebrows. 'That's very kind.'

He shrugged. 'She will be happy for you to use it. It is an honour for her.'

'But how do you know I'll bring it back?'

The smile became almost indulgent. 'When the *kyria* wishes to leave Myros, she must return here. Also, she must eat, and my taverna has good fish. The best.' He nodded. 'You will come back, *thespinis*.'

Cressy hadn't ridden a bicycle for years. She waited while the proprietor, whose name was Yannis, ceremoniously dusted the saddle for her, then mounted awkwardly.

She said, 'I hope it lasts the distance, *kyrie*.'

'A kilometre is not too far.' He paused. 'I do not recommend that you go further than that, thespinis.'

'We'll see,' Cressy said cheerfully. 'Once I get the hang of it, I may do the grand tour.'

Yannis's face was suddenly serious. 'Go to the beach only, *thespinis*. I advise it. Beyond it the road is bad. Very bad.'

Now, why did she get the feeling that Yannis was

warning her about more than the state of the road? Cressy wondered, as she wobbled away.

But he hadn't been exaggerating. Outside the small town, the road soon deteriorated into a dirt track, with olive groves on one side and the sea on the other, and Cressy had to concentrate hard on keeping her eccentric machine upright, and avoiding the largest stones and deepest potholes.

Apart from the whisper of the sea, and the faint breeze rustling the silver leaves of the olive trees, Cressy felt as if she was enclosed in a silent, shimmering landscape. She was glad of the broad straw hat protecting her blonde hair.

The beach was soon reached, but, she saw with disappointment, it was only a narrow strip of sand with a lot of pebbles and little shade.

The others I saw were much better, she thought. Yannis can't have meant this one.

In spite of the road, she was beginning, against all odds, to enjoy her unexpected cycle ride, and decided to press on to one of the secluded coves she'd glimpsed from the ferry.

Ten minutes later, she was beginning to regret her decision. The gradient on her route had taken a sharp upward turn, and her elderly bone-shaker was no mountain bike.

This must have been what Yannis meant, she thought grimly. Certainly it warranted a warning.

She halted, to have a drink from the bottle of water which he'd pressed on her and consider what to do next.

Myros was only a small island, she argued inwardly, and the next beach couldn't be too far away. So, it might be better to leave the bike at the side of the track—after all, no one in his right mind would steal it—and proceed on foot.

She laid the ancient machine tenderly on its side in the shade of an olive tree, blew it a kiss, and walked on.

She'd gone about five hundred yards when she first heard the music, only faint, but unmistakably Greek, with its strong underlying rhythm. Cressy paused, breathless from her continued climb, and listened, her brows drawing together.

She swore softly under her breath. 'I don't believe it,' she muttered. 'I've come all this way in this heat, only to find someone else's beach party.'

She was going to walk on, but then sudden curiosity got the better of her, and, letting the music guide her, she moved quietly through the scrub and stones to the edge of the cliff. There was a track of sorts leading down to the pale crescent of sand below, but Cressy ignored that, moving to slightly higher ground where she could get an overall view of the beach.

The first thing she saw was a small caique, with faded blue paint and its sails furled, moored just offshore. But that appeared to be deserted.

Then she looked down, and the breath caught in her throat.

Below her, alone on the sand, a man was dancing.

Arms flung wide, head back, his face lifted to the sun, he swayed, and dipped to the ground, and leapt, his entire body given over to the sheer joy of living—and the raw power of the music.

And totally absorbed in his response to it, thought Cressy. Clearly nothing else existed for him at this moment.

She dropped to her knees in the shelter of a dried and

spindly shrub and watched, amused at first, but gradually becoming more entranced.

She'd seen demonstrations of *syrtaki* at the hotel, of course, but never performed with this wild, elemental force.

This man seemed completely at home in his solitary environment, Cressy told herself in bewilderment, as if he was somehow part of the sea, and the rocks, and the harsh brilliant sunlight, and shared their common spirit. Or the reincarnation of some pagan god...

She halted right there.

Now she was just being fanciful, she thought with self-derision.

He might be a wonderful dancer, but what she was actually seeing was a waiter from one of the hotels on the other island, practising his after-dinner routine for the tourists.

But not from my hotel, she thought. Or I'd have remembered...

Because he wasn't just a beautiful dancer. He was beautiful in other ways, too.

He was taller than average, and magnificently built, with broad, muscular shoulders, narrow hips and endless legs, his only covering a pair of ragged denim shorts which left little to the imagination.

The thick, dark hair, curling down on to the nape of his neck, gleamed like silk in the sunshine, and his skin was like burnished bronze.

To her shock, Cressy found her mouth was suddenly dry, her pulses drumming in unaccustomed and unwelcome excitement. She realised, too, there was an odd, trembling ache deep within her.

What the hell am I doing? she asked frantically, as she lifted herself cautiously to her feet and backed away. I'm an intelligent woman. I go for brains, not brawn. Or I would if I was interested in any kind of involvement, she reminded herself hastily.

Besides, this brand of obvious physicality leaves me cold. I'm not in the market for—holiday bait.

She was being unfair, and she knew it as she walked on, her pace quickening perceptibly.

After all, the lone dancer could have no idea he had an audience. He'd created his own private world of passion and movement, and if its intrinsic sensuality had sent her into meltdown then that was her problem, not his.

All the same, she was glad when the music faded from earshot. Although the image in her mind might not be so easy to dismiss, she realised ruefully.

'I don't know what's happening to me, but I don't like it,' she said under her breath, lengthening her stride.

A further five minutes' walk brought her to another cove, and this one was deserted, she noted as she scrambled thankfully down to the sand.

She stood for a moment, listening to the silence, then spread her towel in the shade of a rock, kicked off her canvas shoes, and slipped out of her navy cotton trousers and shirt to reveal the simple matching bikini beneath.

The sea was like cooling balm against her overheated skin. She waded out until the water was waist-high, then slid gently forward into its embrace, breaking into her strong, easy crawl.

When she eventually got tired, she turned on her back and floated, her eyes closed against the dazzle of the sun.

She felt completely at peace. London, the office and its problems seemed a lifetime away. Even the rift with her father no longer seemed quite so hurtful—or so insoluble. Eloise had driven a wedge between them, but—with care—wedges could be removed. Maybe she'd needed to distance herself in order to see that.

Back under her rock, she towelled herself down, applied sun cream with a lavish hand, drank some more water, then lay down on her front. She reached behind her and undid the clip of her bikini top. A suntan might not be fashionable, but it was inevitable that she would gain a little colour in this heat, and she didn't want any unsightly marks to spoil the effect in the low-backed dresses she'd brought.

She felt bonelessly relaxed, even a little drowsy, as she pillowed her cheek on her folded arms.

There's nothing I can't handle, she told herself with satisfaction as she drifted off to sleep.

She would never be certain what woke her. There was just an odd feeling of disquiet—a sudden chill, as if a cloud had covered the sun—that permeated her pleasant dream and broke its spell.

Cressy forced open her unwilling eyelids. For a moment she could see nothing, because the dazzle of the sun was too strong.

Then, slowly, she realised that she was no longer alone.

That there was someone lying on the sand beside her, only a few feet away. Someone tall and bronzed in denim shorts, who was—dear God—smiling at her.

She wanted to scream, but her throat muscles seemed suddenly paralysed. And she couldn't move either because she'd undone her top.

When she found her voice, it sounded small and husky. 'What do you want?'

His smile widened. His mouth, she saw, was firm, although his lower lip had a betrayingly sensuous curve, and his teeth were very white. For the rest of him, he had a straight nose, just fractionally too long for classical beauty, strongly accented cheekbones, and deepset eyes the colour of agate flecked with gold.

He also needed a shave.

He said, 'Why did you not come down and dance with me?' His voice was deep, with a distinct undercurrent of amusement, and he spoke in English.

It was the last thing she'd expected him to say, and for a moment she was stunned. Then she rallied.

'I don't know what you mean.'

'Ah, no.' He shook his head reprovingly. 'You should not tell lies—especially when you are so bad at it. Your eyes will always give you away.'

'That's ridiculous,' Cressy said with hostility. 'And also impertinent. You know nothing about me.'

'I know that you were watching me from the cliff, and then you ran away.' The return was imperturbable.

'I didn't run,' Cressy said with as much dignity as she could evoke when she was lying, prone, wearing only the bottom half of a bikini. 'I just wanted to find some peace and quiet. And I didn't mean to disturb you. Please go back to your—rehearsal.'

'That is finished for the day. Now it is time to eat.' He reached behind him and produced a small rucksack.

Cressy groaned inwardly. How on earth was she going to get rid of him, she wondered wildly, without insulting his Greek machismo? She was uneasily aware of how isolated this little beach was. And that they were both almost naked. The last thing she needed to do was provoke him in any way. Even to anger.

She made a business of looking at her watch. 'So, it

is. Well, I must get back to the village. Yannis is expecting me to eat at his taverna.'

'But not in the middle of the day,' he said. 'In the middle of the day he likes to drink coffee and play *tavli*. He'll cook for you tonight.'

'I don't think so.' Cressy made a discreet effort to fasten the hook on her bikini top. 'I have to get the evening ferry back to Alakos.'

Her unwanted neighbour watched her struggles with interest, but didn't volunteer his assistance as she'd been half afraid he might. 'You are staying in a hotel on Alakos?'

'Yes.' At the third attempt, Cressy managed the hook, and felt marginally more secure. 'At the Hellenic Imperial.'

'The Imperial? *Po po po.*' His dark brows lifted. 'You would need to be very rich to stay at such a place.'

'Not at all,' Cressy said with a certain crispness, wondering if he was planning to kidnap her and hold her to ransom. 'I work for my living like everyone else.'

'Ah—you are a model, perhaps—or an actress?' He produced a paper bag from his rucksack and opened it. Cressy saw that it contained pitta bread with some kind of filling.

'Of course not,' she denied swiftly. 'I work in an office—as a taxation accountant.' She reached for her shirt. 'And now I must be going.'

'It is a long time until evening—and your ferry.' He divided the envelope of pitta bread into two and held out half to her, using the paper bag as a plate.

'No,' Cressy said. 'It's very kind of you, but I couldn't—possibly.'

He leaned across and put the improvised plate on the corner of her towel.

'Why are you frightened?' He sounded as if he was merely expressing a friendly interest.

'I'm not.'

He sighed. 'You are lying again, *matia mou*. Now eat, and tell me about your work in England, and later we will swim. And do not tell me you cannot swim,' he added, as her lips parted in negation, 'because I too was watching.'

Cressy sat very upright. She said, quietly and coldly. 'Does it occur to you, *kyrie*, that I might not want to spend the afternoon with you? That I prefer to be alone?'

'Yes,' he said. 'But that will change when you know me better. And no one so young and so lovely should wish to be alone. It is a sad thing.'

There was lamb tucked into the pitta bread. The scent of it was making her mouth water.

She glared at him. 'I've no taste for meaningless compliments, *kyrie*.'

He said, 'Nor do I, *thespinis*. You know that you are young, so accept that you are also beautiful. And my name is Draco.' He smiled at her. 'Now eat your food, and don't be afraid any more.'

But that, thought Cressy, looking down at the pattern on the towel—or anywhere rather than at him—that was easier said than done.

CHAPTER THREE

IN SPITE of all Cressy's misgivings about the risks of her situation—and they were many and various—she supposed she had better accept Draco's offer of food. One placatory gesture, she told herself, and then she would go.

If she was allowed to, said a small, unpleasant voice in her head. She'd seen his athleticism when he was dancing. She might be able to out-think him, but did she really imagine she could outrun him up that lethal track?

So much for striking out and being independent, she derided herself. She should have stayed safely in the hotel precincts.

She had expected she would have to force a few mouthfuls past the unremitting tightness of her throat, but to her astonishment the lamb, which had been roasted with herbs and was served with a light lemon dressing and sliced black olives, tasted absolutely wonderful, and she finished every bite.

'It was good?' Draco asked as Cressy wiped her lips and fingers on a tissue.

'It was terrific,' she admitted. She gave him a taut smile. 'You speak English very well.'

His own smile was slow, touched with overt reminiscence. 'I had good teachers.'

'Women, no doubt,' Cressy heard herself saying tartly, and could have bitten her tongue in half. The last thing she needed to do was antagonise him, and his personal life was none of her business anyway, so what had possessed her to make such a comment?

She saw his face harden, the firm mouth suddenly compressed. For a moment she felt the crackle of tension in the air between them like live electricity, then, totally unexpectedly, he began to laugh.

'You are astute, *thespinis*.' Propped on one elbow, he gave her a long and leisurely assessment, missing nothing, making her feel naked under his agate gaze. 'But my grammar—my pronunciation—are not perfect. I am sure there is room for improvement—with the right help.'

Cressy was burning from head to foot, and it had nothing to do with the sun.

She said, 'I'm afraid that you'll have to find another tutor, *kyrie*. I'm not in the market.'

'Life has taught me that most things are for sale, *kyria*—if the price is right.'

There was real danger here. Every instinct she possessed was screaming it at her.

She said coolly and clearly, 'But I am not. And now I think I'd better go.'

'As you wish.' The powerful shoulders lifted in a negligent shrug. 'But understand this. I take only what is freely given. Nothing more. And, in any case, you are the stranger within my gates, and you have eaten my bread, so you have nothing to fear.'

He lifted himself lithely to his feet. 'Now I am going to swim. Naturally, I hope you will still be here when I return, but the choice is yours, *kyria*.'

For a moment he stood looking down at her. He said softly, 'So beautiful, and such a sharp tongue. And yet so afraid of life. What a pity.'

The damned nerve of him, Cressy seethed, watching

him lope down the sand. Translating her natural caution into cowardice.

And, for all his assurances, it was quite obvious that he was just another good-looking Greek on the make. She'd seen it happening at the hotel. Watched them targeting the single women, the divorcees, the ones with hunger in their eyes.

Cressy had avoided their attentions by being busy and absorbed.

But I should have known I couldn't escape for ever, she thought angrily.

Except that she could. Draco was swimming strongly away from the beach. She could see the darkness of his head against the glitter of the sea.

All she had to do was grab her things, put on her shoes, and she would be free.

Free to go back to the village and wait for the evening ferry, at any rate, she reminded herself with an inward groan. Where Draco would know exactly where to find her…

She was caught in a trap of her own making, it seemed. And to sneak away as if she was genuinely scared appeared oddly demeaning anyway.

It would certainly be more dignified to stay where she was. To treat any overtures he might make with cool and dismissive courtesy. And then return to the village in time for a meal at the taverna and her homeward boat trip exactly as she'd planned.

Maybe Draco needed to learn that, for all his good looks and sexual charisma, not all tourists were pushovers.

And he'd virtually guaranteed that she was safe with him, that traditional Greek hospitality would remain paramount, and, in a strange way, she believed him.

Unless, of course, she chose differently. And there was no chance of that.

So she would stay—for a while. Because she was in control of the situation.

But only because he's allowing you to be, niggled the small, irritating voice.

Ignoring it, Cressy reapplied her sun cream, put on her dark glasses and reached for the book she'd brought with her.

When Draco came back he'd find her composed and occupied, and not prepared to be involved in any more verbal tangles.

Distance was the thing, she told herself. And this beach was quite big enough for both of them.

She did not hear his return up the beach—he moved with the noiseless, feline grace of a panther—but she sensed that he was there, just the same. She kept her shoulder slightly turned and her eyes fixed rigidly on the printed page, a silent indication that the story was too gripping to brook interruption.

At the same time she'd expected her signals to be ignored. That he'd at least make some comment about her decision to remain. But as the soundless minutes passed Cressy realised she might be mistaken.

She ventured a swift sideways look, and saw with unreasoning annoyance that Draco was lying face down on his towel, his eyes closed, apparently fast asleep.

She bit her lip, and turned her page with a snap.

But it was all to no avail, she realised five minutes later. She simply couldn't concentrate. She was far too conscious of the man stretched out beside her.

She closed her book and studied him instead. She wondered how old he was. At least thirty, she surmised. Probably slightly more. He wore no jewellery—no medallions, earrings or other gifts from grateful ladies. Just an inexpensive wristwatch, she noted. And no wedding ring either, although that probably meant nothing. If part of his livelihood involved charming foreign woman holidaymakers, he would hardly want to advertise the fact that he was married.

And she could just imagine his poor wife, she thought with asperity, staring up at the sky. Dressed in the ubiquitous black, cooking, cleaning and working in the fields and olive groves while her husband pursued his other interests on the beaches and beside the swimming pools on Alakos—and nice work if you could get it.

'So what have you decided about me?'

Cressy, starting violently, turned her head and found Draco watching her, his mouth twisted in amusement and all signs of slumber fled.

There was no point in pretending or prevaricating. She said flatly, 'I don't have enough evidence to make a judgement.'

His brows lifted. 'What can I tell you?'

'Nothing.' Cressy shrugged. 'After all, it's unlikely that we'll meet again. Let's be content to remain strangers.'

'That is truly what you want?' His tone was curious.

'I've just said so.'

'Then why did you stare at me as if you were trying to see into my heart?'

'Is that what I was doing?' Cressy made a business of applying more sun cream to her legs. 'I—I didn't realise.'

He shook his head reprovingly. 'Another foolish lie, *matia mou.*'

Cressy replaced the cap on the sun cream as if she was wringing someone's neck.

'Very well,' she said. 'If you want to play silly games. What do you do for a living, *kyrie*?'

He lifted a shoulder. 'A little of this. A little of that.'

I can imagine. Aloud, she said, 'That's hardly an answer. I suppose the caique moored in the next cove is yours, and I've seen you dance, so I'd guess you're primarily a fisherman but you also do hotel work entertaining the guests. Am I right?'

'I said you were astute, *thespinis*,' he murmured. 'You read me as you would a balance sheet.'

'It really wasn't that difficult.'

'Truly?' There was slight mockery in his tone. 'Now, shall I tell you about you, I wonder?'

'There's very little to say,' Cressy said swiftly. 'You already know what my work is.'

'Ah.' The dark eyes held hers steadily for a moment. 'But I was not thinking of work.' He got to his feet, dusting sand from his legs. 'However, you have reminded me, *thespinis*, that I cannot enjoy the sun and your company any longer. I have to prepare for this evening's performance.' He slung his towel over his shoulder and picked up his rucksack.

He smiled down at her. '*Kalispera, matia mou.*'

'You keep calling me that, *kyrie*,' Cressy said with a snap, angrily aware of an odd disappointment at his departure. 'What does it mean?'

For one fleeting moment his hand brushed her cheek, pushing back an errant strand of silky hair.

He said softly, 'It means "my eyes". And my name, if you recall, is Draco. Until we meet again.'

He'd hardly touched her, Cressy repeated to herself for the fourth or fifth time. There was nothing to get upset about. He'd pushed her hair behind her ear, and that was all. He hadn't touched her breast or any of her exposed skin, as he could so easily have done.

All that time she'd carefully kept her distance. Built the usual invisible wall around herself.

And then, with one brief, casual gesture, he'd invaded her most personal space. And there hadn't been a damned thing she could do about it.

Oh, there'd been nothing overtly sexual in his touch—she couldn't accuse him of that—yet she'd felt the tingle of her body's response in the innermost core of her being. Known a strange, draining languor as he had walked away. And a sharp, almost primitive need to call him back again.

And that was what she couldn't accept—couldn't come to terms with. That sudden dangerous weakness. The unexpected vulnerability.

God knows what I'd have done if he'd really come on to me, she brooded unhappily.

But the most galling aspect of all was that he'd been the one who'd chosen to leave, and not herself.

I should have gone the moment I woke up and saw him there, Cressy told herself in bitter recrimination. I should have been very English and very outraged at having my privacy disturbed. End of story.

For that matter, the story was over now, she admitted with an inward shrug. She just hadn't been the one to write *Finis*, that was all. And, while she might regret it, there was no need to eat her heart out either.

When she'd heard the thrum of the caique's engine as it passed the cove she'd tried hard to keep her attention fixed on her book. When she'd finally risked a quick glance she had found, to her fury, that he was waving to her from the tiller.

But at least he had been sailing in the opposite direction to the harbour, and she wouldn't run the risk of bumping into him there while she was waiting for the ferry.

And now she had the cove to herself again, just as she'd wanted. Except that it was no longer the peaceful sanctuary that she'd discovered a few hours before. Because she felt restless, suddenly, and strangely dissatisfied.

She wanted to cry out, It's all spoiled, like an angry, thwarted child.

But there was nothing to be gained by sitting about counting her wrongs, she thought with a saving grace of humour.

She went for a last swim, relishing the freshness of the water now a slight breeze had risen, hoping wryly that it would cool her imagination as well as her body.

She collected the bicycle and stood for a moment, debating what to do next. It was too early for dinner and, now that the searing afternoon heat had abated, she decided she might as well see what remained of Myros. It was only a small island, and the circular tour would probably take no more than an hour.

It was very much a working island, she soon realised. The interior might be rocky and inhospitable, but on the lower slopes fields had been ploughed and vines and olives were being cultivated, along with orchards of citrus fruits. The scattered hamlets she passed through seemed prosperous enough, and the few people she encountered offered friendly smiles and greetings.

And, contrary to what Yannis had suggested, the road to the north of the island even had some sort of surface.

So Cressy was disconcerted to find her path suddenly blocked by tall wrought-iron gates and a stone wall.

It seemed that the public road had suddenly become private.

Cressy dismounted and tried the gates, but they were securely locked and she could only rattle them in mild frustration. Beyond them she could see a drive winding upwards between olive groves, then, intriguingly, curving away out of sight, making it impossible to guess what lay further on.

She walked along the side of the wall for a while, but it seemed to stretch for ever, and eventually she was forced to retrace her steps.

Apparently, a whole section of the island had been turned into a no-go area. And all she could do was turn back.

After that disappointment, the puncture was almost inevitable.

Cressy brought her untrustworthy steed to a juddering halt and surveyed the damage, cursing herself mentally for having been lured into such an extensive trip.

Now she was faced with a long walk back to the port, pushing the bicycle.

The breeze had strengthened, whipping up the dust from the road and sending irritating particles into her eyes and mouth. She'd finished her water some time before, and she felt hot, thirsty and out of sorts. What was more, she suspected she was getting a blister on her foot.

From now on, she promised herself, she'd confine her activities to the grounds of the Hellenic Imperial.

She'd limped on for another quarter of a mile when she heard the sound of a vehicle on the road behind her.

'More dust,' she muttered, dragging herself and the bicycle on to the stony verge.

A battered pick-up truck roared past, but not before Cressy had managed to catch a glimpse of the driver.

She said a despairing, 'Oh, no—it can't be...' as the truck braked sharply and began to reverse back to where she was standing.

He said, 'How good to meet again so soon. I did not expect it.'

She said crisply, 'Nor I. You were on board a boat, *kyrie*. Now you're driving a truck. What next, I wonder?'

'Probably my own two feet, *thespinis*—like you.' Draco slanted a smile at her through the open window. 'Get in, and I will drive you back to the port.'

'I'm enjoying the walk,' Cressy said regally, and he sighed.

'More lies, *matia mou*. When will you learn?' He swung himself down from the truck, picked up the bicycle and tossed it onto a pile of sacks in the back of the vehicle, then gave Cressy a measuring look. 'You wish to travel like that, or with me?'

Glaring at him, Cressy scrambled into the passenger seat. 'Do you always get your own way?'

He shrugged. 'Why not?'

She could think of a hundred reasons without repeating herself, but she said nothing, sitting beside him in mutinous silence as the pick-up lurched down the track.

At least he'd changed out of those appalling shorts, she thought, stealing a lightning glance from under her lashes. He was now wearing clean but faded jeans and a white shirt, open at the neck with the sleeves turned back over his tanned forearms. And he seemed to have shaved.

All ready for the evening conquests, no doubt.

After a while, he said, 'You are not in a very good mood after your day on the beach.'

Cressy shrugged. 'It started well,' she said stonily. 'Then went downhill fast.'

'As you tried to do on Yannis's bicycle?' He was grinning. 'Not wise.'

'So I discovered,' she admitted tautly. 'Now all I want is to get back to Alakos.'

'You don't like my island?'

'It isn't that at all,' she denied swiftly. 'But I'm hot, dusty, and my hair's full of salt. I need a shower, a cold drink and a meal.'

'*Katavaleno*. I understand.' He swerved to avoid a major pothole. 'So, tell me what you think of Myros?'

'I like what I've seen.' Cressy paused. 'But some of it seems to be cordoned off.'

'Ah,' he said. 'You have been to the north of the island. Some rich people have their houses there.'

'They clearly like their privacy.' She frowned. 'Don't the islanders mind?'

'There is enough room for all of us.' He shrugged. 'If they wish to stay behind high walls, that is their problem.'

There was a silence, then he said, 'When I saw you, you were limping. Why?'

Cressy fought back a gasp.

She said curtly, 'You don't miss much, do you? My foot's a little sore, that's all.'

'You have sprained your ankle?'

'No—nothing like that.'

'What, then?'

Cressy hesitated. 'It's just a small blister.' She forced a smile. 'I seem to have lost the knack of walking.'

He nodded. 'And also of living, I think.'

Cressy flushed. 'So you keep saying. But it's not true. I have a terrific life. I'm very successful, and very happy. And you have no right to imply otherwise,' she added hotly. 'You don't know me, or anything about me.'

'I am trying,' he said. 'But you don't make it easy.'

'Then perhaps you should take the hint,' she flashed. 'Find a more willing subject to analyse.'

She was suddenly thrown across the seat as Draco swung the wheel, turning his ramshackle vehicle on to the verge, where he stopped.

'What are you doing?' Cressy struggled to regain her balance, feeling her breath quicken as Draco turned slowly to face her.

'You think you are unwilling?' The agate eyes glittered at her. 'But you are wrong. You are only unaware.'

He allowed that to sink in, nodding slightly at her indrawn breath, then went on, 'As for the happiness and the success you speak of, I see no such things in you. A woman who is fulfilled has an inner light. Her eyes shine, her skin blooms. But when I look into your eyes I see sadness and fear, *matia mou*.'

He paused. 'And not all high walls are made of stone. Remember that.'

Cressy's back was rigid. She said raggedly, 'I'm sure this chat-up line works with some people, but not with me, *kyrie*. You're insolent, and arrogant, and I'd prefer to walk the rest of the way.'

Draco restarted the truck. 'You will hurt no one but yourself, *thespinis*. And you will walk nowhere until that blister has received attention,' he added curtly. 'So don't be a fool.'

She had never been so angry. She sat with her arms

wrapped round her body, damming back the words of fury and condemnation that threatened to choke her. Fighting back tears, too, unexpected and inexplicable.

She didn't move until the truck stopped outside Yannis's taverna, and she turned to make a measured and final exit, only to find herself fighting with the recalcitrant door catch.

Draco had no such problems, she realised with gritted teeth as he jumped out of the driving seat and appeared beside her. In a second the door was open, and Cressy found herself being lifted out of the passenger side and carried round the side of the taverna to a flight of white-painted stone steps.

Gasping, she began to struggle, trying vainly to get her arms free so that she could hit him. 'How dare you? You bastard. Put me down—put me down now.'

She saw Yannis in a doorway with a plump, pretty woman in a faded red dress standing beside him, their faces masks of astonishment. Heard Draco bark some kind of command in his own language as he started up the steps with Cressy still pinned helplessly against his chest.

The door at the top of the stairs was standing open, and Cressy was carried through it into a corridor lined by half a dozen doors in dark, carved wood.

Draco opened the nearest and shouldered his way in. It was a large room, its pale walls tinged with the glow of sunset from the half-open shutters at the window.

The floor was tiled and there was a chest of drawers, a clothes cupboard and a large bed covered in immaculate white linen, towards which she was being relentlessly carried.

And her anger gave way to swift, nerve-shredding panic.

As Draco put her down on the coverlet, she heard herself whisper, 'No—please...' and hated the note of pleading in her voice.

Draco straightened, his face cold, his mouth a thin line. 'Do not insult me. I have told Maria to come to you. Now, wait there.'

As he reached the door, he was met by the plump woman carrying towels, a basket containing soap and shampoo, and, most welcome of all, a bottle of drinking water.

She rounded on Draco, her voice shrill and scolding, and he grinned down at her, lifting his hands in mock surrender as he went out, closing the door behind him.

Maria looked at Cressy, her dark eyes unwelcoming. She said in slow, strongly accented English, 'Who are you, *kyria*, and what are you doing here?'

Cressy said wearily, 'I don't think I know any more.' And at last her precarious self-control slipped, and she burst into a flood of tears.

CHAPTER FOUR

SHE hadn't intended it, but it was probably the best thing she could have done. Because next moment she'd been swept into Maria's embrace and was being cooed at in Greek, while a surprisingly gentle hand stroked her hair.

When the choking sobs began to subside, she was urged into the little tiled shower-room.

'All will be well, little one,' Maria said as she left her alone. 'You will see. Men,' she added in a tone of robust disapproval.

The warm water and shampoo provided a healing therapy of their own, and Cressy felt almost human again as she wandered back into the bedroom with the largest towel wrapped round her like a sarong.

She checked in surprise because her discarded clothing seemed to have vanished. True, she hadn't been looking forward to putting it on again, but, apart from a change of underwear in her bag, it was all she had. And she could hardly travel back to Alakos in a towel.

Then she saw that there was something lying on the bed—a dress in filmy white cotton, with a full skirt and a square neck embroidered with flowers.

She heard a sound at the door, and turned eagerly. 'Oh, Maria,' she began, and stopped, her breath catching in her throat, as Draco strode into the room.

She swallowed, her hand instinctively going to the knot that secured the towel in place.

She said icily, 'Get out of here—now. Or I'll scream for Maria.'

'You will need strong lungs. Maria is busy in the kitchen.' He put down the bowl he was carrying on the table beside the bed. 'And I am here on an errand of mercy. Let me see your foot.'

'My foot is fine.'

'You wish to have an infection?' His tone was inflexible. 'And spend the rest of your vacation in hospital?' He pointed to the bed. 'Sit down.'

'You have an answer for everything,' Cressy said as she mutinously obeyed. 'I suppose you trained as a doctor between fishing and dancing in restaurants.'

His mouth twisted. 'No, *thespinis*. I took a course in common sense.'

He knelt in front of her and lifted her foot gently to examine it. His fingers were gentle and cool, and she felt a strange shiver of awareness glide between her shoulder blades and down her spine. He glanced up.

'I am hurting you?'

'No.' Cressy bit her lip, trying to appear composed. But it wasn't easy. The clean, male scent of him seemed to fill her consciousness, and she found herself breathing more deeply, inhaling the faint fragrance of soap and clean linen. The silky black curls were inches from her hand, and she wondered how they would feel as her fingers caressed them.

Beneath the towel, she could feel her skin warming in swift, unbidden excitement. Feel her hardening nipples graze against the rough fabric...

Oh, God, what am I doing?

Aloud, she said urgently, 'Look—there's no need for you to do this. I can manage—really.'

'You don't like to be touched?'

'I've never thought about it.' She found herself startled into honesty.

'Then think now.' He paused, and there was a sudden harshness in his voice. 'Do you like to be in the arms of your lover?'

'Of course,' she said, and was glad that his head was bent, and that this time he could not look into her eyes and see that she was lying again.

She was expecting more questions, but he was suddenly silent, concentrating, presumably, on what he was doing.

There was disinfectant in the bowl that he'd brought, and Cressy tried not to wince as he swabbed the blister.

'What's that?' she asked dubiously as he uncapped a small pot of pale green ointment.

'It is made from herbs,' he said. 'It will help you to heal.'

When he'd finished, Cressy had a small, neat dressing held in place by a strip of plaster.

'*Efharisto*,' she said unwillingly. 'Thank you. It—it feels better already.'

'Good,' he said, getting to his feet. 'Then you will be able to dance with me tonight.'

'No,' Cressy said, feeling her heart thud painfully against her ribcage. 'No, I couldn't possibly.'

'Why not? Because your lover would not like it if he knew?'

'Perhaps.' Cressy examined her plaster with renewed interest. This non-existent boyfriend was proving useful, she thought. She had a dress ring in her luggage at the hotel. From now on she would wear it—on her engagement finger.

'Then why is he not here with you—making sure that no other man's hand touches his woman?'

She shrugged. 'He didn't want to come. He—he doesn't like very hot weather.'

'He has ice in his veins—this Englishman.' The harshness in his tone was inlaid with contempt.

'On the contrary.' Cressy moved her foot cautiously. 'But we have a modern relationship, *kyrie*. We don't have to spend every minute of every day together. We—like our space.'

He said slowly, 'If you belonged to me, *matia mou*, I would not let you out of my sight.'

She raised her eyebrows. 'Isn't that a little primitive?'

'Perhaps.' His mouth smiled but the agate eyes were oddly hard. 'But it is also—effective.'

He picked up the bowl and the roll of plaster. 'Come down when you are ready, *thespinis*. Yannis is waiting to cook your dinner.'

'I can't come down,' she said. 'I have nothing to wear.'

Draco indicated the dress that was lying on the bed. 'You call this nothing? Maria has put it here for you. It would honour her for you to wear it. And be an honour for you, too,' he added sharply. 'It was her wedding dress.'

'Oh.' Cressy swallowed. 'I had no idea. Then of course I must...' Her voice tailed away.

He replaced the dress carefully, then went to the door.

He said, 'I will tell them to expect you—to dine, and then to dance.'

And was gone.

Maria must have been very much slimmer at the time of her marriage, Cressy reflected, for the dress was almost a perfect fit.

Of course, the canvas shoes didn't really do it justice, but they'd have to suffice.

She'd brushed her damp hair until it hung, sleek and shining, to her shoulders, and applied a touch of colour to her mouth.

Now, she circled doubtfully in front of the long narrow mirror fixed to the wall. No one at her City office would have recognised her, she thought. She hardly recognised herself.

I look about seventeen, she thought. Except that I never looked like this when I was seventeen.

It wasn't just the dress. There was something in her face—something soft, almost wistful, that was new and unfamiliar. Under their fringe of lashes, her eyes were dreaming.

My eyes. That was what he had called her. Matia mou.

Only she wasn't going to think about that any more— what he'd said, or done. She was going to eat her meal, get on her ferry, and go back to the sanctuary of her expensive hotel. And if he turned up there, Security would know how to deal with him.

She nodded fiercely, and went down to the courtyard of the taverna.

Yannis welcomed her with extravagant admiration, and Maria appeared in the kitchen doorway, smiling mistily.

But Draco, as a cautious glance round soon revealed, was nowhere to be seen.

Perhaps the mention of a boyfriend had produced the desired result, Cressy told herself, firmly quashing an unwelcome tingle of disappointment.

To her surprise, the taverna was busy, and not just with local people. One of the tour companies had brought a crowd over from Alakos, it seemed, and most of the tables had been rearranged in a long line under the striped awning, and people, laughing and talking, were taking their seats there.

Yannis took Cressy to a secluded corner, protected by latticework screens covered, in turn, by a flowering vine.

He brought her ouzo, followed by dishes of taramasalata and houmous, and juicy black olives, with a platter of fresh bread.

As she sampled them, Cressy saw that a group of bouzouki players had arrived and were tuning their instruments.

For the dancing, thought Cressy with sudden unease. She sent a restive glance at her watch.

'There is a problem?' No mistaking that deep voice. Cressy looked up, shocked, to see Draco depositing a bottle of white wine on the table and taking the seat opposite.

Her warning antennae had let her down badly this time, she thought, biting her lip.

She hurried into speech. 'I was wondering about the ferry. What time does it leave?'

He sent an amused glance at the exuberant holidaymakers. 'When these people are ready to go. There is no hurry.' He paused. 'Or are you so anxious to leave us?'

She kept her voice even. 'I think it's time that I got back to the real world.'

'Or what passes for reality at the Hellenic Imperial hotel,' he said softly.

'You don't approve of such places?'

He shrugged. 'The islands need tourists, and tourists need hotels. They can prove—lucrative.'

'Especially,' Cressy said waspishly, 'for someone like you.'

His grin was unabashed. 'I do not deny it.' He picked up her glass to fill it with wine.

She said, 'I didn't order that.'

He smiled at her. 'It is a gift.'

'I didn't expect that either.'

'You ask for so little, *matia mou*. It is one of your many charms.'

Cressy flushed. 'If you really want to do me a favour, *kyrie*, you'll stop calling me *matia mou*.'

His brows lifted. 'Why?'

'Because it's—inappropriate. In my country it could be construed as harassment.'

She couldn't believe how prim and humourless she sounded.

He said quietly, 'But you are in my country now. On my island. And things are different here.'

'Is that a warning?' She stiffened.

'Do you feel that you are in danger?'

Yes, she wanted to scream. Yes—and I don't understand what's happening to me. I don't want this.

Aloud, she said lightly, 'I'm the stranger within your gates, *kyrie*. Isn't that what you told me? I've eaten your bread, and now I'm drinking your wine.' She lifted her glass towards him, then took a mouthful. It was cool and crisp against her dry throat. 'So why should I be afraid?'

He raised his own glass. '*Stin iyia sas*. To you, *thespinis*, and to your beauty in that dress. If your lover was here, he would beg on his knees to make you his bride.' He drank, and put down his glass.

He said softly, his gaze holding hers, 'I will make a bargain with you. I will not call you "my eyes" until your eyes promise me that I may. And, in return, you will tell me your given name.'

Under the cool white cotton, her skin felt as if it was on fire.

She lifted her chin. 'Very well, *kyrie*. I'm called Cressida.'

'Cressida,' he repeated thoughtfully. 'The golden one—who was faithless to her lover Troilus.'

'According to Shakespeare, and the other men who wrote about her,' Cressy said crisply. 'She, of course, might have had a different viewpoint. And, if it comes to that, your own namesake isn't much to brag about—a tyrant imposing laws that no one could live under. Although that shouldn't surprise me,' she added with warmth.

'Quarrelling?' Yannis arrived with two plates of grilled swordfish, Greek salads, and a big bowl of fries. 'Not while you eat my food, or you will get bad stomachs.' He wagged an admonishing finger at them both, and went off.

Draco grinned at her. 'He is right. Let us begin again.'

He held out his hand. '*Hero poli*, Cressida. I am pleased to meet you.'

Reluctantly, she allowed her fingers to be enclosed in the warmth of his. '*Hero poli*—Draco.'

'And your name is very beautiful,' he added.

Cressy wrinkled her nose. 'I used to hate it,' she confessed. 'But then I hated everything about being a girl. I wanted so badly to be a boy when I was little that my father used to call me Sid as a joke. My mother was very cross about it, so he'd never use it in front of her. Only when we were on our own.'

'And does he still call you—Sid?' His brows lifted.

Cressy looked down at her plate. 'Not for a long time,' she said quietly.

'I am not surprised.' He gave a faint smile. 'I must tell you, Cressida, that you are no boy.'

She met the sudden intensity of the dark eyes and flushed, reaching hurriedly for her knife and fork.

The swordfish was succulent and delicious, and she ate every scrap, even conducting a laughing battle with Draco over the last few fries.

'It is good to meet a woman who does not wish to starve herself,' he told her as he refilled her glass.

She shook her head. 'One of these days all these calories will suddenly explode, and I'll turn into a mountain.'

'No.' The dark eyes travelled over her in smiling, sensuous appraisal. 'For me, you will always look as you do now, *agapi mou*.'

Cressy frowned. 'What does that mean?' she asked suspiciously.

He laughed. 'It is best that you don't know.'

Cressy felt her colour deepen helplessly. To cover her confusion, she turned to watch the bouzouki players, tapping her fingers on the table to the music.

Draco was watching her. 'You like bouzouki?'

'I don't know very much,' she admitted. 'Just "Zorba's Dance", like everyone else.' She hesitated. 'I liked what you were dancing to this morning.'

'That was also by Theodorakis.' He smiled faintly. 'He is still very much a hero. A man whose music spoke to the people.'

She said, 'I—I hope you're going to dance tonight.'

'Only if you will promise, just once, to be my partner.'

'But I couldn't,' Cressy protested. 'I've never done any Greek dancing.'

'I did not mean that. When the entertainment is over, Yannis plays other music.' The agate eyes glittered at her. 'We will choose something very slow—very sweet—so that you won't hurt your foot.'

'Oh.' Cressy felt hollow inside, but she mustered a smile. 'Thank you.'

'Would you like some dessert? Halva, perhaps—or baklava?'

'Just coffee, please.'

He said, 'I'll fetch it.'

She watched him lithely threading his way between the tables, and saw without surprise that several of the woman holidaymakers from the large party were watching him too, nudging each other and exchanging whispered comments and giggles.

I could always send a note over saying, 'He's available,' Cressy thought sourly. Only people might get killed in the rush.

She'd come away on holiday to relax, yet she'd never felt so edgy and restless in her life.

She'd had her day and her evening neatly planned, but here she was, in another woman's wedding dress, having dinner with a man who supplemented his income by 'befriending' lonely women.

And she wasn't lonely, she told herself vehemently. Yes, she missed her father's company, but she had plenty of friends. She could go out every night, if she wanted. And there were plenty of men who'd be keen to escort her.

Which was fine. It was when they tried to get closer that warning bells started to ring and she felt herself freeze.

No man was prepared to be held at arm's length for ever. She understood that perfectly well. She'd always assumed that one of her casual friendships would eventually bloom into something deeper. Something based on liking and respect, rather than casual physical attraction.

She'd always sworn she'd never be caught in that trap.

So a holiday romance had never been on the cards.

Draco was good-looking, with a sexual aura as powerful as a force field, but this time he'd chosen the wrong target, she told herself with determination.

Their acquaintance would end with dinner, as she would make clear.

I'll pay Yannis for the meal, she thought, and ask him to tell Draco goodbye for me.

And then she'd never set foot on Myros again. She would arrange for the hotel to launder and return Maria's dress and collect her own things. And that would be an end to it.

She looked round for Yannis, but at the same moment the bouzouki players struck up again, and she saw that he and three other men had formed a line and begun to dance, their hands resting on each other's shoulders. It was a slow, intricate dance, but their movements were perfectly synchronised, and strangely dignified, Cressy thought, watching, entranced.

This wasn't just a cabaret act, as it was at the hotel, she realised as she joined the rest of the audience in clapping in time to the music. These were men to whom their own culture was a living, breathing thing.

The music quickened its pace. The dance changed to include Maria and a couple of other women, and, gradually, the crowd from Alakos were persuaded to join in too, weaving their way between the tables in a long, twirling chain.

A waiter appeared at her side with coffee. 'For you, *thespinis*. Kyrios Draco says he is to dance next.'

Giving her an ideal chance to slip away, thought Cressy. As the waiter moved off, she stopped him. *'O logariasimos, parakolo?'* Adding, 'May I have the bill, please?' in case he didn't understand her attempt at Greek.

But he didn't seem to have much grasp of English either, because he shrugged, smilingly spread his hands, and kept on walking.

The dance finished and everyone sat down, laughing and talking.

When the music started again, it was slow and haunting, almost plaintive.

Cressy knew that Draco had appeared, because the chattering voices were stilled suddenly, and there was a new tension in the air. She stared down at her coffee, not wanting to look up—not wanting to watch, but eventually impelled to.

Across the distance that divided them, above the heads of the crowd, his eyes met hers—held them steadily. He inclined his head in silent acknowledgement. Then he began to dance.

Yannis and the other men knelt in a half-circle around him, clapping the rhythm. Tonight, there was none of the exuberance she'd seen that morning. The movements were as passionate, but they spoke of pain and isolation. The music seemed to wail and weep, emphasising the yearning expressed by his taut body.

Cressy, totally enthralled, saw weariness and suffering. And every so often a dangerous flicker of wildness.

She thought, with an odd certainty, This is about love—and the loss of love...

When it stopped, there was silence for a moment, and then the applause broke out, wave after wave of it, and people were standing to take photographs.

When disco music began to play over the sound system it was almost a shock. But no one else could have followed Draco, she thought.

Everyone was up on their feet, joining in, jigging around vigorously. Glad, she thought, to dispel some of the emotion of the last few minutes.

Cressy noticed the girl at once. She was red-haired and pretty, wearing a tiny Lycra skirt and a skimpy top displaying a generous amount of cleavage. Her hand was on Draco's arm and she was smiling up at him, moving closer, her whole body an invitation.

Cressy put down her coffee cup, aware that her hand was shaking. She knew an overwhelming impulse to rush over to them—to drag the redhead away—to slap her—scratch her nails down that simpering face.

But she wasn't a violent person, she told herself vehemently. She never had been.

Except that she'd never been jealous before. And that made all the difference.

The resentment she felt for Eloise didn't even feature on the same scale, she thought, closing her eyes, conscious that she felt slightly sick.

She and Draco came from two different worlds. So how could she possibly feel these things for a total stranger—someone she didn't want? That she couldn't want...

The soundtrack had changed to something soft and dreamy, and Cressy kept her eyes shut, because she didn't want to see the red-haired girl in Draco's arms.

His voice, soft and amused, said, 'It is too soon to sleep, *agapi mou*. You have a bargain to keep.'

She looked up at him, feeling her stomach muscles clench in unwelcome excitement and longing.

She said coolly, 'Shouldn't you be spending time with your adoring public?'

His grin was appreciative. 'She was beautiful, *ne*?' He whistled. 'Such a mouth—such breasts.' Lazily, he scanned Cressy's indignantly parted lips, then let his gaze travel slowly downwards. That was all he did, yet for one dizzy, scared moment she knew how his mouth would feel on hers—recognised the intimate touch of his hands on her body.

He went on quietly, 'But I am here with you, my golden one, so don't disappoint me.'

He held out his hand, and, silently, she rose from her seat and went with him. Felt his arms close round her, drawing her against him. Cressy surrendered, sliding her own arms round his firm waist and resting her cheek against his chest as they moved quietly together to the music, one tune fading effortlessly into another.

She was not an accomplished dancer, yet in Draco's arms she seemed to drift in perfect attunement, as if she was part of him. It might have been a dream, except that she was only too aware of the physical reality of his nearness.

She was trembling inside, her body tingling as the warmth of his skin invaded her thin layers of clothing, giving her the helpless impression that she was naked in his arms. Shocking her by the sudden scalding heat of desire.

There were no pretences anymore. He was as aroused as she was.

He whispered against her ear, his voice raw and urgent, 'You feel it too, *ne*, my girl, my heaven? This need we have for each other?'

She pulled away, staring up at him, her eyes wide, the pupils dilated as she met the glint of golden fire in his.

She said hoarsely, 'I—I can't do this. I have to go—have to...'

And stopped, as she realised they were alone. The courtyard was deserted. Yannis and his helpers had vanished into the taverna, the glass doors discreetly closed behind them, and the crowd from Alakos had gone.

She said on a little sob, 'The ferry—oh, God, the ferry...'

She ran out of the courtyard and down the street towards the harbour, but Draco caught her before she'd gone more than a few yards.

'The ferry has gone,' he said.

'But you knew I had to catch it. You knew that.' Her voice shook. 'Now I'm stranded. Oh, *hell*. What am I going to do?'

'You stay here,' he said calmly. 'It's not a problem.'

'Yes,' she said bitterly. 'Oh, yes, it is. You don't understand...'

'I know more than you think.' He put his hands on her shoulders, looking down into her angry, frightened face. 'You believe I have kept you here to share my bed tonight, but you are wrong. I shall sleep at my own house, and you will stay here with Yannis and Maria.'

Cressy gasped. 'When was this decided?'

'When we realised that there would be no room for you on the ferry. An overcrowded boat is not safe, particularly when many of the passengers have been drinking Metaxa. It is better to wait for tomorrow.'

She bit her lip. 'Very well.' She paused. 'But the hotel. They'll know I haven't come back…'

'Yannis has telephoned them, so all is well.'

She said quietly, 'Then there's nothing left to say.'

The music had stopped when they came back to the courtyard, and the lights were out.

Draco walked beside her, his tread as quiet as a cat's. He did not touch her, but she felt him in every fibre of her being.

He would kiss her, she thought confusedly, and she wanted him to. In fact, she ached for him. But she'd betrayed too much already, while they were dancing. And when his mouth touched hers she would have no defences left.

No strength to say no when he walked up the moonlit stairs beside her to the quiet, cool room with the wide bed. No power to resist when he drew her down into his arms.

His for the taking, she thought. And he would know that, and would take…

They reached the foot of the stone steps and she paused uncertainly, waiting for him to reach for her.

He said softly, 'Until tomorrow—Cressida the golden. But now—*kalinichta*. Goodnight.' And she felt the brush of his lips against her hair, as swift and tantalising as a butterfly's wing.

And then she was free, walking up the stairs alone, and bewildered. She turned at the top of the stairs and looked down at him, the still shadow waiting there. Watching her go.

She said huskily, 'I don't understand. What do you want from me?'

'I want everything, *agapi mou*.' There was a strange

harshness in his voice. 'All you have to give. And nothing less will do.' He paused. 'But I can wait.'

He turned away into the darkness, leaving Cressy standing motionless, her hand pressed to her trembling mouth.

CHAPTER FIVE

'MISS FIELDING—are you all right?'

Cressida started violently, and looked up to see one of the senior nurses standing beside her.

'Yes,' she said. 'I'm fine. I'm sorry—I was miles away.'

A thousand miles, she thought, and another world...

'I'm going to ask you to go to the visitors' room for a little while. The consultant is coming to see your father, and he'll talk to you afterwards.'

'Of course.' She almost stumbled up from her chair and along the corridor. It wasn't a comfortable room. There was a table in the middle of the room with magazines, and a few moulded plastic chairs ranged round the walls.

She went over to the window and looked out at a vista of rooftops.

She felt ashamed. She was supposed to be here for her father, trying to infuse him with her own youth and strength, and instead she'd allowed herself to daydream—to remember things far better forgotten. A time that was past and done with.

Except...

The memory of that enigmatic e-mail message would not be so easily dismissed.

I am waiting for you.

It can't be him, she denied, almost violently. I won't believe it.

She grabbed a magazine from the table and sat down,

only to open it at a page recommending Greek holidays. She looked at the crescent of bleached sand fringed by turquoise water in the picture and realised bleakly that there was no refuge from her memories.

They crowded her mind, filling it. Drawing her inexorably back to Myros.

She'd hardly slept that first night at the taverna. She had been too aware of the danger threatening her to be able to relax. And Draco was the most danger she'd ever encountered in her life.

No wonder he was a fisherman, she had thought, turning over restlessly and thumping the flat pillow with her fist. He knew exactly how to keep a woman hooked and helpless.

But he wouldn't reel her in. She wouldn't allow it to happen. She was her own person, and her plan didn't include casual sex. It never had.

Draco had to learn that no matter how attractive he might be he was not always going to win.

And he'd soon find consolation. Every time he danced there'd be a queue of eager and willing girls vying for his attention. He wouldn't have time to remember the one that got away.

She had nodded fiercely, and closed her eyes with determination.

When she'd awoken, early sun had been spilling through the slats in the shutters across the tiled floor.

The first thing she had seen was that all the things she'd used yesterday, including the beach towel, were lying pristinely laundered and neatly folded on the chair, and the white dress, which had been carefully draped there, had gone. Maria, it seemed, had performed a dawn raid.

Which I didn't intend, Cressy had thought, as she slid out of bed and headed for the shower.

When she had gone down the outside stairs, Maria had been sweeping the courtyard. To Cressy's embarrassment, it had been made immediately clear that she would be allowed to pay nothing for her night's lodging or her meal. Nor would she be permitted to have the white dress cleaned.

'It is my pleasure to do this for you,' Maria declared. 'Everyone say how beautiful you look in the dress.'

Cressy flushed a little. 'Oh?'

'Ah, yes.' Maria gave her a roguish look. 'And one person in particular, *ne*?' She pointed to the table Cressy had occupied the night before. 'Sit there, *kyria*, and I will bring you breakfast. Rolls and coffee, and some of the honey from my sister's bees.' She bustled off, leaving Cressy to take a careful look around, but she had the courtyard to herself, she realised with relief.

She consulted the list of ferry times in her bag, and saw that the first one ran in just over half an hour. She should make it easily.

Her meal also included fresh orange juice and a bowl of creamy yoghurt. By the time she got up from the table she was replete.

'I can't thank you enough,' she told Yannis and Maria when they came to say goodbye to her.

'You are welcome.' Yannis's hand closed over hers. 'Welcome at any time. Your room will always be waiting.'

Cressy's smile was a little taut. 'Maybe—one day,' she said. She hesitated. 'And please would you thank Draco for me? He's been—kind.'

She picked up her bag and headed down to the harbour, determined to be the first one on the ferry. But it wasn't moored at the landing point she'd used yesterday. In fact she couldn't see it anywhere, she realised frantically, shading her eyes and staring out to sea.

'So you did not intend to say goodbye.' Draco got up from the stack of wooden crates he'd been sitting on. The shorts he was wearing were just as disreputable as the previous pair, and he'd topped them with an unbuttoned white cotton shirt.

Cressy lifted her chin. 'I—I left a message with Maria.'

'Now you can give it to me in person.'

Exactly what she hadn't wanted. She said stiltedly, 'Just—thank you, and good luck.'

'I believe in fate more than luck.' He looked her over, smiling faintly. 'Last night you were Cressida,' he said. 'But today you are Sid again. What will you be tomorrow, *agapi mou*?'

She shook her head. She said, almost inaudibly. 'I don't think I know any more.'

'Perhaps you are being reborn,' he said. 'Rising like a phoenix from the ashes of your former life.'

She threw back her head. 'But I don't want that. I'm quite content with things as they are.'

'Content?' There was scorn in his voice. 'Is that the most you can wish for? What a small, narrow word, when there is excitement, passion and rapture to be experienced.'

'Perhaps,' she said, 'I like to feel safe.'

'There is no safety, *agapi mou*. Not in life. Not in love. As you will discover when you stop running away.' He shrugged. 'But if you wish to return to Alakos and the comfort of your hotel, I will take you.'

'Thank you,' she said. 'But I'll wait for the proper ferry.'

'Then you'll wait a long time,' he said drily. 'Kostas drank too much Metaxa last night on Alakos. There will be no ferry until tonight.'

Cressy gasped indignantly. 'Is he allowed to do that?'

Draco grinned. 'He does not usually wait for permission. It is my boat or nothing, *pethi mou*.'

She gave him a fulminating glance, then sighed. 'All right. Your boat. Just as long as I get back to Alakos.'

'Why the hurry? Are you so sure that Myros has nothing more to offer?' There was an undercurrent of mockery in his tone.

'I'm paying to stay at the Hellenic Imperial,' she reminded him tautly.

'Ah, money,' he said. 'That concerns you deeply?'

'I like to get my money's worth. But I'm sure you're far above such considerations.'

He lifted a negligent shoulder. 'It's easier not to think about it, I promise you.'

Cressy bit her lip, aware that she'd been ungracious about his undoubted poverty.

She said, 'You must let me pay you for the trip.'

He sent her a quizzical look. 'Did Yannis and Maria ask you to pay for the meal last night—or your room?'

'No,' she said. 'They didn't. But…'

'And I am no different. There is no charge.' And there was a note in his voice which told her not to argue.

She sat tensely in the bow as the caique pushed its way through the sparkling sunlit water. The faint early haze was clearing and it was going to be another scorching day, she thought, lifting her hair away from the nape of her neck.

Draco said from the tiller, 'You are too warm? There is an awning…'

'No, I'm fine,' she assured him quickly. 'It's just so—beautiful.'

'I think you are falling in love, *agapi mou*, with my country. You will never want to go home.'

She stared at the horizon. 'I think my boss would have something to say about that.'

'You are indispensable?'

'Hardly. I don't think anyone really is. We just fool ourselves, then we go, and our space is filled, and no one even remembers we were once there.'

'That is a sad thought for such a lovely day,' Draco said after a pause. 'But you will be remembered always.'

She shook her head. 'I don't think so.'

'Ah, but you will,' he said. 'By your lover, for one—and your father, for another. And I—I will remember too.'

'You will?' She sent him a look of disbelief. 'That's nonsense.'

'Of course I'll remember. It is not every day I meet a girl with hair like the sun, and moonlight in her eyes, who is called Sid.'

Her heart twisted slowly and painfully. To cover the sudden emotion, she pulled a face. 'I knew I'd regret mentioning that.'

'There is nothing to regret. It is good that your father had this special name for you.' He smiled at her. 'Sometimes when I look at you I can see the little girl you were.'

Cressy turned away and stared at the sea. She said flatly, 'She's been gone a long time.'

'You will find her again when you hold your own daughter in your arms.'

How simple he made it sound, Cressy thought, her throat aching. And how unlikely it really was.

She straightened her shoulders. 'Alakos doesn't seem to be coming any closer.'

He said, 'I thought you would wish to pay a last visit to our beach.'

'And I thought I'd made it clear I wanted to go straight back.' There was sudden ice in her voice as she turned on him, but Draco did not appear chilled.

His eyes met hers steadily. 'You offered to pay for your trip. This is the price—that you swim with me just once.'

She said acidly, 'Dancing last night. Swimming today. Do you set up a full fitness programme for all your women?'

He spoke very quietly. 'That is a suggestion that demeans us both. But if it is really what you think, then there is no more to be said.'

She watched him move the tiller, heading the caique out into the open sea.

Then she looked back at the horizon and found it suddenly blurred with unshed tears.

It was a miserably silent journey. To Cressy's surprise, Draco avoided the main harbour and sailed round to the hotel's private bay, bringing his craft skilfully alongside the small jetty.

In a subdued voice, she said, 'I don't think you're meant to be here.'

He shrugged. 'Does it matter? I shall soon be gone.'

His touch completely impersonal, he helped her ashore, and put her bag on the planking beside her.

She said in a sudden rush, 'Draco—I'm sorry—I didn't mean what I said. I—I don't want us to part bad friends, but I'm just so confused. I can't seem to get my head together...'

He nodded, but the bronze face showed no sign of softening.

'Then start listening to your heart instead, Cressida. And when you do, you know where to find me.' He pointed towards Myros. 'I shall be there—waiting for you.'

She stood on the jetty and watched until the boat was a mere speck, but he never looked back.

Cressy jumped as the door to the visitors' room opened and the consultant came in.

'Miss Fielding.' His handshake was limp for such an eminent man. 'You'll be pleased to hear that your father is making good progress. If it continues, we should be able to send him home next week.'

'Oh.' Cressy sat down on one of the uncomfortable chairs. 'Oh, that's such a relief. And the operation?'

'As soon as we consider he's fit enough.' The consultant looked vaguely round. 'Is your mother not here? I should speak to her about his future care.'

Cressy said evenly, 'My stepmother is—away.'

'Of course,' he said. 'Building up her strength to nurse the invalid at home, no doubt. Admirable.'

Cressida bent her head. 'Now may I go back to my father, please?

'You're going to be all right, Dad,' she whispered to the still figure in the bed. 'Isn't that wonderful news? I just wish you'd give some sign that you can hear me. Although I do understand that you've got to rest.

'And I can work for you, Daddy. I can deal with the bank, and the mortgage company, and everyone. I can't get your money back, but maybe I can stop you losing everything else. I'll talk to them—I'll make them listen. Because I need to work—to stop me from thinking. Remembering...'

In spite of the heat, she shivered.

She had gone straight up to the hotel, she recalled, and lain down on the bed in her air-conditioned room and stared up at the ceiling...

There was a vast, aching emptiness inside her. A trembling, frightened nothingness.

She thought, What am I doing? What have I done?

Draco's face seemed to float above her, and she closed her eyes to shut him out. But she couldn't dismiss her other senses so easily. Her skin burned as she remembered the sensuous pressure of his body against hers. She seemed to breathe the scent of him. To feel the brush of his lips on her flesh.

A little moan escaped her. She was consumed by bewildered longing, her body torn apart by physical needs that she'd never known before.

She twisted restlessly on the bed, trying to find peace and calm, but failing.

She got up and went out on to the balcony, but the indigo shimmer of Myros on the horizon drove her inside again.

She stayed in her room until midday, when she made herself go down and join the queue at the lavish buffet on the hotel's terrace.

She'd never realised before how many couples seemed to be staying at the hotel, wandering around hand in hand, or with their arms round each other.

Making her blindingly—piercingly aware of her own isolation—her own loneliness.

Making her realise that she couldn't bear it any

longer. And that she didn't have to—that she too could choose to be happy for a little while.

A few days—even a few hours, she thought. I'd settle for that. Whatever the ultimate cost.

She could tell herself a thousand times that she was crazy even to contemplate such a thing, but it made no difference. Her will power—her control didn't seem to matter any more. The ache of yearning was too strong, too compelling, and it was drawing her back.

When she told them at Reception that she was going back to Myros to stay for a while she half expected they would try to dissuade her, but her decision was accepted almost casually.

Down at the harbour, she didn't wait for the ferry, but paid one of the local boatmen to take her across to the other island.

She was trembling as she walked up from the quay towards the taverna. This was madness, and she knew it, and it would serve her right if she walked in and found Draco with someone else, she thought, pain twisting inside her. But one swift glance told her that he wasn't there.

Yannis was playing *tavli*, and his jaw dropped when he saw her. Then he recovered himself, and got to his feet smiling broadly.

The *thespinis* was welcome. It was good that she had come back. Especially as he had mended the wheel on his sister's bicycle.

Up in her room, Cressy changed into a black bikini, topping it with a scooped neck T-shirt in the same colour and a wrapround skirt in a black and white swirling print.

All the way to the beach she was straining her ears to hear music, but there was only silence and solitude.

She left the bicycle on the clifftop and scrambled down to the sand. The heat was intense, but she felt cold with disappointment.

She had been so ridiculously sure that he'd be there—waiting for her.

Was it really only twenty-four hours? she wondered, spreading her towel in the same spot. It seemed more like a year.

She slipped off her skirt and top, kicked off her sandals, and ran down to the sea, welcoming its cool caress against her overheated skin.

She needed to work off some of this emotion somehow, and a long, strenuous swim would do the trick. If only it could restore her common sense at the same time.

She drove herself on, pounding up and down as if she was covering lengths in a pool, until her arms and legs were heavy with tiredness and she knew it was time to go back.

She put a foot down, finding sand and shingle, and began to wade towards the beach, wringing the excess water out of her hair.

Out of the dazzle of the sun she saw him, standing motionless on the edge of the sea, small waves curling round his bare feet.

She began to run, cursing the pressure of the water which held her back.

He was holding her towel, she realised, and as she reached him he wrapped it round her, pulling her into his arms. She lifted her face mutely, and for the first time experienced the hungry demand of his mouth on hers.

The kiss seemed to last an eternity, as if, with that first taste, they could not get enough of each other.

He was not gentle, nor did she require him to be. His mouth clung, burned, tore at hers as if he was trying to absorb her into his being.

Her own lips parted breathlessly, welcoming the thrust of his tongue, inciting the dark, heated exploration to go deeper still. Offering herself without reserve.

Sun, sea and bleached sand were performing a crazy, spinning dance around her, and she put up her hands to grip his bare shoulders. She was trembling under this wild onslaught on her senses, her legs shaking under her.

Just as she thought she might collapse on the sand at his feet, Draco lifted her into his arms and carried her up the beach. He'd spread a rug in the shadow of some rocks and he lowered her on to it, coming down beside her, seeking her mouth again, his hand tangling in her damp blonde hair.

She surrendered her lips eagerly to the sensuous rapture of his possession. She felt as if she was drunk—or that she'd entered some other undreamed of dimension.

Her hands caressed his back, holding him to her as his mouth travelled downwards, questing the curve of her throat and the small hollows at its base.

His tongue found the cleft between her breasts and lingered, and she gasped, her body arching involuntarily, her nipples hardening in excitement under the damp fabric.

His lips brushed each soft swell of flesh above the confines of the bikini top as one hand stroked down her body to find and cup the delicate contour of her hip with total mastery. Making no secret of his intention.

He lifted his head and stared down at her, the dark eyes slumbrous, a flush of deeper colour along the high cheekbones, as if he was waiting for some sign from her.

Watching him, Cressy raised a hand and undid the halter strap of her bikini, then released the little clip, freeing the tiny garment completely.

Draco bent his head and with great precision took it from her with his teeth.

He tossed it aside and lowered his mouth fully to her bare breasts, paying them slow and languorous homage, his lips moulding their soft fullness. As she felt the provocative flicker of his tongue across the puckered rose of her nipples a little moan of surprise and longing escaped her.

His mouth enclosed each hot, excited peak in turn, pleasuring them softly and subtly. Eyes closed, Cressy gave herself up to delight, feeling her last remaining inhibitions sliding away.

At the same time his fingers were feathering across her thighs, brushing the delicate mound they guarded, and her body responded with a rush of scalding, passionate heat.

His mouth moved down her body slowly, almost druggingly, paying minute attention to each curve and hollow. He murmured softly in his own language, resting his cheek against the concavity of her stomach.

She was dimly aware that at some point he had discarded the swimming trunks that were his sole covering, but it was only when she felt the glide of his fingers against the heated, throbbing core of her womanhood that she realised that she too was now naked.

He kissed her mouth again, his tongue teasing hers as his hands continued their gentle erotic play, taking her ever closer to some brink she'd never known existed.

As her breathing quickened she felt him move slightly, his body covering hers, his hands sliding under her to lift her for his possession.

For a fleeting moment she experienced the heated pressure of him against her, seeking her. And then there was pain, and she heard her voice, muffled against his shoulder, crying out in shock and sudden panic.

He was instantly still. Then he rolled away from her almost frantically, his breath rasping in his throat.

When she dared look, he was sitting a few feet away, one leg drawn up, his forehead resting on his knee. There was a faint sheen of perspiration gleaming on his skin, and his chest heaved as he fought for control.

She whispered his name, and when there was no response reached across and put her hand lightly on his arm.

He shook her off almost violently. His voice was a snarl. 'Do not touch me. It is not safe.'

She said in a whisper, 'What is it? I don't understand...'

As the silence lengthened between them she said, more urgently, her voice shaking a little, 'Talk to me, please. Tell me what's wrong. What I've done.'

Draco turned and looked at her, his dark eyes hooded, the firm mouth compressed.

He said, 'You have done nothing wrong. The mistake, God help us both, is mine.'

He reached for his trunks and pulled them on, his face taut.

Colour stormed into her face and she grabbed clumsily for her towel, holding it in front of her defensively, just as if there was an inch of her that he'd left undiscovered.

'You lied to me, Cressida. Why?' His voice was harsh.

'Lied?' she repeated uncomprehendingly.

'You let me think you had a lover. But it is not true. So why did you pretend.'

'What did you expect me to do?' Her eyes blurred with humiliated tears. 'It was what you wanted to hear—wasn't it? And it seemed—safer.'

'No,' he said. 'It was not safe. It was a stupid lie, and a dangerous one. You thought I would not know?'

She bent her head. 'I—I didn't think so. I didn't realise it would make any difference...'

She heard him whisper something sharp and violent, then he was beside her again. He drew her towards him, cupping her face gently between his hands, making her meet his searching gaze.

He said quietly, 'It makes all the difference in the world, *agapi mou*. But I am also to blame. I should have realised that you were claiming a sophistication you did not possess.'

She said tautly, 'Of course, you know so much about women.'

'More than you know of men, certainly.'

Cressy bit her lip, unable to deny his curt response. Her voice shook slightly. 'Draco—I'm so sorry...'

'Sorry?' he repeated, his voice incredulous. 'You offer me the ultimate gift—and say you are sorry?'

She said flatly, 'But it's a gift you don't seem to want.'

His mouth relaxed into the shadow of a smile. 'You think I don't want you, *agapi mou*?' He took her hands and carried them fleetingly to his body. 'You are wrong. But a woman's innocence should not be thrown away to feed the hunger of the moment. You deserve better.'

His lips touched hers, swiftly and gently. 'Now dress yourself, and we will go back to the town, where there are more people and less temptations.'

He got to his feet and walked down the beach, where he stood, his back turned, gazing at the sea, while Cressy huddled into her clothing.

When he came back to her, she said, 'I think I'd better go back to Alakos.'

'Why should you do that?' His dark brows drew into a frown.

'Because I'm very embarrassed.' She made a business of folding her towel. 'I've made a real fool of myself.' She added carefully, 'And I'd just be in the way if I stayed.'

'Ah,' Draco said softly. 'You feel you might hinder my search for the next willing body.' He cast a despairing look at the heavens. 'Is that truly what you think of me?'

She said, 'Draco—I don't know what to think. I don't *know* you.'

'Then why did you come back?' He spoke gently, but there was an inflexible note in his voice. 'Just so that I could rid you of your unwanted virginity? I don't believe that.'

She bit her lip. 'Because I found I couldn't stay away. And now I've ruined everything.'

He sighed. 'Nothing is spoiled—unless you wish it to be.' There was a silence, then he stroked the curve of her face with one long finger. 'Is that what you want, *pethi mou*? Or shall we begin all over again? Start to learn about each other, not just with our bodies, but our minds?'

She said on a little sob, 'Oh, Draco, please.'

'Then so be it.' He took her hand, held it in his, his

fingers strong and warm. 'But understand, Cressida, that this changes everything. And if you leave me now, I shall follow. However long, however far.' He paused. 'You accept this?'

And, from some great distance, she heard herself answer, 'Yes.'

CHAPTER SIX

IT HAD just seemed a romantic thing to say on a beach, Cressy told herself as she drove home from the hospital. After all, they'd both known that their time together was going to be limited. That sooner or later the idyll would end, and she would fly back to real life.

What she hadn't foreseen was that it would indeed be much sooner.

At first, as the sunlit days had passed, she'd felt she was living in a dream, or under a spell that Draco had cast around her.

Most of her waking hours had been spent in his company, and even when she'd been asleep the image of him had never been far from her mind.

The first part of the morning she'd usually spent alone. She'd assumed that Draco was out in his boat, fishing, but when she'd mentioned this to Yannis he'd shrugged and said, 'I think he is at his house, Kyria Cressida. He is having some building done.'

Cressy understood. A lot of local houses seemed to be built in instalments, the owners occupying the ground floor until they could afford to add further storeys.

Draco had clearly made enough money to build another floor on to his, and if there was a vaguely troubling query at the back of her mind as to exactly where that money came from, she dismissed it. Nothing was allowed to impinge on her happiness.

Sometimes she wondered wistfully whether she

would ever be asked to see his house, but assumed it would never happen. These close-knit village communities might not be pleased to see one of their number with an *anglitha*, especially if he'd been earmarked for one of their daughters, she thought with a pang.

Anyway, if Draco wished to keep his private life to himself, that was his concern. He would have to go on living here after she'd gone...

She sighed. The realisation that her time in Greece was running out was causing her real pain.

I didn't really want to come here, she thought, grimacing. Now I don't want to leave.

It was hard to separate one day from another, when all of them were touched with gold. Sometimes they went out on the boat, landing on some quiet beach to swim, and cook the fish they'd caught over a wood fire.

At other times Draco drove the pick-up to the island's peaceful beauty spots, along the coast, or up into the high bare hills. And at night they danced together.

She was relaxed with him now. They shared a lot of laughter, but they could be quiet together too. When he teased her, she teased back. They had, she thought, become friends—and that was good.

But she couldn't deny the painful, ecstatic lift of her heart that happened each time he strode into the courtyard of the taverna to find her. Or the sweet, sensual ache that any physical contact with him seemed to evoke.

For much of the time he kept her at a distance, and she knew it. Just sometimes, in the drowsy afternoons, he would draw her into his arms and explore her mouth gently with his. Her hair seemed to entrance him. 'Like pale silk,' he would whisper, winding strands round his fingers and carrying them to his lips.

But—so far and no further, it seemed. The merest touch of his lips could ignite her desire, making her burn and melt with longing for the intimacy of his touch, for the consummation that her aroused flesh had been denied, but if he was aware of that, he gave no sign.

Just once, when he'd kissed her goodnight, she'd tried to hold him, pressing herself against him, her lips parting in mute invitation beneath the pressure of his. Longing to spark the passion that she knew lay just beneath the surface.

But he'd gently detached her clinging hands and stepped back, bending his head to drop a kiss on each soft palm before he let her go. And she had walked away up the stairs, knowing that he would not follow.

His control seemed to be total—and yet there were occasional moments when she felt him watching her. Was aware of a strange tension quivering along her nerve-endings, as if her body had somehow discerned the naked hunger in his and was responding to it.

Someone else was watching her too, she thought. Maria. The older woman was still warmly friendly, but once or twice Cressy had caught an anxious glance, or a little worried frown, and she wondered why.

But not too deeply. Her only real concern was the moment when she would see Draco again—would hear his voice and feel his smile touch her own mouth.

And that was all that mattered.

She didn't realise, of course, how swiftly and how finally things could change.

She woke early that day on Myros, to the bleak realisation that there was just over a week of her holiday left. She sat up in bed, hugging her knees, frowning a little. Maybe this was the time to walk away—while she still could. Before she was in too deep and reduced to begging.

Draco had told her the previous evening that he would come for her just after breakfast.

'So for once you're not going to work on your house.' Cressy had raised her eyebrows. 'I'm honoured.' She'd paused. 'How's it getting on—the house, I mean?'

He had shrugged. 'It is almost finished. It has taken longer than I thought.'

She'd been tempted to say, I'd love to see it, simply to test his reaction, but she had remained silent.

When she considered, the house was the least of it. There were so many things she still didn't know about him, she thought, her frown deepening. He had never spoken of his family, or mentioned friends apart from the crowd at the taverna, and even there he seemed to be treated with a certain respect rather than the usual raucous camaraderie.

But then he was incurious about her background too, she acknowledged.

She knew all kinds of little details about him, of course. She knew that his lashes were long enough to curl on his cheek when he slept. That there was a scar on his thigh, a relic from his boyhood when he'd gashed himself on a rock while swimming.

She was also aware that he could only relax for a certain time before he became restive, and that he secretly preferred her to wear dresses rather than trousers.

There'd been times recently, too, when he'd appeared to retreat so deeply into his own thoughts that it had been impossible for her to reach him, and this had made her feel oddly helpless and a little on edge.

Perhaps he was trying to find a humane way of telling

her that it was over and suggesting she went back to Alakos, she thought desolately as she went to her shower.

'Today we'll do something different,' he told her as they walked down to the harbour. 'There is something I want you to see.'

She felt a little surge of pleasure. Maybe at last she was going to see the mysterious house—or even meet his family.

She said lightly, 'That sounds intriguing.'

They sailed past their usual beach, heading north.

'Where are we going?'

'You have never been all round the island. I think you should.' Draco gave her the tiller.

'Oh.' Cressy masked her disappointment. After a moment, she said slowly, 'Myros is so lovely, Draco. It's like part of a different world. I—I shall hate to say goodbye.'

'So enjoy it while you can,' he said casually. 'And don't run us on to the rocks, *pethi mou*.'

To the north of the island the coastline became more dramatic, with one high promontory standing out from the rest. And on this jutting headland, clinging to it like a lizard on a rock, was the massive sprawl of a villa, white-walled and roofed in terracotta.

'My God.' Cressy shaded her eyes. 'So that's what was behind the stone wall. It's absolutely vast. Who does it belong to?'

'The head of the Ximenes Corporation.' His tone was indifferent. 'You've heard of that?'

'I think so.' Cressy wrinkled her nose. 'They're in shipping, aren't they?'

'And banking, and a hotel chain. The founder of the dynasty was called Alexandros. Like his namesake, he wished to conquer the world before he was thirty.' Draco put his hand over hers to alter the tiller. 'Do not go too close, *agapi mou*.'

'Because intruders aren't welcome?' Cressy pulled a face. 'Poor rich man.'

'You despise money?' His sideways glance was curious.

'On the contrary. I work long hours to earn as much as I can.'

'And that is important to you?'

'Well—naturally.'

'More important than being a woman, perhaps?'

Cressy bit her lip, sudden bewilderment battling with hurt. 'That's a cruel thing to say.'

Draco shrugged a shoulder. 'You are not a child,' he said. 'You live in a society where sexual freedom is accepted, and yet you are still a virgin. Why?'

She removed her hand from beneath his. 'I don't think it's any of your concern.'

'We said we would learn about each other,' he said. 'Yet you refuse to answer a simple question. One that would solve the mystery about you. Why won't you explain?'

'You dare say that to me?' She was angry now. 'You're the one with the secrets. You tell me nothing about yourself.'

'You don't ask.'

'All right.' She drew a deep breath. 'Are your parents alive?'

'No,' he said. 'But I have aunts and uncles and a great many cousins. Now, answer my question.'

Cressy hesitated. 'Perhaps I'm out of touch with today's morality,' she said. 'Or maybe I just haven't met the right man.'

'Ah,' he said softly. 'This great love of which every woman dreams. So, you believe in that.'

I never did before.

Her need for him, her longing, was an aching wound which only he could heal. And it was impossible for him not to know that. So why did he torment her by holding back?

She kept her voice light. 'We're all entitled to our dreams.'

'So, what do you dream of, Cressida *mou*?'

'Oh, dreams are like wishes.' She twisted round, pretending to take a last look at the villa on the headland. 'If you talk about them, they don't come true.'

'Then tell me this,' he said. 'Why did you come back here?'

Cressy swallowed. 'I—I wanted to see more of Myros.'

He sighed impatiently. 'Must I look into your eyes to know the truth, *agapi mou*?'

She said, almost inaudibly, 'And because you asked me...'

'Even though you knew that I wanted you—what I would ask?'

She swung back, tears stinging her eyes. 'Yes,' she said. 'Is that what you want to hear, Kyrios Draco? That I wanted you so much I came back to offer myself...' The stumbling words choked into silence.

'Yes,' he said quietly. 'I—needed to hear that, *agapi mou*.'

His arm encircled her, drawing her against him. 'Don't cry, my golden one—my treasure,' he whispered against her hair as she buried her face in his shoulder. 'And don't be ashamed of what you feel.'

'How can I help it?' Her voice was muffled.

'You imagine I do not want you—because I have been patient?' His voice sank to a whisper. 'I have had to force myself to remain cool, but no longer. I have to speak—to tell you everything in my heart.'

He paused. 'My life is yours, Cressida *mou*. Be my wife and stay with me for ever. Work beside me each day and lie in my arms at night.'

His body was shaking against hers. As she lifted her head she saw the proud face strangely anxious, the firm mouth incredibly vulnerable.

She put up her hand and touched his cheek, brushing her thumb softly across his lips.

She whispered, 'I'll stay...'

He kissed her once, his mouth hard, almost fierce on hers. Telling her beyond doubt how precarious that taut control really was.

'I must wait for more,' he told her as he reluctantly released her, his mouth twisting. 'I want to live with you, my bride, not drown with you.'

She laughed, leaning back in his embrace, the breeze from the sea lifting her hair, happiness warming her like her own private sun.

Lips touching her hair, Draco whispered words of love and need, his voice raw as he switched to his own language.

'I wish I could understand what you're saying,' Cressy sighed, her fingers lightly caressing the strong arm that held her so securely.

'I will tell you one day.' There was a smile in his voice. 'But only when we are married.'

In the hour it took to return to Myros harbour, they also made some practical plans.

It was agreed that Cressy would catch the midday ferry to Alakos, to pack the rest of her things and check out of the Hellenic Imperial. And make a few necessary phone calls, she thought, with a sudden bump of nervousness.

'I would take you myself,' Draco said, frowning. 'But there are things I must do at my house, arrangements I must make.' He paused. 'You'll stay there with me until our marriage, *pethi mou*? You'll trust me?'

'Is that really necessary?' Flushing slightly, Cressy met his gaze directly. 'Draco—I love you. I want to belong to you.'

'And so you will,' he said gently. 'In our house, in our bed, on our wedding night. That is how it must be, Cressida *mou*.'

She shook her head. 'You have a will of iron, *kyrie*.'

His gaze caressed her. 'When you look at me like that, *kyria*, I have no will at all.'

At the taverna, she went up to collect her things, leaving Draco to talk to Yannis.

As she fastened her travel bag she heard a sound behind her, and looked round to find Maria standing in the doorway.

'Maria.' Cressy smiled at her a little shyly. 'You've heard the news? I'm hoping very much that you'll lend me your wedding dress again.'

'Kyria Cressida.' Maria took a step forward, her face troubled. 'Are you sure about this? Kyrios Draco—how well do you know him?'

'I know that I love him.'

'You should take care,' Maria said quietly. 'This is not a marriage of equals.'

Cressy bit her lips. 'I understand what you're trying to say. That we'll have to make more adjustments than other couples. But...'

Maria gestured impatiently. 'That is not what I mean. There are things you do not know.'

Cressy stared at her. 'What sort of things?'

Yannis shouted Maria's name from below and she turned to go. 'I cannot say more. But you must be careful.' She left Cressy staring after her.

She was quiet as she walked down to the ferry with Draco at her side.

'Already regrets?' He smiled at her.

'No,' she denied, a little too quickly. She wanted to ask about Maria's warning, but it needed an oblique approach, and there wasn't time because people were already boarding the ferry.

He kissed her mouth, and she felt his thumb trace the sign of the cross on her forehead.

'Come to me soon,' he whispered. 'I shall be waiting for you, my beloved.'

As she collected her key from Hotel Reception, Cressy wondered what the deferential concierge would say if he knew she was planning to marry one of his countrymen.

She'd had time to think on the ferry trip, but hadn't come to any firm conclusions.

Perhaps Maria simply doubted that Draco had sufficient means to support a wife. After all, Cressy had little real idea of what he did for a living, she realised with a touch of unease.

Or had there been something more cynical in her warning? Did Maria suspect that Cressy's real attraction for Draco was as an affluent tourist?

But I'm not rich, and he knows it, Cressy thought. I'm well paid, but when I stop working that'll be it.

And I've still got rent to pay, and bills to settle back in England.

On the other hand even quite modest savings might seem a fortune to an impecunious fisherman.

She found herself remembering the silences—all the times she hadn't known what he was thinking. And, in spite of herself, began to wonder.

That total certainty about the future—her inner radiance—had taken a jolt, but a few doubts were perfectly natural, surely.

Anyway, she and Draco couldn't get married immediately, she reminded herself. There were all kinds of legal and religious formalities to be completed first.

And plenty of time for any lingering qualms to be assuaged.

She was halfway through her packing when the telephone rang.

'Cressy, my dear.'

'Why, Uncle Bob.' She sat down on the edge of the bed. 'What a surprise. I—I was actually planning to call you—'

'Cressy,' he interrupted firmly, 'I'm afraid you must listen carefully. I've got bad news.'

Ten minutes later she replaced the receiver. Her face was colourless and she felt deathly cold.

Her wonderful golden dream had gone, to be replaced by bleak and frightening reality. A chilling reminder of exactly who she was. Not some silly, lovesick child swept away by a handsome face, but a woman with a career, duties and obligations. A woman with a life far removed from some half-finished shack on a piece of Mediterranean rock.

Her father was not only ruined, but alone and ill. He might even be dying. Their recent estrangement was suddenly meaningless. She had to go back to England at once.

For a moment Draco's face seemed to swim in front of her. Gasping, she wrapped her arms round her body. She couldn't let herself think about him, or the folly of the last ten days. She had quite deliberately to wipe him from her mind, and her memory. There was no place for him in her life now, and never had been outside a crazy dream. He was a luxury she couldn't afford, she thought, biting her lip until she tasted blood.

As it was, no real harm had been done, and she had to be thankful for that.

It made her wince to think how naive she'd been— how easily she'd been beguiled to near disaster.

Draco had been so clever, using his sexuality to keep her in a torment of frustration and longing. All those kisses, she thought bitterly. The fleeting caresses that had aroused without satisfying.

And all leading to what? Not marriage, she was certain. He was probably bluffing about that. No, he was counting on her walking away once he'd shown her the life she could expect. But not until she'd handed over a hefty payment for his injured feelings, no doubt.

It was fate, she told herself as the plane took off from Athens. Fate intervening to stop her making the most hideous mistake of her life.

She had to see it like that or she'd go mad. She had to block the pain or she'd moan aloud. Had to tell herself that Draco was just a beach boy on the make or she'd mourn him for ever.

And she had her father's problems to sort out. She had no time for her own.

All very reasoned, Cressy thought now, as she brought her car to a halt in front of the house. Very rational. If only there hadn't been an unknown factor in her equation. A factor that still seemed to be pursuing her.

Cressy spent most of the afternoon on the telephone and sending e-mails, informing her father's creditors that she'd be negotiating on his behalf during his stay in hospital. But if she'd hoped for instant response or co-operation, she was disappointed.

She was just reluctantly deciding to call it a day when she heard the sound of a car outside and her uncle appeared, accompanied by Charles Lawrence, her father's legal adviser.

Sir Robert spoke without preamble. 'Cressy—have you spoken to the bank?'

She shook her head. 'They put me off with polite noises. Why—have you heard something?'

'I was contacted this morning.' Charles Lawrence was speaking. 'It's an extraordinary business, Cressida. They've had an offer to pay off the mortgage on this house, and your father's other debts. Someone's prepared to—take them over.'

'Just like that?' Cressy stared at both men. 'But that's impossible.'

Mr Lawrence nodded. 'So I thought. But I've since spoken to the other party, and the offer has been confirmed.'

Cressy mentally reviewed her father's close friends. There were several millionaires among them, but she wouldn't have credited any of them with that level of generosity.

She said doubtfully, 'Is it Dad's old company—have they put together a rescue package for him?'

'Nothing like that, I fear. The offer has come from

the Standard Trust Bank. They are based in New York, but they're owned by the Ximenes Corporation. I expect you've heard of it.'

'Yes.' Her voice sounded odd, suddenly, almost distorted. 'Yes—it was mentioned to me quite recently.'

'Well, I don't understand any of it,' Sir Robert said bluntly. 'Who are these people, and what on earth have they to do with James? I wasn't aware he'd had any dealings with them.'

'I'm sure he didn't.' Charles Lawrence shook his head. 'It's a complete mystery, but I hope Cressida may be able to solve it.' He gave her a bleak smile. 'It seems they wish to negotiate with you personally, my dear.'

'Did they give any particular reason?' Cressy felt hollow as weird, incredible suspicions continued to ferment in her mind.

No, she thought. It's not true. It can't be. It's just an odd coincidence. It has to be—*has to*...

'No, but I got the impression that the chairman—a chap called Viannis—is a law unto himself.' He consulted some notes. 'He's staying in London at the Grand Imperial—occupies the penthouse, apparently. You're to phone for an appointment.'

'Well, I don't like the sound of it,' Sir Robert said restively. 'You're James's solicitor. He should be talking to you.'

'I suggested as much, but they were adamant. It has to be Cressida. Although she can always refuse,' he added quickly.

'No,' Cressy said. 'If this Viannis is prepared to throw my father a lifeline, then I'll talk to him, or anyone. I'll call tomorrow and fix up a meeting.'

'Well,' Sir Robert said dubiously, 'if you're quite sure, my dear.'

After their departure Cressy sat for a while, staring into space. Then she rose and went over to the desk and her laptop.

The e-mail icon was waiting for her, as she'd suspected it would be.

Swallowing, she clicked on to the message.

'Sid,' she read. 'I am waiting for you. Come to me.'

And that meant there could no longer be any doubt at all.

'Oh, God,' she whispered, her clenched fist pressed against her mouth. 'What am I going to do?'

CHAPTER SEVEN

As THE gates closed and the lift began its smooth rush to the penthouse, Cressy drew a deep breath.

Whatever—whoever—was waiting for her, it was essential that she appear composed and in control. She couldn't afford to let the mask slip for a moment and reveal the turmoil of emotion inside her.

She had dressed carefully for this meeting. Her navy blue suit was immaculate, the skirt cut decorously to the knee. The heavy cream silk blouse buttoned to the throat, and she wore neat navy pumps with a medium heel and carried a briefcase. Her hair had been brushed severely back from her face and confined at the nape of her neck with a gilt clip.

Her make-up had been meticulously applied to cover up the tell-tale signs of another sleepless night.

She looked, she thought, cool and businesslike. She hoped she was going to be treated accordingly.

She thought, not for the first time, her throat tightening uncontrollably, Oh, let him be a stranger. Please—*please* let me be wrong about this...

She was met on the top floor by a tall blonde man with a transatlantic accent, who greeted her unsmilingly and introduced himself as Paul Nixon, Mr Viannis's personal assistant.

He led her down the thickly carpeted corridor and knocked at the double doors at the end.

He said, 'Miss Fielding is here, sir,' and stood aside to allow Cressy to go in.

The room was full of light. There were huge windows on three sides, permitting panoramic views all over London.

But Cressy was only aware of the tall, dark figure silhouetted against the brightness. For a moment she was scarcely able to breathe, and she halted abruptly, feeling as if a giant fist had clenched in her stomach, all her worst fears finally and inevitably confirmed.

He was very still, but with the tension of a coiled spring. Across the room, his anger reached out and touched her, and she had to fight an impulse to flinch. Or even run...

He said softly, 'So, you have come to me at last—Cressida, my faithless one.'

There was a note in his voice which sent a shiver between her shoulder blades, but it was vital not to seem afraid.

She lifted her chin. 'Mr Viannis?'

'What charming formality.' The mockery in his tone was savage. 'You feel it's appropriate—under the circumstances? After all, how do you address your ex-fiancé—someone you've so signally betrayed?'

She said steadily, 'I came here to negotiate a deal for my father, not indulge in useless recriminations.'

'No,' he said. 'You came here to accept my terms. There is nothing to negotiate.'

She'd hoped to find a stranger and in some ways her wish had been granted, because this wasn't Draco. This man had never worn scruffy denims or danced in the sunlight. Had never kissed her, or smiled at her with lazy desire. Could never, even for a few breathless moments, have held her naked in his arms.

This man looked thinner—older, she thought, her eyes scanning him with sudden bewilderment. His charcoal suit with its faint pinstripe was exquisitely cut, his tie a paler grey silk.

The tumbled black hair had been tamed and trimmed. And there was no golden light in the dark eyes that met hers. They were cold—impenetrable.

Even his voice was different. Now he spoke with hardly any accent at all.

She thought, How could I not have seen it—the ruthlessness behind the golden sunlit charm?

He walked over to the big desk in the centre of the room and sat down, curtly indicating that she should occupy the chair set at the opposite side.

She obeyed reluctantly. Her legs were shaking and her heart was thudding unevenly.

She said, struggling to keep her voice level, 'How did you find me?'

'You were staying in one of my hotels, so that provided the basic information.' He shrugged. 'After that, I had enquiries made.'

'You checked up on me?' Her voice was taut. 'Was this before or after you asked me to marry you?'

His smile did not reach his eyes. 'Oh, long before. When we first encountered each other. I needed to be sure that you were just as you seemed.'

'I'm glad I measured up to your exacting requirements.' She spoke with deliberate disdain, trying to cover her growing unease.

'That was then,' he said. 'This is now.'

Cressy touched the tip of her tongue to her dry lips, realising too late that Draco had seen and marked that tiny act of self-betrayal.

She hurried into speech. 'And that's how you discovered my father's—difficulties, I suppose?'

'Yes,' he said. 'But they are hardly "difficulties". Your father is facing total ruin.'

'I know that,' she said. 'Which is the reason I'm here today.'

'No,' he said. 'You are here because you ran away. Because you left me without a word. You are here to explain.'

'My father collapsed,' she said flatly. 'He was in Intensive Care. I—had to come back.'

'Without one word to the man you had just promised to marry?' His voice bit.

Cressy's hands were clenched so tightly in her lap that her fingers ached. She said, 'I didn't think that either of us took that seriously. A lot of women have—flings on foreign holidays.'

'Ah.' Draco leaned back in the tall leather chair. 'So you saw our relationship as some trivial, transient affair. A thing of no consequence.' His tone suggested courteous interest, but she wasn't fooled.

'In some ways,' she said uncertainly.

He said slowly, 'If that was true, I would have taken you on the beach that first afternoon and you would have spent the rest of your holiday in my bed.'

'And eventually gone on my way with a diamond necklace, I suppose,' Cressy flashed.

'Perhaps.' He sounded indifferent. 'If you'd pleased me sufficiently.'

'I can't think why you held back.'

'Because I was fool enough to respect your innocence, Cressida *mou*.' His tone was harsh. 'I did not see it was just a physical attribute. That, in reality, you were just as calculating and heartless as your namesake.'

Cressy leaned forward. 'You think I've treated you badly,' she said hotly. 'But you weren't honest with me either. You deliberately let me think you were poor. Why?'

'An unaccountable need to be wanted for myself only, and not for my worldly goods,' he drawled. 'It was so refreshing to meet someone who had no idea who I was, *pethi mou*.'

'And how long did you plan to go on deceiving me?' She realised now why Maria had tried to warn her. To tell her that she was involved with a man who was not only very rich, but powerful. A man who would live up to his name if crossed.

'It would have been over as soon as you returned from Alakos. You see, *agapi mou*, I had planned a big party for our engagement at my house.'

She stared at him. 'It belongs to you, doesn't it? That wonderful villa on the headland?'

'Yes,' he said. 'My family and friends were flying in from all over the world to meet you—my future wife— there.'

'Oh.' Cressy felt sick.

'At first I thought you had simply missed the ferry,' he went on, as if she hadn't spoken. 'I called the hotel, and they told me you had checked out, so I waited for a message. I waited a long time. I cannot remember the precise moment I realised you were not coming back.'

'My father needed me,' she said desperately. 'I had to get to Athens—to go to him.'

'And it never occurred to you to turn to me—the man you'd professed to love?' His mouth twisted contemptuously. 'What a mistake, Cressida *mou*. My helicopter would have flown us to Athens. My private plane would have taken us on to London. You would have been there in half the time.'

'But I had no means of knowing that,' she protested.

'If you had come to me you would have known. Only you didn't. And that is the worst thing of all. To know that you were in trouble—in pain—yet you didn't want to share this with me. Even if I'd been as poor as you thought, at least I had the right to put my arms around you and hold you.

'As it was, I could have taken you straight to your father and been with you to comfort and care for you, as a man should with his woman.' He paused, the dark eyes merciless. 'Tell me, *pethi mou*, had you any intention of contacting me again—ever? Or was I simply to be—erased, like an unfortunate mistake in a calculation?'

Cressy shook her head, feeling tears thickening in her throat. 'Draco—I don't know—I was worried—confused...'

'Then let me tell you the answer,' he said. 'You didn't love—and you didn't trust either. That was the bitter truth I had to learn. I was poor, so I could be discarded, as if I had no feelings. And one day you will discover how that feels. Because I shall teach you.'

He smiled at her. 'You will discover, Cressida *mou*, that I am not so easily forgotten.'

She said in a low voice, 'I suppose you mean to use my father's problems against me. Well—I'm prepared for that.'

'Are you?' he asked softly. 'I had originally intended to present the settlement of his debts as a gift to you when we announced our engagement. Since then I have had time to think again.'

She said urgently, 'Draco—whatever you think of me—please don't punish my father any more. He's a sick man.'

'And when he leaves hospital he will need a home

to go to,' he said. 'The house that now belongs to me. Is that what you're trying to put into words?'

She said on a note of desperation, 'I could pay rent...'

'Yes, you will pay,' he said quietly. 'But not with money. I have enough of that already.'

'Then how?' Her voice was barely more than a whisper.

'Don't you know?' he said. 'Don't you understand that I still want you?'

The room was very still suddenly. She stared across the desk at him. At the hard bronze face and the cool mouth that looked as if it would never smile again. Watched and waited for some softening—some warmth. But in vain.

She swallowed. 'You mean—in spite of everything— you're going to marry me?'

His laugh was harsh. 'No, not marriage, my sweet. I will not be caught again. This time I'm offering a less formal arrangement.' He added cynically, 'And spare me the pretence that you don't understand my offer.'

'I understand.' Her voice seemed to come from a long way away. 'You're saying that if I—sleep with you— you won't enforce the mortgage or my father's other debts.'

'Yes,' he said softly. 'I am saying exactly that. And what is your answer?'

She said hoarsely, 'Draco, you can't mean this. If you loved me, you wouldn't...'

'I said that I wanted you, Cressida *mou*. I did not mention love.'

Pain ripped at her, tearing her apart. She hadn't realised it was possible to hurt so much. Or to be so afraid.

She said, her voice shaking, 'Is this your idea of revenge? To rape me?'

'No,' he said. 'Because you will come to me willingly, Cressida, as we both know.'

'Never.'

He shrugged. 'Then regard it simply as a business transaction. You understand those better than you know yourself, I think.'

'Business?' Her voice cracked. 'How can it be that?'

'I have something you want.' His smile mocked her. 'You have something I want. That's how deals are made.'

'You make it sound so simple.'

'It is hardly complicated.' His voice was cool, and oddly impersonal. 'You will come to me, and stay with me as long as I require. When our liaison ends, I will hand over the mortgage and other papers—instead of a diamond necklace,' he added, his mouth twisting.

'And if I refuse this—degrading offer?'

He leaned back in his chair. He said quietly, 'We have already established that your father's well-being is your sole priority. So I do not think we need consider that possibility—do you?'

'No.' Her voice was barely audible. 'No, I don't—really—have a choice.'

He smiled thinly. 'You've made the right decision.' He got to his feet and came round the desk to her side. He took her hand, pulling her out of the chair.

He led her across the room to a door, which he opened, revealing a large and luxurious bedroom.

'You mean—now?' Her voice rose, and she recoiled, swinging round to face him. 'Oh, God, you can't be serious.'

His brows lifted. 'Why not?'

She said wildly, 'Because it's the middle of the morning.'

He began to laugh. 'How conventional you are, *agapi mou*,' he mocked. 'When we were on Myros there was not one minute of the day or night that we did not want each other.'

She bit her lip. 'That was different.'

'Did you expect me to seduce you over dinner with flowers and moonlight?' His tone was cynical. 'It is too late for that. Once, perhaps, I would have made it beautiful for you. Now—' he shrugged '—regard it as the signature on a contract.'

'Draco.' Her voice broke. 'Please—don't do this to me—to us.'

'Us?' he echoed contemptuously. 'There is no "us". I have bought you, Cressida *mou*. That is all. And this time you will not have the opportunity to run away.' He glanced at his watch. 'I have a couple of calls to make. I will join you in a few minutes.'

She said bitterly, 'You're enjoying this, aren't you?'

'I intend to,' he said. 'Whether or not you share my pleasure is your own concern. But I think you will.'

He pulled her towards him, his arm a steel band forcing her compliance. His dark face swam momentarily in front of her startled eyes. Then he bent his head and kissed her breast.

The sudden heat of his mouth scorched through her thin blouse and lacy bra as if she was already naked. His lips found her nipple, tugging at it, creating a sharp, exquisite pain that triggered a scalding flood of need in return.

Surprised and shamed at the physical fierceness of her response, Cressy gasped, her hands curling into impotent fists at her sides.

When he lifted his head he was smiling faintly. He reached for one small clenched hand and raised it to his lips with insolent grace.

His other hand slid down over her hip to her thigh, and lingered there suggestively.

He said softly, 'Nothing has really changed between us, Cressida *mou*. Only the terms of our coming together. Shall I prove it to you? Show you exactly how much you still want me?'

Helpless colour warmed her face. She shook her head, staring down at the carpet, not daring to meet the intensity of his gaze. Scared of what else she might betray.

She had not bargained for the overwhelming force of instinct. But that could be harnessed, she told herself. Hidden.

For her own sake, she had to try.

She found herself impelled gently but inexorably into the bedroom. She began a last protest, but Draco laid a finger on her parted lips, silencing her.

He said, 'I shall try not to keep you waiting too long.'

The door closed behind him, shutting her in. She stood, her arms wrapped defensively across her body, staring round.

It was a big room, and the bed was its dominant feature, wide and low, with a dark green cover tailored in heavy linen, matching the drapes at the windows.

A very masculine room, she thought, comfortable but impersonal. A suitable place for a bargain, but not for love. Never for love.

She walked across and tugged at the cords, swinging the curtains across to block out the brilliant sunlight. She wanted shadows, she thought. Shadows and darkness to hide in.

She needed, too, to blot out the searing memory of those other golden days on Myros when she had turned to him, eagerly offering her mouth—her body.

Her whole body seemed to stir in sudden yearning, and regret, and she stiffened, bringing her rebellious senses back under control once more. She could not allow herself such weakness.

Whatever Draco did to her—no matter how he made her feel—somehow she had to stay aloof—and endure.

Presently, she thought, I shall wake up and find all this was just a nightmare.

She looked back, dry-mouthed, at the bed, pain searing through her as she realised how different it could have been.

But she'd made her choice—a whole series of choices—and she had to live with the consequences. Starting now...

She left her clothes in the adjoining dressing room. The carpet was soft under her bare feet as she walked to the bed. The percale sheets felt crisp and cool against her burning skin as she lay tensely, waiting for the door to open.

Which, eventually, just as her nerves had reached screaming point, it did.

'Shy, *agapi mou*?' He was a dark shape at the end of the bed. He turned away, walking over to the windows and flinging back the drapes again, flooding the room with sudden light.

Draco came back to the bed. For a moment he stood staring down at her, then he reached down, twitching the covers from her outraged fingers and tossing them to the foot of the bed.

He said softly, 'A man likes to look, as well as touch.'

Teeth set defiantly, Cressy withstood his lingering scrutiny, deliberately not covering herself with her hands, nor looking away, even when he began, almost casually, to remove his clothes.

Only when he came to lie beside her on the bed and drew her into his arms did she finally close her eyes, her body rigid against his naked warmth.

The scent of his skin, once so familiar and so precious, now admixed with a trace of some expensive cologne, pervaded her mouth and nose, so that she seemed to be breathing him, absorbing him into every atom of her consciousness.

She remembered one day on the beach, kissing his shoulder, tasting the heat of the sun and the salt of the sea on its curving muscularity. But she couldn't afford those kind of memories. She had to lie still and unyielding—and hate. Resentment would be her only salvation.

But it wasn't easy, not when his hands had begun to caress her, the warm fingers skimming over her flesh in exquisite, tantalising exploration.

As they softly brushed her taut nipples Cressy had to bite back a gasp, her body clenching in hot, shamed excitement.

Where his hands touched, his mouth followed. He kissed her breasts softly, his tongue unhurriedly circling each puckered rose peak in turn. Sensation, knife-sharp and honey-sweet, pierced through her, making her quiver and arch towards him involuntarily, and she felt his lips smile against her skin.

His hand parted her thighs and began to stroke her, delicately, subtly, making her moan and writhe against the intimate play of his fingers as they promised—tantalised—and then denied.

Every sense, every atom of consciousness was focused painfully on that tiny, pulsating centre of her being as she felt herself being drawn slowly and exquisitely to some undreamed of brink. As she felt her breath quicken and heard the frantic drumming of her own heart.

She made a small, wounded sound in her throat. A wordless plea for him—somehow—to end this beautiful torment.

'Not yet.' His tongue caressed the whorls of her ear. 'Not yet, but—soon...' And his hand moved fractionally, deepening the caress. Imposing a more compelling demand.

She was blind, deaf—mindless. Aware of nothing but the fierce concentration of pleasure that he was creating for her. As if the sun, beating against her eyelids, was blooming and growing inside her.

And when, at last, he gave her the release she craved, she cried out in harsh animal delight as ripple upon ripple of pure feeling engulfed her—convulsed her. As she was flung out into space, where she fell into the centre of the sun and was consumed.

She was totally relaxed, her body still throbbing with pleasure, as Draco moved above her, and, with one deep thrust, into her.

For a fleeting instant she was scared by the memory of pain, then shocked by its absence. Because now there was only joyous acceptance, and a sense of completion.

As if, she thought, this was the moment she had been made for.

She raised her languid lids and stared up at him, letting herself enclose him. Hold him.

Allowing herself to savour how alien it felt, yet at the same time how totally familiar—and precious.

The bronze face was stark, his eyes like pits of darkness as he began to move, slowly and powerfully, inside her.

Instinct lifted her hands to his shoulders and clasped her legs round his lean hips, so that she could partner him completely. Could mirror each compelling stroke.

As the rhythm and intensity increased, Draco groaned something in his own language. She kissed his throat, licking the salt from his skin, feeling the thunder of his pulse against her lips.

At the same time, deep within her, she was aware of the first flutterings of renewed delight. Incredulous, gasping, she held him closer, her sweat mingling with his as the spiral of pleasure tautened unbearably, then imploded.

Her whole body rocked as the tremors of rapture tore through her, echoed by the wild spasms of his own climax.

When it was over, he lay very still, his face against her breasts.

She wanted to hold him. To put her lips against the damp, dark tangle of hair and whisper that she loved him. That as he'd been the first, so would he be the last.

As his cherished bride, it would have been her right to open her heart to him. As his mistress—she sank her teeth into her swollen lower lip—she had no rights at all. And that was something she must never forget. That her role in his life was at best transient.

At last he stirred, lifting himself away from her. He reached for his watch from the night table, grimaced at the time, and fastened the thin gold bracelet back on his wrist. Then he turned and looked down at Cressy, his dark eyes almost dispassionate.

'Thank you.' His voice was cool, even faintly

amused. 'I had not expected such—enchanting co-operation. You learn quickly.'

'Is—is that all you have to say?' Her voice shook. She felt as if she'd been slapped.

'No, but the rest must wait. I have a meeting in the City. But you don't have to leave,' he added swiftly as Cressy half sat up. 'No one will disturb you if you wish to sleep.'

'I don't,' she said curtly. 'I haven't visited my father today. I need to get back there.'

He nodded, unfazed. 'Paul will contact you with your instructions.'

'Instructions?'

'I shall soon be returning to Greece. I require you to accompany me.'

'But my job—my father,' Cressy protested. 'I can't just—go.'

'You will find that you can. Your employer has been most understanding. Your—services are on temporary loan to me. I did not explain the exact nature of the services,' he added with a shrug. 'So you can tell him as much or as little as you wish.'

She swallowed. 'My God,' she said. 'You don't allow much to stand in your way, do you? Suppose I'd turned you down.'

'I was certain you wouldn't.' His mouth twisted. 'Apart from other considerations, your sexual curiosity had been aroused, *agapi mou*, and needed to be satisfied.' His hand touched her shoulder, then travelled swiftly and sensuously down her body. It was the lightest of caresses but it brought her skin stinglingly alive.

Draco's laugh was soft. 'You see, Cressida *mou*, even now you are eager for your next lesson. How sad that I have not more time to devote to you.'

Cressy reached down and dragged the discarded sheet up over her body. She recognised that it was basically a meaningless gesture, but it made her feel marginally better.

She forced herself to meet his gaze. She said, 'You mentioned I was on loan to you. For how long, exactly?'

Draco swung his long legs to the floor. 'I said three months initially.'

She said, 'I—see.'

The blissful euphoria which had followed their lovemaking had gone. In its place, pain and shame were dragging her apart.

'I suggest you see a doctor as a matter of urgency,' he tossed over his shoulder as he walked to the bathroom. 'Today I used protection, but even so we must ensure there's no chance of you becoming pregnant.'

Cressy was suddenly very still, her eyes enormous as she stared after him.

With a few casual words, she thought, he'd relegated her to the status of a non-person.

Yet this was the reality of the situation. She was no longer his golden love. She was a temporary sexual partner. And the skill and artistry he'd brought to her initiation had simply been a means to an end. Draco had ensured her pleasure merely to increase his own.

And if she'd hoped in some secret corner of her mind that the glory of their coming together would soften his attitude towards her, she knew better now, and disappointment twisted inside her like a claw.

There were tears crowding in her throat, stinging the backs of her eyes, but she would not shed them in front of him.

She said quietly. 'No—of course not.'

The bathroom door closed behind him, and presently she heard the sound of the shower running.

She released a trembling breath. Somehow she had to come to terms with the relationship that he'd offered her, and all its limitations, when the most she could hope for was that it would soon be over.

'Oh, God,' she whispered brokenly. 'How can I bear it?'

And she turned her face into the pillow and lay like a stone.

CHAPTER EIGHT

SHE pretended to be asleep when Draco came back into the bedroom, lying motionless, her eyes tightly shut, as she listened with nerves jangling to his quiet movements, the rustle of clothing as he dressed.

When, at last, he came across to the bed, she forced her tense body into deep relaxation, keeping her breathing soft and even.

She thought she heard him sigh as he turned away, but she couldn't be sure.

It was some time after she heard the bedroom door click shut behind him that she ventured to sit up, and make sure she was really alone.

She thought, I have to get out of here. I don't want anyone to see me—to know…

She knew she was being ridiculous. That there wasn't a member of Draco's staff who wouldn't be perfectly aware of the situation. She just didn't want to find herself face to face with any of them.

She was scared, too, that if she gave way to sleep she might still be here when Draco returned.

She showered swiftly, but if she hoped to wash away the touch and taste of him it was in vain. His possession had been total. He was irrevocably part of her now, and there was nothing she could do about it.

She shivered as she towelled her damp hair.

What had happened to all her high-flown plans about fighting him—about remaining indifferent? she wondered bitterly.

One kiss—his hand on her breast—and all her resolution had crumbled. Indeed, she could hardly have made it easier for him. She wanted to hate him for the way he had made her feel, but she hated herself more.

There were mirrors all round the bathroom, throwing back images of a girl whose eyes were heavy with newly learned secrets. The cool lady she'd been so proud of had vanished for ever, swept away on a frantic tide of passion.

Yet the encounter had left no visible marks on her skin, she thought, with detached surprise. Her mouth was reddened and slightly swollen, and she ached a little, but that was all.

I got off lightly, she told herself. But she knew in her heart that it wasn't true.

When she was dressed, she looked at herself and winced. All those carefully chosen garments—the business suit and prim shirt—had been worn as armour, yet they'd proved no protection at all.

She went back to her flat and changed into a plain black shift, sleeveless and severe, stuffing the discarded clothing into a refuse sack. She never wanted to see any of it again. She thrust her bare feet into sandals and grabbed a simple cream linen jacket before going down to her car.

It was a nightmare journey, a battle between her need to concentrate on the road and the storm of bewildered emotion within her. But at last she reached the hospital.

In one piece, but only just, she thought grimly.

As she waited for the lift to take her up to the ICU, she was waylaid by a nurse.

'Your father's been moved, Miss Fielding. He's made such good progress over the last twenty-four hours that he's in a private room on "A" wing now.'

'You mean he's getting better? But that's wonderful.' Cressy's mouth trembled into a relieved smile. 'Because he looked so ill when I was here last.'

'Oh, he's still being carefully monitored, but everyone's very pleased with him.' The older woman beamed. 'Mind you, I think all the goodies he's been receiving—the fruit and flowers from Mrs Fielding—have cheered him up a lot.'

'Eloise has sent fruit and flowers?' Cressy repeated incredulously.

'Well, there wasn't an actual card, but he said they must be from her. He was so thrilled.' She paused. 'Is Mrs Fielding not with you today? What a shame.'

When she reached her father's room, it looked like a florist's window.

As she paused in the doorway, admiring the banks of blooms, James Fielding turned an eager head towards her, his welcoming smile fading when he saw who it was.

'Cressy, my dear.' He spoke with an effort, failing to mask the disappointment in his voice. 'How good to see you.'

'You look marvellous, Daddy.' She went to the bed and kissed his cheek. 'I've never seen so many flowers. I'd have brought some, but they didn't allow them in ICU, and now everyone else has beaten me to it.' She was aware she was chattering, trying to cover up the awkward moment. Attempting to hide the instinctive hurt provoked by his reaction.

He didn't want it to be me, she thought with desolation. He hoped it was Eloise. That she'd come back to him.

'Those lilies and carnations over there, and the fruit basket, came without a card,' her father said eagerly.

'But I think I know who they're from.' He smiled tenderly. 'In fact, I'm sure. I just wish she'd signed her name. But perhaps she felt diffident about that—under the circumstances.'

Diffident? Cressy wanted to scream. Eloise hasn't an insecure bone in her body.

Instead, she forced a smile as she sat down beside his bed. 'Yes—perhaps…'

He played with the edge of the sheet, frowning a little. 'Has she been in contact—left any message at all?'

Cressy shook her head. 'There's been nothing, Daddy. Don't you think I'd have told you?'

'I don't know,' he said with a touch of impatience. 'Certainly there's never been any love lost between you.'

'Well, that's unimportant now.' She put a hand over his. 'All that matters is that you get well.'

'The consultant says I can go home soon, if I keep up this progress. But he wants me to have a live-in nurse for a while. He feels it will be too much for Berry.'

His frown deepened. 'I wasn't sure that my insurance covered private nursing, but he says it's all taken care of.' He paused. 'What I need to know is—do I still have a home to go to?'

She said gently, 'Yes, you have, darling. I've managed to do a deal with your creditors. You can go on living at the house.'

He nodded. 'That's good. I'd have hated Eloise to find the place all shut up, or occupied by strangers, and not know where to find me. Because it won't last—this Alec Caravas thing. She's had her head turned by a younger man, that's all.'

Cressy's lips parted in a silent gasp of incredulity.

For a moment she could feel the blood drumming in her ears and felt physically sick.

Was that really his only concern—providing a bolt-hole for his worthless wife—if she chose to return? Didn't he realise she'd been Alec Caravas's full accomplice—and that the police would want to interview her if she ever dared show her face again?

She'd expected her father to ask all sorts of awkward questions about the exact accommodation she'd reached over his debts, but he didn't seem remotely interested. Instead he just took it for granted that she'd managed to get things sorted.

Just as he'd tacitly accepted the estrangement between them that Eloise had imposed, she realised with a sudden ache of the heart.

And he would never have any conception of the terrible personal price she'd been forced to pay on his behalf.

I've ruined my life to get him out of trouble, Cressy thought with anguish. And he doesn't even care. Nothing matters except this obsession with Eloise.

She got clumsily to her feet. 'I—I'd better go. I promised the nurses I wouldn't tire you.'

'Perhaps it would be best.' He leaned back against his pillows, reaching for the radio headphones.

She took a deep breath. 'But there's something I must tell you first. I—I have to go abroad very soon—to work. It's a special contract. It may take a few months.'

'Well, that's excellent news.' His smile held some of the old warmth. 'I hope it means more money—or a promotion. You deserve it, you know.'

She said quietly, 'I'm not sure what I deserve any more. And I'm not certain if I should go—if I should leave you.'

'Nonsense, darling. Of course you must go. We both have our own lives to lead. We can't be dependent on each other. And the last thing I want is you fussing round me. Berry and this nurse will be bad enough.'

'No,' she said. 'You're probably right. I—I'll see you tomorrow.'

She went quietly to the door and let herself out. In the corridor, she stopped and leaned against the wall, aware that her legs were shaking so badly she thought she might collapse. She closed her eyes as a scalding tear forced its way under her lid and down her cheek.

She thought brokenly, Oh, Daddy...

'Miss Fielding—is something wrong?' A nurse's anxious voice invaded her torturous thoughts.

Cressy straightened quickly. 'No—it's all right.' She tried a little laugh. 'I think the worry of the past few days has just caught up with me, that's all.'

'I'm not surprised. Oh, and talking of surprises...' The girl felt in the pocket of her uniform. 'You know the fruit and flowers that arrived for your father with no name on them? Well, they've just found this card in Reception. It must have fallen off when the delivery was made.' She beamed. 'One mystery solved.' She lowered her voice significantly. 'Although I think he was hoping they were from Mrs Fielding.'

Cressy held out her hand. 'May I look?'

The signature was a slash of black ink across the rectangle of pasteboard. *'Draco Viannis.'*

She wasn't even surprised. She closed her hand on the card, feeling its sharp edges dig into her palm. Wanting it to hurt. Needing a visible scar to counterbalance all the inner pain.

She said quietly, 'Thank you. I'll—see that he gets

it. Now, is it possible for me to have a word with the consultant?'

She didn't go straight back to the house. There was a National Trust property a few miles away, whose grounds were open to the public. There was an Elizabethan knot garden, and a lake with swans, and Cressy had always loved it there.

She found an unoccupied bench and sat, gazing across the sunlit waters with eyes that saw nothing and a heart without peace.

Her father had needed her, she thought, so she'd turned her back on the love that Draco was offering and gone running to him. She'd wanted, just once more, to be the cherished only daughter—to bask in the old relationship. To be important to him again.

But that was always going to be impossible, she realised wearily. Because they were not the same people any longer. Life had moved on for both of them.

So why this last vain attempt to cling on to her childhood?

She looked down at her hands, clenched in her lap. She remembered other hands, dark against her pale skin, and shivered.

She thought, Was I really so afraid of becoming a woman? Was that the true reason I ran away from Draco?

Under the circumstances, her reluctance to face the challenge of her own sexuality was ironic. Because Draco himself had changed all that in one brief, but very succinct lesson.

And now she was left stranded, between his desire for revenge and her father's indifference.

I've wrecked everything, she told herself desolately.

Sacrificed the only chance of real happiness I've ever been offered.

But she couldn't let herself think about that, or she would break down completely. And she had to be strong to get through the next few weeks or months, living on the edge of Draco's life. Strong enough, too, to walk away with her head high when it was over.

And before that she had other problems to deal with.

Her father might be too preoccupied with the loss of his wife to question this 'job abroad' too closely, but her aunt and uncle might not be so incurious. They would want a full explanation, and she couldn't imagine what she would say to them—or to Berry, who would find it unthinkable for her to leave her father in this way.

And how could she explain why her father's debts were now in abeyance, and the house reprieved, without mentioning the precise terms of her 'contract' with Draco?

Her conversation with the consultant had been uncomfortably revealing. Over the years her father's health cover had been reduced to a minimum. The top-grade private room he was occupying, and the services of the live-in nurse, were being paid for by Draco.

'I thought you knew and approved, Miss Fielding,' the consultant had told her, frowning. 'He described himself as a close friend of the family.'

'Yes,' she'd said, dry-mouthed. 'Yes, of course.'

It seemed there was not a part of her life that Draco didn't control. And the fact that in this instance his influence was totally benign somehow made it no better.

Oh, God, she thought. It's all such a mess.

And began, soundlessly and uncontrollably, to cry until she had no more tears left.

It was the sudden chill of the evening breeze across the lake and the clang of the bell announcing that the grounds were closing that eventually roused her from her unhappy reverie.

It was more than time she was getting back. Berry would have dinner waiting for her and would be worried about her non-appearance, she thought, sighing, as she returned reluctantly to her car.

The hall lights were on when she let herself into the house, but there was no sign of the housekeeper—or of dinner either. No place laid in the dining room or welcoming aroma of food in the air. Just—silence.

She called, 'Berry—I'm home,' and waited, but there was no response.

Maybe she'd gone into the garden, to pick some last-minute fruit for dessert or bring in some washing, Cressy thought, subduing an unwelcome tingle of apprehension.

She walked to the drawing room door, twisted the handle, and went in.

Draco was standing beside the fireplace, one arm resting on the mantelshelf as he stared down at the empty grate. He turned slightly, the dark eyes narrowing as Cressy paused in the doorway, her hand going to her throat in shock.

He said softly, 'So here you are at last, *agapi mou*. I have been waiting for you.'

She said shakily, 'So I see. Where's Berry? What's happened to her?'

His brows lifted. 'Naturally, I have murdered her and buried her body under the lawn,' he returned caustically. 'Or so you seem to think.'

She bit her lip. 'I don't think anything of the kind,' she denied curtly, aware that her heart was hammering in a totally unwelcome way at the sight of him. But then he'd startled her—hadn't he?

'I was just a little anxious about her,' she added defensively.

'So many anxieties about so many people.' His smile did not reach his eyes. 'What a caring heart you have, my golden girl. The truth is that I gave your Mrs Berryman the evening off. I believe she means to go to a cinema.'

'You gave Berry the evening off?' She stared at him, open-mouthed. 'And she agreed?'

His mouth twisted. 'She was a little reluctant at first, but I can be very persuasive.'

'To hell with your powers of persuasion,' Cressy lifted her chin. 'You had no right to do anything of the sort.'

'I have all kinds of rights, Cressida *mou*.' His tone hardened. 'And I mean to enjoy all of them.' He held out a hand. 'Now come and welcome me properly.'

Mutinously, she walked forward and stood in front of him. When he kissed her she stood unmoving, unresponding to the warm, sensuous pressure of his lips on hers.

After a moment, he drew back.

'Sulking?' he asked. 'What's the matter? Did I hurt you, perhaps, this morning?'

Colour rushed into her face. She stared down at the carpet. 'I don't know.'

He said, 'Look at me, *matia mou*. Look at me and say that.'

Cressy raised her eyes unwillingly to him. His smile was faintly mocking, but there was an odd watchfulness in his gaze which she found unnerving.

She said, 'No—no, you didn't. As you know quite well.'

'Where you are concerned, my beautiful one, I suspect I know very little.' His tone was dry. 'But I am glad you did not find your first surrender too much of an ordeal.'

She threw her head back defiantly. 'Your words, *kyrie*. Not mine. And now perhaps you'd tell me what you're doing here.'

'I thought I should pay a visit,' he said. 'To make sure that all was well with my property.' He paused. 'But I see it is not.' He took her chin in his hand, studying her, ignoring her gasp of outrage. 'You have been crying, *pethi mou*. Why?'

'Do you really need to ask that?' She freed herself stormily and stepped back. 'Or did you imagine I'd be turning cartwheels for joy because the mighty Draco Viannis had sex with me today.'

His mouth tightened. 'Would you have wept if Draco the fisherman had taken you that day on Myros?'

'He didn't exist,' she said. 'So how can I know?'

'You could always—pretend.'

She shook her head. 'There's been too much pretence already. Now we have a business arrangement.'

'Ah, yes,' he said softly. He removed his jacket, tossed it over the arm of one of the sofas and sat down, loosening his tie.

He smiled at her. 'Then perhaps you would take off your dress—strictly in the line of business.'

Her skin warmed again, hectically. 'My—dress?'

'To begin with.' His tie followed the jacket, and he began, unhurriedly, to unbutton his shirt.

She said, 'You—you actually expect me to strip for you?'

'It is hardly a novelty.' His tone was dry. 'After all, Cressida *mou*, the first time I saw your beautiful breasts it was your own idea.'

Her voice trembled. 'I—hate you.'

He laughed. 'That should add an extra dimension to the way you remove your clothes, my lovely one. I cannot wait.'

She said, 'But someone might come...'

He grinned at her. 'More than one, I hope, *agapi mou*.'

To her fury, she realised she was blushing again. 'You know what I mean.'

'Yes,' he said. 'And why do you think I gave the housekeeper leave of absence? Precisely so we should not be disturbed. Now, will you take off your dress, or do you wish me to do it for you?'

'No.' Her voice was a thread. 'I'll do it.'

She unfastened the long zip, slid the dress from her shoulders and let it pool round her feet.

'Tell me,' she said. 'If we'd been married, would you have degraded me like this?'

'And if we'd been on our honeymoon, Cressida *mou*, would you have expected either of us to remain fully clothed for very long?'

'You,' she said bitterly, 'have an answer for everything.'

'And you, my lovely one, talk too much.' Draco leaned back, watching her through half-closed eyes. 'Now take off the rest—but slowly.'

They lay together on the thick rug in front of the fireplace, his hands making a long, lingering voyage of rediscovery.

This time, she thought fiercely, she wouldn't let it happen. She wouldn't become some mindless—thing, subject to his every sexual whim. She had a will of her own and she would use it.

But it wasn't easy. Not when he was kissing her slowly and deeply, his tongue a flame against her own. Not when her breasts were in his hands and the tight buds of her nipples were unfurling slowly under his caress. Or when he was stroking her flanks, cupping the roundness of her buttocks in his palms.

And not when she needed him so desperately, so crazily, to touch her—there—at the very core of her womanhood.

He whispered against her lips. 'This time you have to ask, *agapi mou*. You have to tell me what you want.'

Her voice cracked. 'Draco—please...'

'Not good enough, my sweet one. Is it this?' He kissed her breasts, taking each soft, scented mound into his mouth in turn.

'Yes,' she said. 'No. Oh, God...'

'Or this?' His fingertips brushed her intimately, as lightly as a butterfly kiss and as fleeting.

Her only answer was a soft, involuntary whimper of yearning.

'Or even—this?' His voice sank to a whisper as he bent his head and his mouth found her.

She cried out, and for a moment her body went rigid, all her inhibitions rearing up in shock.

But her one prim attempt to push him away was unavailing. He simply captured her wrists in one strong hand and did exactly as he wanted.

Which, Cressy realised, as her whole body began to shake in sudden wanton delight, was exactly what she wanted too.

The last vestiges of control were dissolving under the warm, subtle flicker of his tongue. She was going wild, her head twisting from side to side, the breath bursting hoarsely from her lungs. Pleasure was filling her like a dark flame, driving her to the limits of her endurance. And beyond.

Her whole being seemed to splinter in a rapture so intense she thought she might die.

As awareness slowly returned, she realised she was kissing him, her parted lips clinging to his in abandoned greed. She had marked him too, she saw. There were small crescents on the smooth skin of his shoulders that her nails had scored in those final fainting seconds.

She felt bewildered—and ashamed that her resistance could be so easily and swiftly destroyed. And she was angry, too, because she didn't want to be Draco's creature, locked into this—sexual thrall.

He raised his head and looked down at her.

He said, his voice slurred, 'I couldn't concentrate at my meeting for thinking of your loveliness—your sweetness. I should be at a dinner tonight with a group of other bankers, but I had to find you—to be with you...'

She turned her head, avoiding his gaze. 'Am I supposed to be grateful?'

'No,' he said with sudden harshness. 'Just willing.'

He lifted her hips towards him, and smoothly and expertly joined his body to hers.

She could not fight him physically—she was no match for his hard, virile muscularity—but she could close her mind against him. Force herself to lie passive and unresponsive beneath him—refuse herself the delicious agony of consummation that his powerful body was offering her once more. That, she discovered with shock, her own sated flesh was incredibly, impossibly eager to accept.

And Draco knew what she was doing. Because he too was holding back, deliberately tempting her to abandon her self-denial and join him on the path to their mutual delight.

His mouth touched hers, softly, coaxingly, then brushed her closed eyelids. His lips tugged at the lobe of her ear and explored the vulnerable pulse in her throat. He whispered her name almost pleadingly against her breast.

And, in spite of everything, her iron resolve was beginning to falter, her aroused body making demands she could no longer ignore.

But Draco's patience had cracked too. He was no longer teasing, or even very gentle. Instead, he was driving himself with a kind of grim determination towards his own climax.

At its height, he cried out something in his own language, his voice harsh, almost broken.

When it was over, he rolled away from her and lay, one arm covering his eyes, as his rasping breath slowly returned to normal.

Cressy sat up slowly, pushing her hair from her eyes. She supposed she had scored a small victory, but it seemed a barren, sterile thing, especially when her newly awakened body was aching for the fulfilment she'd spurned.

She felt cold, and a little frightened. She didn't dare look at him, or say anything, even when, a long time later, he got to his feet and walked to the sofa and his discarded clothing. A brooding silence enclosed them both.

At last he said, 'You made me use you. Why?'

She said, 'I assumed you wished to be repaid for my

father's medical bills. You can't always choose the currency.'

He whispered something under his breath, and the controlled violence of it made her flinch. He picked up her dress and tossed it to her. 'Cover yourself.'

She slipped it over her head, but didn't fasten it. She didn't trust her shaking hands to deal with the zip.

He was fully dressed when he spoke again, his tone clipped, remote. 'You will find food in the kitchen. I brought a hamper from London. There is chicken, and champagne and peaches.'

She ran her tongue across her dry lips. 'Aren't you hungry?'

'I find I do not wish to eat with you,' he returned curtly. 'Besides, I think it best if I go before I do something I shall regret.'

He walked to the door and she followed him, barefoot, holding the slipping dress against her.

She said, her voice faltering a little, 'Did you drive yourself here? I didn't see another car.'

'I parked at the back of the house. The housekeeper directed me.'

'In my father's place?' Her voice rose. 'Oh, God, how could she do such a thing?'

'Because, unlike you, Cressida *mou*, she seems able to accept that I am the master here now.'

Hurt exploded inside her, and an odd sense of desolation.

She said thickly, 'Damn you,' and swung back her hand. She wanted to hit him—to drive the expression of cold mockery from his face.

But he was too quick for her, grabbing her wrist with hard fingers, shaking her slightly, so that the damned dress slid off her shoulders again, baring her to the waist.

She saw his face change, become starkly intent. He said softly, 'There is only one way to deal with a woman like you.'

He swung her round so that her back, suddenly, was against the closed door. She tried to cover her breasts with her hands, but his fingers closed round her wrists, lifting them above her head and holding them there.

He said, 'It is a little late for such modesty. Rage suits you better.'

She said breathlessly, 'Let me go—you bastard...'

'When *I* choose,' he said. 'Not you.'

She heard her dress tear as it fell to the floor. He took her quickly, his anger meeting hers in an explosive fusion that stunned the senses.

She thought, This is an outrage... And then she stopped thinking altogether.

Because his hands were under her thighs, lifting her so that she had to clamp her legs round his waist, join the driving rhythm of his possession.

His mouth was crushing hers passionately, drinking the salty, angry tears from her lips. She was moaning in her throat, gasping for breath, dizzy and drowning in the merciless forces he had released in her.

She tried to push him away, but it was already too late. Deep within her she could feel the first harsh tremors of her approaching climax. As the pulsations overwhelmed her, tore through her, she sobbed her release against his lips, then hung in his arms, limp as a rag doll, incapable of speech, hardly able to think.

Draco stepped back from the door and carried her across the room, dropping her almost negligently on to the sofa.

Cressy lay, staring up at him, her face hectically flushed, her hair wildly dishevelled and her eyes wide and enormous.

His smile was mocking as he casually fastened his clothing. He reached into the inside pocket of his jacket for his wallet.

A shower of fifty-pound notes fluttered down on her.

He said softly, 'I think I have ruined your dress, *agapi mou*, so buy yourself a new one. Something that does not make you look as if you are in mourning for your virginity, hmm?'

He paused. 'And do not ever try to reject me again.'

She wanted to reach out to him, to say his name, to ask him to stay with her, but she was too shattered by the impact of the last few minutes to be able to move or formulate coherent words.

She could only watch helplessly as he turned and walked to the door, where he paused.

'And do not wait for me to apologise,' he flung back at her. 'Because I find, after all, I do not regret a thing.' And he went out, slamming the door behind him.

CHAPTER NINE

'I'M GOING to hire a detective,' said James Fielding. 'Someone who knows what he's doing. He'll find her—persuade her to come home. Of course it will cost a great deal of money, but that's not a problem. It's time I was back in the workplace, anyway. I was a damned fool to be talked into early retirement.'

There was an awkward silence. Cressy saw the swift, worried glance exchanged by her aunt and uncle, and looked down at her hands gripped together in her lap.

Every day it was the same, she thought wearily. Schemes to make new fortunes. Plans to win Eloise back. Her father could talk of nothing else. He seemed to have lost all touch with reality.

His financial difficulties—the fact that the house no longer belonged to him—were simply brushed aside as temporary difficulties.

But then who am I to criticise? she wondered. With the nightmare I've created for myself?

It had been a week since Draco had slammed out, and since then she hadn't heard a word from him.

And she was scared.

After he'd gone, she'd lain on the sofa for a long time, limbless, weightless in the aftermath of that raw, savage ecstasy. She'd never dreamed she was capable of such a primitive intensity of feeling. Was stunned by her capacity for passion.

It was as if she'd lived her life only knowing half of herself.

When she'd been able to move again, and think, she had gone up to her room, showered, and changed into jeans and a thin sweater. She had burned the torn dress, along with the money, in the kitchen range, and had thrown away the food and wine. She'd felt too numb to eat. Besides, it had all been too reminiscent of the picnics they'd shared on Myros, and she hadn't been able to bear to remember the uncomplicated happiness of those days.

Days, she'd thought, when I was falling in love…

And could have wept for the innocence and tenderness of that lost time.

She had recalled the way his arm had held her, fitting her to the curve of his body. The beat of his heart under her cheek. How he'd smiled at her. The reined-back hunger in his eyes. The huskiness in his voice when he'd asked her to marry him.

Everything, she'd thought bleakly, that she'd thrown away with both hands.

And no amount of sex, however mind-blowing, would ever make up for that.

By the time Berry had returned she'd managed to regain some kind of composure. She'd spent the evening in the study, working on her computer, tying up some loose ends from work and listening to music.

'Has your visitor gone, Miss Cressy?' Berry looked around her as if she might find him hiding in a corner. 'You could have knocked me down with a feather when he told me he was the new owner and showed me the papers.' She lowered her voice. 'I didn't really want to leave him here, but he was so persuasive.' She shook her head. 'Not an easy gentleman to say no to. But did I do the right thing?'

'Yes, of course.' Cressy smiled at her with a tranquillity she was far from feeling. 'I suppose he thought it was time he saw what he was getting for his money.'

'And he told me Mr Fielding will be renting the house from him and we won't have to move out. Oh, that's such a relief, Miss Cressy. I've been so worried.'

So have I, Cressy thought bleakly. And my worries aren't over yet.

As each long day passed, she felt as if she was living on a knife-edge, waiting for the phone to ring. Scanning her e-mail box for messages.

But the nights were even worse. She lay awake for hours, staring into the darkness, her body aching for him—longing for him. She felt bereft—like a child crying unheard for comfort.

Perhaps he'd decided to cut his losses and shut her out of his life altogether. That was the thought that tortured her every waking moment.

She told herself that she was concerned for her father. Because if Draco had really decided to finish their relationship, it did not follow that he would write off her father's debts.

But in her heart she knew it would never be as simple as that. That she was using her father's problems as a barrier—as self-protection against a hurt that might tear her in pieces. Against feelings she dared not examine too closely in case they destroyed her.

'Cressy, dear.' Her aunt's voice reached her from some far distance. 'I think it's time we went, and let James rest.'

'Yes, of course.' She rose, reaching for her bag, aware that Lady Kenny was watching her with a faint frown.

'Coffee, I think,' Sir Robert said when they were in the corridor.

In the hospital cafeteria, he joined the queue at the counter while Cressy and Barbara Kenny found a corner table.

'It doesn't get any better, does it?' Lady Kenny said abruptly. 'Poor James is like a dog with a bone. He won't let go.'

Cressy shook her head. 'And he gets so agitated when he talks about her. I know it's not good for him. What he'll be like when he gets home...'

'I wonder if that's such a good thing.' Her aunt played with her wedding ring. 'Whether he wouldn't be better living somewhere with no memories. But he'll have the nurse to keep an eye on him, and dear Berry, so we must hope for the best.' She gave Cressy a searching glance. 'Now tell me about this new job of yours.'

'There's nothing to tell,' Cressy hedged. 'I'm not even sure it's happening.'

'I gather it's connected with the Standard Trust Bank,' Lady Kenny went on, as if she hadn't spoken. 'And that the head of the bank—some Greek tycoon—has made himself personally responsible for your father's debts. Isn't that a little unusual?'

Cressy shrugged. 'I suppose so. I haven't really thought about it.'

'Even when he insisted on conducting the negotiations with you personally?' Her aunt's tone was acerbic. 'And when you'd only just come back from Greece?' She gave an exasperated sigh. 'Cressy, I'm not a fool. Are you involved with this man?'

Cressy bit her lip. 'Not in the way that you think, Aunt Bar.'

Which was no more than the truth, she thought unhappily. No one would believe the complexities of her relationship with Draco.

'I have a short-term contract,' she continued, 'which necessitates my working abroad. After what he's done for Dad, I could hardly refuse. And I can look after myself,' she added, infusing her tone with brightness.

Lady Kenny snorted. 'Oh, really? Have you looked in a mirror lately? You're all eyes and cheekbones.' She leaned forward. 'Darling, men like Draco Viannis are not philanthropists. You don't know what you're getting yourself into. Your uncle and I are both worried sick. And if your father would come down to earth for a few minutes, I know he'd put a stop to it.'

'It's for three months,' Cressy said quietly. 'If I go at all.' She swallowed. 'Mr Viannis may be having second thoughts.'

'I can't vouch for this coffee.' Sir Robert deposited a tray on the table and sat down, fixing his niece with a penetrating look. 'Now then, Cressy, I want a word about this Viannis chap. Are you sure you know what you're doing?'

They were both so kind, Cressy thought as she drove home later, and so anxious about her. And she knew she'd done nothing to set their minds at rest.

But what could she say—what reassurance could she possibly give? Especially when she herself felt as if she was operating in some kind of vacuum.

There was a strange car, large, powerful and glossy, parked in front of the house, and Berry was waiting to open the door for her.

'You've a visitor, Miss Cressy. I've shown him into the drawing room.'

Cressy's heart thudded, and her throat tightened painfully as she walked towards the drawing room. Ever since her last encounter with Draco she hadn't been inside the room, unsure if she could handle the memories it would evoke. In fact, she'd made a point of using her father's study instead.

Now she had to face him there. Brave whatever he had to tell her.

Swallowing, she twisted the handle and went in.

The anticlimax when she found herself confronted by a stranger was almost ludicrous.

Except that she did know him, she realised after a stunned moment. It was Paul Nixon, who worked as Draco's PA. She'd seen him briefly in London.

She felt sick. Draco wasn't even going to break their agreement in person.

'Miss Fielding. I'm sorry I didn't make an appointment, but Mr Viannis called from New York last night to say he'll be returning to Myros next week and wishes you to meet him there. And that doesn't leave much time.'

She felt as if she'd been reprieved from a death sentence, and was ashamed of the relief and joy that flooded through her.

She said quietly, 'I understand. Won't you sit down? Can I offer you some tea or coffee?'

'Your housekeeper already did that, ma'am.' He delved into a briefcase. 'I have a file here, with your itinerary. You'll fly first class to Athens, and transfer to Myros by helicopter. Also details of the personal allowance that you'll receive while you remain Mr Viannis's—companion, and the final settlement he is prepared to make.'

Caught on the raw, Cressy took the folder he handed her.

'What a lot of paperwork,' she said coolly, hiding her hurt. 'All to get a man into bed with a woman.'

Paul Nixon's solemn face reddened uncomfortably and he gave Cressy an austere look. 'The details of Mr Viannis's private life are no business of mine, Miss Fielding. I'm just here to do a job.'

'You do it well,' she said. 'But I'm sure you've had plenty of practice.'

He looked more po-faced than ever. 'You'll also be requested to sign a contract of confidentiality,' he went on. 'Guaranteeing that no details of your time with Mr Viannis will ever be made public.'

'In case I write a kiss-and-tell story for the tabloids?' Cressy asked with disbelief. 'My God, I'm the last person in the world who'd want to go public.'

'I'm sure that's how you feel now, ma'am. But things can change, and Mr Viannis would not wish any future marriage he might contract to be compromised by unwelcome revelations.'

She felt as if she'd been punched in the stomach, but she recovered and managed a taut smile. 'In other words, hell hath no fury, Mr Nixon. Tell your boss I'll sign his guarantee.'

She took the pen he handed her, and wrote her name where indicated.

Then she showed him to the door, wished him a pleasant drive back to London, and returned to the drawing room.

The folder was lying on the coffee table. The next three months of her life all spelled out for her in clauses, sub-clauses and settlements.

She picked it up, weighed it speculatively for a moment, then, with a small choking cry, threw it across the room as hard as she could. It hit the wall and fell, disgorging its contents on to the carpet.

And then she burst into tears.

Cressy finished rubbing sun screen on to her legs, and put the cap back on the bottle.

It would be tempting, she thought with detachment, to allow Draco to arrive and find her burned to a crisp, and consequently unavailable, but she could not risk the damage to her skin.

The sky above Myros was cloudlessly blue, the sun relentlessly hot, and the swimming pool beside her deliciously cool. If only she could relax and enjoy it...

But that was impossible.

She found herself stealing another glance at her watch, and swore under her breath. He would be here only too soon. She didn't have to mark the passage of every minute until then.

She'd arrived the previous day, leaving rain and a chill, unseasonal breeze in England.

Her father, immersed in the letters he was writing to various companies offering his services as a consultant, had wished her an almost casual goodbye.

At one time she would have been wounded by his self-absorption. Now she had her own immediate problems to deal with.

The resident nurse, a Miss Clayton, was a kind, sensible woman, and Cressy had liked her at once. But it was clear she had a struggle on her hands to induce James Fielding to rest.

'It's not just a question of medication,' she'd told Cressy as they shook hands. 'He needs to relax more.'

Don't we all? thought Cressy, with irony, reaching for the iced lemonade on the table beside her. She might be in the equivalent of Eden, but she was like a cat on hot bricks just the same.

However disapproving Mr Nixon might be, there had been nothing wrong with his travel arrangements. It had been VIP treatment all the way.

The villa was just as beautiful as she'd imagined, with large airy rooms and exquisitely tiled floors, and a magical view of the sea from every window. And although it was luxurious, it wasn't stridently so. The furniture tended to be on the heavy, old-fashioned side, suggesting it had been passed down over several generations, and Cressy found it charming.

And the service was faultless, she thought. Courteous and unobtrusive.

If Vassilis, Draco's elderly major-domo, had reservations about his employer's choice of guest, he gave no sign of it.

She knew now what building work Draco had found it necessary to supervise, because she was living in it.

It was a guest bungalow, completely separate from the villa itself, with its own garden and pool, tucked away in a corner of the grounds.

It had a large living room, where her meals were served, a bathroom, with a big sunken tub as well as a conventional shower, and a huge bedroom, with walls painted in pale gold and a king-size bed with an ivory cover, draped in matching filmy curtains.

The perfect love nest, she'd thought, lips twisting, as Vassilis had shown her round it. All that was lacking was the perfect love.

But at least she was the first one to stay there. She hadn't had to spend her first sleepless night speculating on the women who'd occupied this bed before her. Her successor could worry about that.

Pain knifed at her, but she couldn't let that matter. She had to keep reminding herself of the tenuous nature of her position. Accustom herself to the idea that she had no permanent role in Draco's life.

And perhaps by the time it ended she would have learned to live with the pain.

In the distance, she heard the sound of a helicopter. She scrambled off the cushioned lounger and stood, staring upwards, her hand shading her eyes, her heart thumping against her ribcage.

It came in low enough for her to be aware of a figure—a face looking down at her—then descended towards the pad on the far side of the main house.

She took a deep, steadying breath, and thought, He's here.

And now, as Vassilis had tactfully indicated, she must wait to be summoned.

Fright and excitement warred inside her for control. After a moment, she resumed her place on the lounger. She didn't want to be found standing beside the pool as if she was planning to drown herself.

She picked up the magazine she'd been glancing through and tried to concentrate on it as the minutes dragged by.

It was over an hour later when Vassilis's upright figure appeared in the gap in the high flowering hedge that divided the bungalow from the rest of the grounds.

He said in his careful English, 'Mr Viannis presents his compliments to you, madam, and asks if you will dine with him this evening. He suggests ten o'clock.'

Six hours to go, Cressy thought. Draco was playing it cool. Whereas she might well become a nervous wreck.

Aloud, she said sedately, 'Please thank Mr Viannis,

and tell him I'd be delighted.' She paused. 'Am I to join him at the main house?'

'Yes, madam. I shall conduct you there.' He made her a small half-bow, and turned away.

Well, what had she expected? she asked herself with self-derision as she went back to her magazine. That Draco was going to rush to her side and smother her with kisses?

She was being taught her place, she thought, in one unequivocal lesson.

But, she told herself forlornly, she would have preferred the kisses.

She spent a lot of time that evening deciding what to wear. In the end she chose a cream silk shift, with bootlace straps and a deeply slashed neckline that skimmed the inner curves of her breasts. The minimum of underwear and a pair of cream strappy sandals with high heels completed the outfit.

Dressing the part, she thought, as she brushed her hair to fall in a silky curtain on her shoulders. But wasn't that what he was paying for?

She noticed that Vassilis kept his eyes discreetly lowered when he came to collect her.

It was a warm, sultry night, and the cicadas were busy as she walked through the garden. There were lights on inside the villa, and on the terrace which surrounded it.

One massive pair of sliding glass doors stood open, leading, she knew, to the *saloni*, and Vassilis paused outside, indicating politely that she should precede him into the lamplit room.

Lifting her chin, she obeyed, aware of him closing the doors behind her. Shutting her in.

He was standing at a side table, pouring himself a

drink. He was wearing jeans, and a dark polo shirt, unbuttoned to reveal the shadowing of hair on his chest, and for a brief moment her heart lifted as she saw the lover she'd first met.

Then he turned and studied her, the firm mouth unsmiling, and she knew she was mistaken.

He said softly, 'So, here you are.'

'As you see,' she said, masking her real emotions with flippancy. 'Stripped, bathed, and brought to your tent.'

His tone was flat. 'You are not amusing.' He pointed to the cloudy liquid in his glass. 'I am drinking ouzo. May I get you some?'

'I'd prefer plain water.'

He gave her a cynical look. 'How abstemious of you, *agapi mou*,' he drawled. 'You don't feel that alcohol might dull the edge of your coming ordeal?'

'Is that how you regard it?'

Draco shrugged. 'I want you very badly.' The dark eyes met hers in a frankly sensual challenge. 'And I am not in the mood to make allowances.'

Her throat tightened. She was aware that her skin was tingling, her entire body stirring with irresistible excitement under its thin silken covering.

Faint colour rose in her face, but she didn't look away.

She said, 'I'll take the risk.'

He lifted a sceptical brow, then turned back to the table, dropping ice cubes into a tumbler and filling it with water.

When he came across to give her the glass, Cressy felt her pulses surge. She thought that he would touch her, run his fingers down her bare arm, take her hand, kiss her mouth.

But he stepped back, lifting his own glass in a mocking salute. 'To courage, *pethi mou*,' he said, and drank.

They had dinner on the terrace, the table lit by glass-shaded candles. Vassilis brought them a light creamy soup, delicately flavoured with lemon, then fish baked with herbs, served with tiny potatoes and a green salad.

The food was delicious but Cressy had to force herself to eat. She was too aware of the shadowed face of the man who sat opposite her. Conscious of the caress of his dark eyes on her lips, her shoulders, her breasts. And she felt deep within her the slow ache of anticipation.

The silence between them was electric—alive with tension. As if, she thought, a storm was brewing.

She said, trying to introduce an element of normality, 'How was New York?'

'Like an oven. I prefer to go there in the fall.'

'Was your trip successful?'

'Thank you, yes.' There was faint amusement in his voice.

'And was the flight back tiring?'

'Yes, but I have amazing powers of recovery.' He was grinning openly now, and she felt herself blush.

After a pause, he said, 'You sound as if you have been taking lessons.'

'In what?' She sent him a puzzled look.

'Polite conversation for difficult situations,' he said silkily. 'And don't glare at me like that, or Vassilis will think we have quarrelled,' he added as the older man came soft-footed along the terrace.

He brought dessert—a bowl of fresh peaches and glossy black grapes—and when he had filled tiny cups with strong, bitter coffee, he discreetly vanished.

Cressy said, constrainedly, 'He's been very kind.'

His mouth twisted. 'He is paid to be.'

She drank some of the smoky brew. 'Is that what I'm paid for, too?'

He said harshly, 'No, it is not kindness I want from you. And you know it.'

'Then what?'

His smile was crooked. 'For tonight, *agapi mou*, I want you naked in my arms, and I cannot wait any longer. Come with me now.'

Her high heels made it difficult for her to keep up with his stride as they went through the moonlit garden, so she kicked off her sandals and ran beside him, barefoot.

Instantly he lifted her into his arms and carried her the rest of the way. As they reached the bungalow he stopped and kissed her, his mouth fierce and hungry, and she put her arms round his neck and held him, her lips parting eagerly beneath his.

A lamp had been lit in the bedroom, the covers were turned back, and a bottle of champagne on ice had been placed on the night table.

She thought, The stage is set, and wished it hadn't been. That no outsider had intruded on their first night together.

And then Draco kissed her again, and she forgot everything as her need for him surged through her.

He undid the single button which held her dress at the back, and it slid down her body to the floor. He knelt, stripping off her remaining covering, then buried his face against the slight concavity of her abdomen.

He whispered, 'I have dreamed of this, Cressida *mou*, of the scent of your skin—the taste…'

He picked her up and put her on the bed, shrugging

off his own clothes as he came down beside her. He kissed her mouth, and her breasts, then entered her, and she was so very ready, her body opening sweetly for him.

His taking was strong and powerful, and she gave without reserve, glorying in the muscled heat that filled her, taking him deeper and deeper, her mouth soft and moist under his, her fingers grazing his spine.

The final dark rapture took them both unawares. She cried out against his mouth, startled by the force that convulsed her, and heard his deep groan of pleasure in reply.

There were tears on her face, and his eyelashes were wet, but his lips were warm and sure against hers, and the fingers that stroked her body were endlessly tender.

And it was the most natural thing in the world to fold herself into the strong curve of his body and sleep.

But some time later, when she stirred drowsily and reached out to him, the place beside her was empty. And cold, too, as if he'd been gone a long time.

She had expected him to be there. Had counted on waking to the new day in his arms. Instead, loneliness was an icy hand at her throat.

She could just catch the fragrance of the cologne he used on his pillow. It was all that was left of him in the moonlit room, so she pulled the pillow into her arms and held it tightly, breathing the scent of him as she waited for the dawn alone.

CHAPTER TEN

CRESSY turned at the end of the pool, and cut back through the turquoise water with her clean, easy stroke. She'd already completed ten lengths, hoping that strenuous exercise would clear her mind and calm the agony of emotional confusion raging inside her.

Last night when she made love with Draco she had felt that it wasn't just a mating of their bodies, but their spirits too. And she was sure he'd been as moved by their attunement as she had.

She'd expected—she'd needed to sleep in his arms, and wake to feel his mouth warm and drowsy against hers. She'd hoped he would feel the same.

But he'd walked away. And realising that, for him, it had just been another sexual encounter—enjoyable, but soon forgotten—had been a cruel lesson to learn.

Vassilis had brought her breakfast as usual to the little vine-covered pergola, and it had taken all her resolve not to ask where Draco was, if he would be joining her. Or even if he'd sent her a message...

Well, she knew the answer to that too. Because he had not.

Underlining yet again that she had no real importance in his life, apart from the fact that he found her body desirable.

And perhaps she'd needed that kind of reminder, or she might have allowed the euphoria of the previous night to betray her into saying something really stupid. Something he would not want to hear.

She reached the other end of the pool and paused, shaking the drops of water from her face. As she did so she felt strong hands slide under her arms and draw her bodily up out of the water.

'*Kalimera,*' Draco said, as he set her down on the tiled surround. He was wearing elegant pale grey pants, and a white shirt, open at the neck.

'I—I didn't know you were there.' She made a business of wringing the excess water from her hair.

'I have been watching you,' he said. 'Tell me, *pethi mou*, are you training for the next Olympic Games?'

She shrugged. 'Swimming is good exercise.'

He said softly, 'I know another,' and pulled her towards him.

She hung back. 'I'm soaking. Your clothes will be ruined.'

'Then I'll take them off,' he said, and began to unbutton his shirt.

'Your staff…'

'Know better than to interrupt us. Besides, the maids have finished.'

She knew that. She had seen them leave while she was having breakfast, carrying the unwanted champagne and talking and giggling together. No doubt mulling over the fact that Kyrios Draco had found nothing to celebrate during his night with his *anglitha*. She'd felt stung, and his casual reference galled her all the more.

She said breathlessly, 'Is this what you expect? That I just—perform to order at any hour of the day and night?'

His shirt went to join the grey suit jacket and silk tie which, together with a briefcase, were already lying on one of the sun loungers.

He said, 'I was not aware, *agapi mou*, that I had asked you to perform at all.' He unzipped his trousers and stepped out of them, revealing brief black swimming trunks.

He regarded her bleakly. 'I have been in a meeting on Alakos since early morning. Perhaps I should have stayed there rather than hurry back to be with you. Or maybe you would prefer me to return to the main house for my swim?'

She said, stumbling a little, 'No—stay—please.' She looked at him appealingly. 'Draco, try to understand. This—isn't easy for me.'

His voice was cold. 'It was not intended to be.' He walked to the edge of the pool and dived in.

Cressy towelled herself down, then retired rather miserably to her lounger under the sun umbrella. Somehow he'd managed to wrongfoot her again, she thought.

When Draco eventually emerged from the pool, he dried himself quickly, then stretched out on one of the spare loungers a few feet away. He did not speak, or look at her, but busied himself with some papers he took from his briefcase.

With a smothered sigh, Cressy reached for the sun screen and began to apply it to her legs, aware that Draco's eyes had flickered briefly in her direction.

Making her wonder at the same time exactly how much of his attention it would be possible to attract.

He had put her firmly in her place, but how strong was his resolution to keep her at a distance?

She spent a long time smoothing on the lotion, lifting each slender leg in turn and running her hands slowly over her calves and up to her thighs, aware that his gaze was straying for longer and longer periods in her direction.

When she'd finished her legs, she began on her abdomen, using just her fingertips and upward circular movements until her bikini bra got in the way.

She unhooked it, and dropped it to the tiles, and began gently and very delicately to rub sun screen on to her breasts, paying particular attention to her nipples.

A lightning glance from under her lashes at Draco revealed that he'd abandoned all pretence of studying his papers, and instead was lying on his side, propped up on one elbow, watching her with undisguised appreciation.

He said softly, 'For a lady who does not perform, you're putting on quite a show, Cressida *mou*.'

She said, 'I don't want to burn...'

'No,' he said. 'You wish me to do so, instead.'

She gave him a small, cool smile, lifting her hands to push her hair back from her face, so that her breasts tilted upward in deliberate provocation.

'I thought you liked to look at me.'

'I do. You are very lovely. That is why I had your bedroom designed in gold and ivory—so that it would match your hair and your skin. Even if, as I thought then, I could only enjoy the picture you'd make in my imagination. Or on our wedding night,' he added almost casually.

She winced inwardly. She said, 'I hope I didn't disappoint you.'

'Not physically, *agapi mou*. Your body is all that a man could dream of.' His smile did not reach his eyes.

'But?' Cressy lifted her chin. 'Isn't that what you were going to say?'

He said, 'I was going to quote from your Shakespeare's *Troilus and Cressida*—when Troilus realises he has been betrayed.' His voice was quiet, almost reflective. '"If beauty have a soul, this is not she".'

Colour flared in her face. She reached for her discarded towel and pulled it across her body.

She said quietly, 'That's—cruel...'

'Perhaps,' he said. 'I am not in the mood for kindness.' He stood up, stretching indolently, then picked up his clothes.

He said, 'However, I'm hungry and I'm tired. I'm going up to the house to have some food, and then sleep for an hour or two. *Herete*, Cressida *mou*.'

She said quickly, before her courage deserted her, 'You don't have to go. You could have lunch here, and then we could—sleep together—in the beautiful room you made for me.'

There was a silence, then Draco shrugged, his eyes hard. 'I fear that is not possible. You see, to me, sleep is the ultimate surrender between a man and a woman. It signifies trust—mutual dependence, commitment. And I swore a long time ago that it was an intimacy I would only share with my wife.'

She hadn't known it was possible to hurt so much. She said, 'I see,' and was astonished that her voice didn't break.

His smile grazed her skin. 'But if you feel inclined to "perform" again at some time, you have only to let me know. I will be delighted to join you.'

And he walked away, leaving her staring after him, her eyes blurred with tears.

I suppose, Cressy told herself drearily, that this is what's known as stalemate.

She'd found her way out of the garden and was standing on the headland itself, staring out to sea, her hair whipping about her face.

The wind had risen in the night, and below her the water had been stirred into little foam-capped waves.

There was no way down to the shore that she could see, but it was good just to get away from the immediate vicinity of the bungalow.

There were times, she thought restively, when she felt as if she was in solitary confinement.

She hadn't seen Draco for nearly a week now. True, he wasn't always there. The helicopter had been buzzing backwards and forwards regularly. But when he was at home he made no attempt to seek her company.

And pride, as well as fear of another rejection, prevented her from asking him to come to her.

'Kyria Fielding.' She looked round to see Vassilis hurrying towards her. 'I could not find you. I was concerned.'

'Did you think I'd run away again—or that I was going to throw myself over?' Cressy asked drily.

'That is not a subject about which to make jokes,' he said reprovingly, and she sighed.

'I'm sorry, Vassilis. Is there a problem?'

'I have brought your lunch, *kyria*. It will be getting cold.'

She sat, as she always did, at the small table he'd laid for her on the terrace. Her napkin was spread on her lap, and wine was poured into her glass.

The service remained impeccable, she thought, wondering if Vassilis found it strange that his employer's mistress should be spending her days and nights alone. Whatever his views, he was too well-trained to betray them.

He took the lid from a dish and served her a tiny

boned chicken stuffed with a delicately savoury rice. It was delicious, as usual, but as she ate Cressy thought with nostalgia of the meals she'd eaten at Yannis's taverna.

Instead of this evening's gourmet treat, she wondered if she could persuade Draco to take her out to eat. Spit-roasted lamb, she thought, and a Greek salad, and some rough red wine.

And maybe he would dance for her, and smile at her because he saw once more the girl he'd fallen in love with.

It was worth trying, anyway. Anything, she thought, was better than this limbo she was currently occupying.

She began to plan. She would ask Vassilis to arrange transport for her to Myros town, so that she could tell Yannis and Maria they were coming and get them to reserve the usual corner table.

She would also get her hair trimmed, she thought, combing its tangles with her fingers. She might even buy something to wear—something demure, and pretty, and very Greek.

But first she had to see Draco, and invite him formally to have dinner with her. And when he arrived at the bungalow that evening she would tell him he was driving her to Myros instead.

All she needed now was an excuse to go up to the house.

The telephone, she thought, with sudden inspiration. She could say she needed to call her family in England, which was no more than the truth. She'd rung home on her first evening, to tell them all she'd arrived safely, but she'd been reluctant to call again, in case she was faced with questions she couldn't answer.

I'll just have to risk it, she told herself.

She changed into a pair of slim-fitting white trousers, topping them with a dark blue cotton knit sweater with short sleeves and a discreet neckline.

Neat, she thought, as she brushed her hair and tied it back at the nape of her neck with a scarf, but not over-seductive.

Vassilis was clearly surprised to see her when she presented herself at the main door a few minutes later, but he nodded when she mentioned the telephone.

'I will ask for you to use the one in Kyrios Draco's study, madam. It is more private there.'

He led the way to a thick, heavily carved wooden door, and tapped. There was a moment's low-voiced conversation in Greek, then he stood back.

'Go in, madam, if you please.'

So far so good, thought Cressy, pinning on the casually pleasant smile she'd been practising.

But it wasn't Draco who rose with formal politeness as she entered, but Paul Nixon.

'Miss Fielding.' His tone held faint surprise. 'If you're looking for Draco, he's in Athens.'

Disappointment was like a slap in the face.

She said, 'I didn't realise. I didn't hear the helicopter.'

'He went very late last night,' he said. 'I guess you were asleep.' He paused. 'I understand you wish to use the phone?'

No, she thought. I want to make an assignation with my lover.

She said, 'Yes, if that's possible. I'm feeling guilty about my family.'

'And we can't have that.' There was something in his tone, as he gathered up the papers he was working on, which needled her. At the door, he paused. 'You know the code for the UK? Then I'll leave you to it.'

She spoke to her aunt first. 'Aunt Bar—how's everything going? How's Dad?'

'I'm not altogether sure,' Lady Kenny said slowly. 'Your uncle and I went to lunch there yesterday, and he seemed quiet, almost subdued. And he didn't mention Eloise once.' She sighed. 'I think he's finally coming to terms with the fact that she's never coming back.'

'But that's a good thing—isn't it?'

'We must hope so.' Her aunt paused. 'And you, Cressy—how are things with you?'

'Oh, fine,' she said brightly, crossing her fingers in the folds of her skirt. 'You don't have to worry about me.'

When she rang her home, Nurse Clayton told her that her father was proving a model patient, if a little low-spirited.

'A call from you could be just what he needs to cheer him up,' she added.

Her father's voice sounded quiet and tired. He said, 'Sid, darling, I was hoping you'd ring. I've been doing a lot of thinking, and I realise I haven't been very fair or very kind to you for a long time now.'

'Oh, Dad.' Her throat constricted. 'You don't have to say this. Not now.'

'Yes,' he said. 'I must. I don't even know how much personal responsibility you've taken for my financial mess. No one seems prepared to give me any straight answers.' He paused. 'And it matters, because you're all I've got, and you're precious. So, tell me the truth, Sid. This Viannis—is he treating you well?'

'Yes,' she said steadily. 'Yes, he is. And I'll be home very soon now. We'll talk properly then.'

'It's good to hear your voice,' he said. 'I just needed to tell you I was sorry. Bless you, Sid, and take care always.'

She replaced the receiver, frowning a little. She'd never heard him like that before, speaking as if every word was an effort.

She thought, I'll arrange with Draco to ring each day from now on.

She found Paul Nixon waiting in the big square entrance hall.

She said, 'Thank you for the use of the room. I wonder if I could put you to some more trouble.'

'You can always ask.'

It didn't sound particularly hopeful, she thought, bewildered, but she pressed on.

'I was wondering if someone could drive me to Myros town?'

'For what purpose?'

This time his curtness was undisguised.

She flushed. 'Because I haven't been outside the grounds of this villa since I got here.' She ticked her reasons off on her fingers. 'Because I need a hairdresser, and because I'd like to visit Yannis and Maria at the taverna again. I hope that's all right,' she added with a touch of sarcasm.

He said, 'I'll arrange for a beautician from the hotel to visit you here.'

She stared at him. 'I said I'd like to go out.'

'I'm afraid that's not possible, Miss Fielding. Draco wishes you to remain in the environs of the Villa Hera.'

She laughed disbelievingly. 'You mean I can't even go for a walk? But that's ridiculous.'

'This is a small island, Miss Fielding,' he said quietly. 'With traditional views and values, which Draco respects. And your status has changed since you were last here.'

She stiffened as she realised what he was implying. 'You mean Maria might not want to meet Draco's whore?'

'Precisely. Also your presence here is a matter of total discretion. Draco does not wish that compromised—largely for your own sake. One day you won't have his protection. And as his discarded mistress you'd be a fair target for the gutter press.'

There was a note almost like relish in his tone.

The breath caught in her throat. She said. 'You don't like me very much, do you?'

'I work for Draco, Miss Fielding. I don't judge how he chooses to amuse himself.'

'Really?' Cressy raised her eyebrows. 'I get the impression you've been judging me ever since I stepped out of that penthouse lift in London.'

He looked at her icily. 'Okay, Miss Fielding. You want to hear it—you'll get it. Draco and I go way back. We were at school together in the States, and at college. He was best man at my wedding, and I planned to stand up for him when he married this shy Aphrodite that he'd found on a beach. A girl he worshipped, and who loved him for himself alone. Someone he'd thought he'd never find.

'Only there was no wedding, and you know why. My wife and I were right here when he realised you'd dumped him and run.'

He drew a harsh breath. 'I had to watch my best friend go to pieces in front of me, and it wasn't pleasant. He was torn apart—going crazy. You damn near destroyed him, and if you're suffering a little in return, that's fine with me.'

He shook his head. 'I never wanted him to get involved with you again, but I guess this is his way of finally getting you out of his system, so I sure hope it works.

'And don't bother running to him to get me fired when he comes back tonight, lady,' he added curtly. 'My letter of resignation will already be on his desk.'

She made herself meet the cold accusation, the hostility in his eyes.

She said tonelessly, 'Why should you lose your job for telling the truth? I—I shan't say anything to Draco. And I hope you'll stay and go on being his friend.'

She walked past him towards the door and the sunshine beyond, then turned. Her voice trembled. 'And, for the record, you can't possibly blame me more than I do myself.'

The breeze was still strong, so she spent the remainder of the afternoon inside the bungalow, curled up in a corner of the big, deeply cushioned sofa which dominated the living area, her arms wrapped round her body in a vain attempt to stop herself shaking.

Paul Nixon's words had brought home to her as never before exactly what she'd done. She thought of Draco, scorned and humiliated, like an eagle brought low, and pain tore at her.

I'm no better than Eloise, she thought. I left, too, without considering the ruin and desolation I was leaving behind. And I did that to the man I loved, whereas I don't believe she ever cared for my father.

But her father had forgiven. Had gone on loving Eloise in spite of everything.

Which Draco had not. And once his need for revenge was satisfied, she would be out of his life for ever.

'I'd go to him on my knees,' she whispered. 'If I thought it would do any good. If he'd hold me just once more as if he was keeping me safe against the world. But it's too late.'

A short while later she heard the helicopter passing overhead. And fifteen minutes afterwards became aware of approaching footsteps striding swiftly across the terrace.

She scrambled to her feet, and waited for the door to open.

The wind had ruffled his dark hair. As she looked at him, she felt her heart contract with helpless yearning.

He said, 'Paul tells me you were asking for me.'

'Only to get your permission to telephone England.'

He frowned slightly. 'Naturally, you have it. You do not need to ask. I will arrange to have a phone installed here for your personal use.'

'That's kind,' she said. 'But there's no real need.'

He said quietly, 'Please allow me to do this for you.' He paused. 'Was your call satisfactory?'

'I suppose so.' It was her turn to hesitate. 'I'm worried about my father.'

'I'm sorry.'

'It's probably nothing,' she said. 'He just sounded so defeated somehow.' She sighed. 'But he called me Sid. And he hasn't done that for a very long time.'

He looked her over, smiling slowly. 'And is that who you are now?'

'Only until the sun goes down.' She met his dark gaze. 'Will you have dinner with me this evening?'

'Why, *agapi mou*?' he drawled. 'Is this your way of telling me that you're available again?'

No, she thought, it's my way of telling myself that if

a few hours of lovemaking are all I'm allowed of you, then I'll settle for that.

She shrugged, watching him through her lashes. 'Find out for yourself, *kyrie*—after dinner.'

His brows lifted in mocking acknowledgement. He walked across to her and pulled her against him, his lips exploring hers in warm, sensuous appreciation. At the same time he untied the scarf confining her hair, separating the silky strands with restless fingers and drawing them forward to frame her face.

She laughed and shook her head. 'It needs cutting.'

'I forbid it,' he said huskily. 'It would be a crime against humanity.'

He drew her down to sit beside him on the sofa. He said, 'I have to go away again tomorrow.'

'Must you?' She moved slightly so that his fingers could more easily cup her breast. 'Where this time?'

'New York.'

'I thought you didn't like it there in summer.'

'I have no choice. I have business to settle, and a possible merger to arrange.'

'Tell me about it.' She slipped a hand into the open neck of his shirt, her fingers tracing patterns among the crisp dark hair.

He shook his head. 'I never talk about deals before they are concluded.'

'My father used to say that.'

'Presumably before his business acumen deserted him.' His tone was faintly acerbic.

'It wasn't entirely his fault,' she protested. 'He was under pressure from my stepmother, and he could never refuse her anything. She helped con him out of the money, and now she's gone off with the man who ruined him, and he'd still have her back if he could.'

He gave her a cynical look. 'Love drives you crazy, *pethi mou*. Didn't you know?' He kissed her again. 'I'll go now. I need a shower and a drink before dinner, and I have some calls to make.'

'Is it always like this?' she asked. 'Phone calls and meetings, and dashing from city to city?'

'Not always.' He ran a caressing hand down her spine. 'And when I come back I shall make sure I have some free time to devote to you alone.' He paused. 'Do you miss me when I'm away?'

She wriggled away from his hand and the question at the same time. 'I've never been to New York.'

He was silent for a moment. 'I have too hectic a schedule for you to accompany me this time,' he said quietly. 'There'll be other trips.'

She put on one of her favourite dresses, a simple button-through style in dark green linen, with a square neck and a skirt that flared slightly. She brushed lustre on to her lips, and mascara on to her long lashes, and stroked scent on to her throat and breasts. Preparing herself for love, she thought, her mouth twisting sadly.

When she emerged from her bedroom, she was confronted by a procession of people with table linen, cutlery and glassware, all milling round in the living room.

She beckoned to Vassilis. 'Will you tell them all to go, please?'

'To go, madam?' He was clearly shocked. 'But we must make things ready for Kyrios Draco.'

'I can do that myself,' Cressy said briskly, ignoring his horrified expression. 'I can lay a table, arrange flowers and light candles.'

'But the *kyrie*...'

'The *kyrie* wants peace and privacy, and so do I.'

Cressy offered him a winning smile. 'Please make them understand I wish to be alone with him.'

He was clearly scandalised by such candour—the fiction that she was just another guest and this was an ordinary dinner party had to be maintained somehow—but he had the room emptied in minutes.

As she moved round the table, putting the final touches, Cressy let herself pretend that she was back in London, in her own flat, waiting for Draco to arrive. That once again they were lovers, with a wedding to plan and a future to dream about.

As it could have been, she thought. Only I was too much of a coward to take the risk.

When everything was as good as she could make it, she sat down and tried to compose herself. It was impossible that she should still feel shy with Draco, yet she did. Because in many ways he was still an enigma.

He made love to her with breathtaking skill and artistry, but that was such a minor part of his life. And the doors to the rest were closed to her.

Restlessly, she reached for the pile of magazines that Vassilis provided on an almost daily basis. They were mostly high-fashion glossies, which didn't interest her greatly, but there was the odd news magazine sometimes, reminding her that there was a real world outside Myros.

She picked up the latest edition and began to flick through the politics and reviews which made up most of its content.

She turned to the business pages and stopped, her whole body suddenly rigid, because Draco was there. And not alone. The full-length photograph of him in evening dress, taken outside some restaurant, also featured the beautiful girl clinging to his arm. She was tall and dark, with sultry eyes and a pouting mouth, and her spectacular figure was enhanced by a piece of designer glamour that had probably cost more than a thousand dollars per square centimetre.

'Draco Viannis with shipping heiress Anna Theodorous', ran the caption, and, numbly, Cressy turned to read the accompanying story.

> Insiders, expecting to hear that the Ximenes Corporation's bid for the Theodorous tanker fleet has been successful, were intrigued last week by rumours of a more personal merger between the two giants.
>
> Draco Viannis seems likely to surrender his bachelor status at last when his engagement is announced to Dimitris Theodorous's lovely twenty-year-old daughter Anna.
>
> While boardroom negotiations were said to have temporarily stalled, the couple seemed inseparable at a series of fashionable Manhattan niteries, and a Ximenes source confirmed they were close.
>
> Maybe all Dimitris has to do is wait for his rival to become his son-in-law.

Someone was moaning, a small, desolate sound in the stillness.

It was a moment before she realised that the noise was coming from herself, and pressed a hand to her mouth to stifle it.

She closed the magazine and thrust it back into the middle of the pile, as if she could somehow, by so doing, make it disappear altogether.

But there would be other stories in other newspapers and magazines that she would have to confront eventually. This would be a big business marriage, and it would not be celebrated quietly.

A whimper escaped her. But she couldn't let herself go to pieces.

It would be pointless anyway. He had made it coldly clear all along that he would marry eventually. She just hadn't expected it to be so soon. But it was none of her business. She'd forfeited all rights the day she'd agreed to his terms.

Nor was it any use telling herself that this was a political marriage rather than a love match. How many men with his money and power did follow their hearts, anyway? And Draco wouldn't risk being caught in that trap again.

Besides, having Anna Theodorous as a wife would be no hardship to any red-blooded man.

She'll be the one, thought Cressy, to sleep in his arms and be the mother of his children.

And I shall have to remember that every day for the rest of my life.

CHAPTER ELEVEN

'YOU are very quiet.' Draco watched her meditatively across the candlelit table.

She smiled at him. 'I thought you might like to eat in peace.'

'And I thought perhaps you were worn out by domesticity, *agapi mou*.' He indicated the table. 'Vassilis tells me you did all this yourself.'

'Yes,' Cressy said lightly. 'I'm amazing, aren't I? Imagine knowing where knives and forks go.'

His lips twitched. 'Can you cook as well? Does my chef have to worry?'

'I'm a very good cook, but I wouldn't dare invade his domain.'

How can I do this? she asked herself. How can I sit and chat about trivia when my heart is breaking?

He said softly, 'There seems no end to your talents, my beautiful one.'

She leaned back in her chair, letting her fingers play gently with the long stem of her wine glass, caressing the slender shaft with sensuous enjoyment. 'I try to please.'

Draco watched what she was doing with undisguised amusement. He said gently, 'Behave, Cressida *mou*.'

She let her lashes sweep down to veil her eyes. 'That's for wives, *kyrie*. Mistresses are allowed to do as they like. It goes with the territory.'

'You seem to know a great deal about it.'

'I've had to learn fast. After all, I don't want your successor to feel I'm lacking in any respect.'

'My successor?' His fork clattered to his plate. 'What in hell do you mean?'

She shrugged. 'Well, this certainly beats accountancy. I expect a long and lucrative career. Of course, I shall need you to introduce me to your friends when my three months is up,' she added casually.

He said with a snap, 'I'll make a note in my diary.'

'You sound put out.' Cressy raised her eyebrows. 'But I have to be practical. And I really should become more demanding too. After all, I'm still wearing my own clothes,' she added, frowning. 'Why wasn't there a wardrobe full of top designer gear waiting for me?'

'Perhaps because I felt you would almost certainly throw it in the sea,' he said.

'I wouldn't throw jewels in the sea,' she said. 'Or furs.'

'I admit I did not think of furs.' Draco picked up a peach and began to peel it. 'But the average temperature on Myros may have affected my judgement.'

'I could always save them,' she said. 'For New York in the fall.'

'But if you want jewels, you shall have them,' he went on, as if she hadn't spoken. 'Do you prefer diamonds or pearls?'

'Both,' she said.

His brows lifted. 'Take care, *pethi mou*. You may price yourself out of the market.'

'I'll be careful,' she said. 'And I'll be very selective next time, too, about my choice of benefactor.' She looked thoughtfully into space. 'A lonely widower, perhaps—whose daughter's just got married...'

'What is this nonsense?' There was no amusement in his voice now.

She shrugged. 'You'll be going on to the next lady. I'll have to go on to the next man.' She paused on the very edge of the abyss. Then jumped. 'You will introduce me to Dimitris Theodorous, won't you?'

Draco put down the knife he was using very carefully. 'What are you talking about?' His tone was ice.

'The merger,' she said. 'I've been reading all about it.'

'It's no secret,' he said. 'Ximenes has been negotiating for those tankers for a long time.'

'I wasn't,' she said, 'talking about tankers.'

'I did not think so.' The agate eyes glittered at her.

'Miss Theodorous photographs beautifully,' she went on recklessly. 'I loved her dress—what there was of it. Do tell her so.'

He leaned back in his chair. 'With pleasure,' he drawled. 'Which particular dress did you have in mind? She has so many.'

She had to guess. 'The Versace.'

He smiled reminiscently. 'Ah, yes.'

Cressy brought her fist down on the table. 'You bastard.' Her voice shook. 'You were with her every night in New York. Then you came back here—to me.'

He shrugged. 'What good is a woman in New York when I am on Myros?' His voice was silky.

'You're despicable.'

'No,' he said. 'Practical—like you.' His eyes blazed at her suddenly. 'And you forfeited the right to dictate to me about other lovers when you ran out on our wedding.'

She said fiercely, 'And you forfeited the same right when you forced me into bed with you.'

'You think I used force?' His chair grated across the tiled floor as he stood up. 'You are a child, Cressida *mou*. But perhaps it is time you learned another lesson. Perhaps I should show you what to expect when you find yourself in the bed of Dimitris Theodorous or any of his type.'

He strode round the table, and pulled her up from her chair by her wrist. She tried to struggle free and failed.

'Let go of me...'

'No,' he said. 'You obey orders, not give them.' He took hold of the neckline of the green dress and tore it apart, the strong fingers negligent.

She said breathlessly, 'Draco—what are you doing?'

He said, almost conversationally, 'When Theodorous goes cruising on his yacht, he takes three girls at a time. As soon as they get on board their clothes are removed, and they spend the rest of the voyage naked, even in front of the crew. Is that how you wish to be treated? Because I am willing.'

He picked her up and carried her into the bedroom, dropping her on the bed.

She stared up at him, trembling, as he began to unfasten his clothing.

She said, 'Draco—you're frightening me.'

'But this is only a demonstration, Cressida *mou*.' His smile seared her. 'The reality would be infinitely worse, I promise you.'

She shrank, sudden tears hot in her throat. 'Draco—no, please.'

There was an endless, terrible silence, then she heard him sigh. He sat down on the bed beside her and took her chin in his hand, making her look at him.

He said quietly, 'One night with Theodorous, *agapi*

mou, and you would never feel clean again, I promise you.'

He put her into the bed and drew the sheet gently over her.

Her clenched fist was pressed against her mouth. She said, 'What will happen to me when you're married?'

'Hush,' he said. 'Get some rest. We will talk about it when I get back from New York.'

He half rose, and she caught at his hand. 'Stay with me—please.'

He hesitated. 'For a little while, then.' He lay down beside her, on top of the covers, sliding an arm round her shoulders and drawing her against him.

'Aren't you going to undress?'

'No.'

'Don't you—want me?'

'Yes,' he said. 'But I do not trust myself with you, Cressida *mou*. Too much has happened tonight.'

'Oh.' She closed her eyes and put her head against his chest, soothed by the strong beat of his heart. When she spoke again, her voice was quiet. 'Are you leaving very early tomorrow?'

'Around five. I have a meeting in Athens before my plane leaves.'

She said, 'Can I see you off?' and felt him smile.

'You will be asleep.'

'No,' she said. 'No, I'll be there. I promise.'

His lips touched her forehead, and he began to talk to her very softly in his own language. She did not know what he was saying, but it didn't seem to matter, because his arms were holding her, and she felt so safe—so secure that her eyelids began to droop...

She awoke with a start, and lay, watching the grey light stealing through the shutters. She was alone, but then she'd expected to be. And who was to say that she might not soon be alone for the rest of her life?

She peered at her watch, and realised with shock that it was almost five a.m., that he would be leaving.

There wasn't time to dress or even get to the helicopter pad. She grabbed a thin white cotton robe and thrust her arms into the sleeves, fastening its sash as she ran. The tiles were icy under her bare feet, and the stones on the path outside were painful, but she didn't falter.

She flew down through the garden, her lungs on fire, as at last she panted out on to the chill, damp grass of the headland.

The sun was a sullen red disc on the horizon. Behind her, coming over the house, she heard the beat of the rotors, and she swung round, staring up into the sky, waving frantically, willing him to look down and see her.

The noise was earsplitting. The chopper was right overhead now, but she could see him, and knew that he saw her too as he lifted his hand in greeting.

And she put her hands to her mouth and shouted, 'I love you,' into the vibrating air, knowing as she did so that he couldn't hear her. That her words would be eaten, fragmented and thrown away by the machine that was taking him away from her.

She stood watching, and waving, until the helicopter was just a speck in the distance, then she turned and went slowly back to the bungalow.

'You do not eat enough, madam,' Vassilis said sternly. 'You will make yourself ill.'

'It's too hot to eat,' said Cressy.

The temperature had soared in the last few days, and the sea looked like glass, the horizon shrouded in a permanent haze. Even the big parasols near the pool were no defence against the sun's fierceness, and after her swim Cressy preferred to retreat to the shade of the terrace.

She wondered if it was equally warm in New York, but didn't dwell on it. What might or might not be happening on the other side of the Atlantic was a no-go area for her. It had to be if she was to retain any peace of mind.

And when he came back they would talk...

She watched as Vassilis, clucking, removed the remnants of her half-eaten lunch, then settled back in her chair. She hadn't slept well the previous night. She'd had a series of small hateful dreams which still hung over her like a pall, and made her feel restless and uneasy.

Or maybe a storm was brewing somewhere which would end this still, brazen heat.

She found herself wishing that the newly installed telephone would ring, and she'd pick up the receiver and hear Draco's voice saying *agapi mou*. But she knew she might as well cry for the moon. He'd called twice since he'd been away, each time asking briefly and politely if she was all right. She'd said, 'Yes' and 'Thank you' and that had been that.

He hadn't mentioned when he was coming back, and she hadn't dared to ask. Or if he would be alone when he came...

She heard the sound of footsteps and sat up with sudden incredulous hope, only to see Paul Nixon approaching.

Since their confrontation up at the Villa Hera she

hadn't set eyes on him, and as far as she knew he'd never come down to the bungalow before. Now he walked up to the terrace, and halted awkwardly in front of her.

He said, 'Miss Fielding—Cressida—there's been a phone call. I have some bad news for you.'

She felt sick, her eyes scanning his grave face. She said, 'It's Draco, isn't it? Something's happened—I knew it...'

'No,' he said quickly. 'No, Draco's fine. The call was from England—from your uncle. I'm afraid your father's had another heart attack.'

She scrambled to her feet. 'Oh, God—when? Is he back in hospital? I must go to him...'

He took both her hands in his, which was odd of him, when he disliked her so much.

He said, 'He's not in hospital. He was at home when it happened.'

Her voice seemed to belong to a stranger. She said, 'He didn't make it—did he?' And saw him bow his head in acquiescence.

He said, 'I've spoken to Draco, and I'm to escort you back to England for the funeral at once.'

She moved sharply. 'There's no need for that.'

'Yes, there is,' he told her firmly. 'You can't face this alone. If you'll pack what you need, I'll start making our travel arrangements.'

'I knew there was something wrong,' she said, her voice shaking. 'I—I dreamed it.'

'Can I get you something? Some brandy, maybe, or some tea if you'd prefer?'

She shook her head. 'I don't want anything. I'd just like to be on my way. My aunt will need me.'

'Yes.' He patted her shoulder clumsily. 'Miss Fielding—I'm truly sorry.'

She tried to smile. 'Just now you called me Cressida. If we're going to be travelling companions, perhaps you should stick to that.'

He nodded. 'I'll send one of the maids to help you pack.'

She stood watching him walk back up the path. She wanted to cry, but no tears would come.

She thought, It's over. It's all over. And, in spite of the intense heat, she shivered.

When she reached home the following day, her aunt and uncle were waiting for her.

'Cressy.' Lady Kenny took her in her arms. 'My poor darling. What a terrible homecoming.'

Cressy kissed her cheek. 'I think I was expecting it,' she said quietly. 'He sounded so different lately—like a shadow of himself. As if he'd given up.'

Her aunt hugged her, then turned to Paul Nixon, who was waiting in the doorway.

She held out her hand. 'I don't think we've met. I'm Barbara Kenny.'

'This is Paul,' Cressy said, offering him a strained, grateful smile. 'He's a friend of Draco's, and he made all the arrangements for me. He's been very kind. I—I couldn't have managed without him.'

'Yes,' Sir Robert said, shaking hands with him, 'Mr Viannis said he'd look after you.'

'You've spoken to Draco?' He seemed to have been in contact with everyone but herself, she thought painfully.

'I could hardly avoid it, my dear. He's in the drawing

room. Took an overnight flight from the States, I understand.'

Draco was standing by the window as she went in. He came towards her quickly, and she waited for him to enfold her in his arms, but instead he embraced her formally, with a kiss on each cheek, leaving her feeling faintly chilled.

'You are well?' The dark face was concerned.

She nodded. 'I didn't know you'd be here.'

'I thought I should come,' he said. 'For all kinds of reasons. I hope you will tell me what I can do to help.'

She thought, You're with me, and that's enough...

He stepped back. 'Now I will leave you with your family,' he added, and, making them all a slight bow, he went out.

A little later she saw him walking in the garden with Paul Nixon, both of them deep in conversation.

'I didn't expect to like him,' Barbara Kenny said abruptly. 'But I can't deny his charm. I gather he proposes to stay here, so you'd better come to us.'

Cressy smiled at her wearily. 'Aunt Bar,' she said, 'you know quite well that I've been living with him in Greece. It's a bit late to consider the conventions. Besides,' she added with a touch of constraint, 'this house does belong to him.'

'Well, yes.' Lady Kenny flushed slightly. 'But you're in mourning—he can hardly expect...'

Cressy bent her head. She said quietly, 'You don't have to worry, Aunt Bar. I don't think he's expecting anything.'

The door opened and Berry came in, pushing a trolley laden with tea things. Her eyes were red and puffy, and her mouth trembled when she saw Cressy.

'Oh, Miss Cressy, my dear. Poor Mr Fielding. It

shouldn't have happened. He should have had many more years—seen his grandchildren born.'

Cressy bit her lip, aware that Lady Kenny was staring at her in sudden horrified speculation.

She gave a slight, almost wistful shake of her head, then turned back to the housekeeper, her voice gentle. 'It's terrible for us, Berry, but I really don't think he wanted to go on living.'

'No, he didn't,' Berry said forcefully. 'Not after he got that awful letter from *her*.'

Cressy was startled. 'Did Daddy hear from Eloise?'

'Nancy—Nurse Clayton took the post into him. She wasn't to know, of course, but if I'd seen Mrs Fielding's writing I'd have held it back, that I would. Given it to Sir Robert first.'

'What did it say?'

'I don't know, Miss Cressy. Mr Fielding burnt it in an old ashtray in the study, so that no one else would see it. All he'd say was that she was never coming back. White as a sheet he was too, and looked as if he'd been crying. And he was never the same, after.'

'Whatever we all thought of Eloise,' Cressy said, 'Daddy truly loved her. And he didn't want to go on living without her.' She swallowed. 'I really think it's that simple.'

And I, she thought, as pain tore at her, I am my father's daughter.

It was a quiet funeral. None of James Fielding's former colleagues attended, but all the neighbours paid their respects, and the little church was full.

Draco stayed at Cressy's side throughout, which raised a few eyebrows, and she knew there were already various rumours spreading about his ownership of the house, but she didn't care.

Whatever anyone thought about their relationship, they were wrong, she told herself unhappily.

Apart from taking her arm in church, he hadn't touched her at all during the past difficult days.

At night, she remained in her old room, while Draco slept on the other side of the house. And he'd never given the slightest hint that he wished to change these arrangements.

She thought, It's over, and realised that when she'd thought the same words on Myros, she hadn't simply been referring to her father.

She felt sick and empty inside. Grief for James Fielding was now commingling with the agony of this other loss, draining the colour from her face and haunting her eyes.

She supposed he had already asked Anna Theodorous to marry him before he came away, but she wished he would tell her openly rather than leave her in limbo like this.

He promised he'd talk to me when he came back from New York, she told herself. And talk to me he will.

Nearly everyone who'd been to the church had come back to the house afterwards, and Cressy was ashamed at her own impatience when some of them showed a disposition to linger.

The last of them had just gone, and she was collecting the used sherry glasses in the drawing room, when Paul Nixon came in. He was carrying a large buff envelope.

He said, 'Draco's had to go back to London, Cressida, but he asked me to give you this.'

'He's gone?' She stared at him, the colour draining

from her face. She put the glasses down carefully. 'But he can't have done. And without even saying goodbye?'

Paul sighed. 'I guess he felt it was for the best.' He put the envelope in her hands and gave her a constrained smile. 'After all, you're a free woman now.'

'A free woman?' God, she thought, I sound like an echo.

He said, 'Look in your package.' He bent and gave her a quick peck on the cheek. 'Goodbye, honey, and good luck.'

When he'd gone, she tore open the envelope, letting its contents spill out on to the sofa. The first document was the deeds to the house, and there was a note from Draco attached to it which she seized upon.

> Your father's debts died with him, Cressida, and with them any obligation to me. So you are free to take up your own life again, and forget, if you can, all the unhappiness I have caused you.
>
> Perhaps we were fated to make each other unhappy, my beautiful one.
>
> I am also giving you back the house, with the hope that you will make your home there and find some true joy at last. I ask God to bless you.

She lifted the note and held it against her heart, staring silently, sightlessly into space.

Lady Kenny came in. 'Well, I have to confess, darling, I'm glad that's over.' She sat down with a heavy sigh. 'It's been such a horrible time for everyone. Your uncle thinks it would do us all good to go away for a few days, so what do you think?'

'It's a lovely idea,' Cressy said, putting all the papers

carefully back in the envelope. 'But I'm already going away.'

'You are?' Her aunt stared at her. 'But where?'

'To London first. To New York, maybe—if I have to. Or an island called Myros, Or anywhere.' She forced a smile. 'Wherever Draco is.'

'Oh, my dearest child, do you think that's wise?' Lady Kenny looked distressed. 'I know he's incredibly good-looking—and he's been amazingly sweet and thoughtful—in fact Robert really likes him—and I've grown quite attached myself, but—' She broke off. 'Where was I?'

'I think,' Cressy said gently, 'that you were about to tell me I'm making a big mistake.'

'Well, I have to think so. All that money and power. He can do exactly what he likes, and probably always has. And what if he gets tired of you, and breaks your heart?'

'That's a risk I'll just have to take.' Cressy bent and kissed her. 'Because I love him, Aunt Bar, and I always will. And I don't want to go on living without him either, whatever the terms.'

She saw her aunt's face change suddenly, and glanced round.

Draco was standing in the open doorway, his body as rigid as if he'd been turned to stone, his face bleak and strained.

Across the room, his gaze captured hers. Held it.

He said hoarsely. 'Are they true? Those things you were saying?'

She said, 'You came back...'

'I did not intend to. I wanted to release you completely. But I found I could not go. Not without a word. Or without holding you in my arms one last time.'

He walked slowly forward, halting a few feet away from her, while Lady Kenny rose quietly and tiptoed, unnoticed, from the room. 'I heard what you said, *agapi mou*. Every word. Did you mean it? Do you—can you love me?'

'Yes.' She looked at him pleadingly, her heart in her eyes. 'Draco—don't leave me, or send me away. Take me with you, please. I'll do anything you want. Be anything you want. I won't make waves. I'll live anywhere, if I can just be part of your life sometimes. And I won't be a threat to your marriage, I swear it.'

'You have been a threat to me since I first saw you peeping down at me on that beach on Myros.' He came to her, pulling her into his arms without gentleness. 'If you knew how I have longed to touch you through all these long sad days—to comfort you.'

'But you did.' She put up a hand and touched his cheek. 'You've been there for me all the time.'

'I used to come to your room,' he said. 'Sit in a chair and watch you sleep, counting how many more hours I had to spend with you. Feeling time slipping through my fingers. Telling myself that I had ruined everything, and that you would be glad to be rid of me.'

She said, 'Why didn't you wake me up—make love to me?'

'You were grieving for your father,' he said. 'I could not intrude on that.'

She bent her head. 'I think I did my grieving a long time ago. This time, I was just—letting him go.'

He said softly, 'Ah, *pethi mou*...'

He lifted her into his arms and sat down on one of the sofas, cradling her on his lap.

He said gently, 'Why did you leave me, my dear one? Why didn't you turn to me?'

She drew a deep breath. 'Because I was scared. My father's illness was an excuse to leave, not a reason. I—I didn't believe in love. I'd seen the damage it could do. Saw my father change completely when my stepmother came into his life, and that frightened me. I didn't want that to happen to me. I wanted to stay in control—not be at someone else's mercy for the rest of my life.

'When that call from England came, it seemed like a sign telling me I didn't have to change after all. That I could just go back to my old life and pretend nothing had happened. That I'd be safe that way.

'Only it was already too late.' She beat suddenly on his chest with her fists. 'Why didn't you tell me it was too late? Because you knew—didn't you?'

'Yes,' he said. 'I knew.' He was silent for a moment. 'So, I made you afraid of love.'

'I was more frightened of myself,' she said. 'Of the way you could make me feel. Although I didn't know the half of it then.'

He shook his head. 'How can you still love me, Cressida *mou*, when I've treated you so badly?'

'It could have been worse,' she said. 'You could simply have cut me out of your life.'

'That was never a possibility.' His voice was suddenly harsh. 'Even when I was hurt and angry, you were in my blood. I could not let you go. So I told myself you were just another tramp, who cared only for money and material things. And that I would have you on those terms.'

He stroked her hair back from her forehead. 'After our first time together, I was so ashamed—so angry with myself. You had been so sweet—so giving. You turned my revenge back on me, *pethi mou*—and I suffered.

'Every time I came to you it became more difficult to pretend. That's why I could never stay with you afterwards—hold you in my arms all night as I longed to do—because I knew I might break down and tell you how I truly felt. And you might not care.'

He sighed. 'And because I knew how temporary an arrangement it was. That your father might have another fatal attack at any time. And you would be free to walk away again, and this time I would have no power to bring you back.'

'You always had power over me.' She pressed a kiss to his tanned throat. 'The power of love—right from the first. Even when you offered me your bargain. I—I wanted to hate you, but I couldn't.'

'That last morning on Myros,' he said, 'you promised you would say goodbye to me, but you didn't come, although I delayed the takeoff. And then something made me look down, and you were there, waving to me, all in white, like the bride I'd dreamed of.

'And I told myself that when I came back from New York I would go on my knees to you if necessary, and beg you to forgive me—and to marry me.'

Her heart missed an incredulous, joyous beat. She said, 'I thought you were going to marry Anna Theodorous.'

'That was her father's plan, not mine. And he leaked the story to the newspapers to pressure me over the tanker deal.' His mouth tightened. 'He is a man who regards women as commodities, *agapi mou*. Even his own child.'

The hands that cupped her face were trembling suddenly. He said, 'Cressida—can you forgive me—after all that has happened between us? Will you be my wife?

She said wonderingly, 'Do you doubt it? Draco—you must know how you make me feel.'

'You do not have to love someone to like being in bed with them, *pethi mou*,' he told her quietly. 'As it was, each time we made love I could only think of how much happiness I had thrown away.'

'And I thought the same. Oh, why didn't you tell me?'

'I did tell you.' He smiled into her eyes. 'On our last night together on Myros. You must learn to speak Greek, my love, then you would know.'

She slid her arms round his neck, pressing herself against him. 'Can I have my first lesson now?'

He groaned. 'No, Cressida, because I have to find your aunt and arrange for you to stay at her house until the wedding. You see—I am belatedly trying to do the right thing,' he added wryly.

She said, 'Won't it be awkward for you to take me back to Myros as your wife? Perhaps we should leave things as they are. I mean—you don't *have* to marry me...'

He kissed her softly, and lingeringly. 'But you are so wrong, my heart. I do have to marry you, and very soon. I cannot wait any longer. Besides, Vassilis requires it. He told Paul while I was away that you did not eat because you were pining for me.'

'Oh,' she said. 'So you're marrying me just to please your staff.'

'And because I cannot go many more nights without sleep,' Draco added, straight-faced.

'And those are your only reasons?' Cressy sat up in mock outrage.

'There are others.' He pulled her back into his arms.

'Which we will discuss when we are less likely to be interrupted,' he added, his mouth softly exploring hers.

'What a pity,' she whispered against his lips. 'Because I have some wonderful memories of this room...

'But I want to make one thing clear,' she went on, when he allowed her to speak again. 'I'm staying with you, not Aunt Bar.'

'You will do as you're told, Cressida *mou*.' He sounded like the autocrat again, and she ran a loving finger across his lips.

'Then I shall sue you for breach of contract.' She smiled up at him. 'You bought me for three months. There are still two left—and I want them. I want *you*. Besides,' she added, 'if you'd really been going to marry Anna, you wouldn't have stopped making love to me. So why should you stop because you're marrying me instead?'

'I think there is something wrong with your logic,' Draco said, trying not to laugh. 'But I don't think I care. I am certainly not going to argue.'

She reached up and kissed him in turn, letting her tongue flicker softly along his lower lip. 'So will you dine with me tonight, Kyrios Draco? And after dinner will you please take me to bed and make love to me for hours?'

'I will.' His mouth took hers with a deep, sensual yearning that made her body melt against his. 'And after we have made love, Kyria Cressida, will you sleep in my arms for what is left of the night?'

She took a deep breath. 'Oh, yes, darling. Yes, I will.'

His arms tightened round her. 'Then it seems, my bride, that we have a bargain.'

'For three months?' Her smile was misty.

'No.' Draco looked deep into her eyes, shining for him with love and trust. 'For the whole of our lives, *matia mou*.'

Modern
romance™

...international affairs – seduction and passion guaranteed

Tender
romance™

...sparkling, emotional, feel-good romance

Historical
romance™

...rich, vivid and passionate

Medical
romance™

...pulse-raising romance – heart-racing medical drama

Sensual
romance™

...teasing, tempting, provocatively playful

Blaze

...scorching hot sexy reads

27 new titles every month.

Live the emotion

MILLS & BOON®

MB5

Next month don't miss –

HOT SUMMER LOVING

Sit back and enjoy the sun with these sizzling summer stories. They're hot, passionate and irresistibly sexy!

On sale 6th August 2004

Available at most branches of WHSmith, Tesco, Martins, Borders, Eason, Sainsbury's and all good paperback bookshops.

0704/05

GRAHAM/RTL/2

MILLS & BOON

Volume 2 on sale from 6th August 2004

Lynne Graham

International Playboys

A Savage Betrayal

Available at most branches of WHSmith, Tesco, Martins, Borders, Eason, Sainsbury's and all good paperback bookshops.

MILLS & BOON

You're invited to a...

White Wedding

Margaret Way, Jessica Steele,
Judy Christenberry

On sale 20th August 2004

Available at most branches of WHSmith, Tesco, Martins, Borders, Eason, Sainsbury's and all good paperback bookshops.

0804/024/MB103

MILLS & BOON

Strictly Business

When the fun starts... after hours!

Liz Fielding **PENNY JORDAN** **Hannah Bernard**

On sale 3rd September 2004

Available at most branches of WHSmith, Tesco, Martins, Borders, Eason, Sainsbury's and all good paperback bookshops.

MILLS & BOON®
Live the emotion

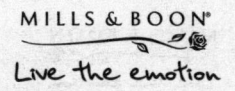

Regency Brides

A wonderful six-book Regency collection

Two sparkling Regency romances in each volume

Volume 2 on sale from 6th August 2004

Available at most branches of WHSmith, Tesco, Martins, Borders, Eason, Sainsbury's, and all good paperback bookshops.

MILLS & BOON®

Live the emotion

Modern
romance™

MISTRESS OF CONVENIENCE by Penny Jordan

Suzy has never been called a security risk before – but Colonel Lucas Soames insists she is. In order to safeguard his top secret mission, the suave millionaire forces her to pose as his mistress. Secreted away in a luxurious Italian villa it isn't long before their attraction reaches boiling point...

THE PASSIONATE HUSBAND by Helen Brooks

Marsha Kane is shocked to see her soon-to-be ex-husband again. She hasn't seen Taylor since she left him for cheating on her; now she's trying desperately not to fall for him all over again. Taylor is determined to get Marsha back – and he always gets what he wants...doesn't he?

HIS BID FOR A BRIDE by Carole Mortimer

Skye O'Hara's life is rocked by tragedy and she's reunited with Falkner Harrington – her father's enigmatic business partner. Needing some time to adjust, she accepts when Falkner offers her the sanctuary of his home. However, Skye soon suspects that he has a secret agenda...

THE BRABANTI BABY by Catherine Spencer

Gabriel Brabanti wants to see the baby he's been told is his daughter – but not his ex-wife. So Eve Caldwell arrives at his Maltese villa with the child. Eve captivates him – but Gabriel is convinced she's lying. Eve leaves Gabriel's house, and his bed, but her heart is breaking...

On sale 6th August 2004

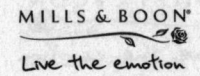

Available at most branches of WHSmith, Tesco, Martins, Borders, Eason, Sainsbury's and all good paperback bookshops.

MILLS & BOON®

Live the emotion

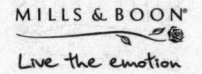

Modern
romance™

THE ITALIAN TYCOON'S MISTRESS by Cathy Williams

When tycoon Rocco Losi takes over Losi Construction he tries to sack Amy Hogan. But his belief that she'll leave quietly is soon challenged – by Amy! Who is this little spitfire who thinks she can out-argue him – and turn him on? Rocco decides that Amy can stay after all...

THE GREEK'S SEVEN DAY SEDUCTION by Susan Stephens

When Charlotte joined in a dance traditionally performed only by men – she didn't expect Iannis Kiriakos's passionate reaction! She can't resist the incredible sexual current flowing between them, so why not indulge in a holiday? But she has no idea who Iannis really is...

THE SHEIKH'S BARTERED BRIDE by Lucy Monroe

After a whirlwind courtship, Sheikh Hakim bin Omar al Kadar proposes marriage. Shy, innocent Catherine Benning has fallen head-over-heels in love, and accepts. After the wedding they travel to Hakim's desert kingdom – and Catherine discovers that Hakim has bought her!

BY ROYAL COMMAND by Robyn Donald

Lauren's only escape from the war-torn island of Sant'Rosa is to marry Guy, a total stranger, in a fake ceremony. Later, reunited with Guy, Lauren is overwhelmed by an explosive desire. But Guy has news for her. Their marriage vows were legal and, what's more, he's really a prince...

On sale 6th August 2004

Available at most branches of WHSmith, Tesco, Martins, Borders, Eason, Sainsbury's and all good paperback bookshops.

MILLS & BOON®

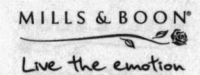

Live the emotion

Medical romance™

BUSHFIRE BRIDE by Marion Lennox

Dr Rachel Harper just wanted to escape her busy emergency ward for a weekend. Now she's stranded in the Outback, working with the area's only doctor, the powerfully charming Hugo McInnes. Soon their attraction is raging as strongly as the bushfires around town – but Rachel's secret means she can't give in to her awakened feelings...

THE DOCTOR'S SECRET FAMILY by Alison Roberts

It was love at first sight for Dr Hannah Campbell and surgeon Jack Douglas. But all too soon Hannah learned that Jack had been keeping a crucial secret from her. Now Jack is working on her paediatric ward, and she wants nothing to do with him. She can't risk him seeing her daughter...*his* daughter!

THE PREGNANT MIDWIFE by Fiona McArthur

(Marriage and Maternity)

Midwife Kirsten Wilson has been trying to forget Hunter Morgan since returning to Sydney. Getting up in the helicopter again, to rescue tiny babies, is just what she needs. At least until Hunter arrives as the new doctor in charge! Then a huge helicopter crash forces them to put their priorities in order – and changes their lives for ever...

On sale 6th August 2004

Available at most branches of WHSmith, Tesco, Martins, Borders, Eason, Sainsbury's and all good paperback bookshops.

MILLS & BOON®

Live the emotion

Medical romance™

EMERGENCY: BACHELOR DOCTOR
by Gill Sanderson (Special Care Baby Unit)

On her first day at the Wolds Hospital, Dr Kim Hunter was not expecting to work in the Special Care Baby Unit – and neither was she expecting the impact that her new colleague, Dr Harry Black, had on her! Kim found herself falling for him, and then discovered the heartbreaking reasons behind his fear of commitment...

RAPID RESPONSE *by Jennifer Taylor*

(A&E Drama)

Two years ago Holly Daniels's fiancé walked out without warning – and now the two specialist registrars are reunited, forced to work side by side in the Rapid Response team of a busy emergency unit. Holly's surprised at how fast her heart reacts to Ben Carlisle, and Ben is just as quick to react – so why did he walk away in the first place...?

DOCTORS IN PARADISE *by Meredith Webber*

Tranquillity Sands is a health resort set on a coral-fringed island surrounded by the Pacific – what could possibly go wrong in this perfect place? Everything, as far as Dr Caroline Sayers is concerned! She finds herself in the midst of intrigue, superstition and medical emergency – and through it all strolls Dr Lucas Quinn: laid-back, caring...and utterly irresistible!

On sale 6th August 2004

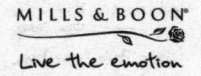

Available at most branches of WHSmith, Tesco, Martins, Borders, Eason, Sainsbury's and all good paperback bookshops.

MILLS & BOON®
Live the emotion

Tender romance™

GINO'S ARRANGED BRIDE by Lucy Gordon
(The Italian Brothers)
All Laura's little girl wants is a daddy to love her. So Laura marries Italian Gino Farnese, believing a paper marriage is the best they can hope for. But there are two rules: no sharing a bed and no falling in love. And they're in danger of breaking them both...

A PRETEND ENGAGEMENT by Jessica Steele
Varnie was startled when she found a man in her bedroom – even more that the man was Leon Beaumont, her brother's boss! But her brother's job was at risk if Varnie didn't let Leon stay. It seemed they were stuck with each other – especially when the newspapers annouced their engagement!

HER SPANISH BOSS by Barbara McMahon *(9 to 5)*
When Rachel Goodson starts working for Luis Alvares he's prickly and suspicious. But soon they draw closer and secrets spill out. Luis's heart is still with his late wife, so Rachel is stunned when he wants her to pose as his girlfriend. Luis wants more than just a pretend relationship...

A CONVENIENT GROOM by Darcy Maguire
(The Bridal Business)
When Riana Andrews woke to find an engagement ring on her finger she was more than a little confused! The guy she *thought* had proposed was Joe Henderson, a sexy photographer. He was certainly acting like her fiancé, and she wasn't imagining the tingles she got around him!

On sale 6th August 2004

Available at most branches of WHSmith, Tesco, Martins, Borders, Eason, Sainsbury's and all good paperback bookshops.

0704/14

MILLS & BOON
Live the emotion

Blaze™

SCORING *by Kristin Hardy*
Under the Covers
As a massage therapist Becka Langdon has the expert touch. She can't wait to get her hands on sexy Mace Duvall – though in a purely professional capacity, of course! Mace is a playboy with a reputation to match and Becka is determined she won't be another notch on his bedpost – but maybe Mace can be one on hers?

JUST TOYING AROUND... *by Rhonda Nelson*
Meg Sugarbaker lives a secret life. By day she is a successful chef, but by night she becomes the infamous Desiree Moon – online sex toy critic. This shouldn't be a problem, except Meg is a virgin! She's good at her job, but could do with a little help to make her fantasy become reality... Nick Deveraux is a lawyer and is determined to prove that the notorious Desiree Moon is in fact a fraud. But after meeting her all he wants to do is play...

On sale 6th August 2004

Available at most branches of WHSmith, Tesco, Martins, Borders, Eason, Sainsbury's and all good paperback bookshops.

MILLS & BOON®

Live the emotion

Sensual romance™

HOT PROSPECT by Julie Kistler
Chicago cop Jake Calhoun is used to playing it by the book. But when he ends up working undercover as a newlywed with a stunning stranger, Jake wants to ignore the rules and create his very own naughty ones…

HOW TO BE THE PERFECT GIRLFRIEND
by Heather MacAllister
Sara Lipton wants to meet Mr Right; if only she could figure out how to be the perfect girlfriend!. All she needs now is a man to practise on and sexy Simon Northrup is a prime candidate…

PURE INDULGENCE by Janelle Denison
Kayla Thomas is counting on her latest idea to make her bakery a huge success – aphrodisiac chocolates! But first she needs an unsuspecting test subject and Jack Tremaine is more than happy to sample *anything* Kayla's offering…

IT'S ALL ABOUT EVE by Tracy Kelleher
Eve Cantora's sexy lingerie shop is causing quite a stir and some items have also been stolen! But when handsome detective Carter Moran arrives to investigate the thefts, Eve realises her troubles are only just beginning…

On sale 6th August 2004

Available at most branches of WHSmith, Tesco, Martins, Borders, Eason, Sainsbury's and all good paperback bookshops.

MillsandBoon.co.uk

books | authors | online reads | magazine | membership

Visit millsandboon.co.uk and discover your one-stop shop for romance!

Find out everything you want to know about romance novels in one place. Read about and buy our novels online anytime you want.

- Choose and buy books from an extensive selection of Mills & Boon® titles.

- Enjoy top authors and *New York Times* best-selling authors – from Penny Jordan and Miranda Lee to Sandra Marton and Nicola Cornick!

- Take advantage of our amazing **FREE** book offers.

- In our Authors' area find titles currently available from all your favourite authors.

- Get hooked on one of our fabulous online reads, with new chapters updated weekly.

- Check out the fascinating articles in our magazine section.

Visit us online at
www.millsandboon.co.uk

…you'll want to come back again and again!!